ISOLA

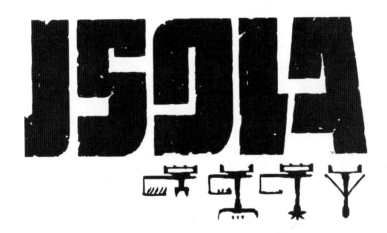

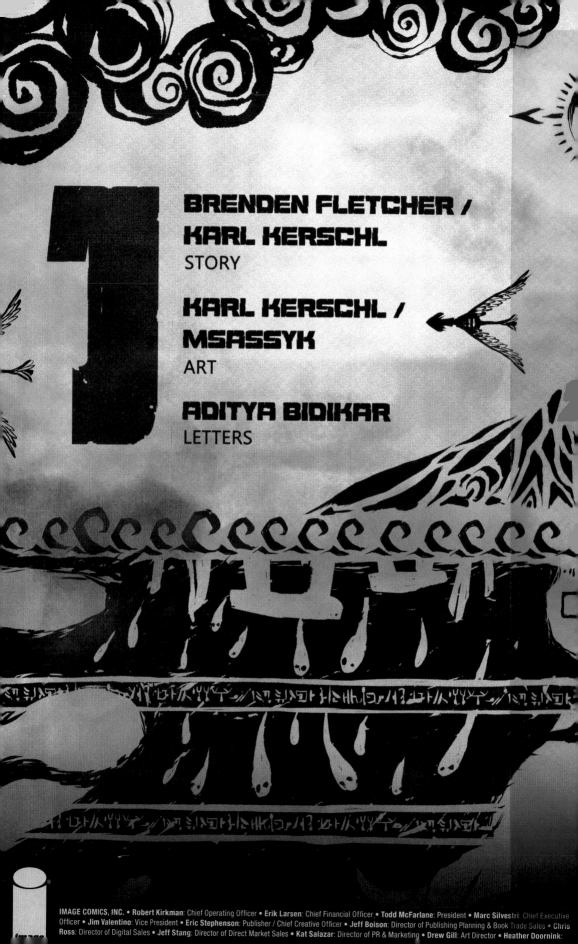

1

BRENDEN FLETCHER / KARL KERSCHL
STORY

KARL KERSCHL / MSASSYK
ART

ADITYA BIDIKAR
LETTERS

IMAGE COMICS, INC. • **Robert Kirkman:** Chief Operating Officer • **Erik Larsen:** Chief Financial Officer, • **Todd McFarlane:** President • **Marc Silvestri:** Chief Executive Officer • **Jim Valentino:** Vice President • **Eric Stephenson:** Publisher / Chief Creative Officer • **Jeff Boison:** Director of Publishing Planning & Book Trade Sales • **Chris Ross:** Director of Digital Sales • **Jeff Stang:** Director of Direct Market Sales • **Kat Salazar:** Director of PR & Marketing • **Drew Gill:** Art Director • **Heather Doornink:**

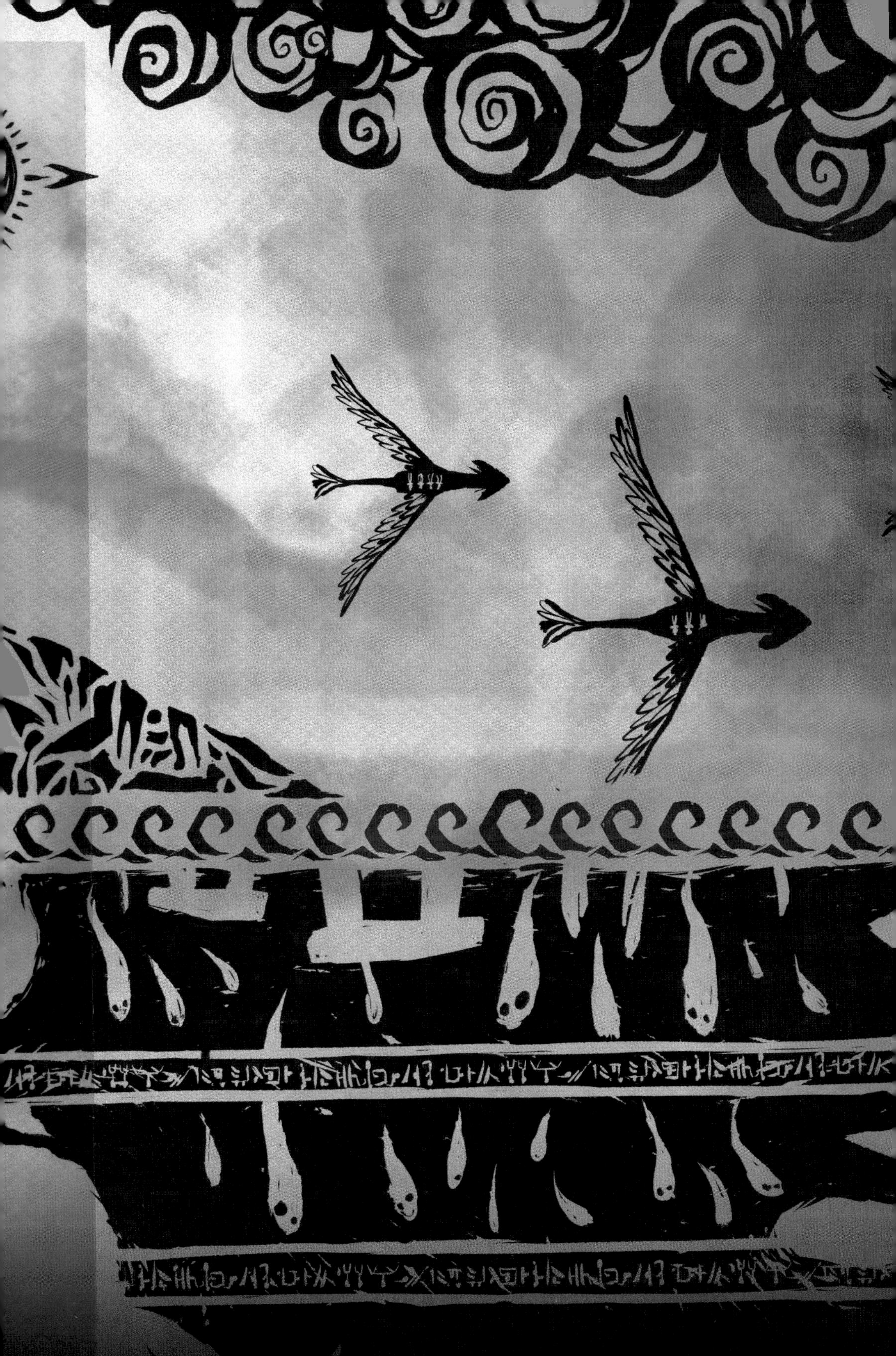

oduction Assistance by Ryan Brewer

OLA, VOL. 1. Third Printing. August 2019. Published by Image Comics, Inc. Office of publication: 2701 NW Vaughn St., Suite 780, Portland, OR 97210. Printed in the USA. For information regarding e CPSIA on this printed material call: 203-595-3636. Representation: Law Offices of Harris M. Miller II, P.C. (rights.inquiries@gmail.com). ISBN: 978-1-5343-0922-7

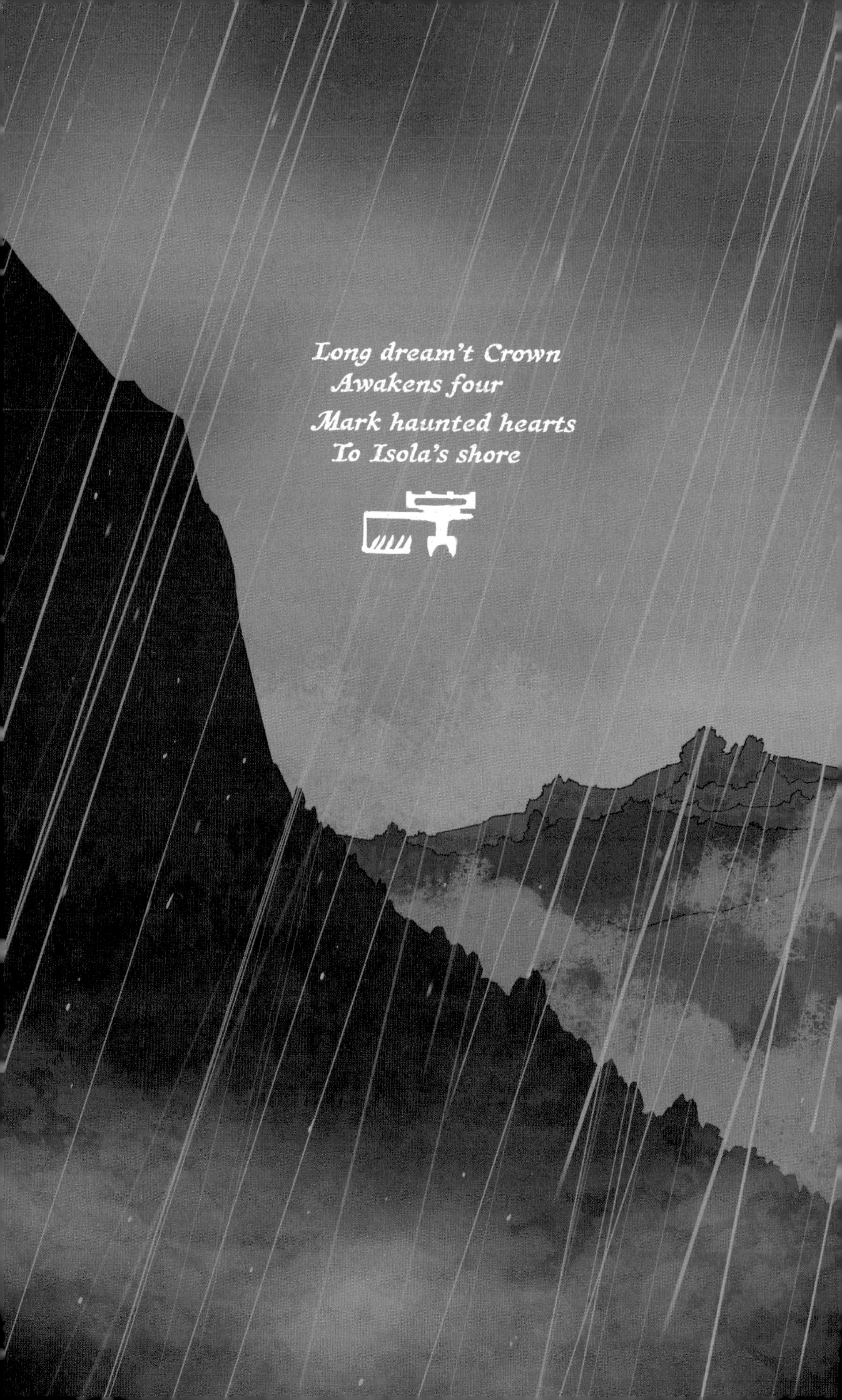
Long dream't Crown
Awakens four
Mark haunted hearts
To Isola's shore

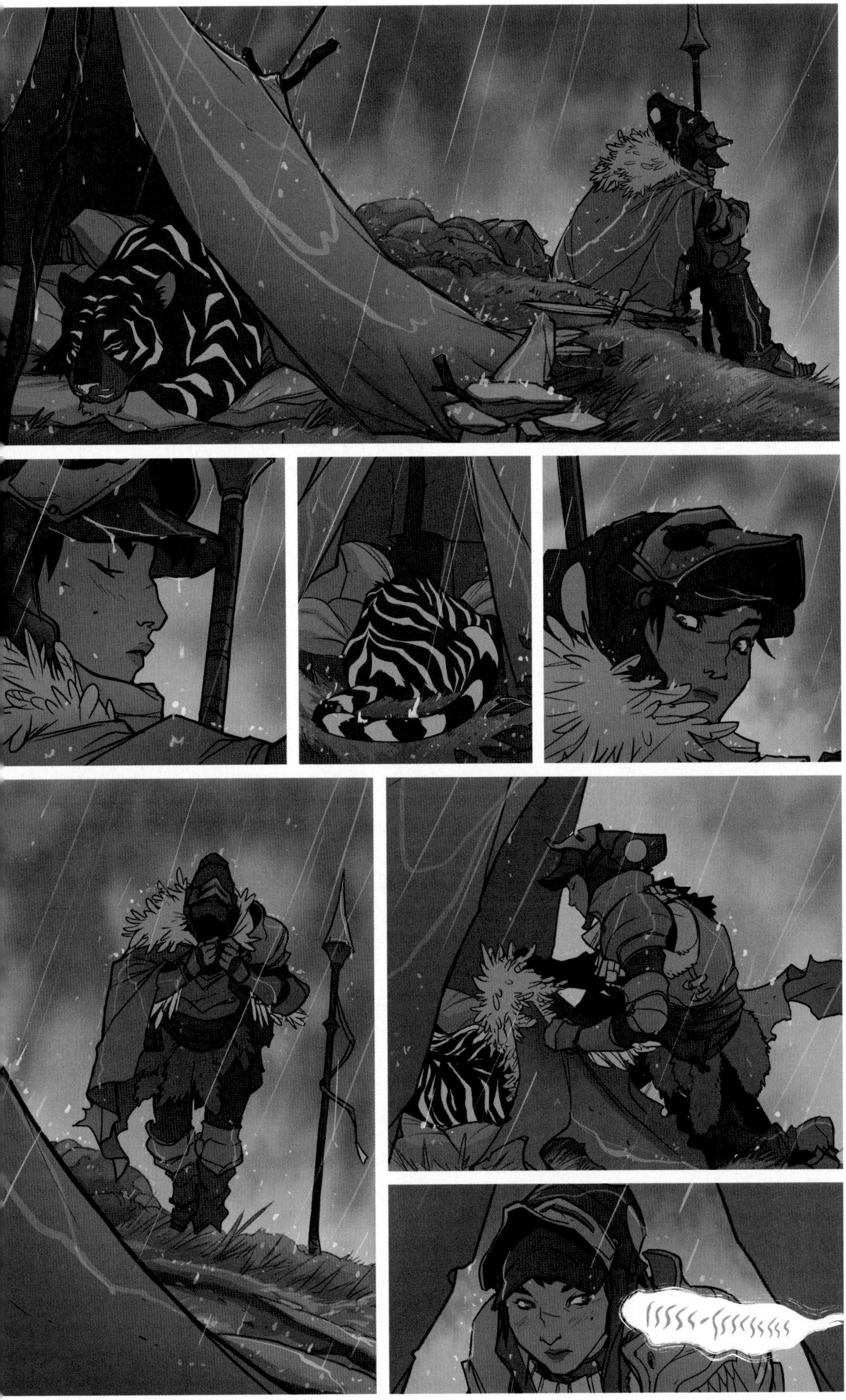

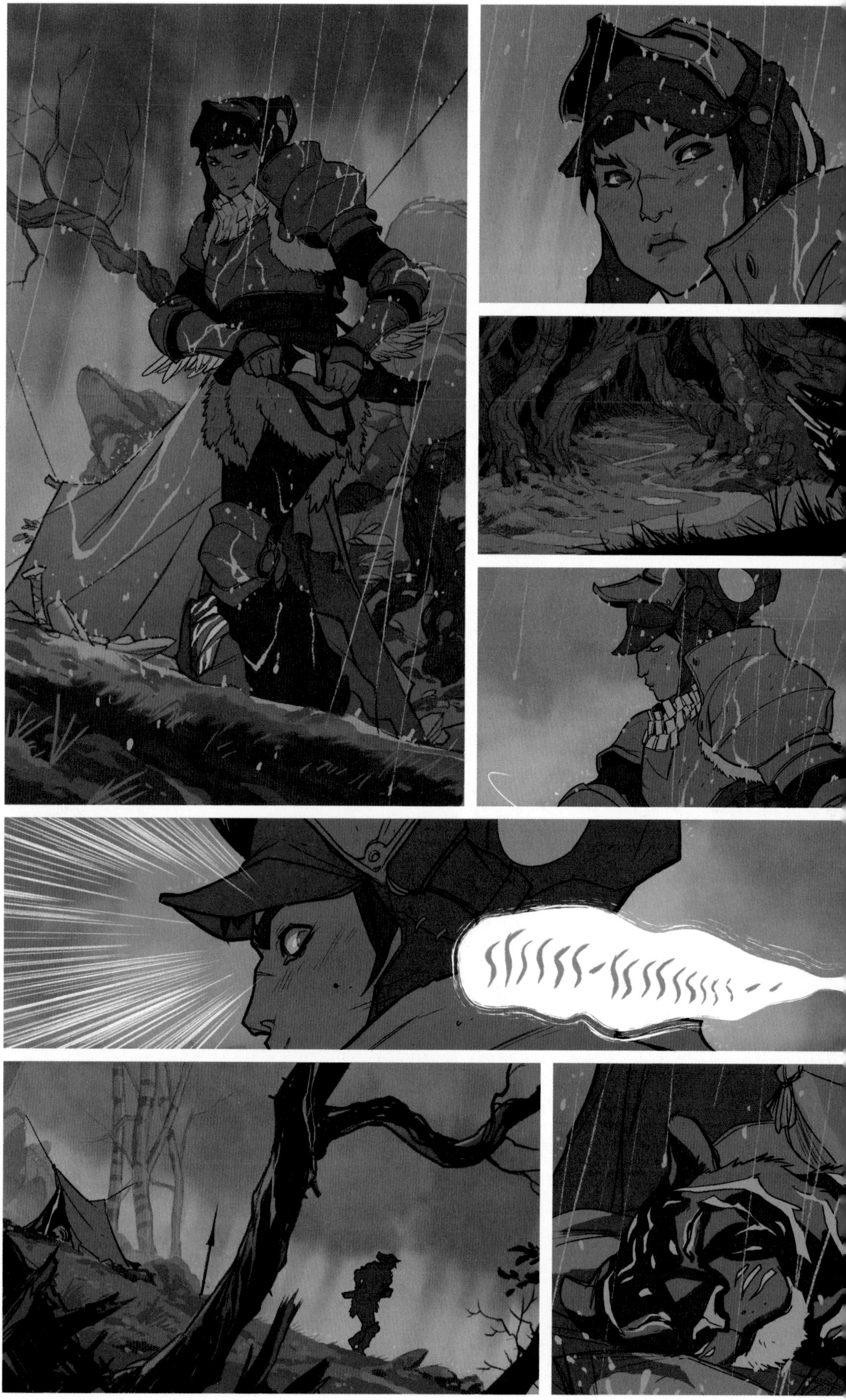
SSSSSS-SSSSSSSSS--

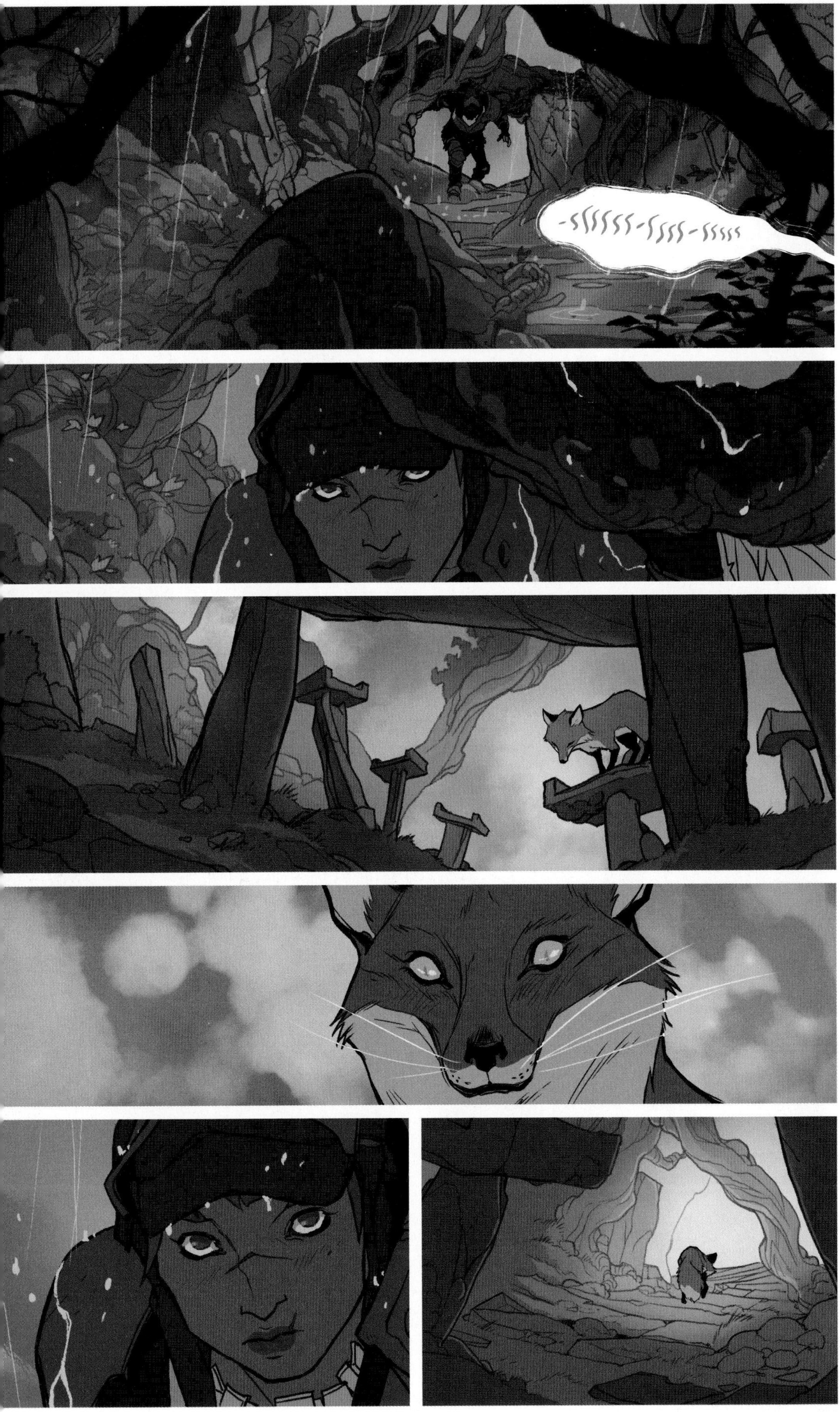

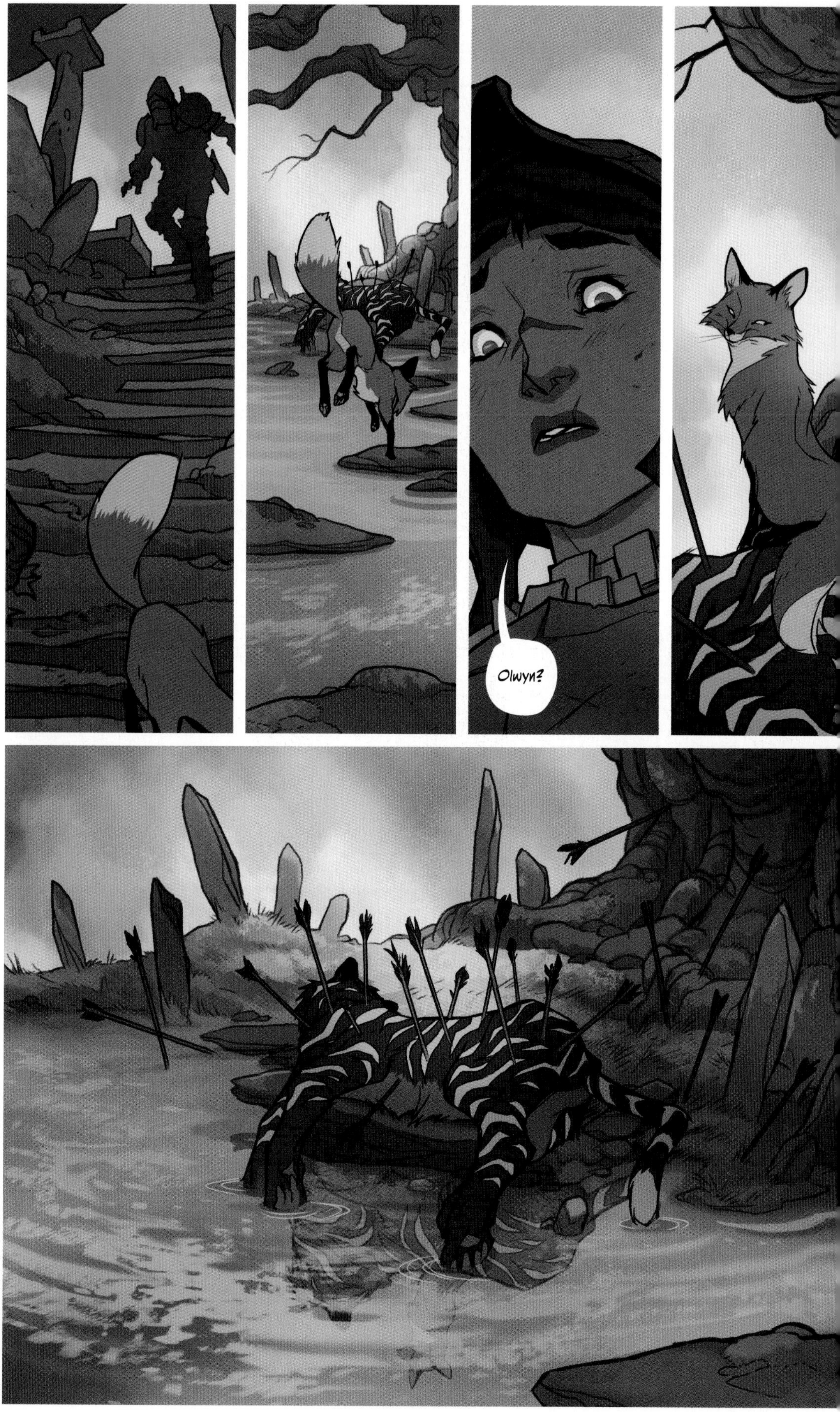
Olwyn?

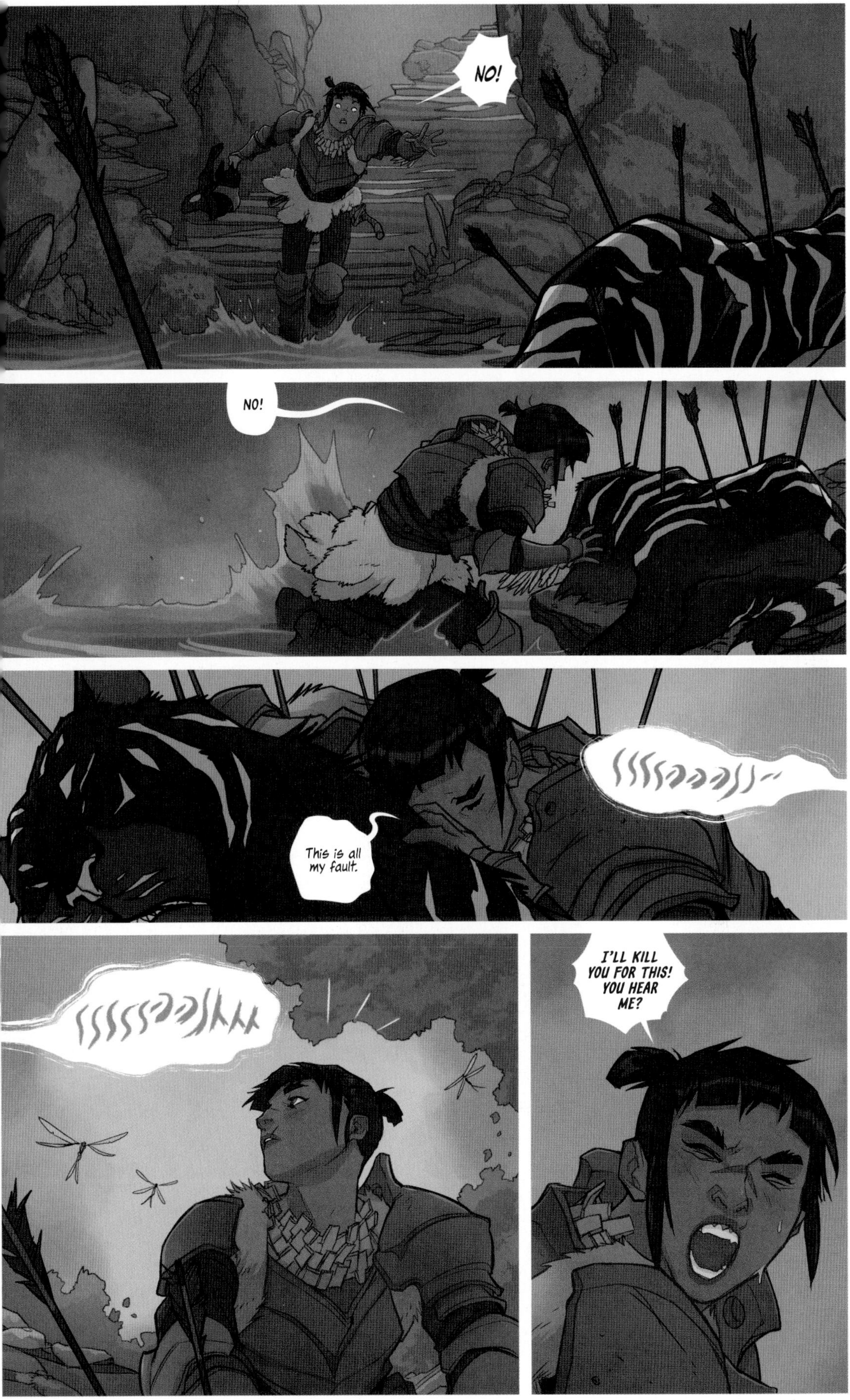
NO!
NO!
This is all my fault.
I'LL KILL YOU FOR THIS! YOU HEAR ME?

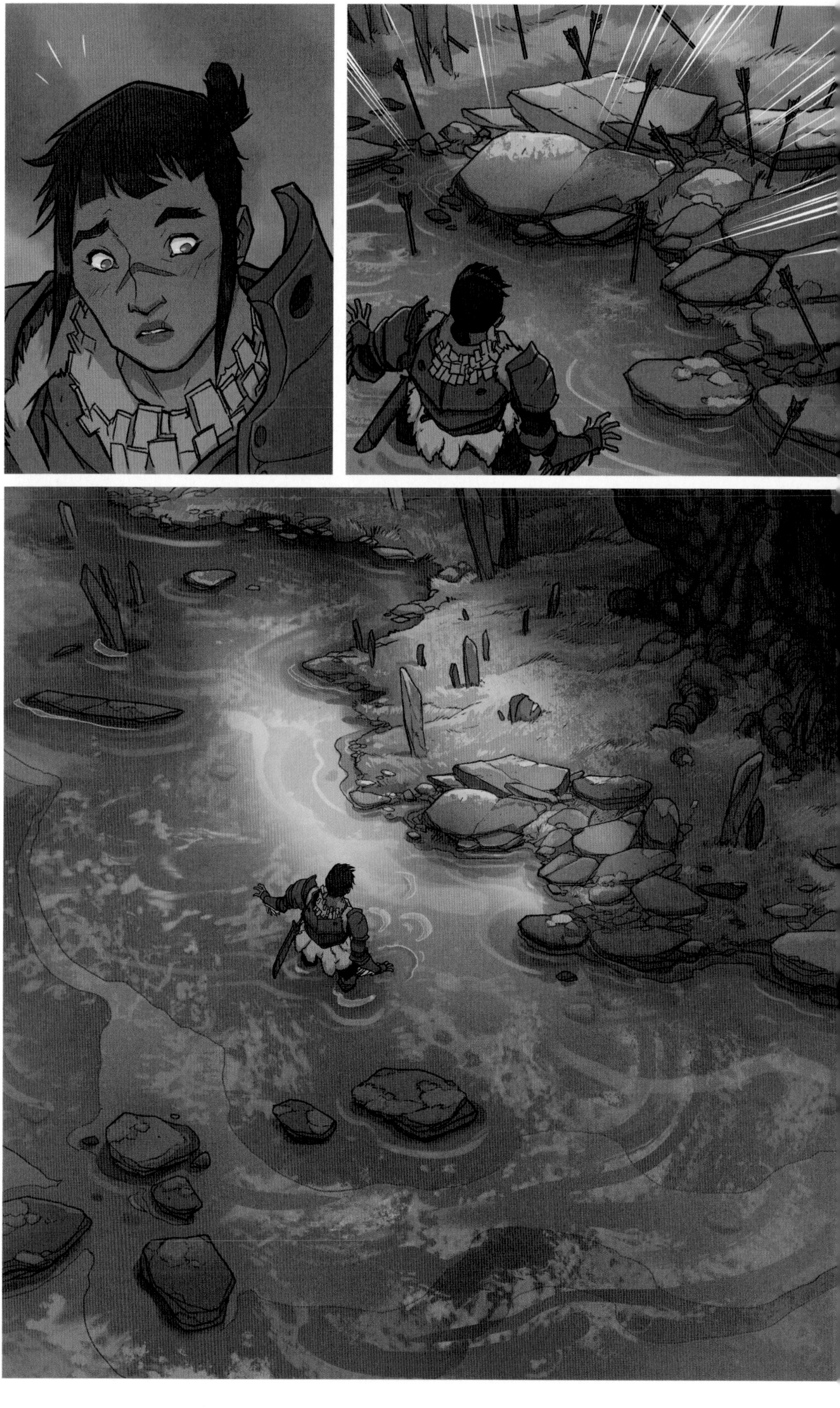

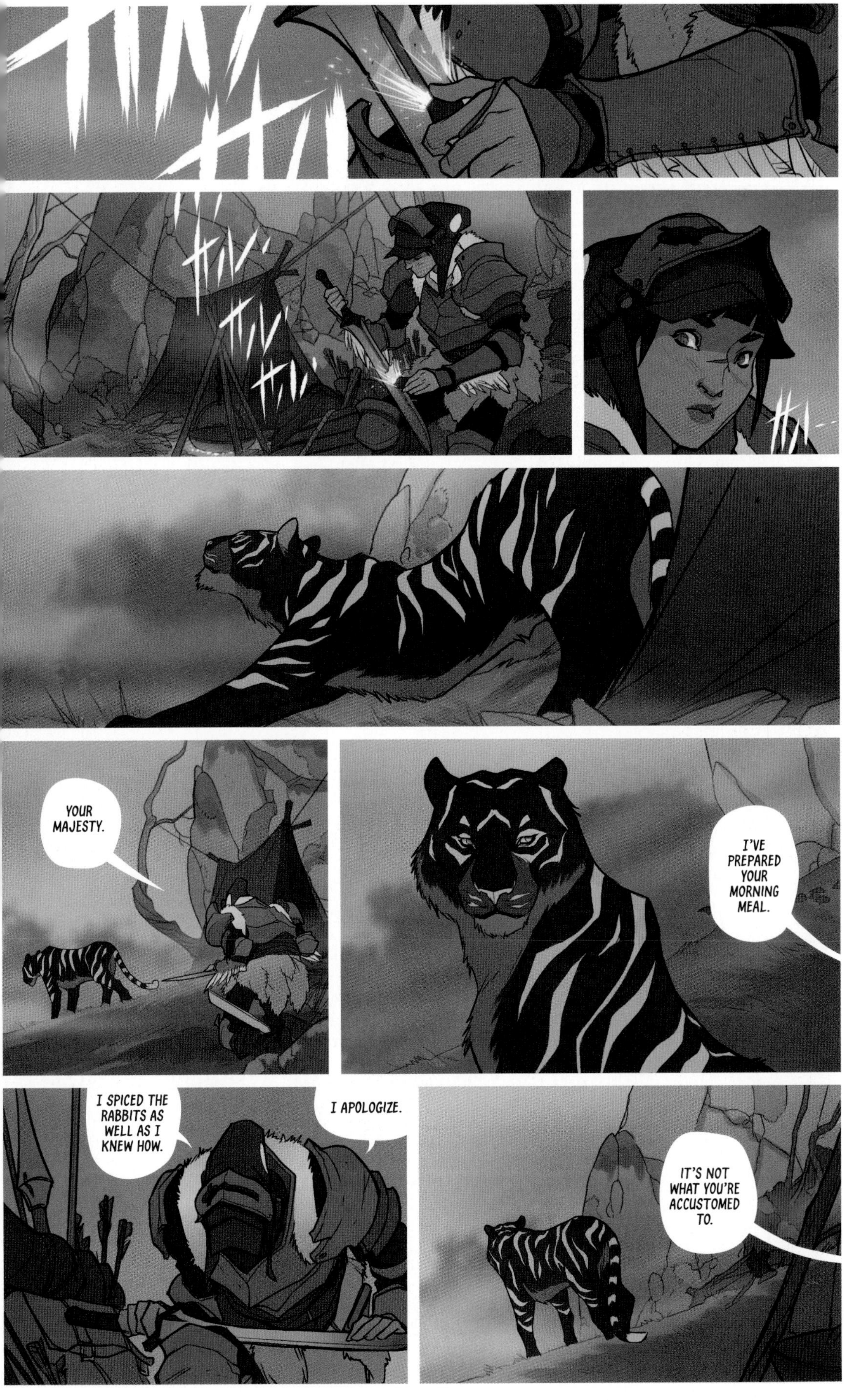
YOUR MAJESTY.
I'VE PREPARED YOUR MORNING MEAL.
I SPICED THE RABBITS AS WELL AS I KNEW HOW.
I APOLOGIZE.
IT'S NOT WHAT YOU'RE ACCUSTOMED TO.

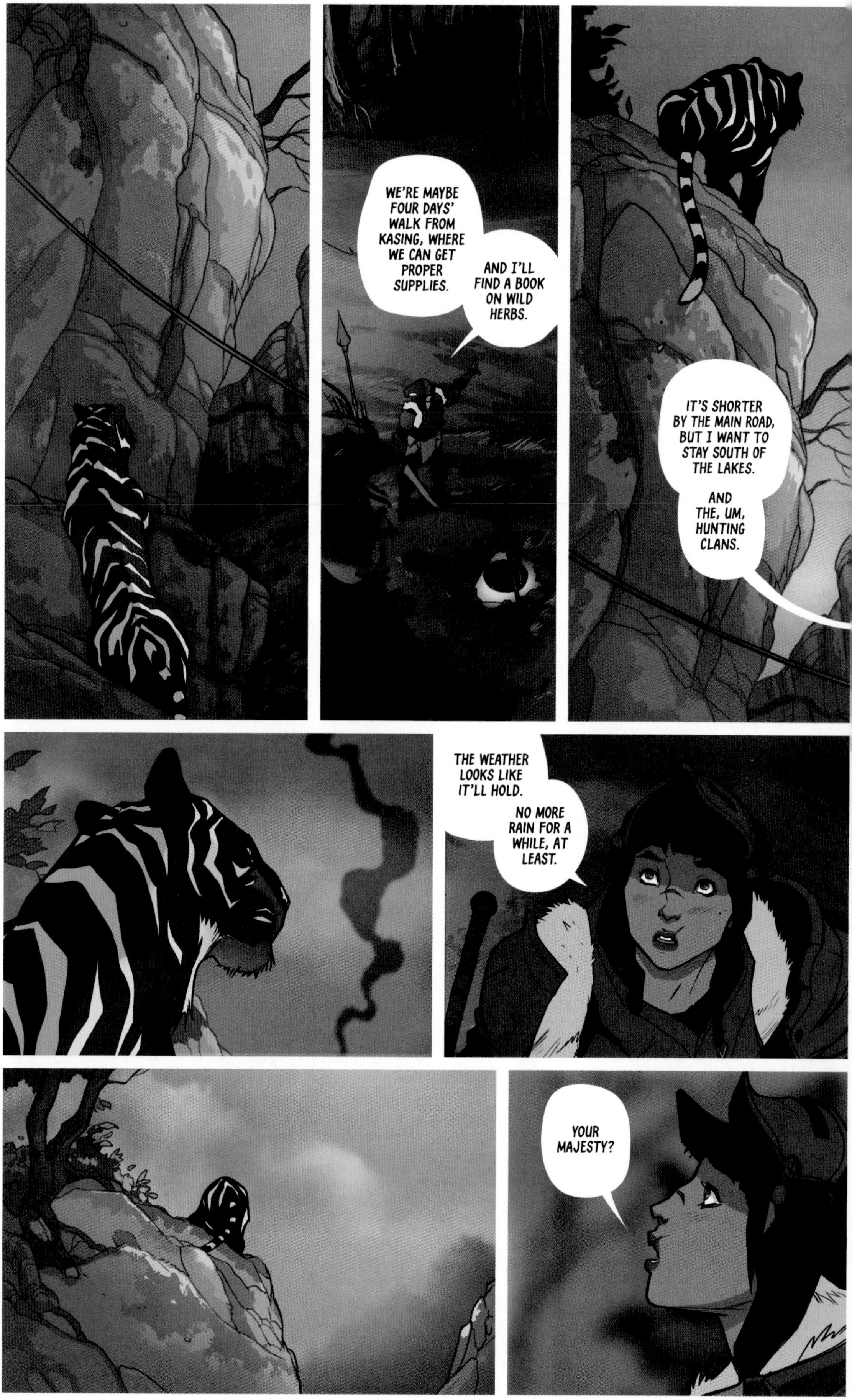
WE'RE MAYBE FOUR DAYS' WALK FROM KASING, WHERE WE CAN GET PROPER SUPPLIES.
AND I'LL FIND A BOOK ON WILD HERBS.
IT'S SHORTER BY THE MAIN ROAD, BUT I WANT TO STAY SOUTH OF THE LAKES.
AND THE, UM, HUNTING CLANS.
THE WEATHER LOOKS LIKE IT'LL HOLD.
NO MORE RAIN FOR A WHILE, AT LEAST.
YOUR MAJESTY?

WE CAN'T GO BACK TO AAR. I'M SORRY BUT WE JUST CAN'T.
NOBODY IS GONNA RECOGNIZE YOU AS A... AS A...CAT.
IF I TAKE YOU BACK HOME THROUGH THE CITY GATES THEY'LL JUST KILL YOU OR ME OR BOTH OF US.
IF YOU CAN TRUST ME...JUST A LITTLE WHILE LONGER.
I CAN FIX ALL OF THIS.
ISOLA EXISTS, YOUR MAJESTY.
I KNOW IT DOES.
BUT I WILL DO ANYTHING YOU COMMAND.
I AM YOURS, ALWAYS.

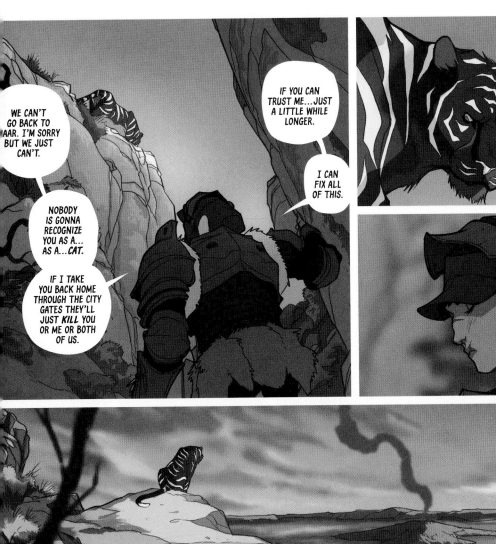

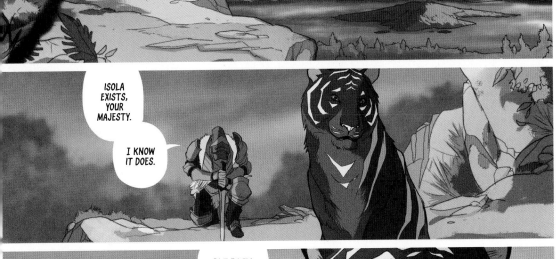

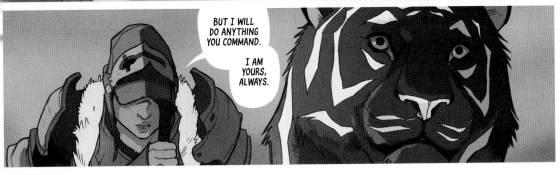

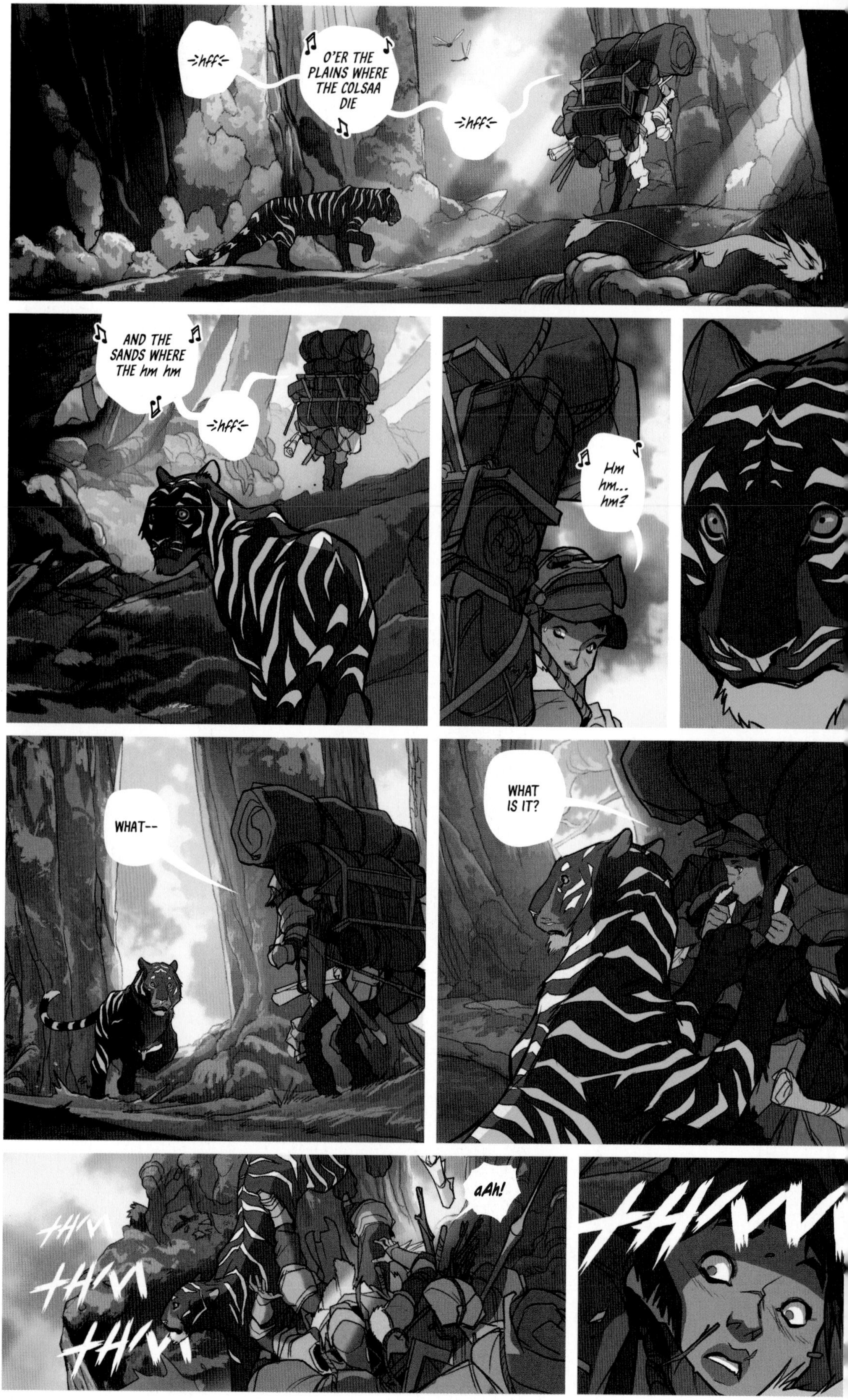

-hff-
O'ER THE PLAINS WHERE THE COLSAA DIE
-hff-
AND THE SANDS WHERE THE hm hm
-hff-
Hm hm... hm?
WHAT--
WHAT IS IT?
aAh!
THWV
THWV
THWV
THWV

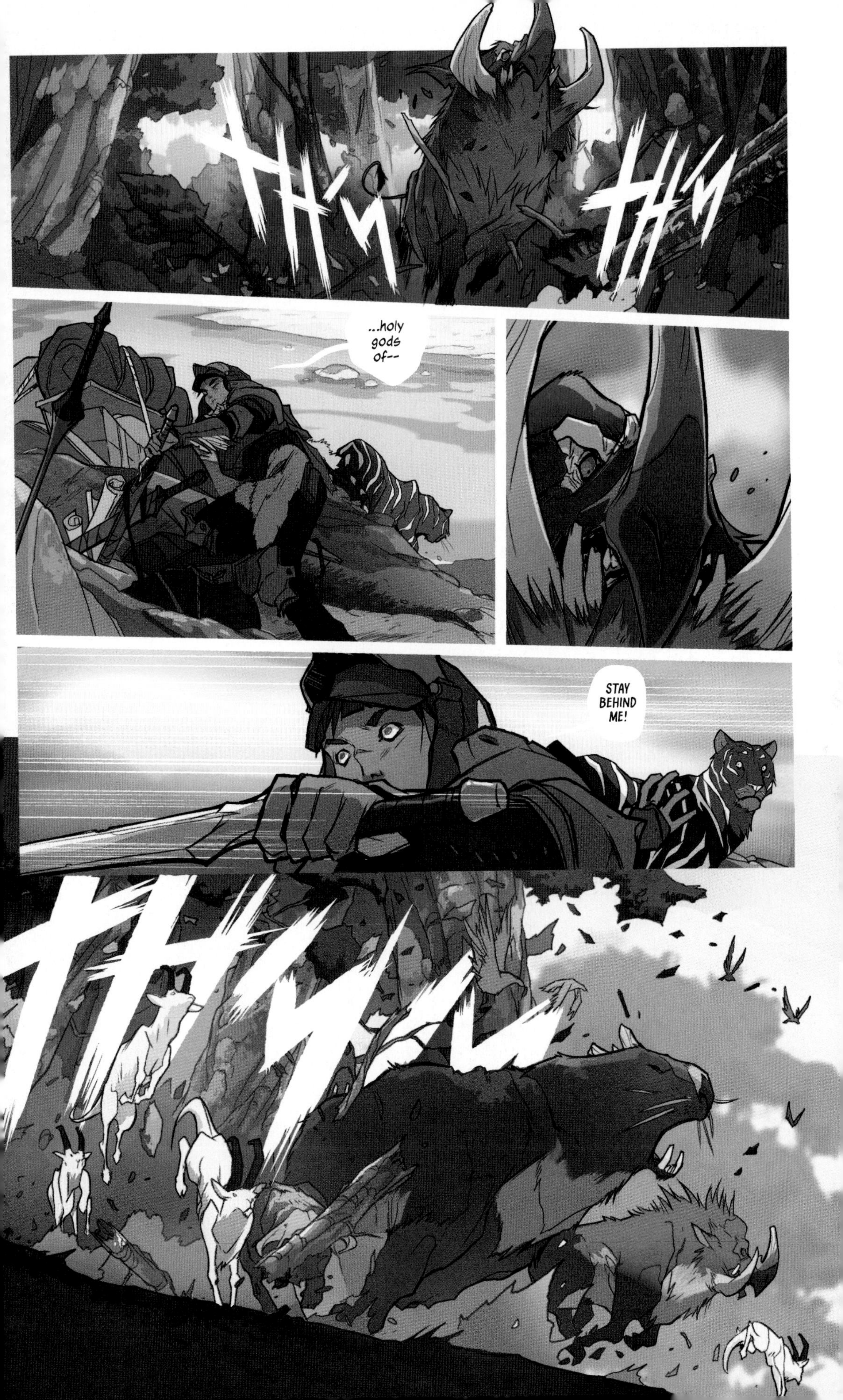

...holy gods of--
STAY BEHIND ME!

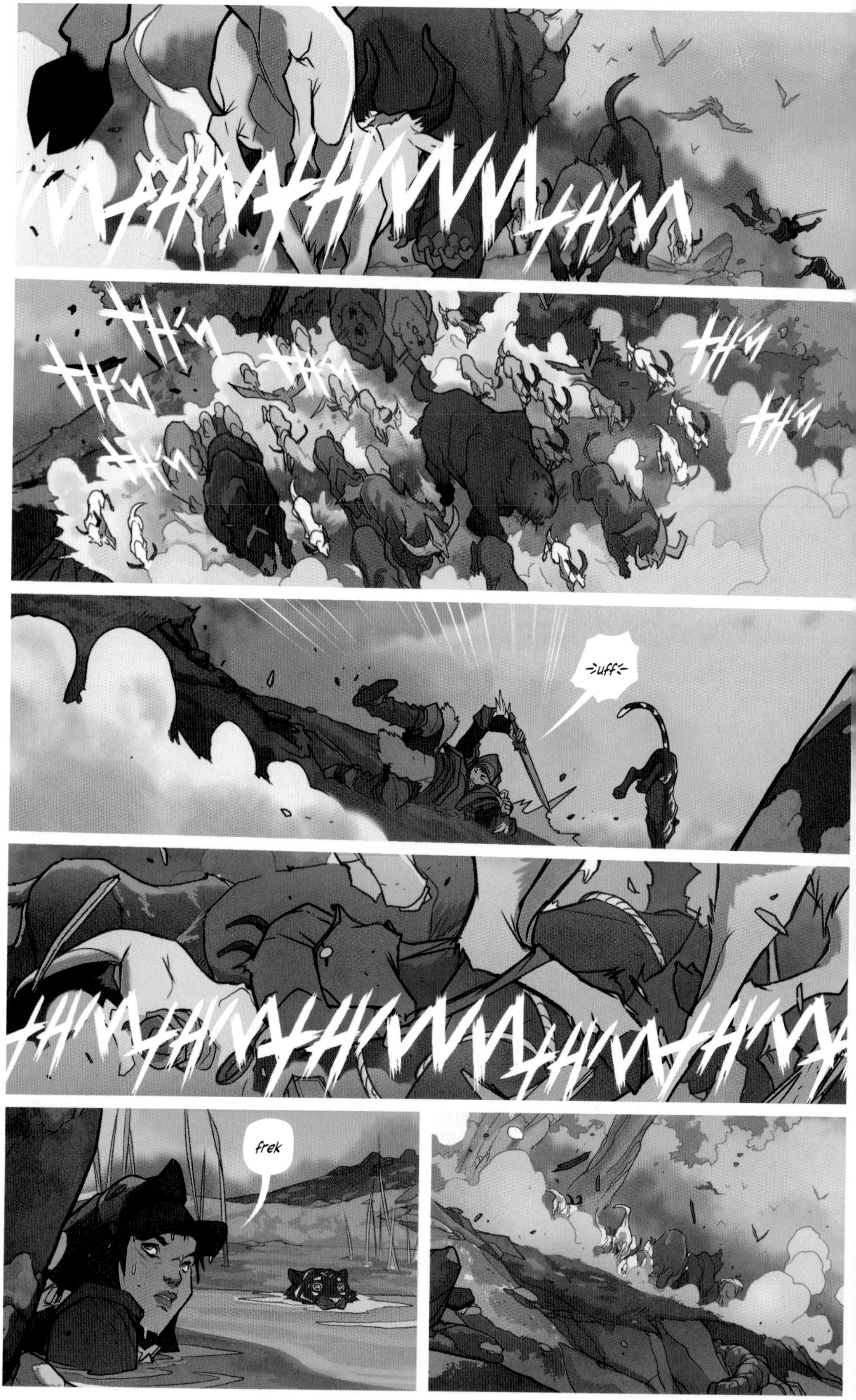
uff
frek

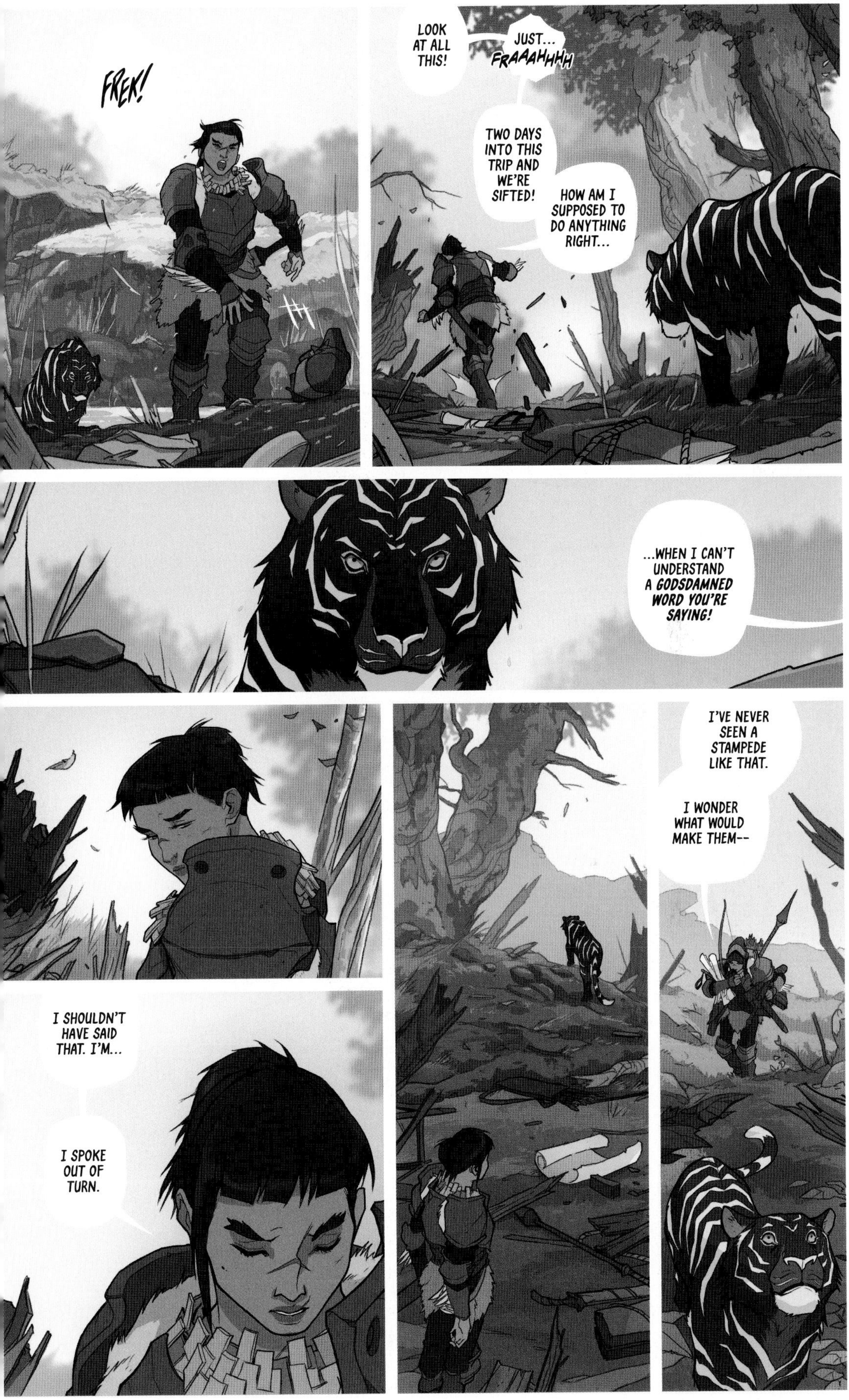
FREK!
LOOK AT ALL THIS!
JUST... FRAAAHHHH
TWO DAYS INTO THIS TRIP AND WE'RE SIFTED!
HOW AM I SUPPOSED TO DO ANYTHING RIGHT...
...WHEN I CAN'T UNDERSTAND A GODSDAMNED WORD YOU'RE SAYING!
I SHOULDN'T HAVE SAID THAT. I'M...
I SPOKE OUT OF TURN.
I'VE NEVER SEEN A STAMPEDE LIKE THAT.
I WONDER WHAT WOULD MAKE THEM--

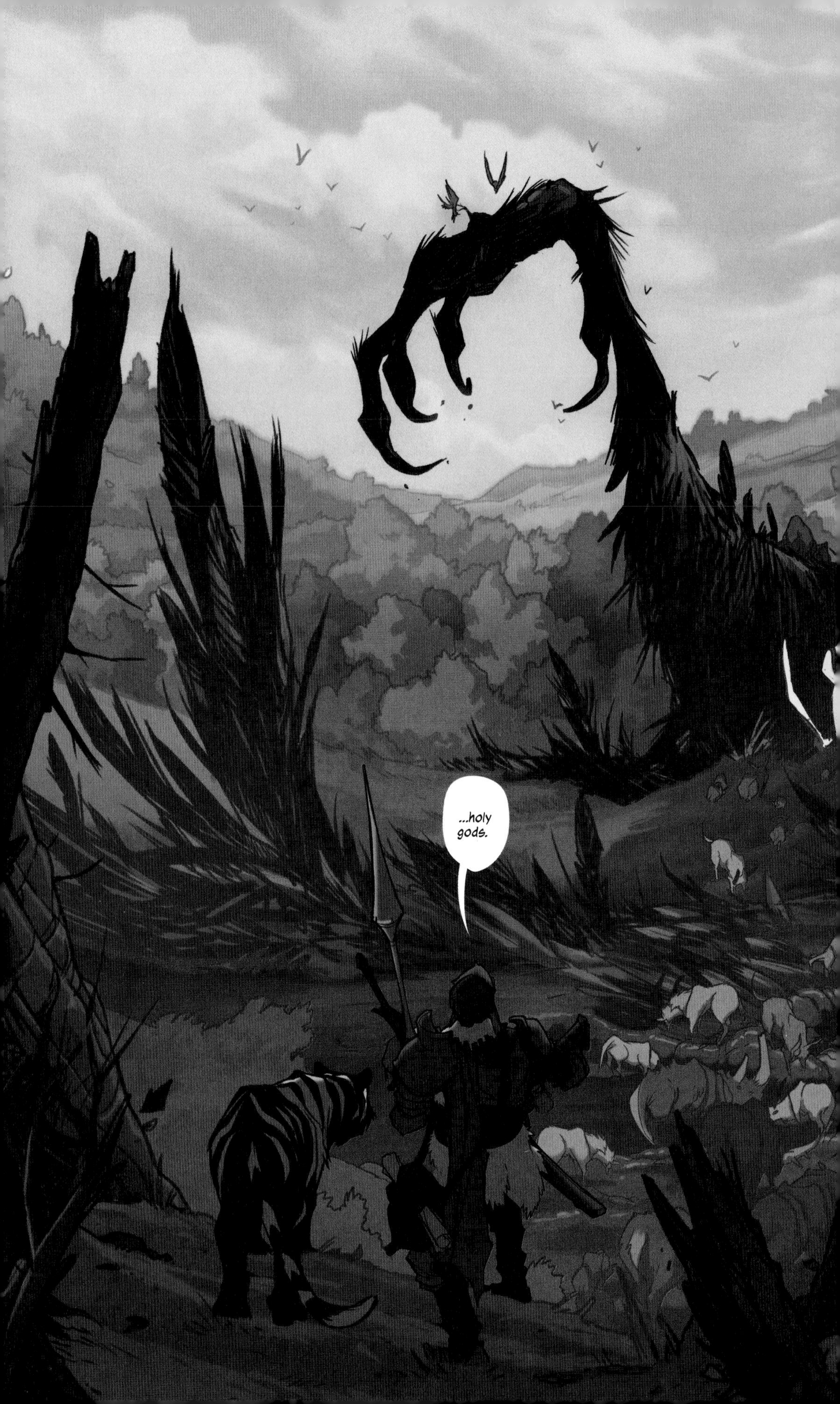
...holy gods.

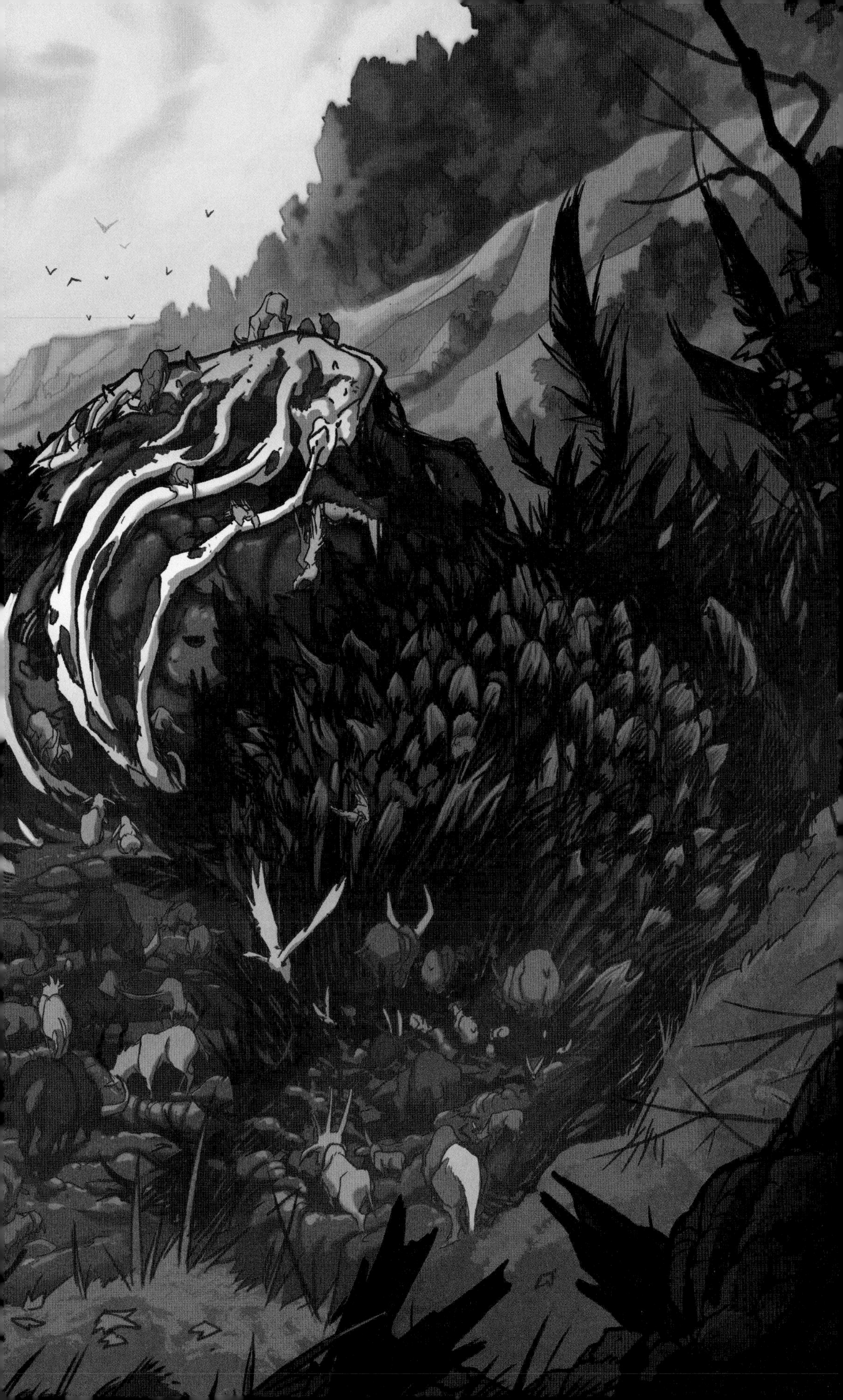

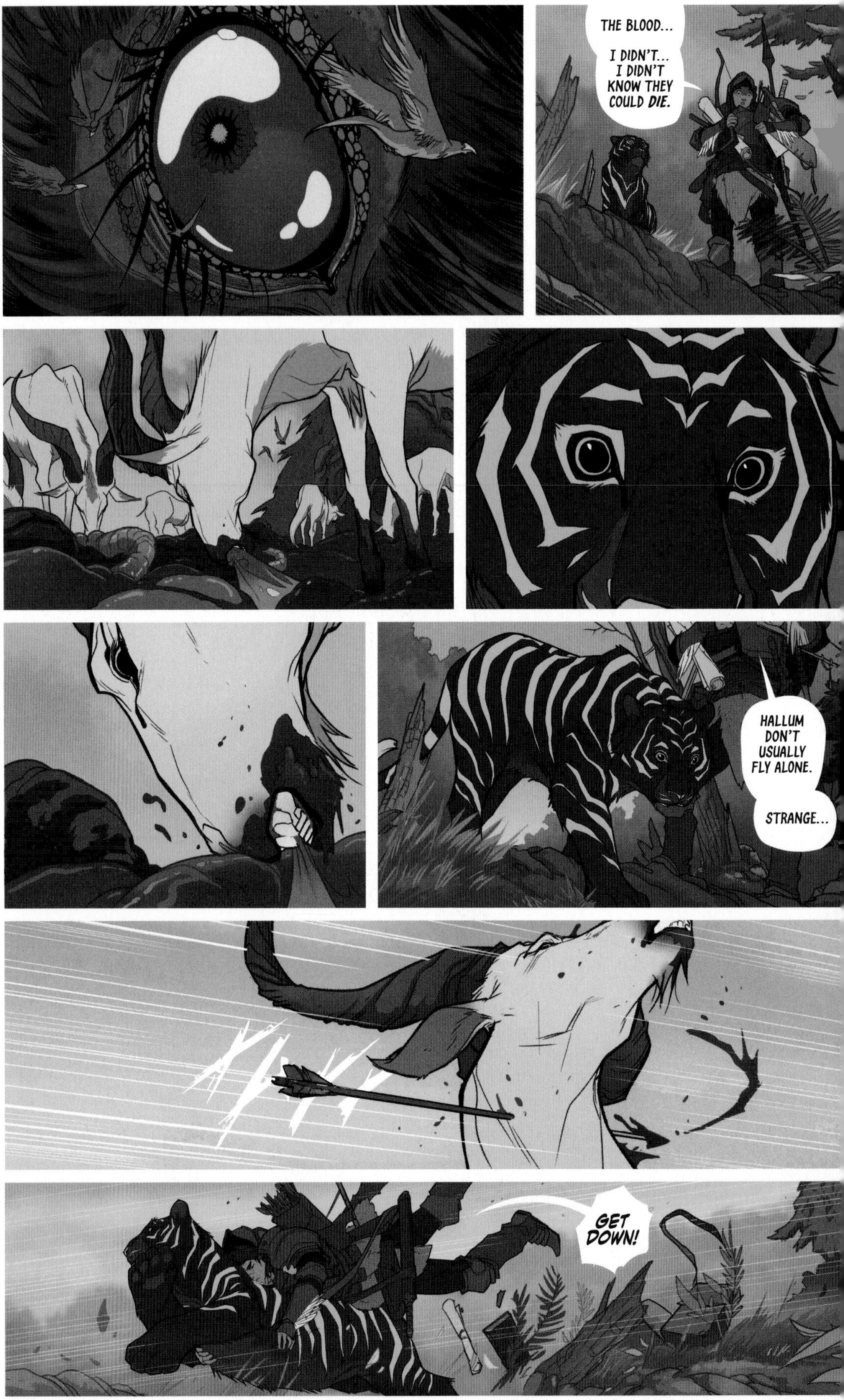
THE BLOOD...
I DIDN'T... I DIDN'T KNOW THEY COULD DIE.
HALLUM DON'T USUALLY FLY ALONE.
STRANGE...
GET DOWN!

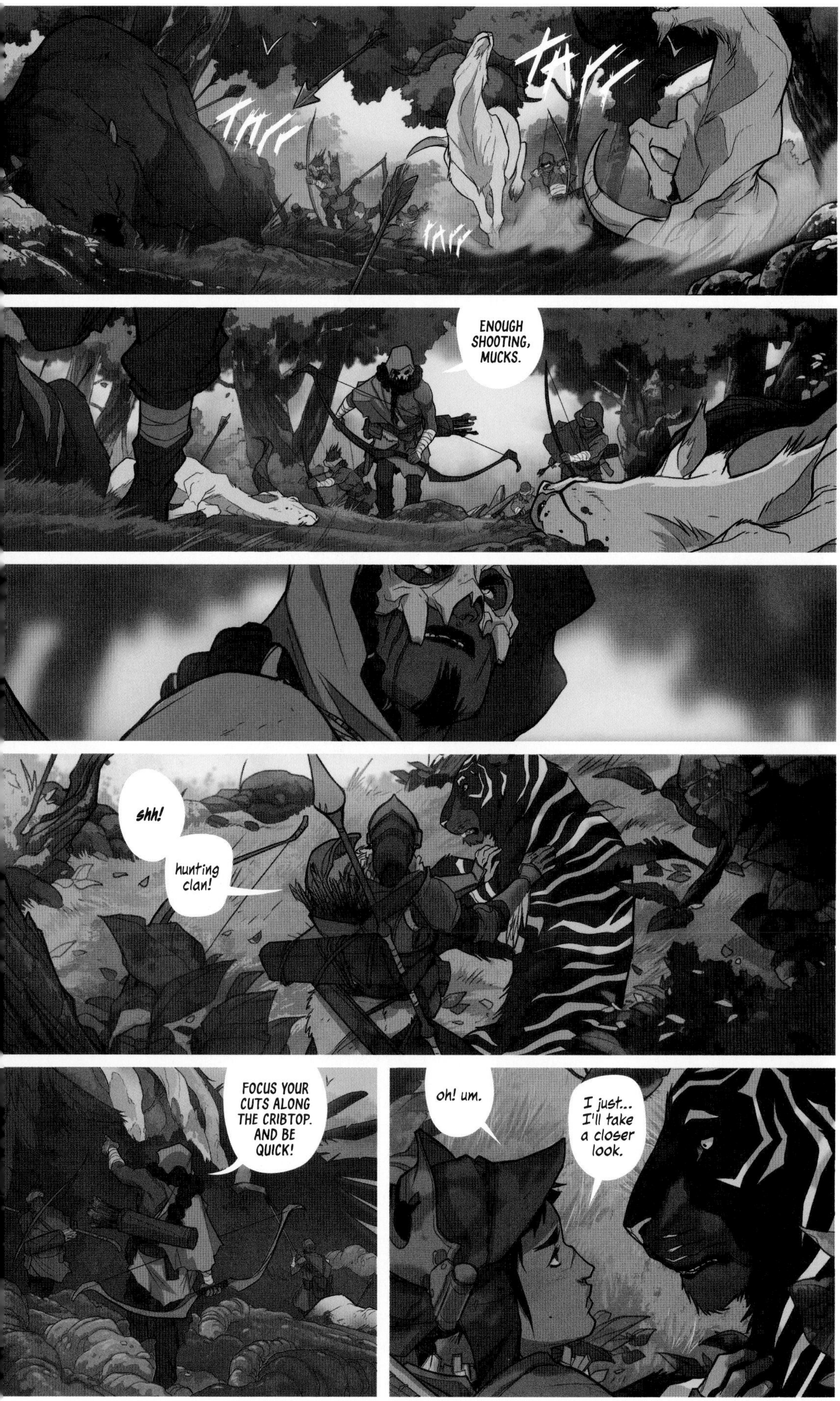

THUNK
THUNK
THUNK
ENOUGH SHOOTING, MUCKS.
shh!
hunting clan!
FOCUS YOUR CUTS ALONG THE CRIBTOP. AND BE QUICK!
oh! um.
I just... I'll take a closer look.

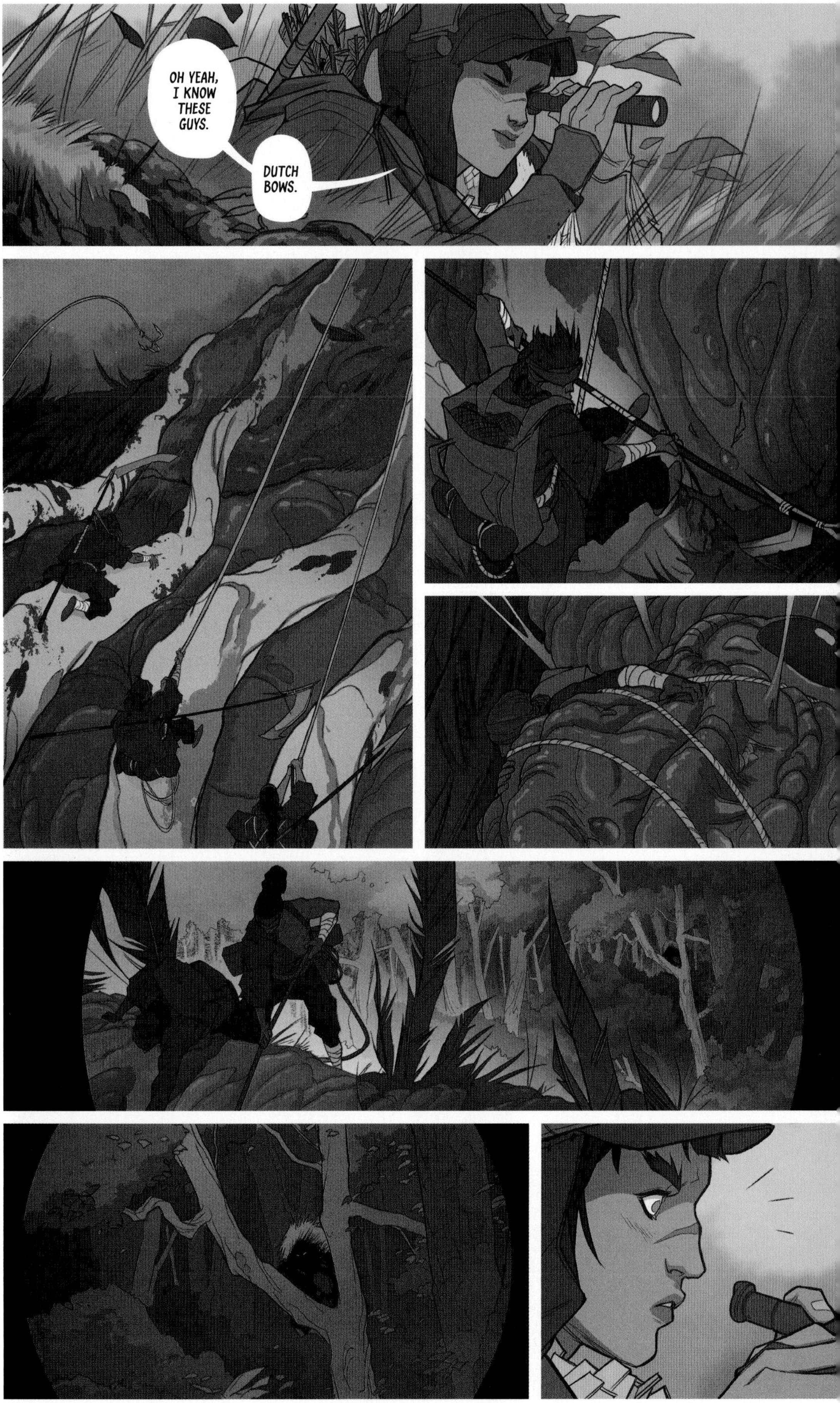
OH YEAH, I KNOW THESE GUYS.
DUTCH BOWS.

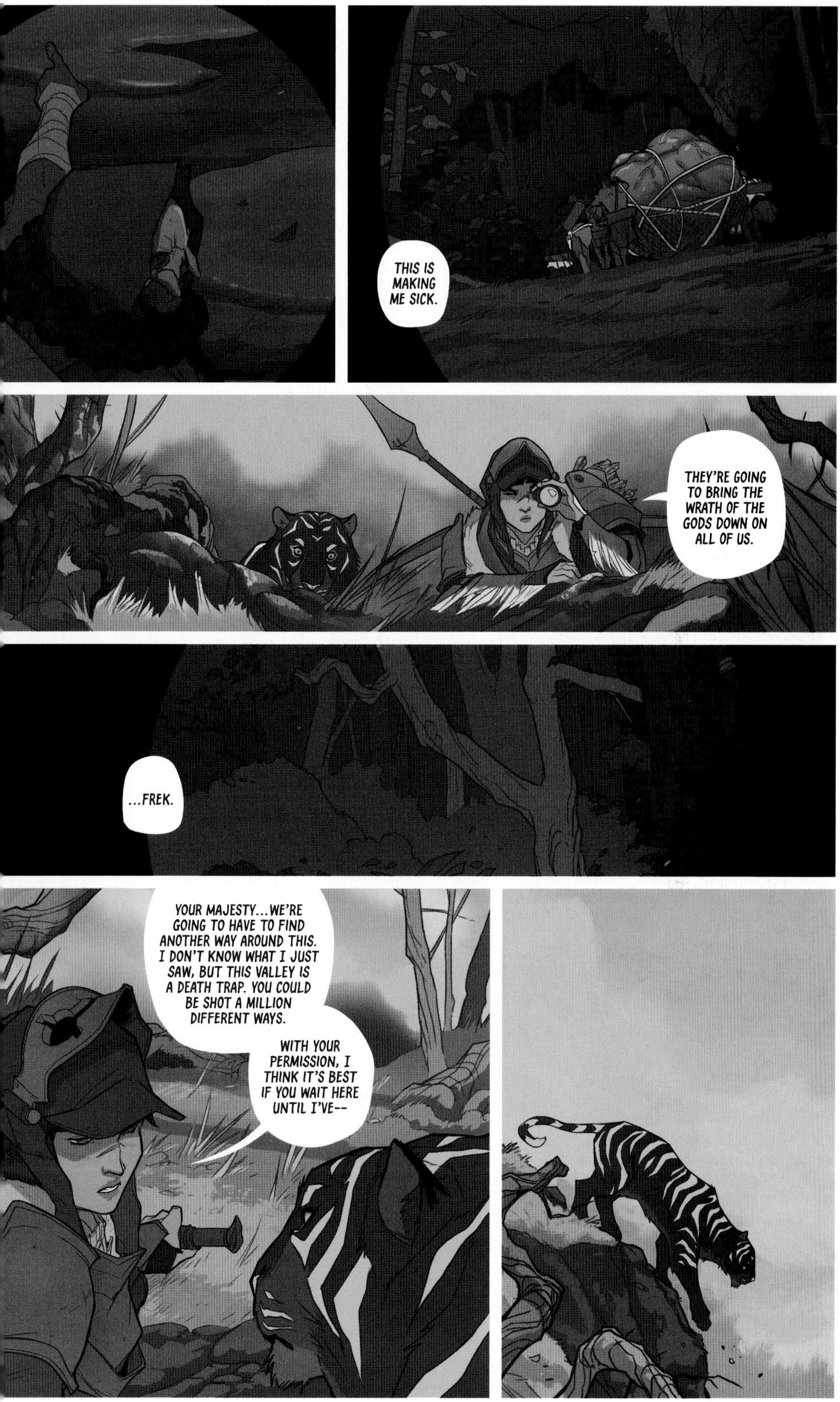

THIS IS MAKING ME SICK.
THEY'RE GOING TO BRING THE WRATH OF THE GODS DOWN ON ALL OF US.
...FREK.
YOUR MAJESTY...WE'RE GOING TO HAVE TO FIND ANOTHER WAY AROUND THIS. I DON'T KNOW WHAT I JUST SAW, BUT THIS VALLEY IS A DEATH TRAP. YOU COULD BE SHOT A MILLION DIFFERENT WAYS.
WITH YOUR PERMISSION, I THINK IT'S BEST IF YOU WAIT HERE UNTIL I'VE--

Please forgive us, Hallum.

May your spirit find its way to Isola.

YOURS TOO, LITTLE PECK.

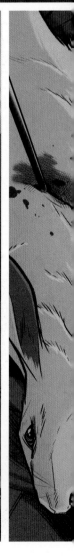

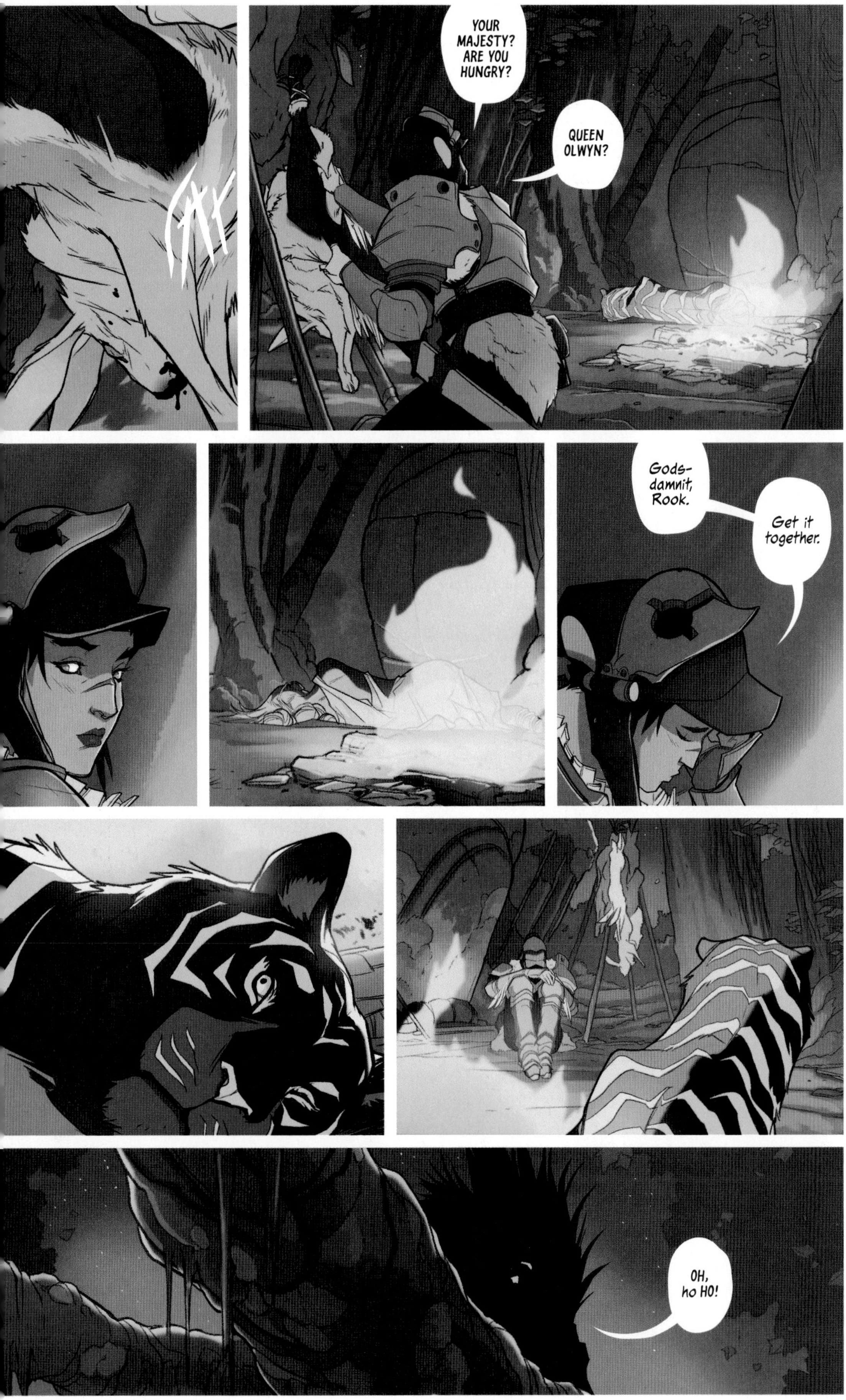
YOUR MAJESTY? ARE YOU HUNGRY?
QUEEN OLWYN?
Gods-damnit, Rook.
Get it together.
OH, ho HO!

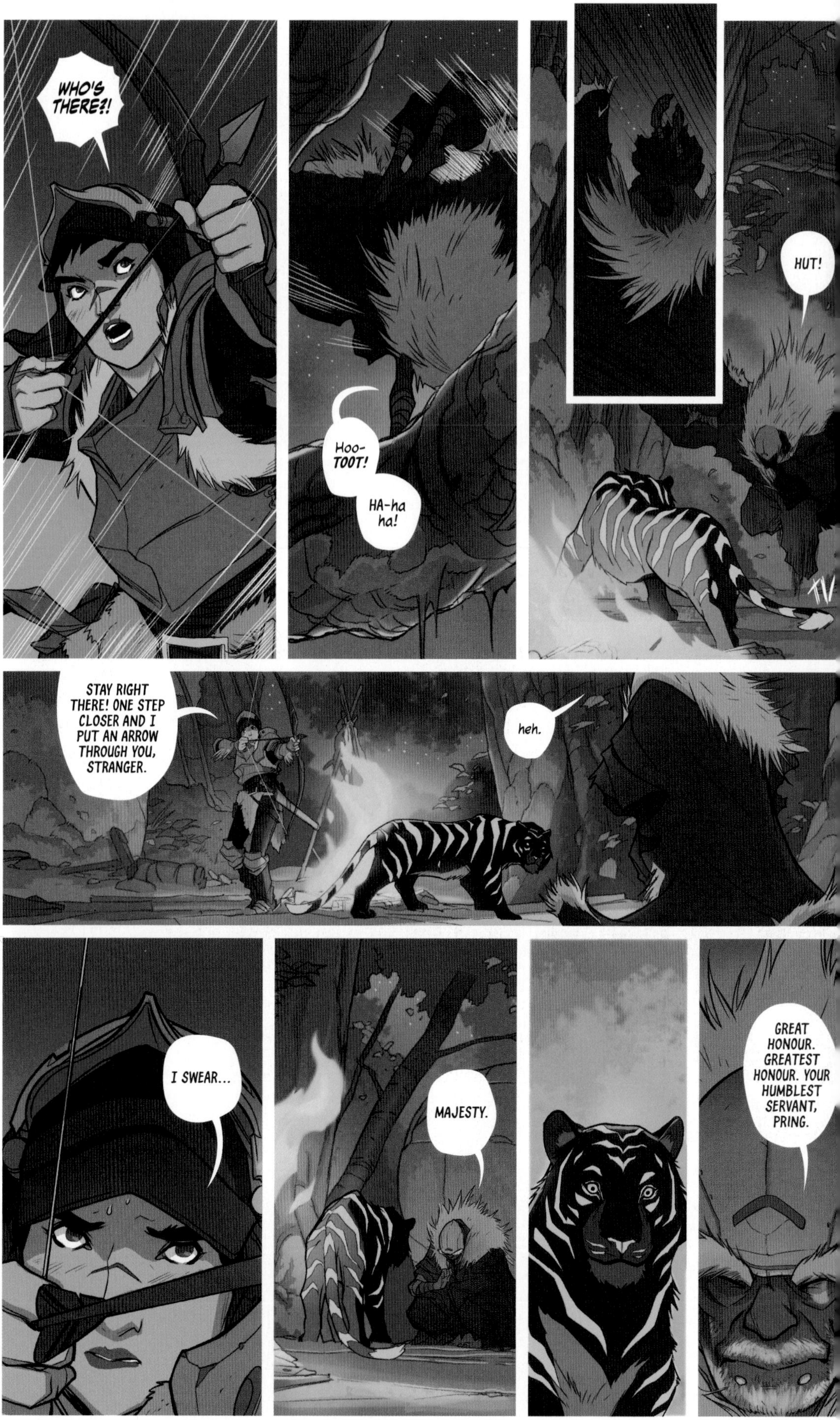
WHO'S THERE?!
Hoo-TOOT!
HA-ha ha!
HUT!
STAY RIGHT THERE! ONE STEP CLOSER AND I PUT AN ARROW THROUGH YOU, STRANGER.
heh.
I SWEAR...
MAJESTY.
GREAT HONOUR. GREATEST HONOUR. YOUR HUMBLEST SERVANT, PRING.

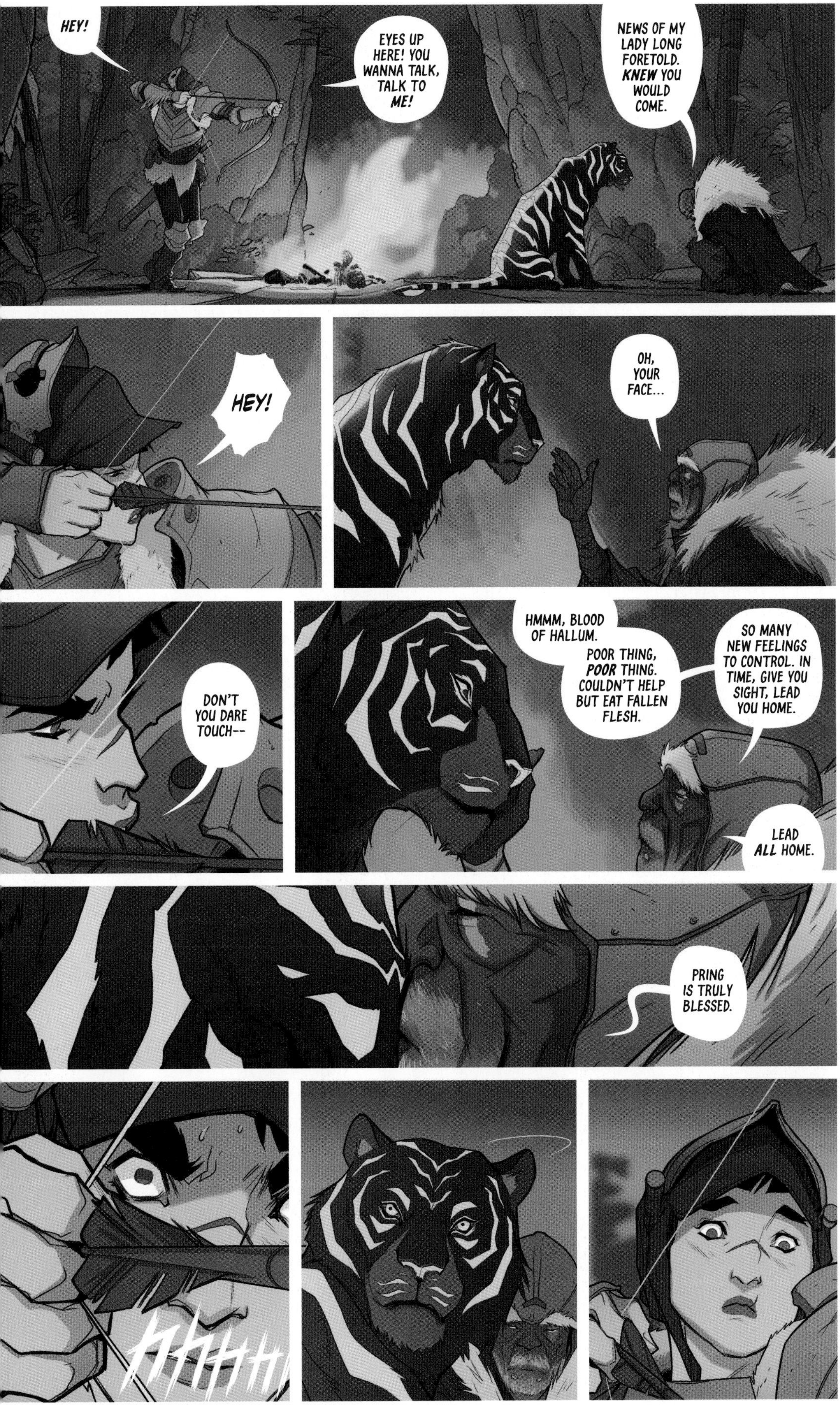
HEY!
EYES UP HERE! YOU WANNA TALK, TALK TO ME!
NEWS OF MY LADY LONG FORETOLD. KNEW YOU WOULD COME.
HEY!
OH, YOUR FACE...
DON'T YOU DARE TOUCH--
HMMM, BLOOD OF HALLUM.
POOR THING, POOR THING. COULDN'T HELP BUT EAT FALLEN FLESH.
SO MANY NEW FEELINGS TO CONTROL. IN TIME, GIVE YOU SIGHT, LEAD YOU HOME.
LEAD ALL HOME.
PRING IS TRULY BLESSED.
hhhhh

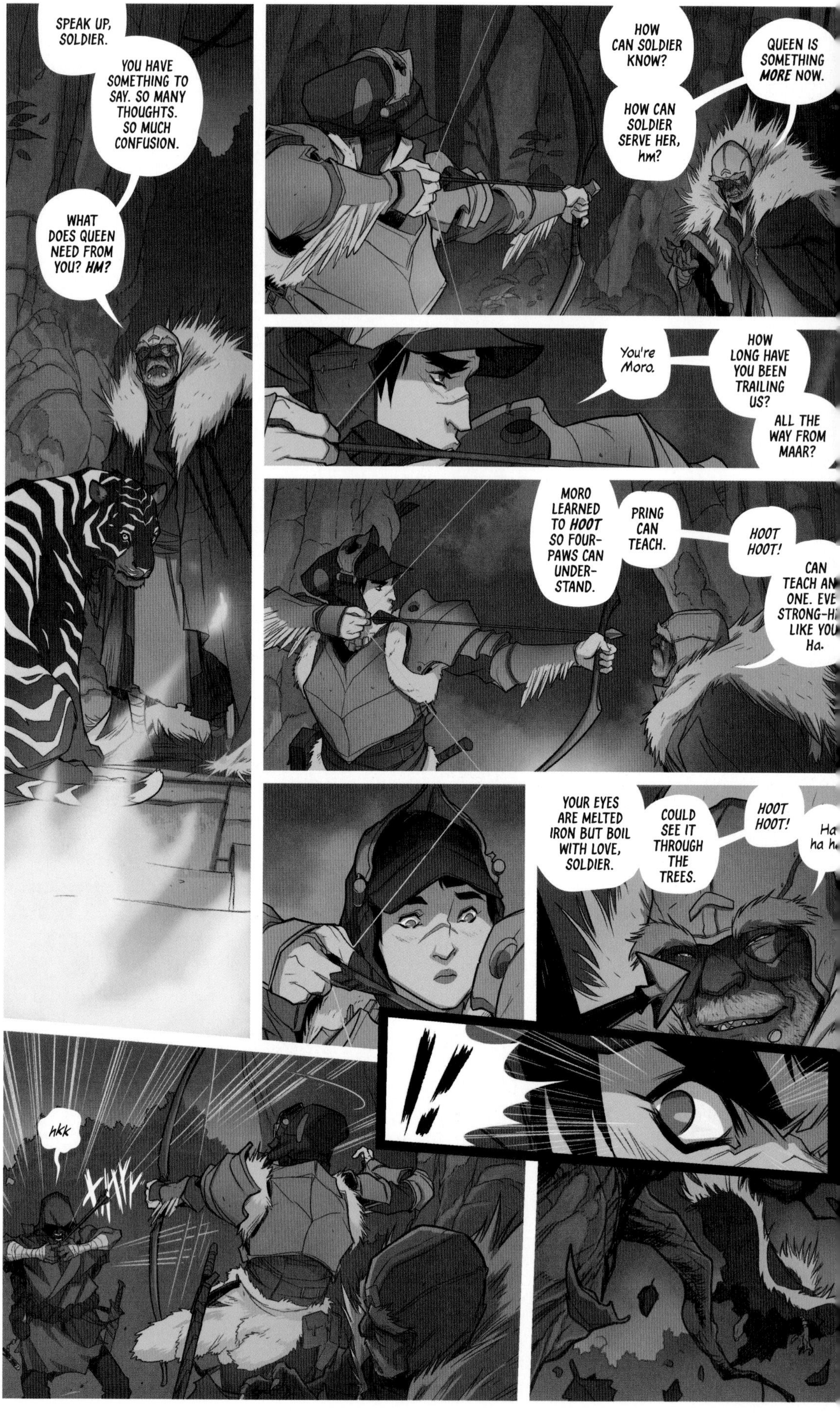

SPEAK UP, SOLDIER.
YOU HAVE SOMETHING TO SAY. SO MANY THOUGHTS. SO MUCH CONFUSION.
WHAT DOES QUEEN NEED FROM YOU? HM?
HOW CAN SOLDIER KNOW?
HOW CAN SOLDIER SERVE HER, hm?
QUEEN IS SOMETHING MORE NOW.
You're Moro.
HOW LONG HAVE YOU BEEN TRAILING US?
ALL THE WAY FROM MAAR?
MORO LEARNED TO HOOT SO FOUR-PAWS CAN UNDER-STAND.
PRING CAN TEACH.
HOOT HOOT!
YOUR EYES ARE MELTED IRON BUT BOIL WITH LOVE, SOLDIER.
COULD SEE IT THROUGH THE TREES.
HOOT HOOT!
!!
hkk

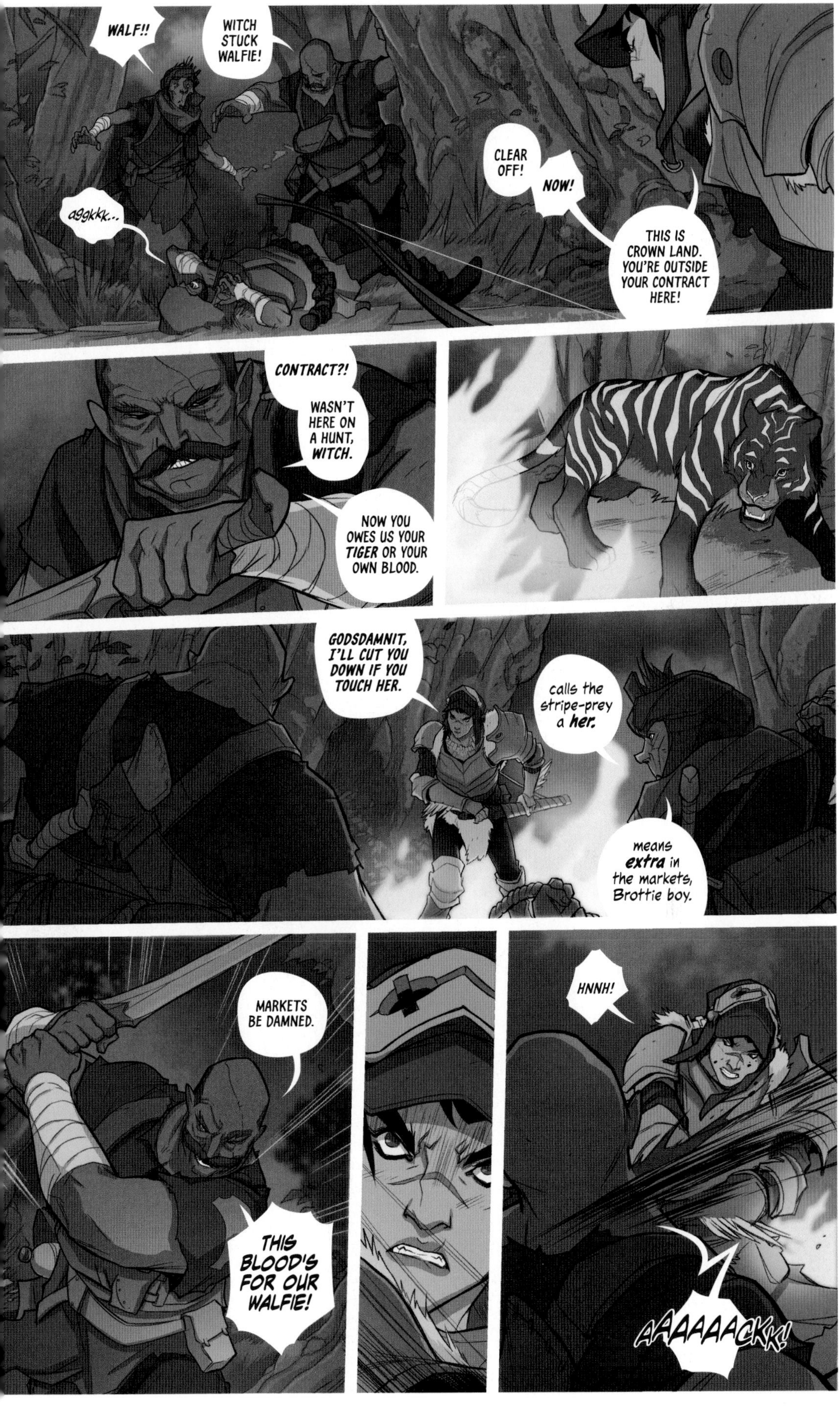
WALF!!
WITCH STUCK WALFIE!
aggkkk...
CLEAR OFF!
NOW!
THIS IS CROWN LAND. YOU'RE OUTSIDE YOUR CONTRACT HERE!
CONTRACT?!
WASN'T HERE ON A HUNT, WITCH.
NOW YOU OWES US YOUR TIGER OR YOUR OWN BLOOD.
GODSDAMNIT, I'LL CUT YOU DOWN IF YOU TOUCH HER.
calls the stripe-prey a her.
means extra in the markets, Brottie boy.
MARKETS BE DAMNED.
THIS BLOOD'S FOR OUR WALFIE!
HNNH!
AAAAAACKK!

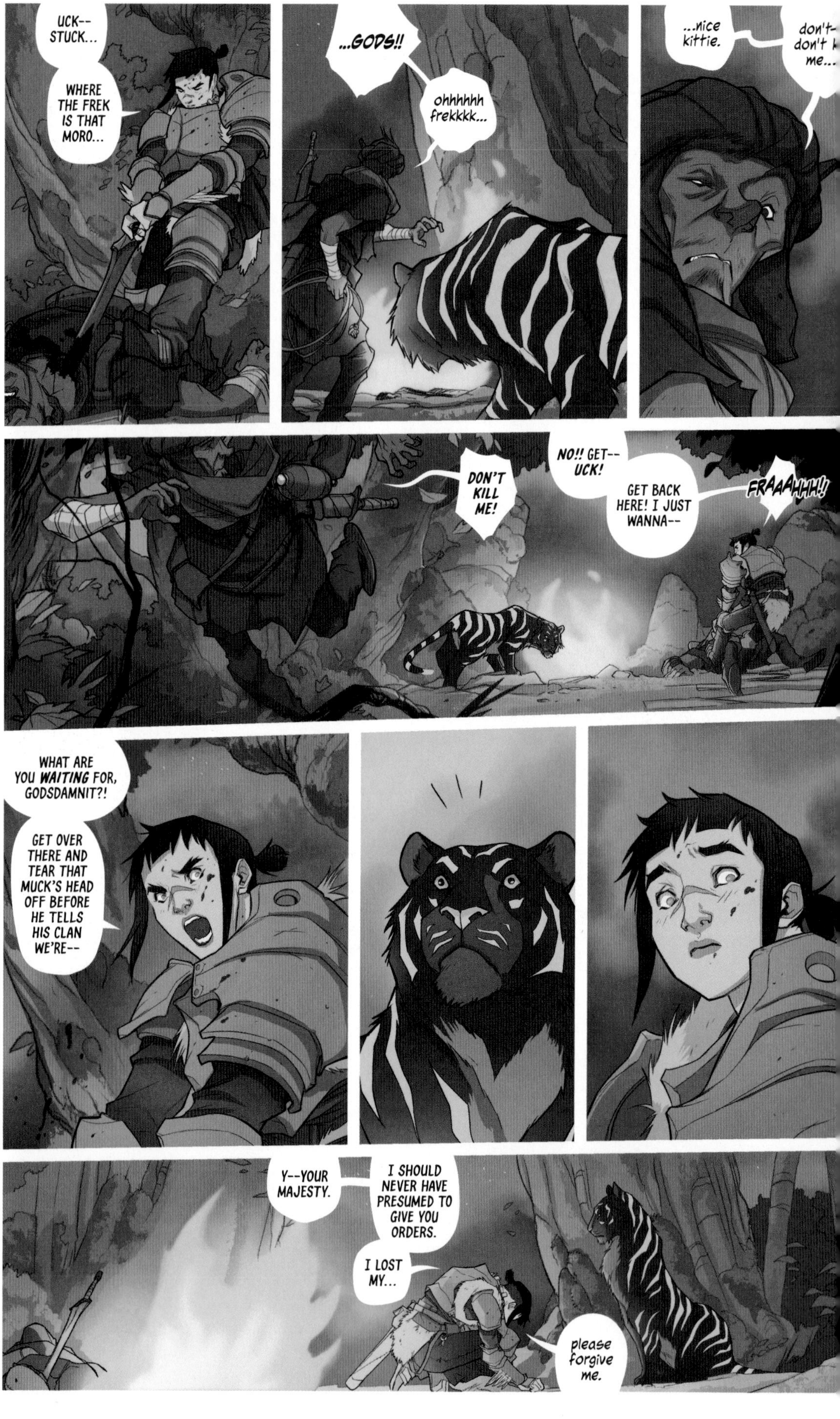
UCK--
STUCK...
WHERE THE FREK IS THAT MORO...
...GODS!!
ohhhhhh frekkkk...
...nice kittie.
don't-- don't k me...
DON'T KILL ME!
NO!! GET--
UCK!
GET BACK HERE! I JUST WANNA--
FRAAAHHH!!
WHAT ARE YOU WAITING FOR, GODSDAMNIT?!
GET OVER THERE AND TEAR THAT MUCK'S HEAD OFF BEFORE HE TELLS HIS CLAN WE'RE--
Y--YOUR MAJESTY.
I SHOULD NEVER HAVE PRESUMED TO GIVE YOU ORDERS.
I LOST MY...
please forgive me.

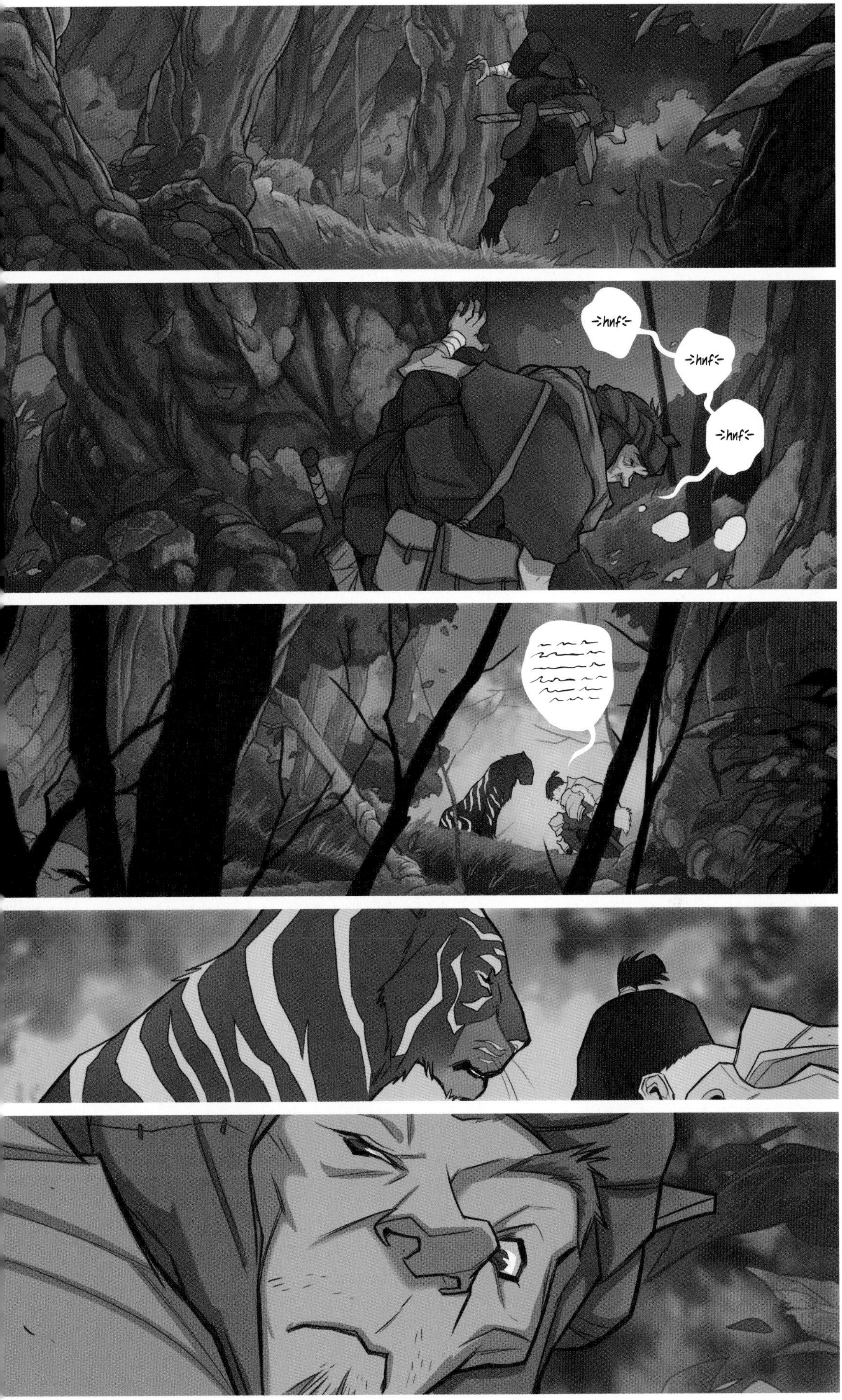
-hnf-
-hnf-
-hnf-

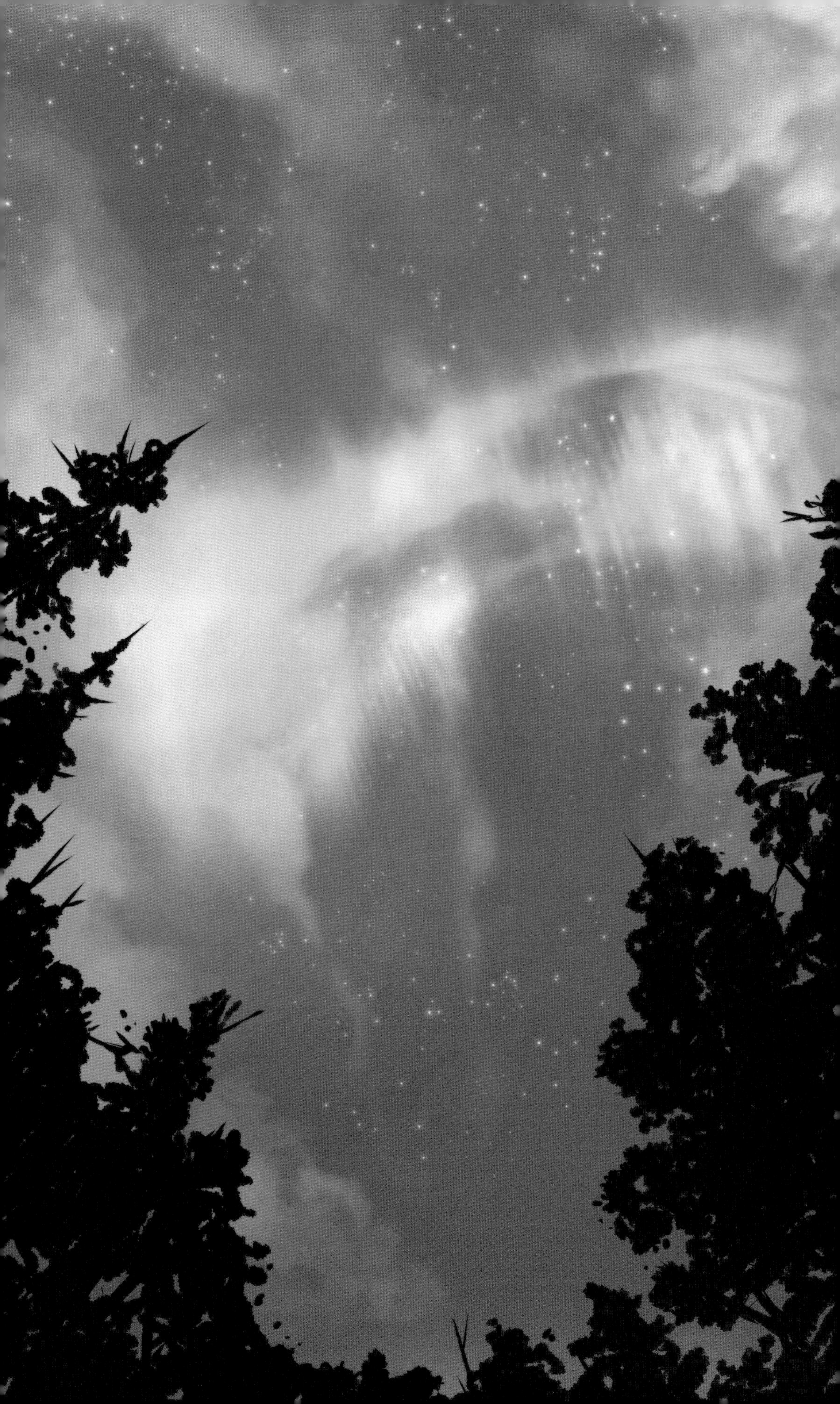

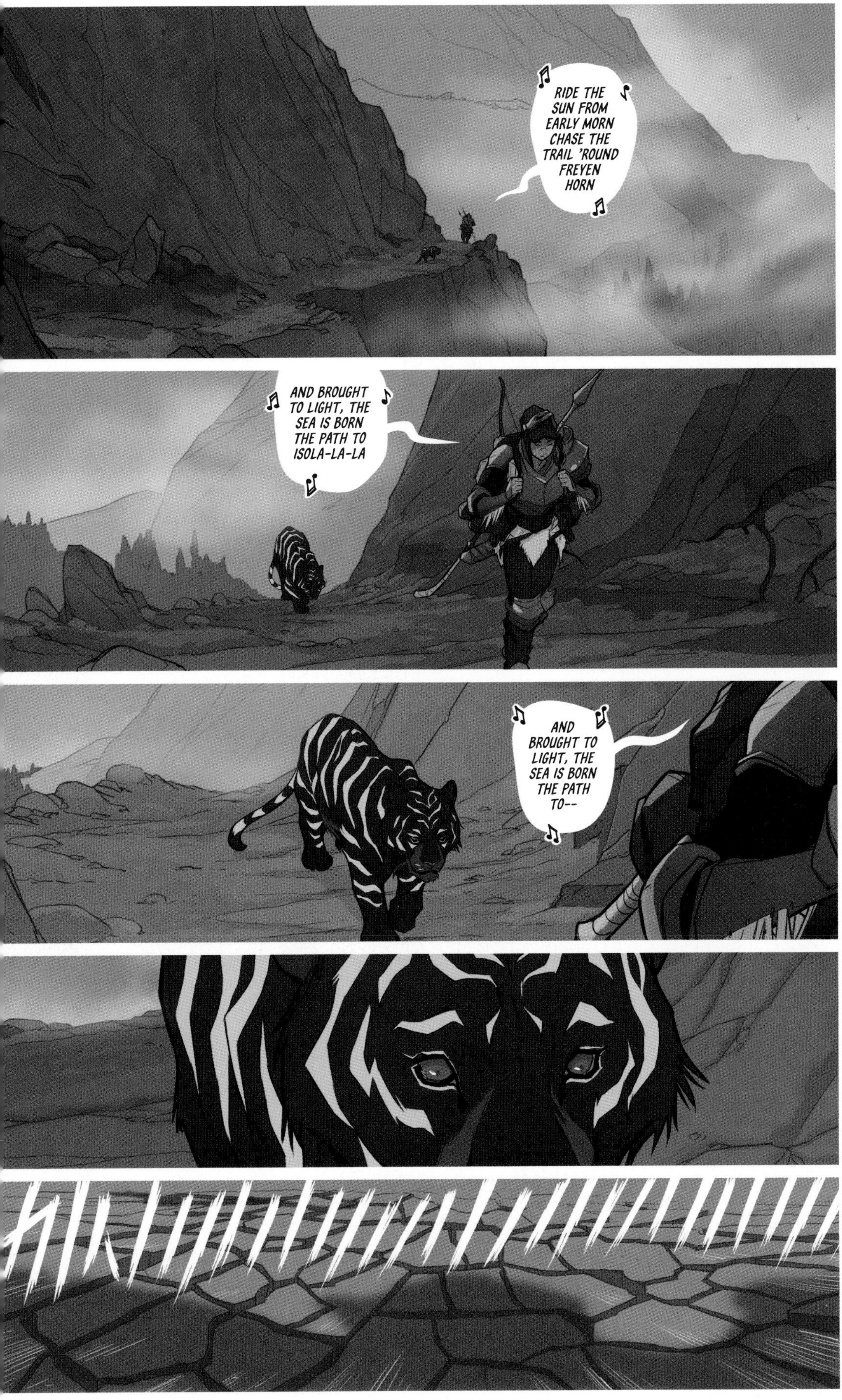
RIDE THE SUN FROM EARLY MORN CHASE THE TRAIL 'ROUND FREYEN HORN
AND BROUGHT TO LIGHT, THE SEA IS BORN THE PATH TO ISOLA-LA-LA
AND BROUGHT TO LIGHT, THE SEA IS BORN THE PATH TO--

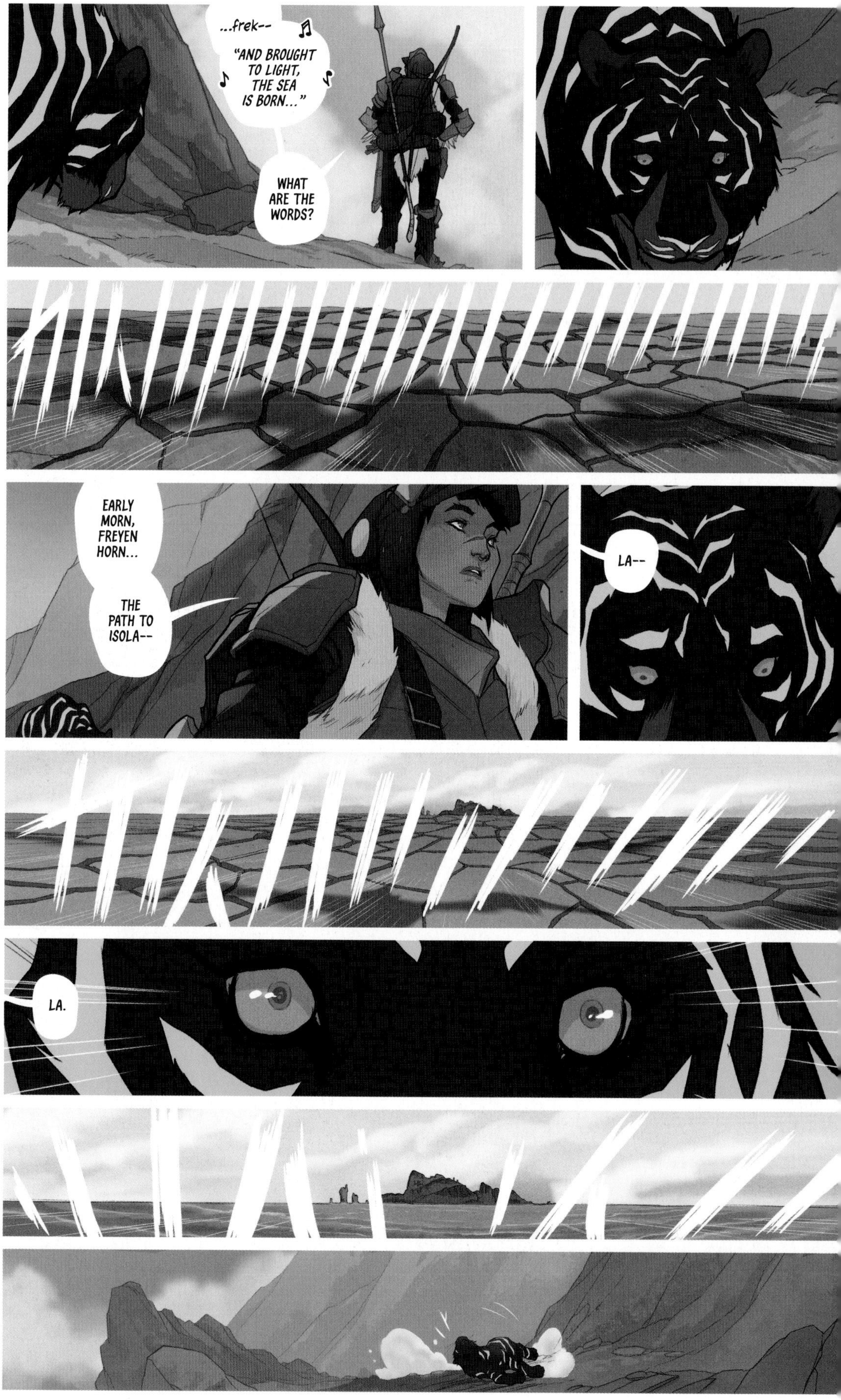
...frek--
"AND BROUGHT TO LIGHT, THE SEA IS BORN..."
WHAT ARE THE WORDS?
EARLY MORN, FREYEN HORN...
THE PATH TO ISOLA--
LA--
LA.

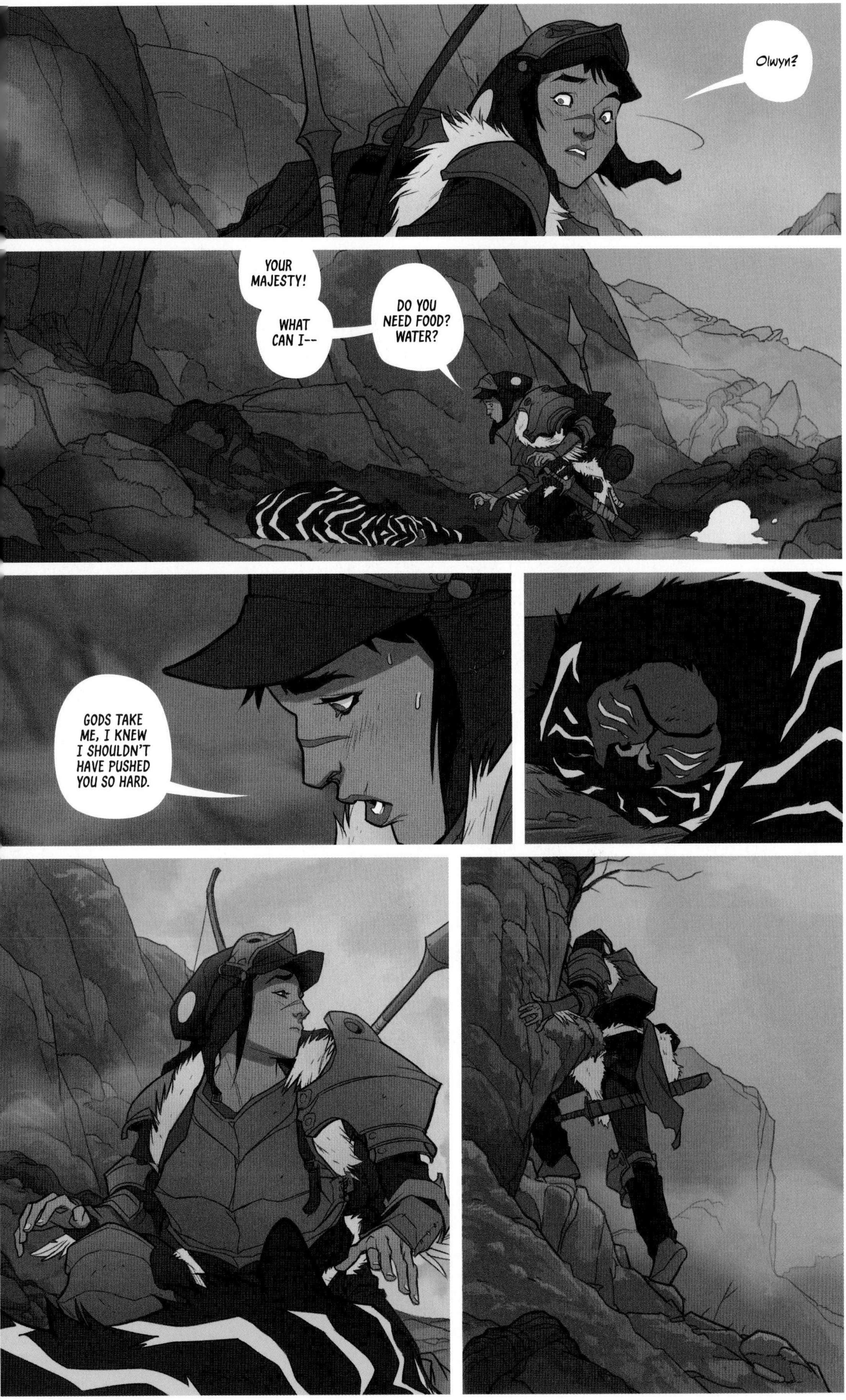
Olwyn?
YOUR MAJESTY!
WHAT CAN I--
DO YOU NEED FOOD? WATER?
GODS TAKE ME, I KNEW I SHOULDN'T HAVE PUSHED YOU SO HARD.

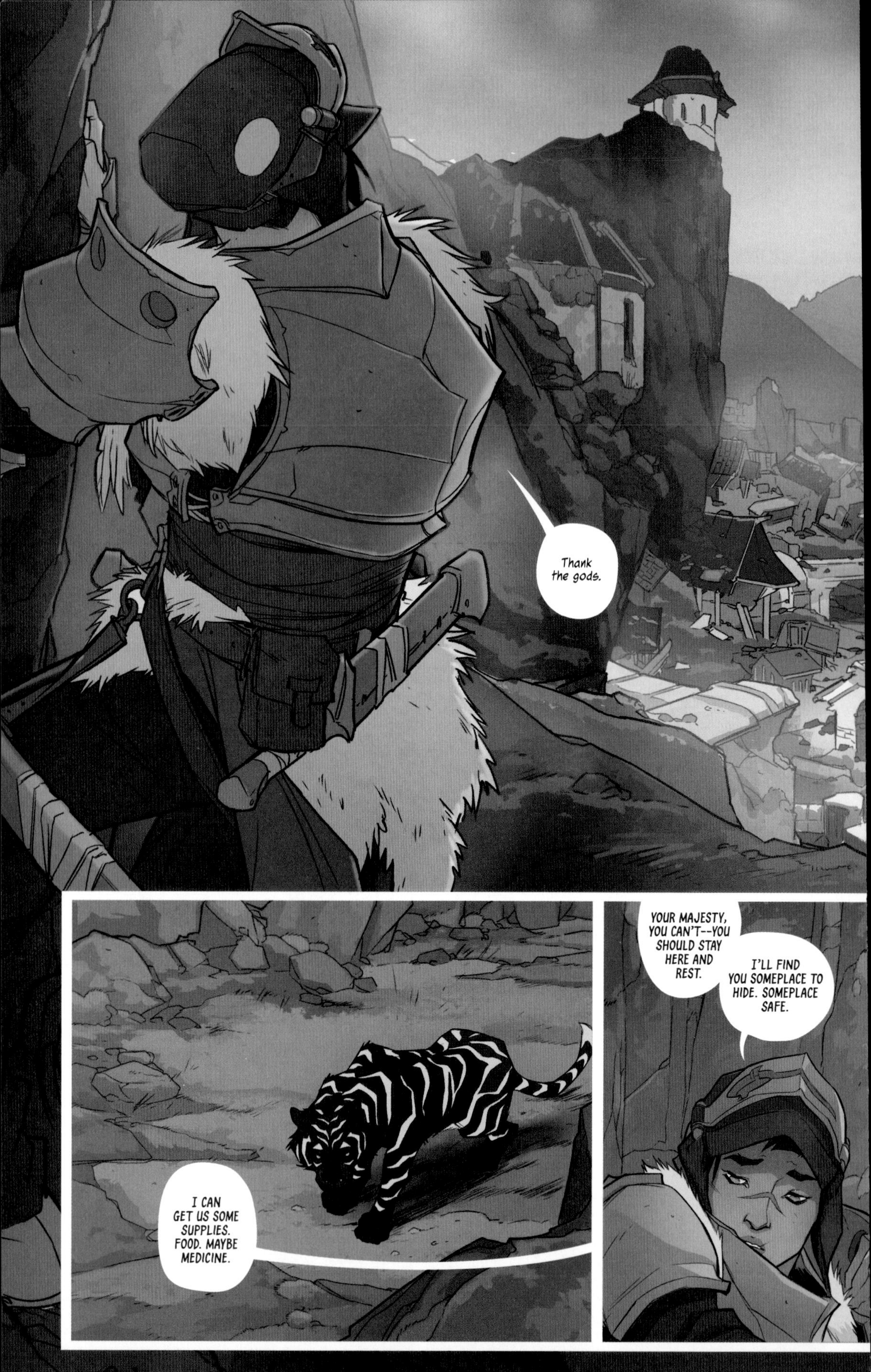
Thank the gods.
I CAN GET US SOME SUPPLIES. FOOD. MAYBE MEDICINE.
YOUR MAJESTY, YOU CAN'T--YOU SHOULD STAY HERE AND REST.
I'LL FIND YOU SOMEPLACE TO HIDE. SOMEPLACE SAFE.

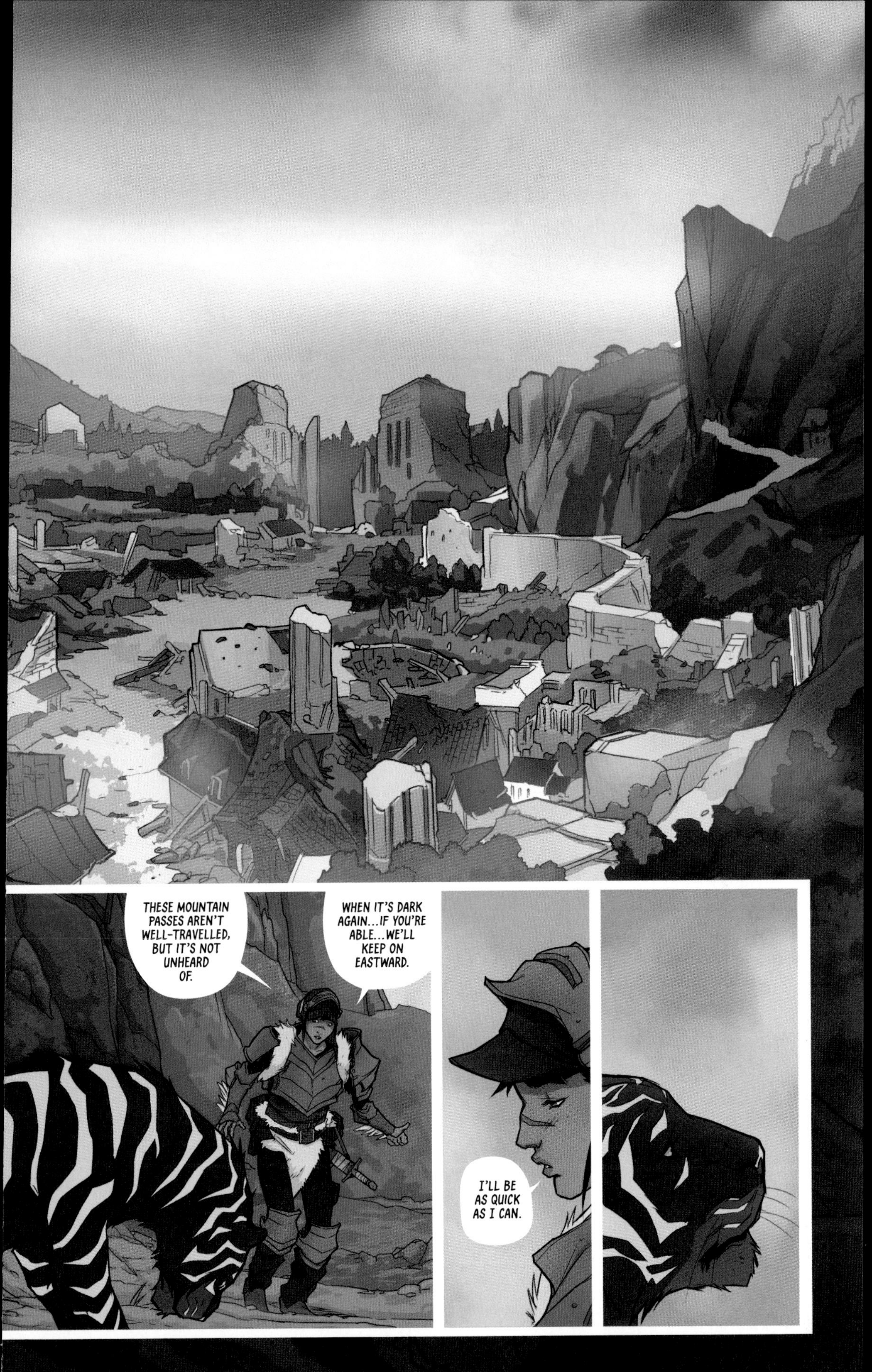
THESE MOUNTAIN PASSES AREN'T WELL-TRAVELLED, BUT IT'S NOT UNHEARD OF.
WHEN IT'S DARK AGAIN...IF YOU'RE ABLE...WE'LL KEEP ON EASTWARD.
I'LL BE AS QUICK AS I CAN.

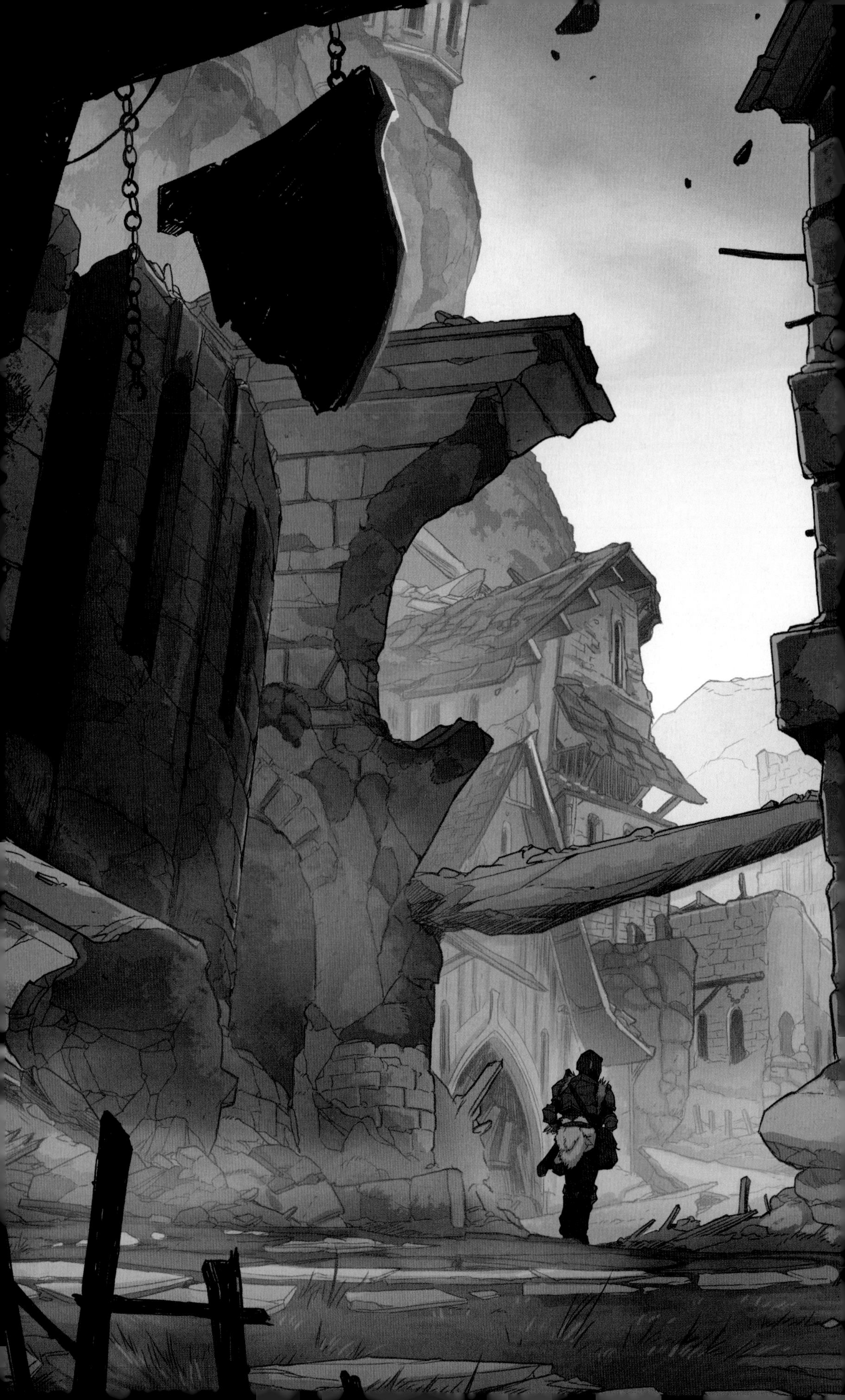

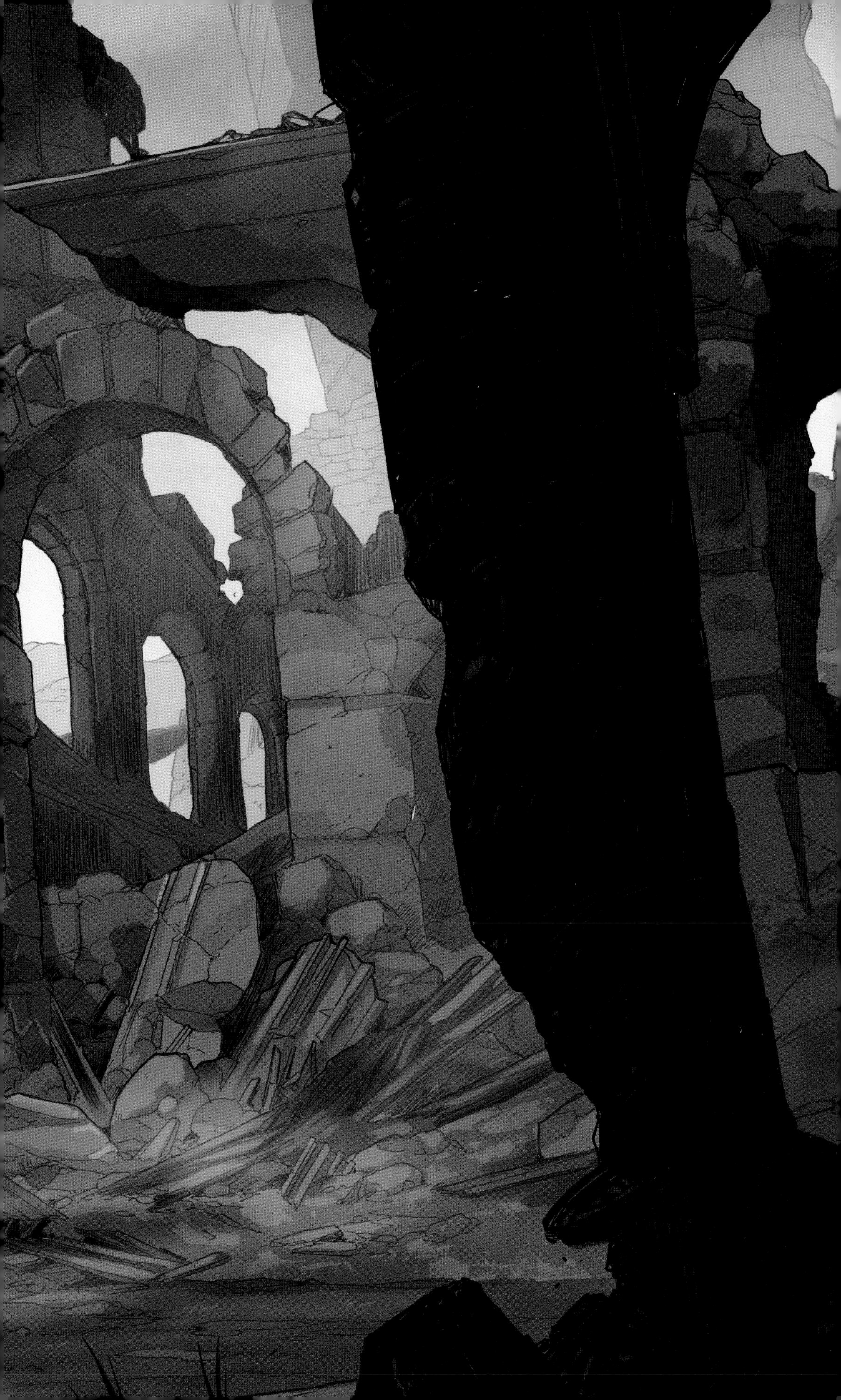

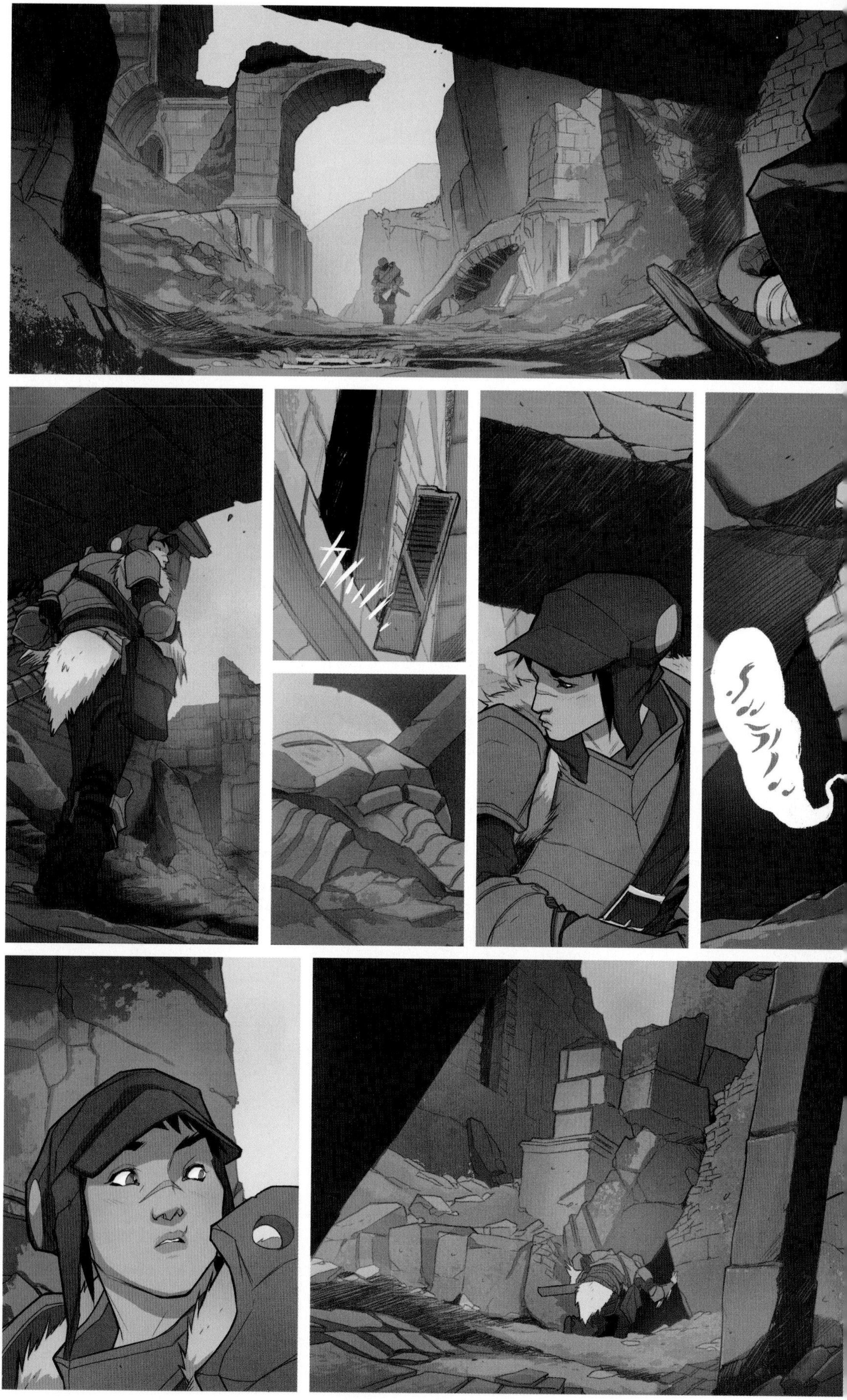

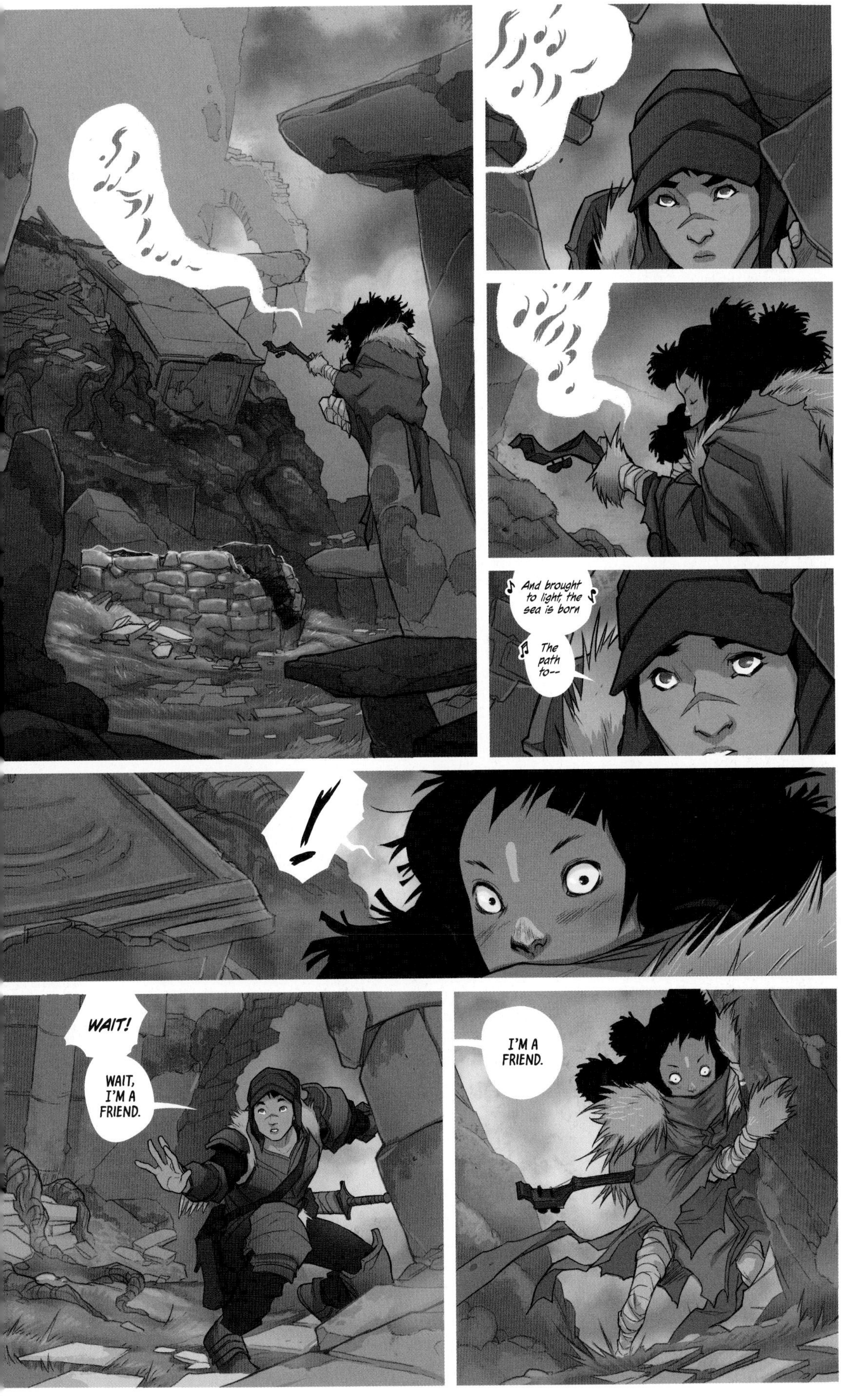
And brought to light, the sea is born
The path to--
!
WAIT!
WAIT, I'M A FRIEND.
I'M A FRIEND.

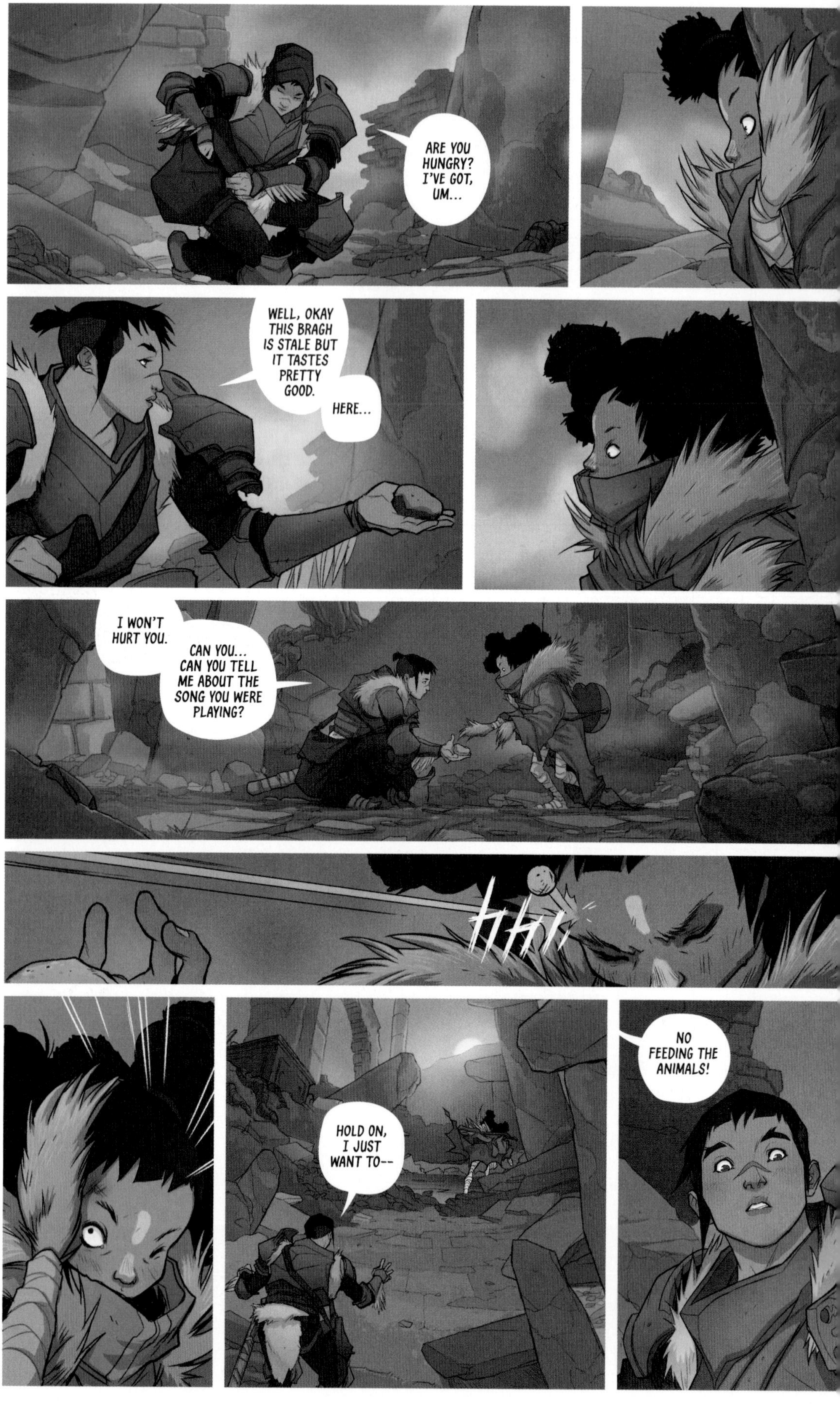
ARE YOU HUNGRY? I'VE GOT, UM...
WELL, OKAY THIS BRAGH IS STALE BUT IT TASTES PRETTY GOOD.
HERE...
I WON'T HURT YOU.
CAN YOU... CAN YOU TELL ME ABOUT THE SONG YOU WERE PLAYING?
HOLD ON, I JUST WANT TO--
NO FEEDING THE ANIMALS!

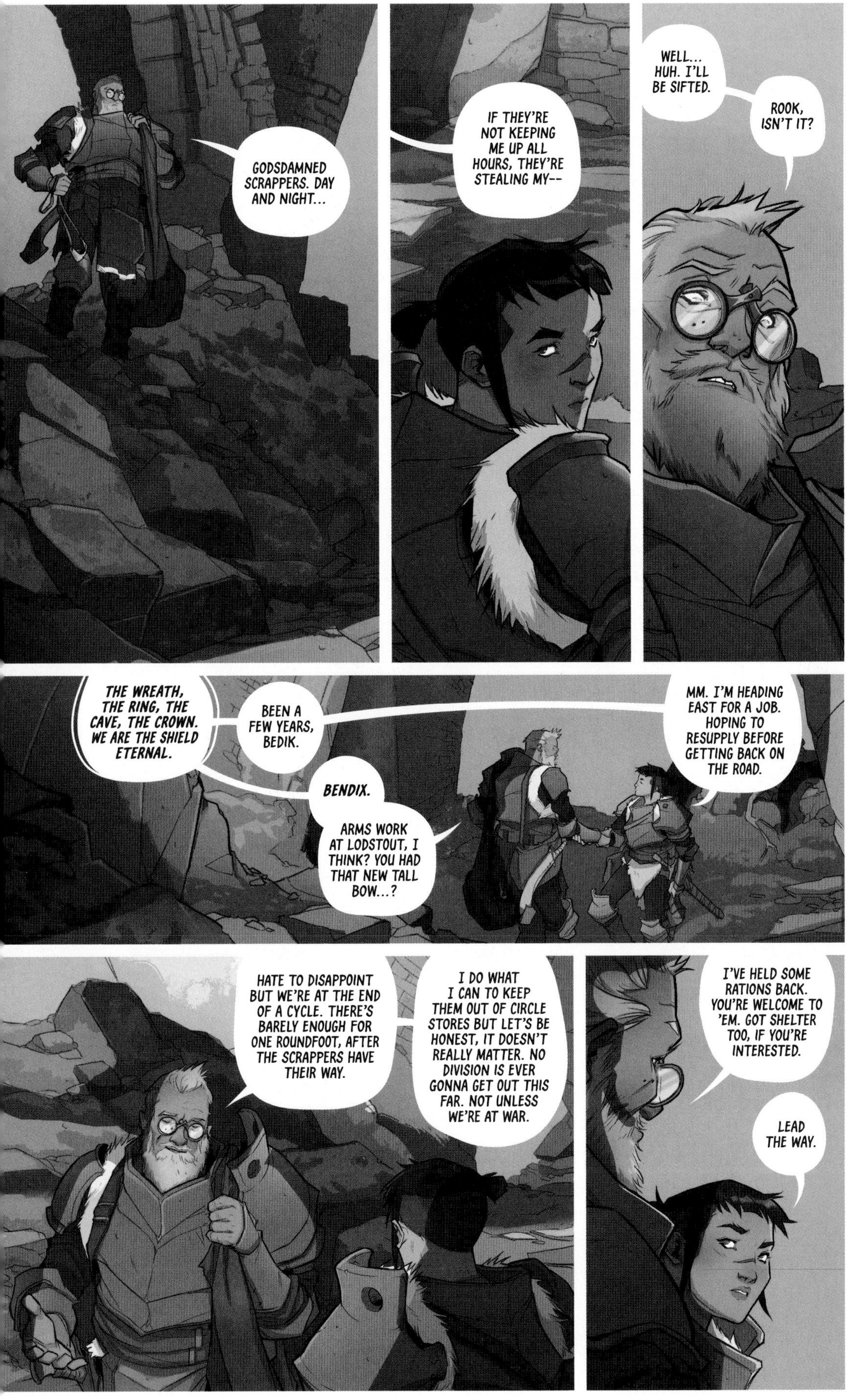
GODSDAMNED SCRAPPERS. DAY AND NIGHT...
IF THEY'RE NOT KEEPING ME UP ALL HOURS, THEY'RE STEALING MY--
WELL... HUH. I'LL BE SIFTED.
ROOK, ISN'T IT?
THE WREATH, THE RING, THE CAVE, THE CROWN. WE ARE THE SHIELD ETERNAL.
BEEN A FEW YEARS, BEDIK.
BENDIX.
ARMS WORK AT LODSTOUT, I THINK? YOU HAD THAT NEW TALL BOW...?
MM. I'M HEADING EAST FOR A JOB. HOPING TO RESUPPLY BEFORE GETTING BACK ON THE ROAD.
HATE TO DISAPPOINT BUT WE'RE AT THE END OF A CYCLE. THERE'S BARELY ENOUGH FOR ONE ROUNDFOOT, AFTER THE SCRAPPERS HAVE THEIR WAY.
I DO WHAT I CAN TO KEEP THEM OUT OF CIRCLE STORES BUT LET'S BE HONEST, IT DOESN'T REALLY MATTER. NO DIVISION IS EVER GONNA GET OUT THIS FAR. NOT UNLESS WE'RE AT WAR.
I'VE HELD SOME RATIONS BACK. YOU'RE WELCOME TO 'EM. GOT SHELTER TOO, IF YOU'RE INTERESTED.
LEAD THE WAY.

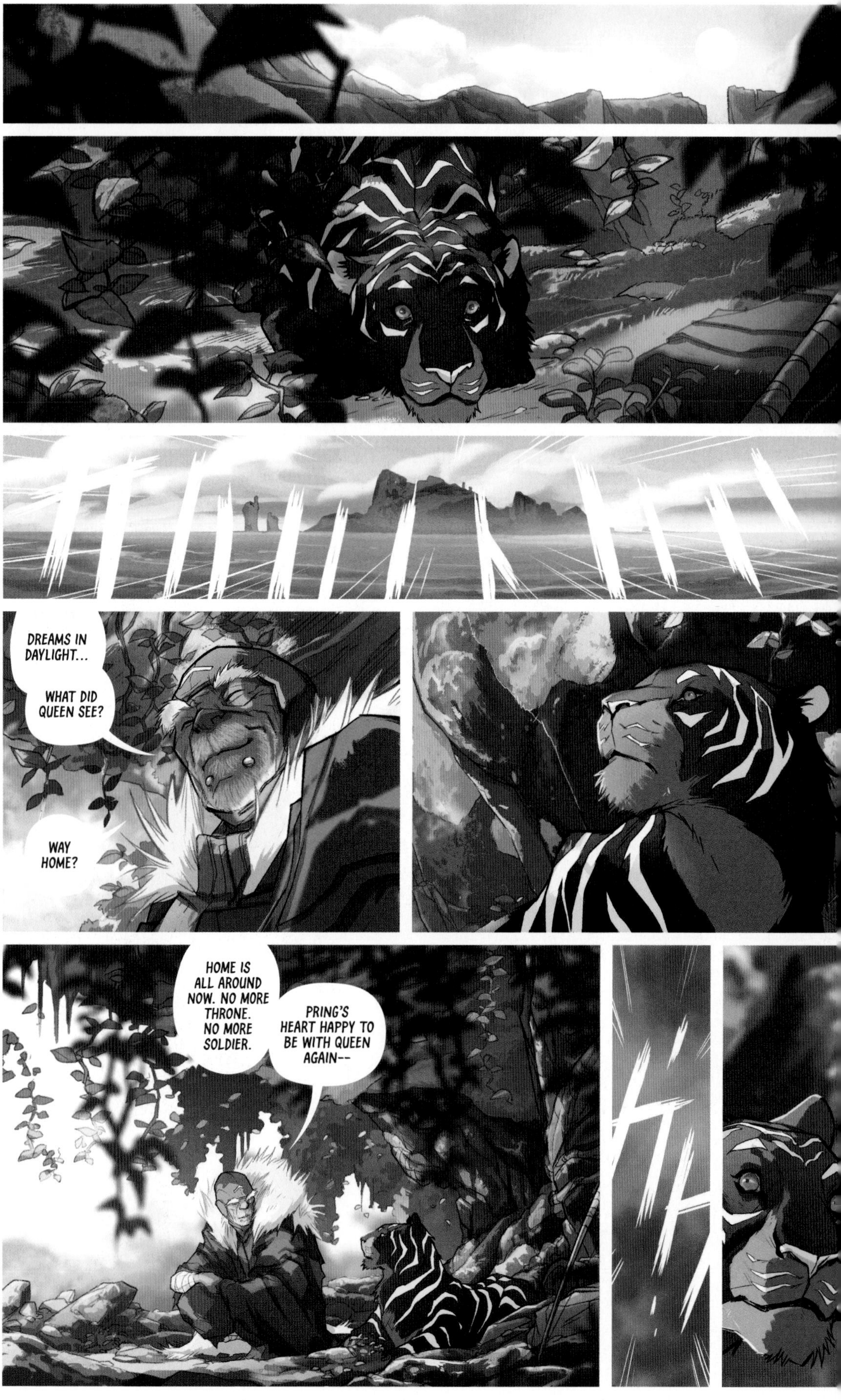

DREAMS IN DAYLIGHT...
WHAT DID QUEEN SEE?
WAY HOME?
HOME IS ALL AROUND NOW. NO MORE THRONE. NO MORE SOLDIER.
PRING'S HEART HAPPY TO BE WITH QUEEN AGAIN--

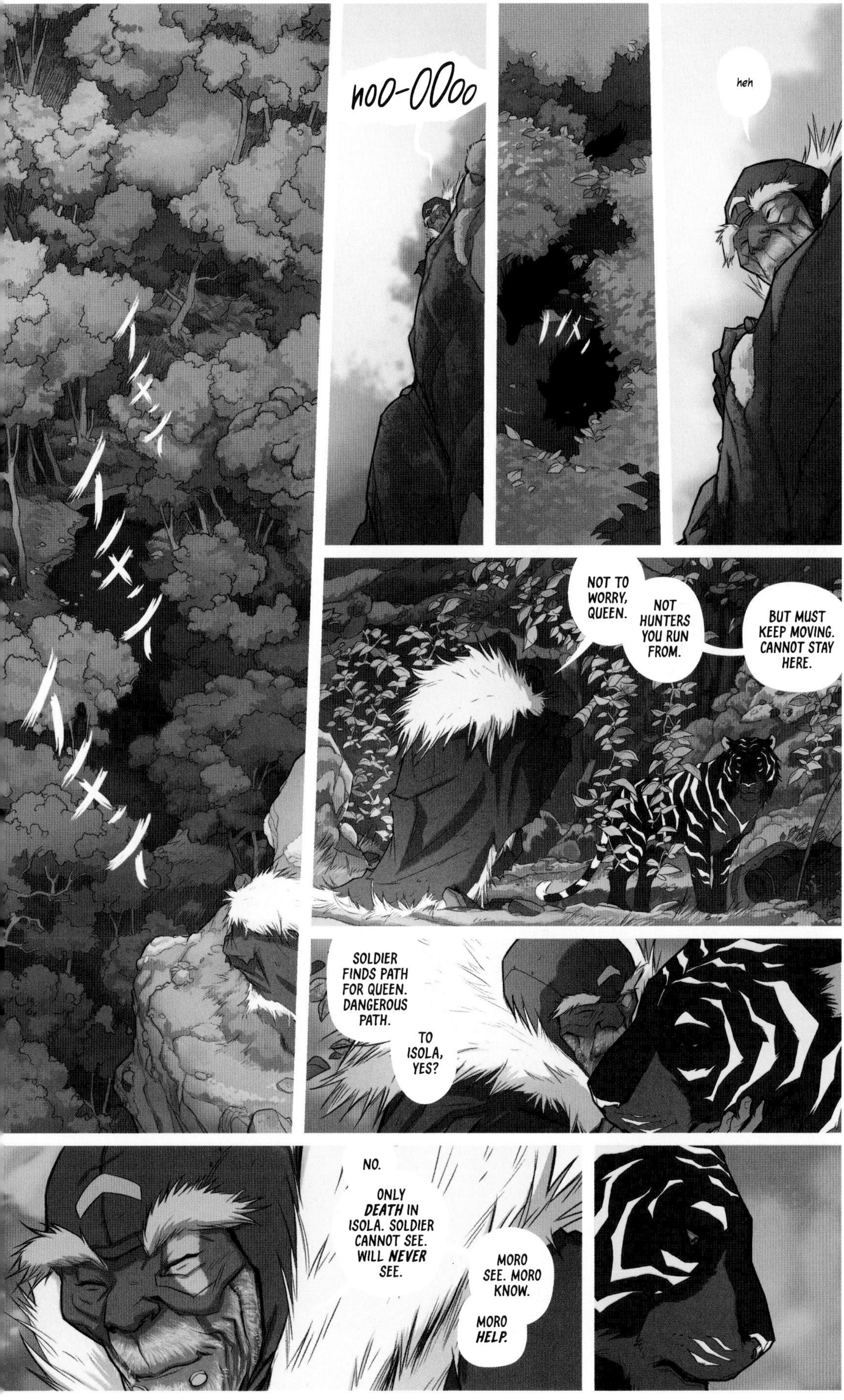

nOO-OOoo
heh
NOT TO WORRY, QUEEN.
NOT HUNTERS YOU RUN FROM.
BUT MUST KEEP MOVING. CANNOT STAY HERE.
SOLDIER FINDS PATH FOR QUEEN. DANGEROUS PATH.
TO ISOLA, YES?
NO.
ONLY DEATH IN ISOLA. SOLDIER CANNOT SEE. WILL NEVER SEE.
MORO SEE. MORO KNOW.
MORO HELP.

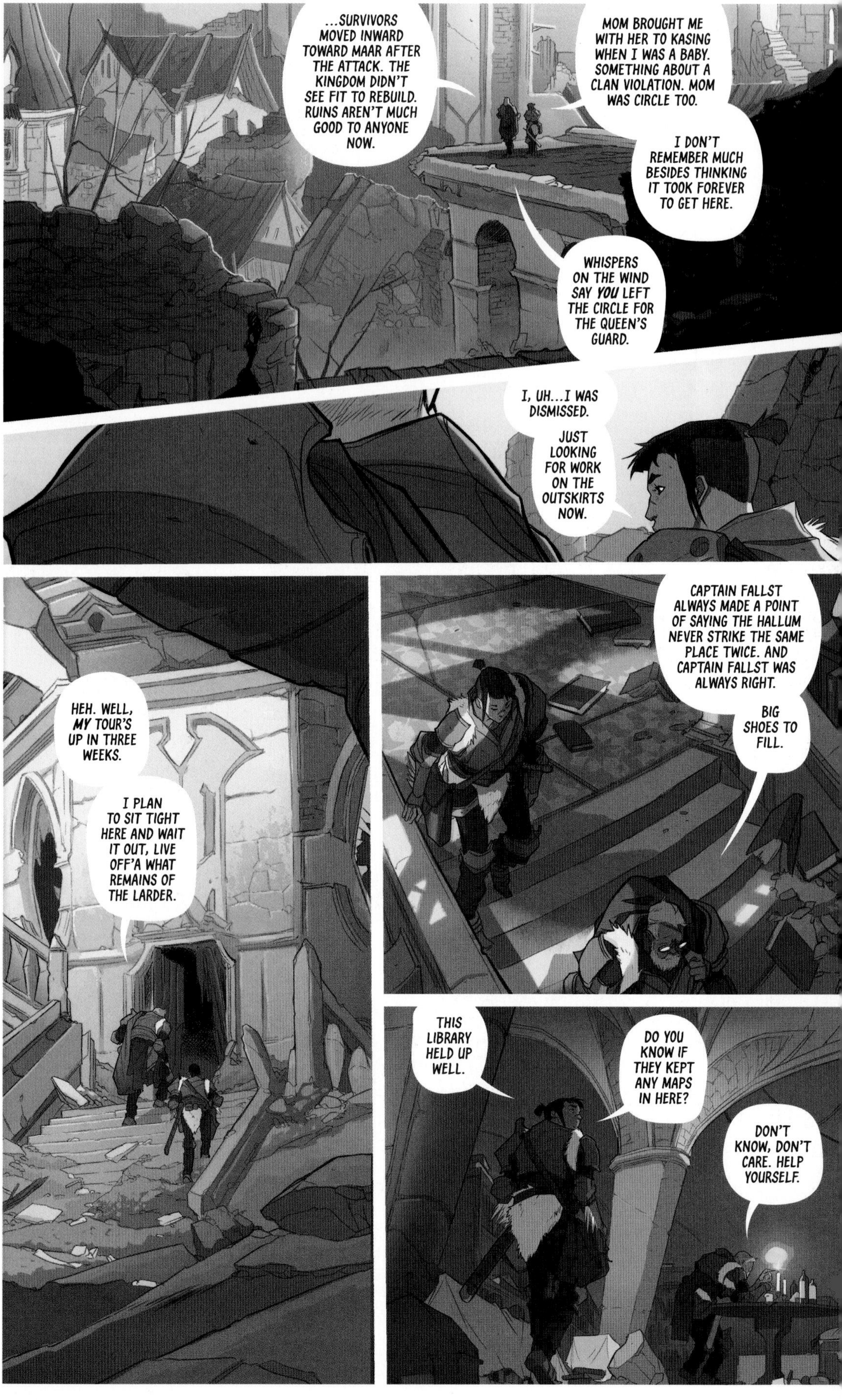
...SURVIVORS MOVED INWARD TOWARD MAAR AFTER THE ATTACK. THE KINGDOM DIDN'T SEE FIT TO REBUILD. RUINS AREN'T MUCH GOOD TO ANYONE NOW.
MOM BROUGHT ME WITH HER TO KASING WHEN I WAS A BABY. SOMETHING ABOUT A CLAN VIOLATION. MOM WAS CIRCLE TOO.
I DON'T REMEMBER MUCH BESIDES THINKING IT TOOK FOREVER TO GET HERE.
WHISPERS ON THE WIND SAY *YOU* LEFT THE CIRCLE FOR THE QUEEN'S GUARD.
I, UH...I WAS DISMISSED.
JUST LOOKING FOR WORK ON THE OUTSKIRTS NOW.
HEH. WELL, *MY* TOUR'S UP IN THREE WEEKS.
I PLAN TO SIT TIGHT HERE AND WAIT IT OUT, LIVE OFF'A WHAT REMAINS OF THE LARDER.
CAPTAIN FALLST ALWAYS MADE A POINT OF SAYING THE HALLUM NEVER STRIKE THE SAME PLACE TWICE. AND CAPTAIN FALLST WAS ALWAYS RIGHT.
BIG SHOES TO FILL.
THIS LIBRARY HELD UP WELL.
DO YOU KNOW IF THEY KEPT ANY MAPS IN HERE?
DON'T KNOW, DON'T CARE. HELP YOURSELF.

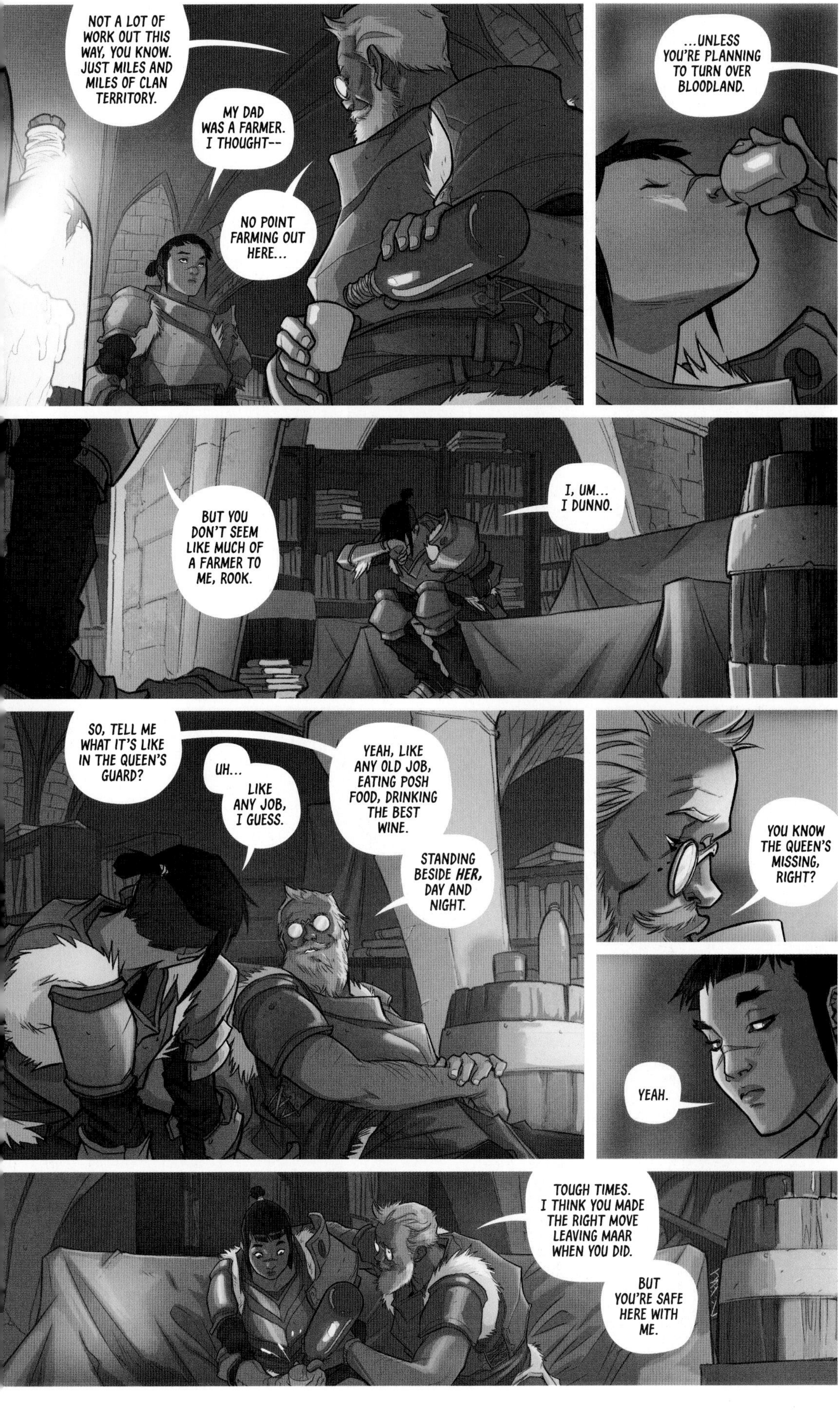
NOT A LOT OF WORK OUT THIS WAY, YOU KNOW. JUST MILES AND MILES OF CLAN TERRITORY.
MY DAD WAS A FARMER. I THOUGHT--
NO POINT FARMING OUT HERE...
...UNLESS YOU'RE PLANNING TO TURN OVER BLOODLAND.
BUT YOU DON'T SEEM LIKE MUCH OF A FARMER TO ME, ROOK.
I, UM... I DUNNO.
SO, TELL ME WHAT IT'S LIKE IN THE QUEEN'S GUARD?
UH...
LIKE ANY JOB, I GUESS.
YEAH, LIKE ANY OLD JOB, EATING POSH FOOD, DRINKING THE BEST WINE.
STANDING BESIDE *HER*, DAY AND NIGHT.
YOU KNOW THE QUEEN'S MISSING, RIGHT?
YEAH.
TOUGH TIMES. I THINK YOU MADE THE RIGHT MOVE LEAVING MAAR WHEN YOU DID.
BUT YOU'RE SAFE HERE WITH ME.

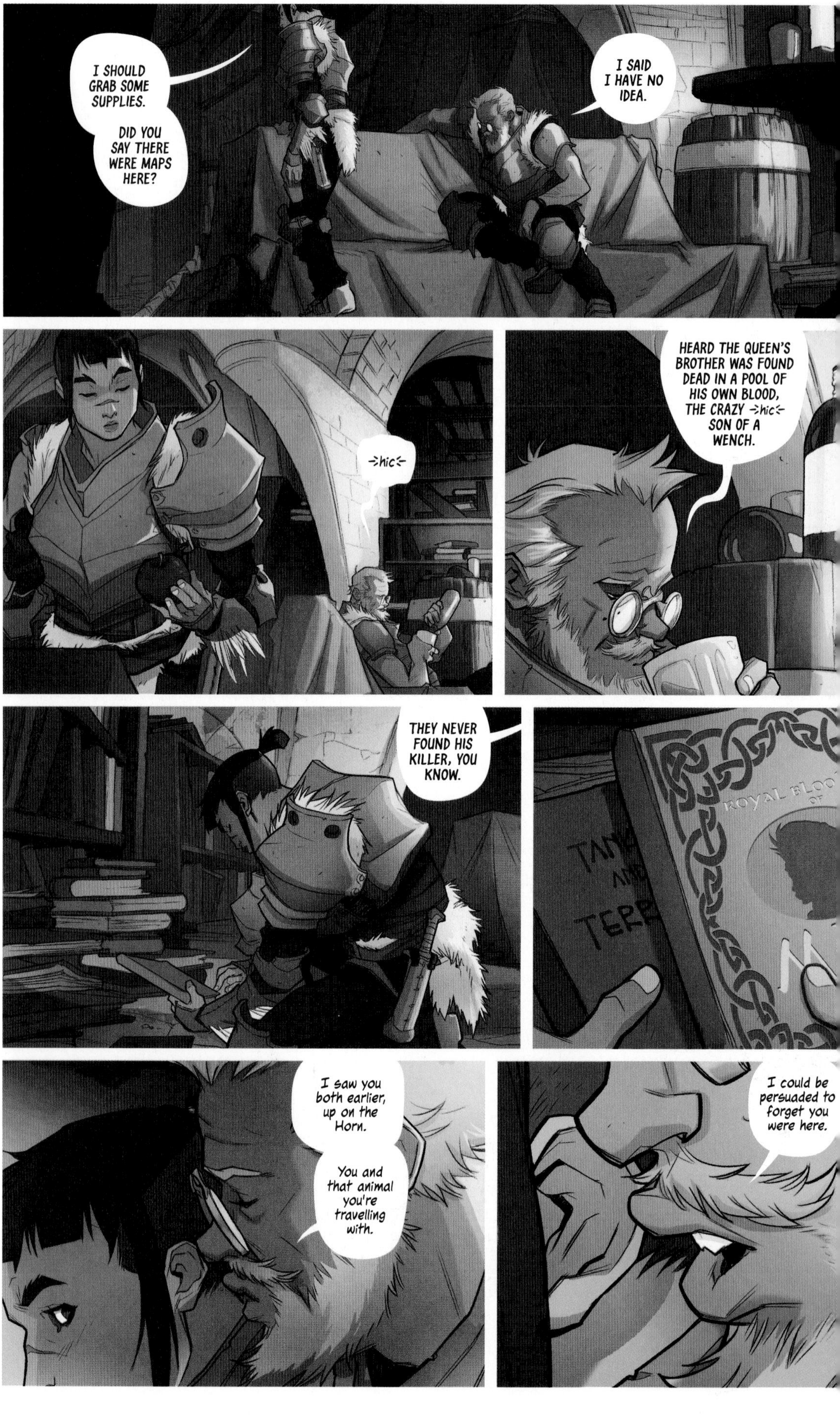

I SHOULD GRAB SOME SUPPLIES.
DID YOU SAY THERE WERE MAPS HERE?
I SAID I HAVE NO IDEA.
-hic-
HEARD THE QUEEN'S BROTHER WAS FOUND DEAD IN A POOL OF HIS OWN BLOOD, THE CRAZY -hic- SON OF A WENCH.
THEY NEVER FOUND HIS KILLER, YOU KNOW.
I saw you both earlier, up on the Horn.
You and that animal you're travelling with.
I could be persuaded to forget you were here.

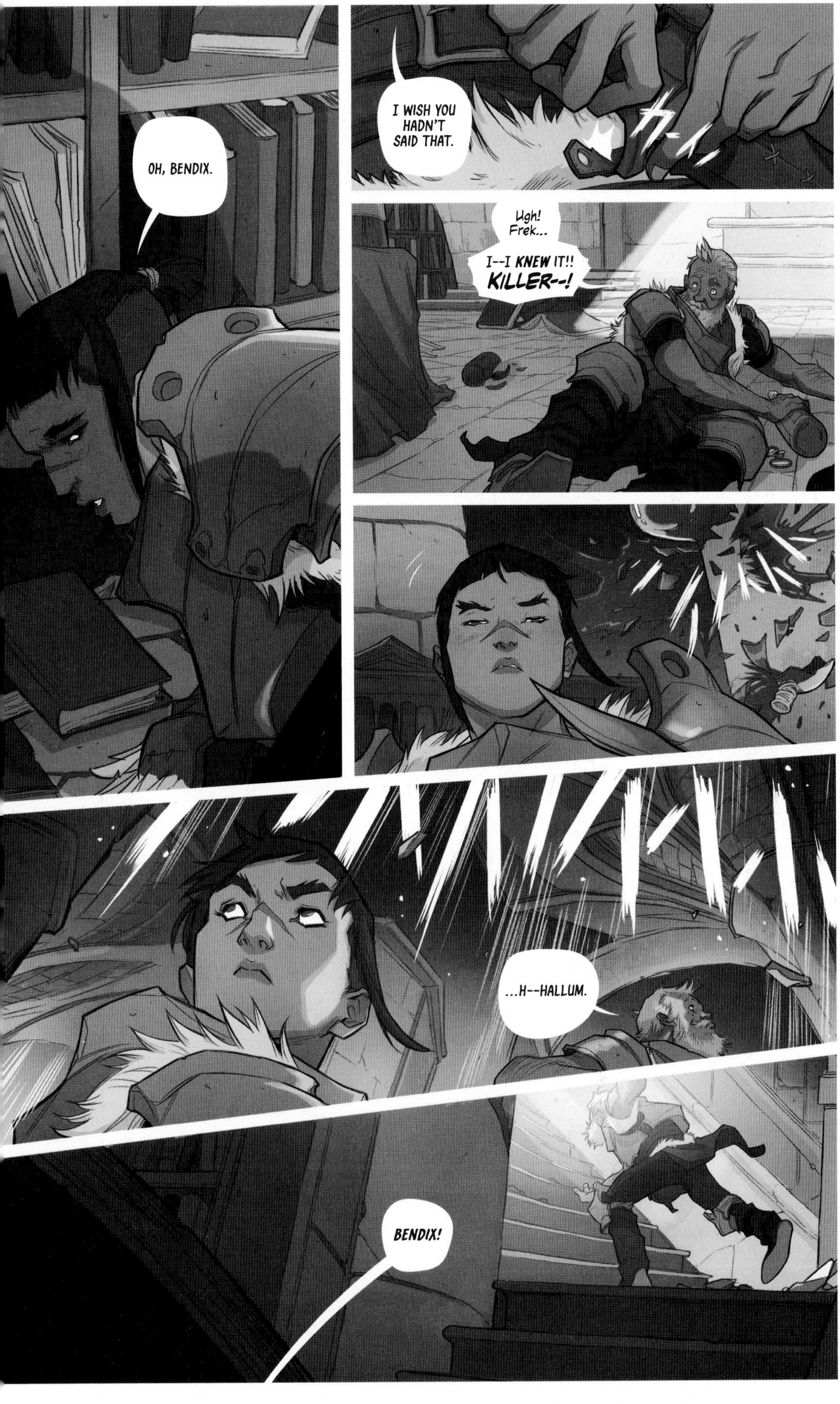
OH, BENDIX.
I WISH YOU HADN'T SAID THAT.
Ugh! Frek...
I--I KNEW IT!! KILLER--!
...H--HALLUM.
BENDIX!

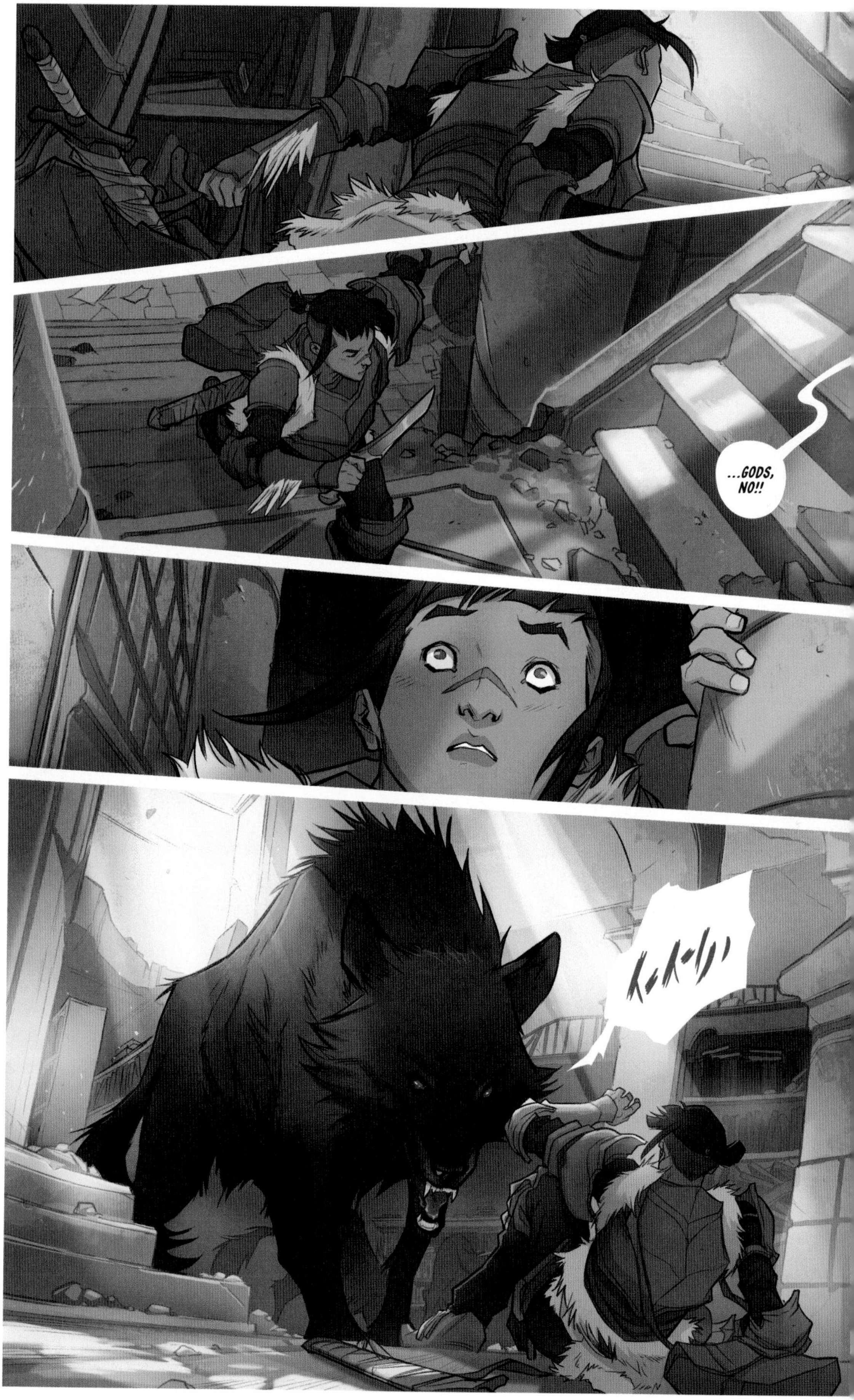
...GODS, NO!!

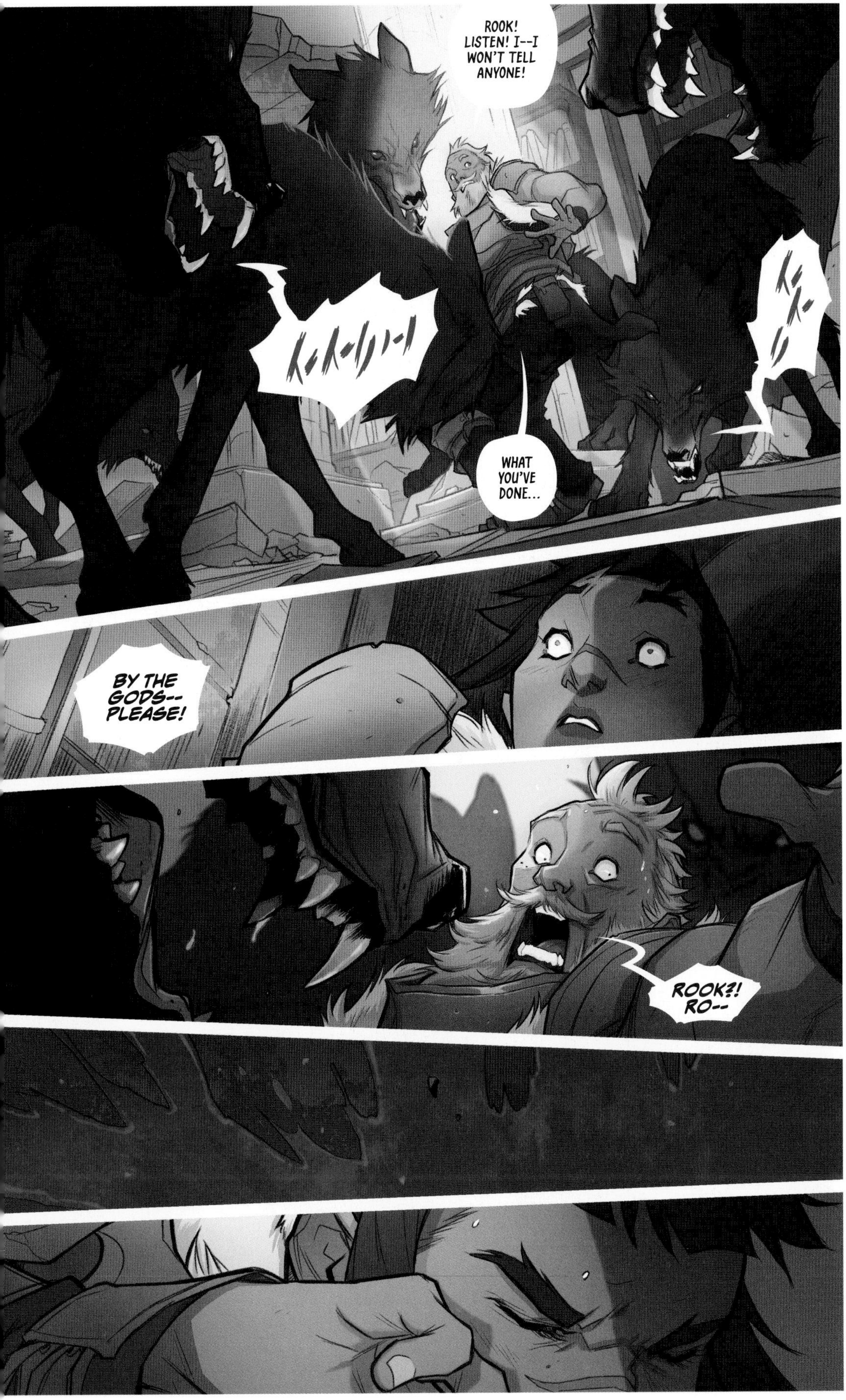
ROOK! LISTEN! I--I WON'T TELL ANYONE!
WHAT YOU'VE DONE...
BY THE GODS-- PLEASE!
ROOK?! RO--

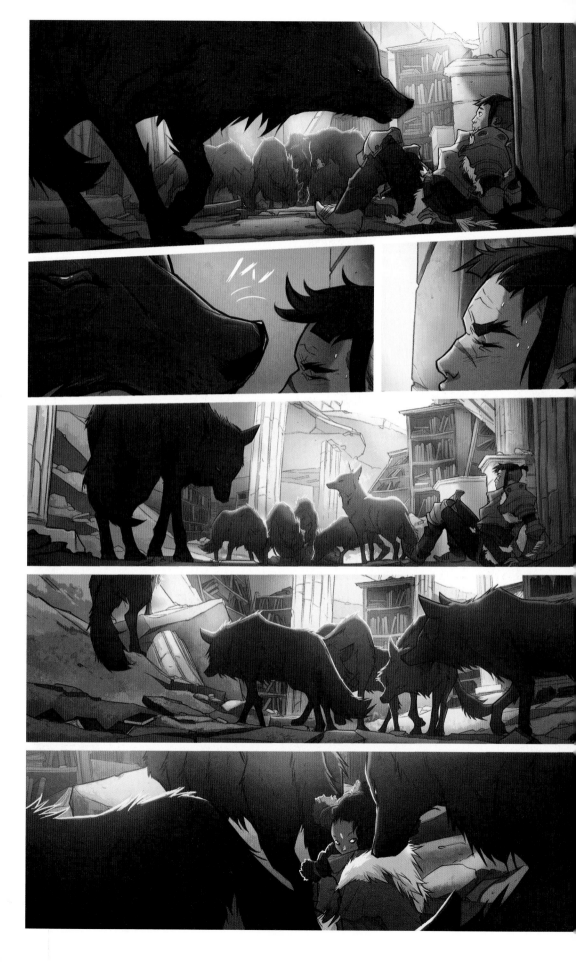

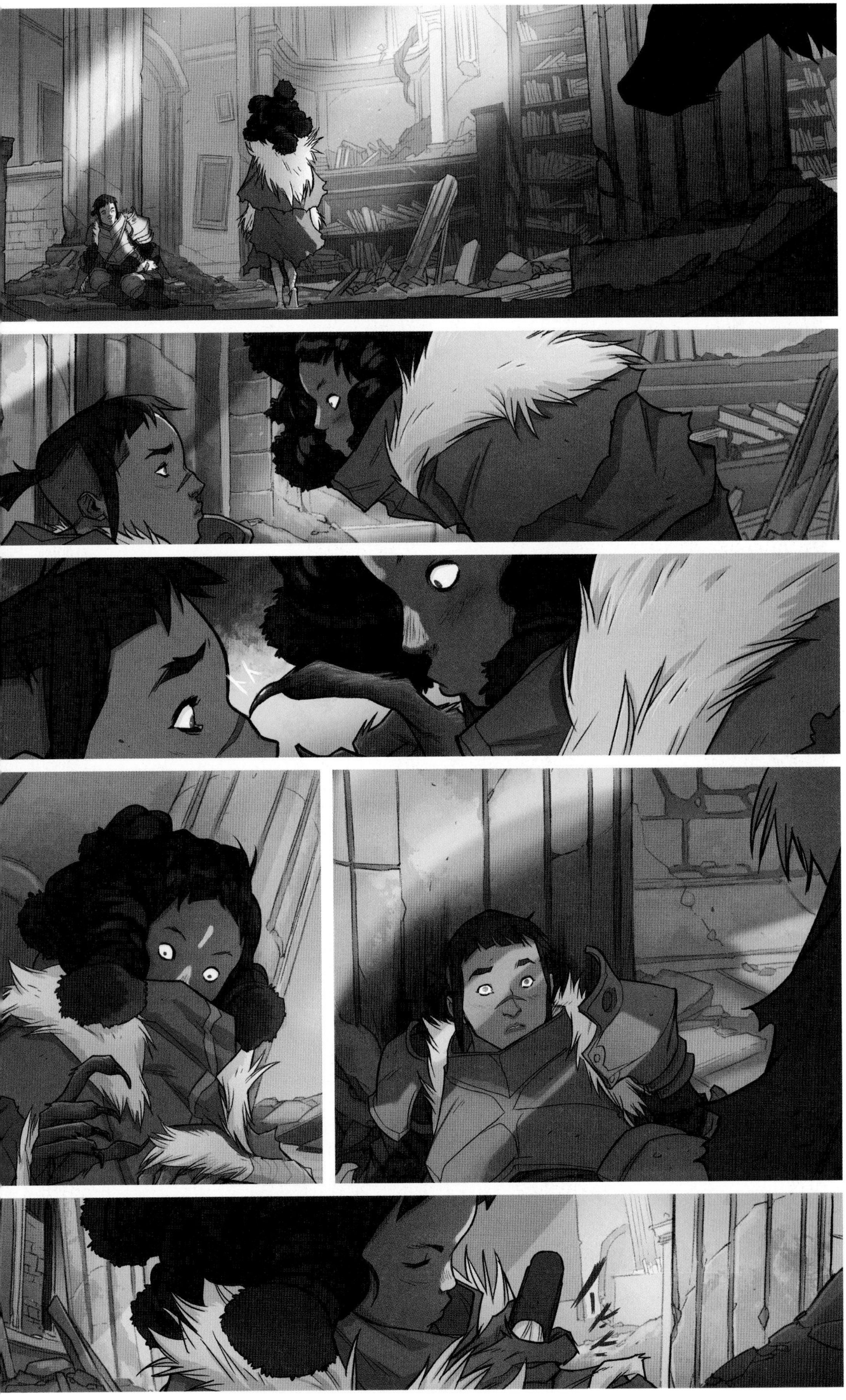

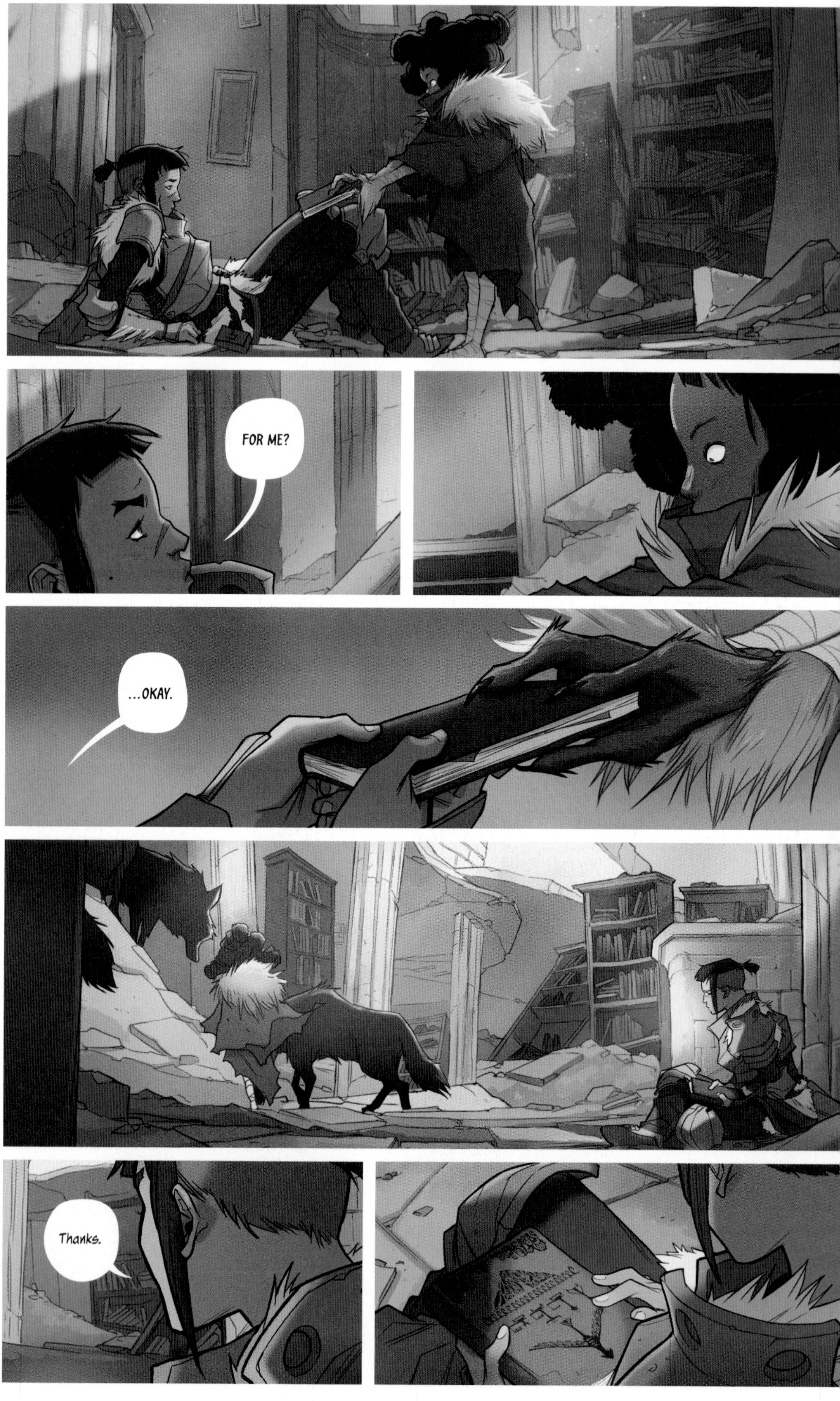
FOR ME?
...OKAY.
Thanks.

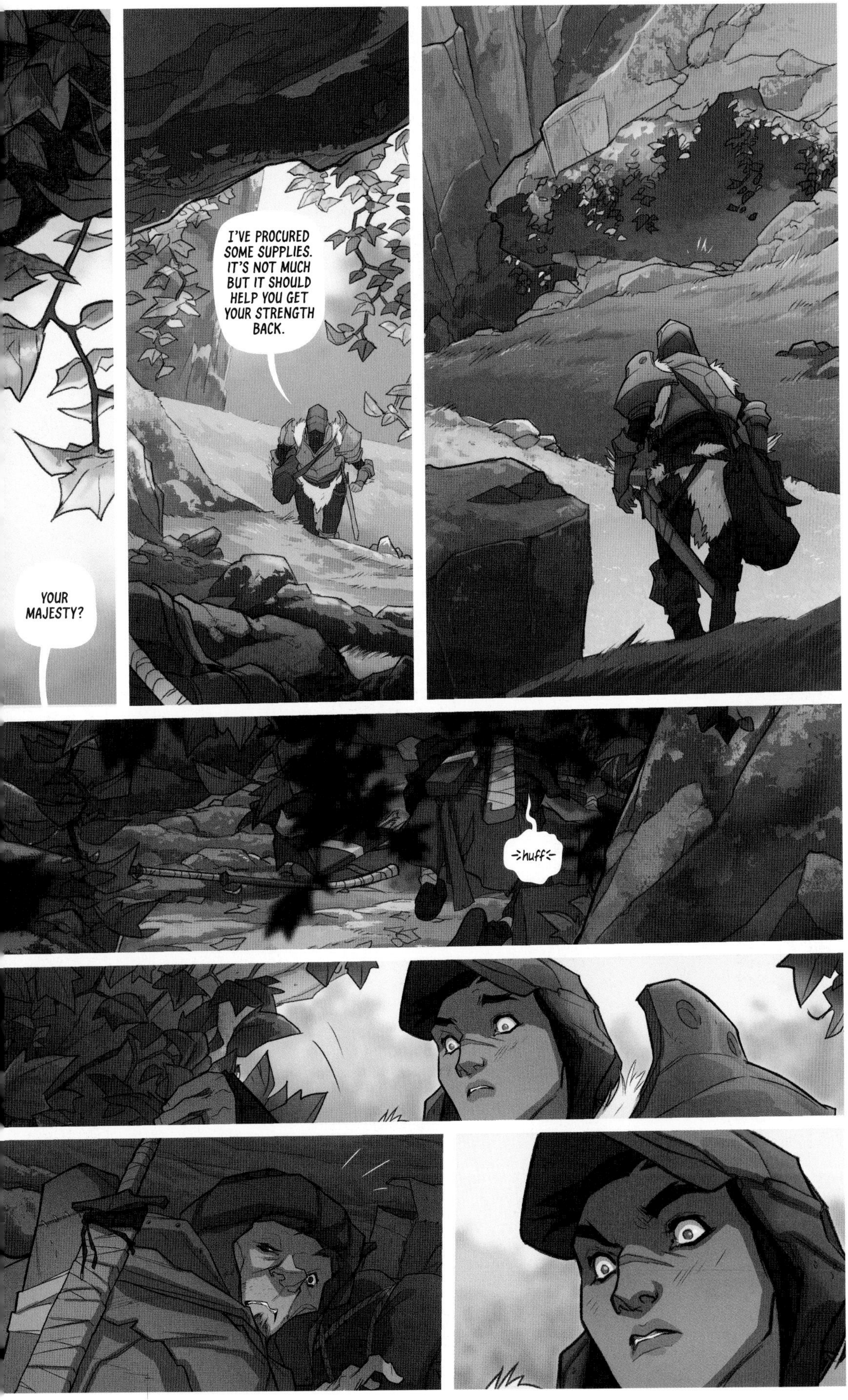
YOUR MAJESTY?
I'VE PROCURED SOME SUPPLIES. IT'S NOT MUCH BUT IT SHOULD HELP YOU GET YOUR STRENGTH BACK.
huff

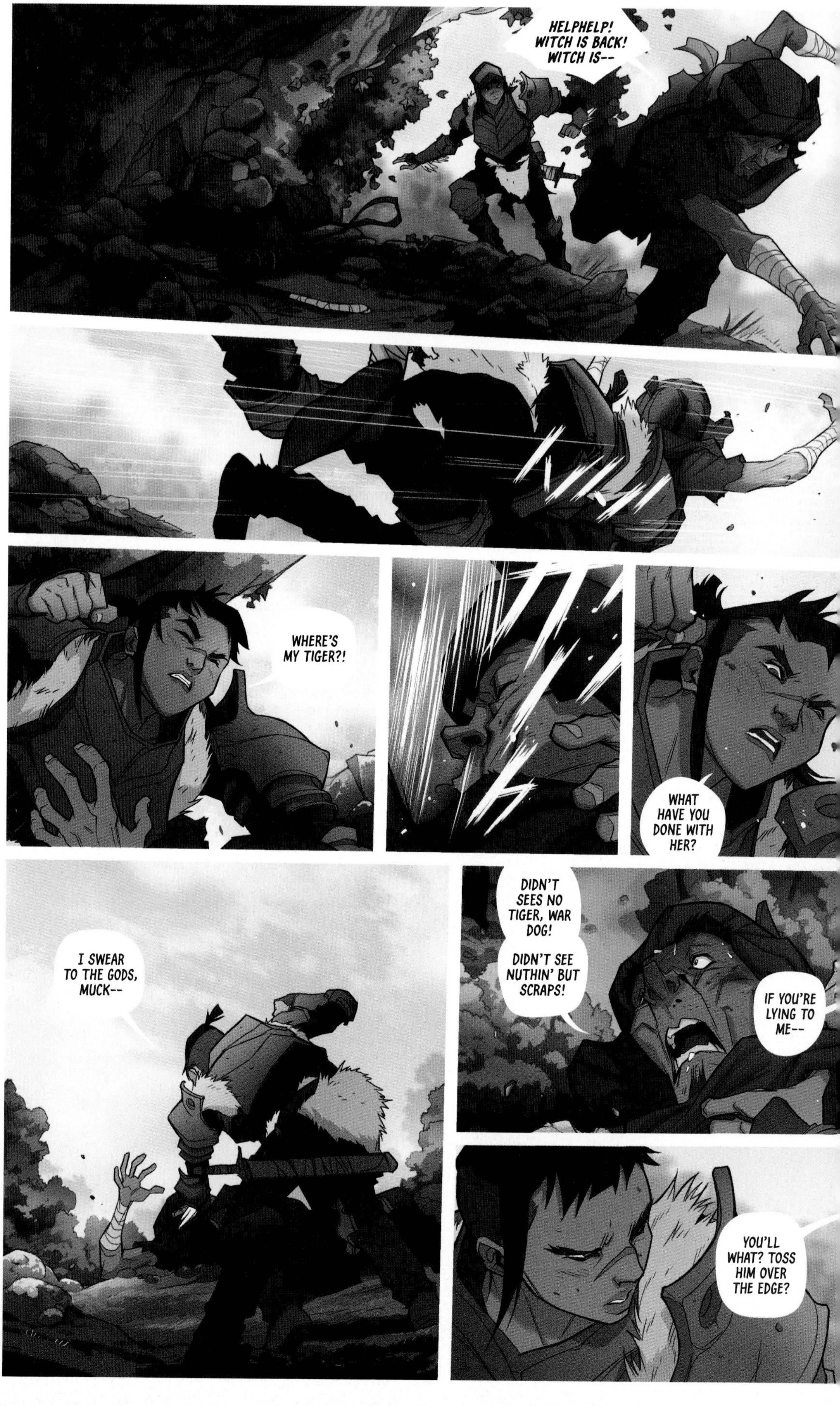
HELPHELP! WITCH IS BACK! WITCH IS--
WHERE'S MY TIGER?!
WHAT HAVE YOU DONE WITH HER?
I SWEAR TO THE GODS, MUCK--
DIDN'T SEES NO TIGER, WAR DOG!
DIDN'T SEE NUTHIN' BUT SCRAPS!
IF YOU'RE LYING TO ME--
YOU'LL WHAT? TOSS HIM OVER THE EDGE?

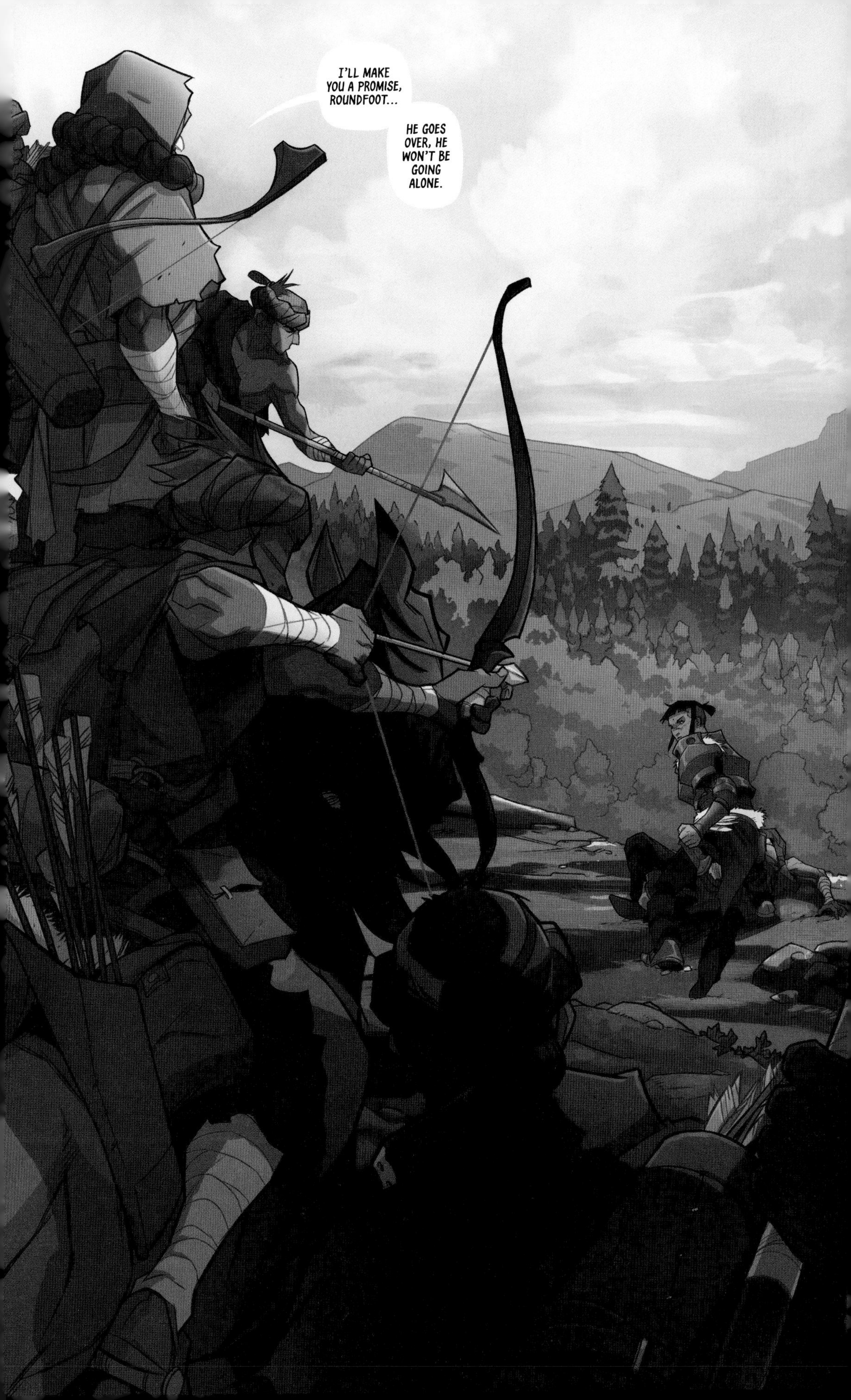
I'LL MAKE YOU A PROMISE, ROUNDFOOT...
HE GOES OVER, HE WON'T BE GOING ALONE.

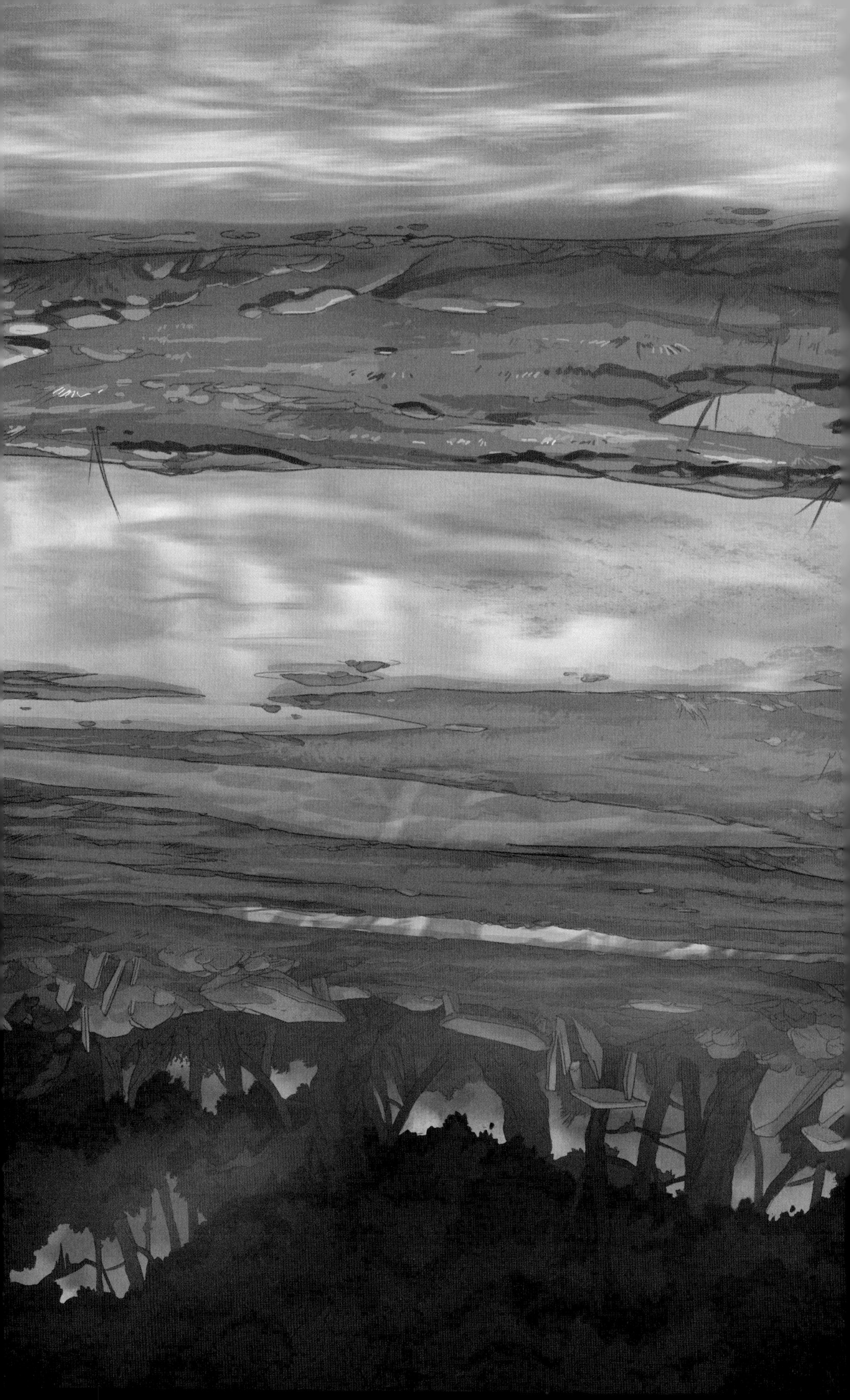

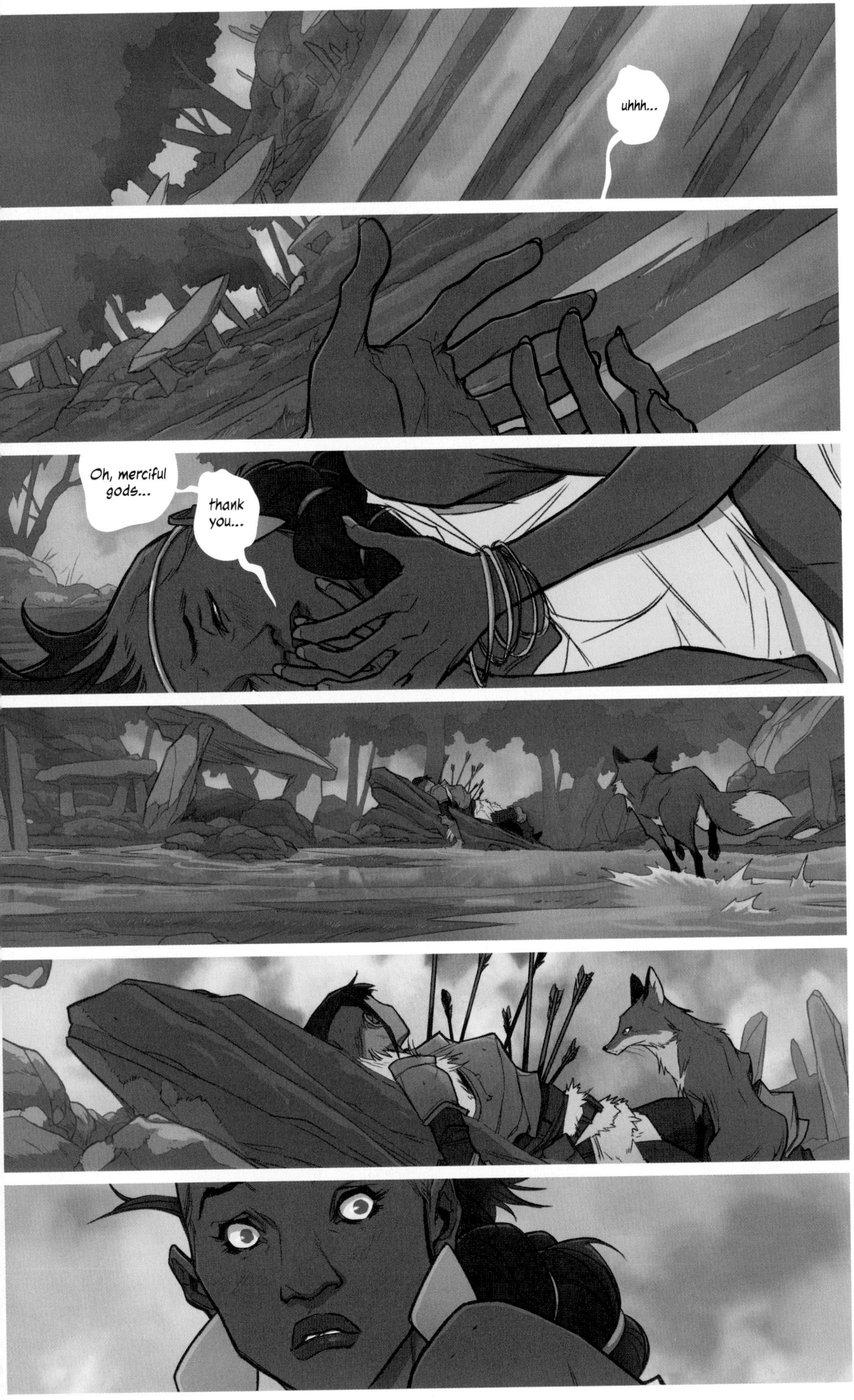
uhhh...
Oh, merciful gods...
thank you...

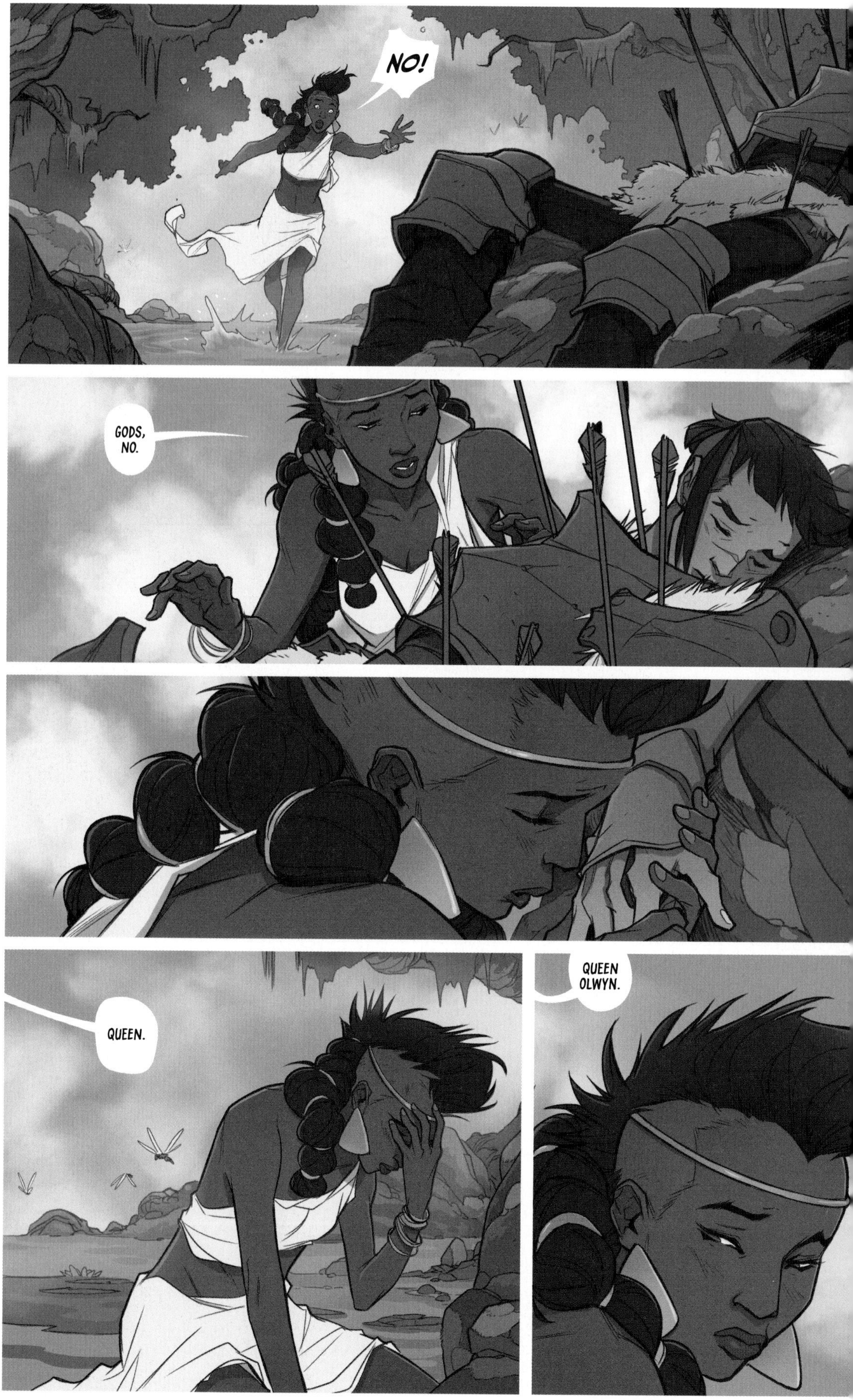
NO!
GODS, NO.
QUEEN.
QUEEN OLWYN.

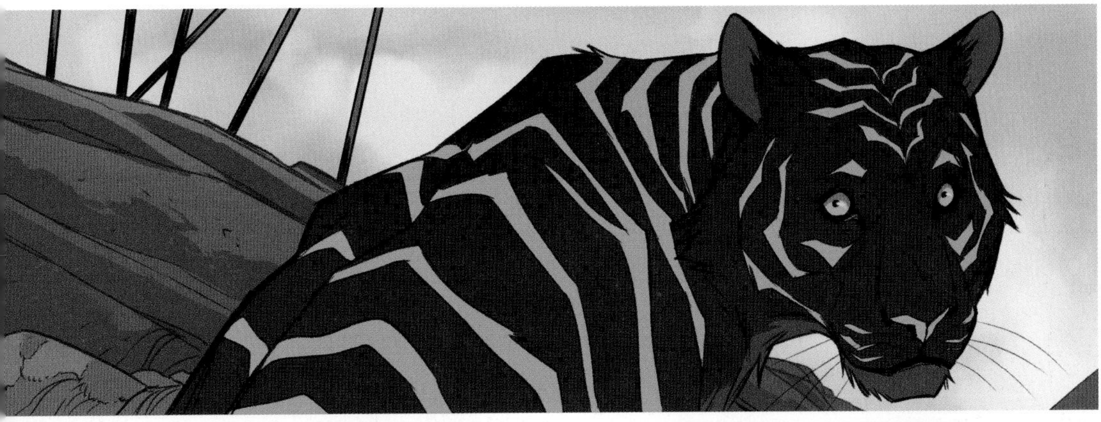

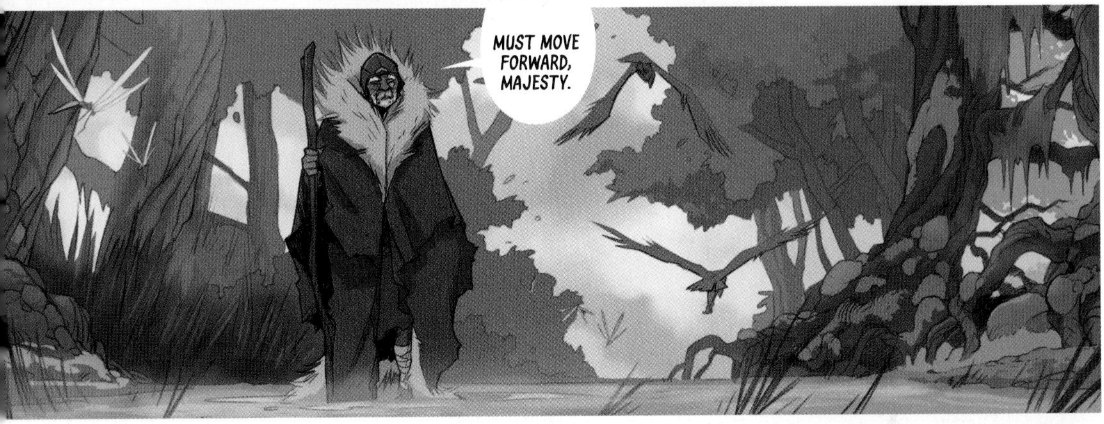
MUST MOVE FORWARD, MAJESTY.

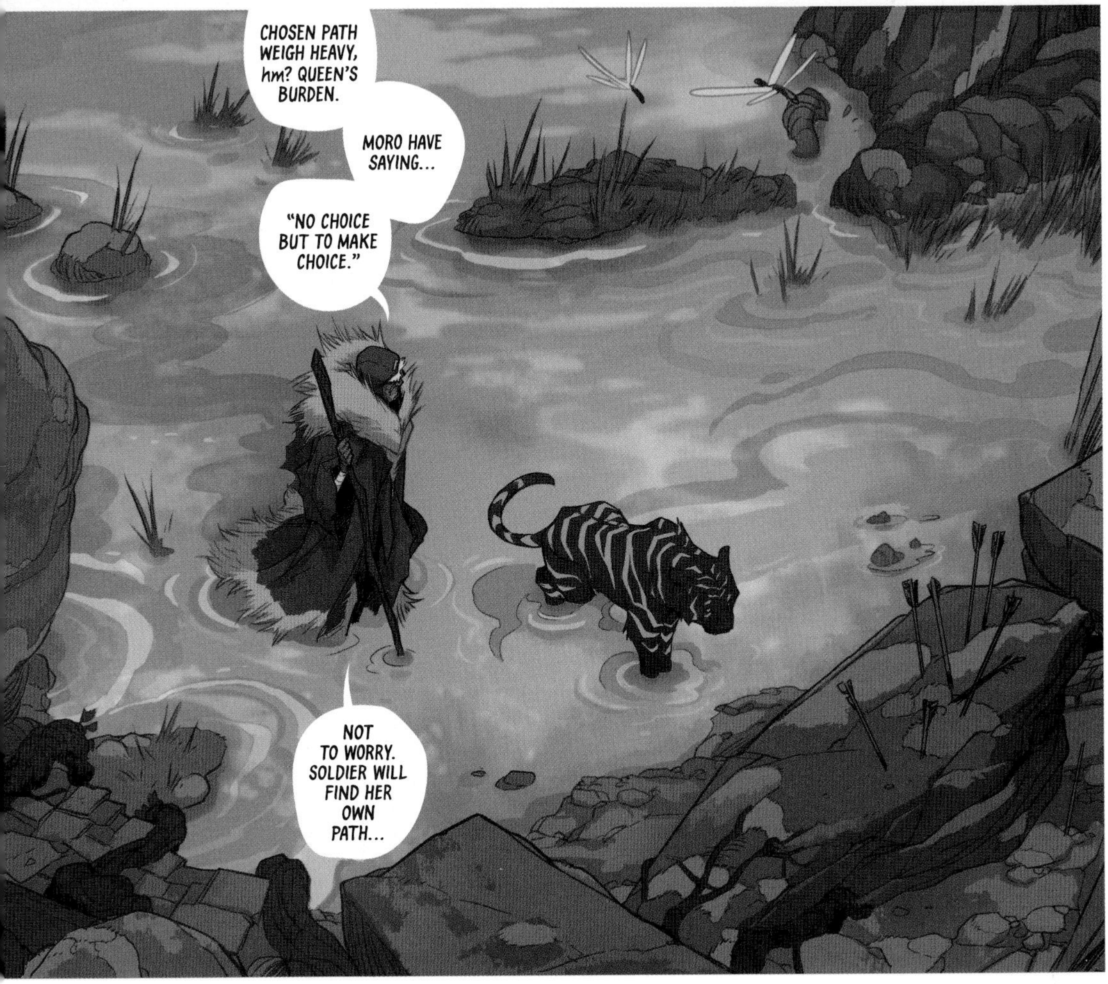
CHOSEN PATH WEIGH HEAVY, hm? QUEEN'S BURDEN.
MORO HAVE SAYING...
"NO CHOICE BUT TO MAKE CHOICE."
NOT TO WORRY. SOLDIER WILL FIND HER OWN PATH...

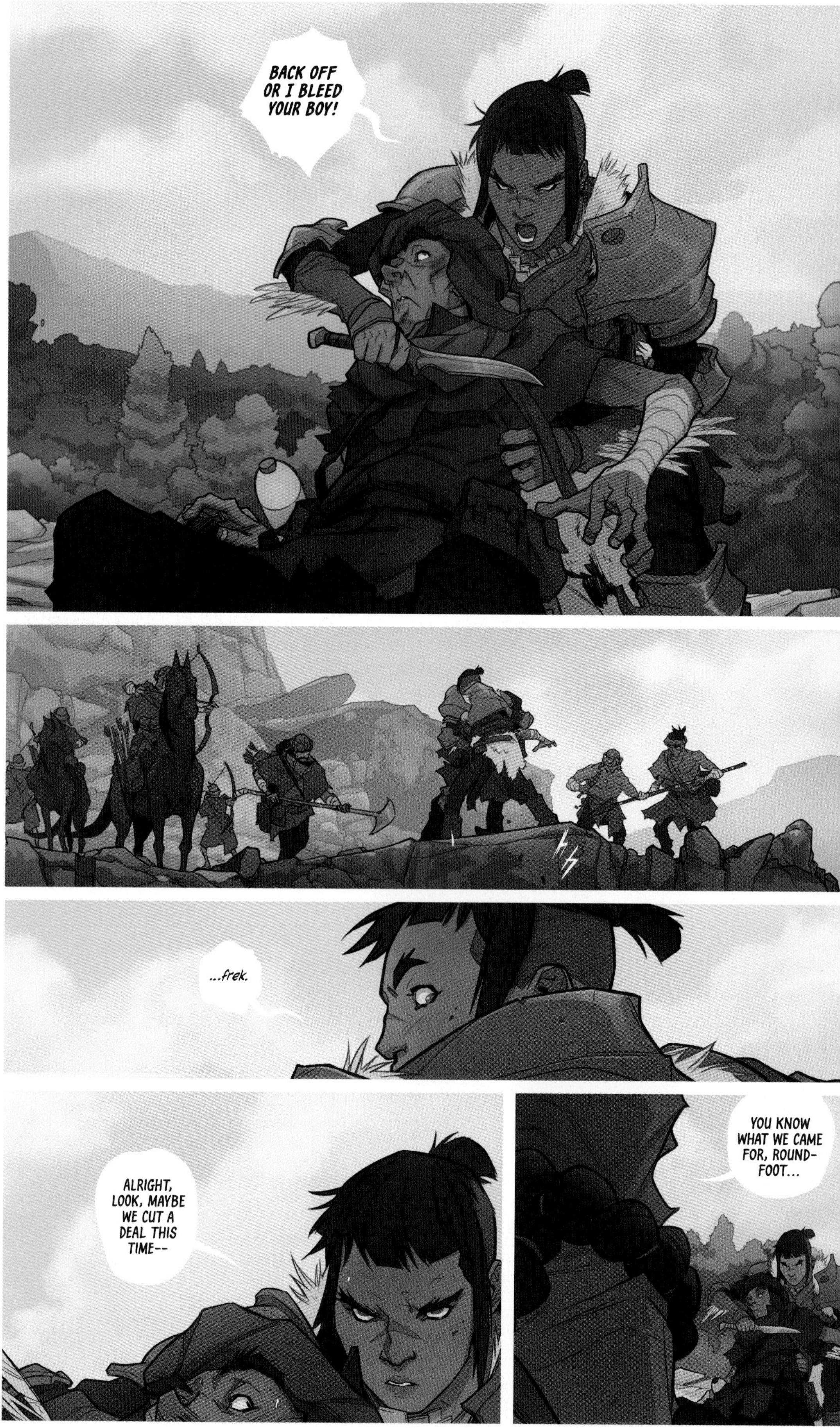
BACK OFF OR I BLEED YOUR BOY!
...frek.
ALRIGHT, LOOK, MAYBE WE CUT A DEAL THIS TIME--
YOU KNOW WHAT WE CAME FOR, ROUND-FOOT...

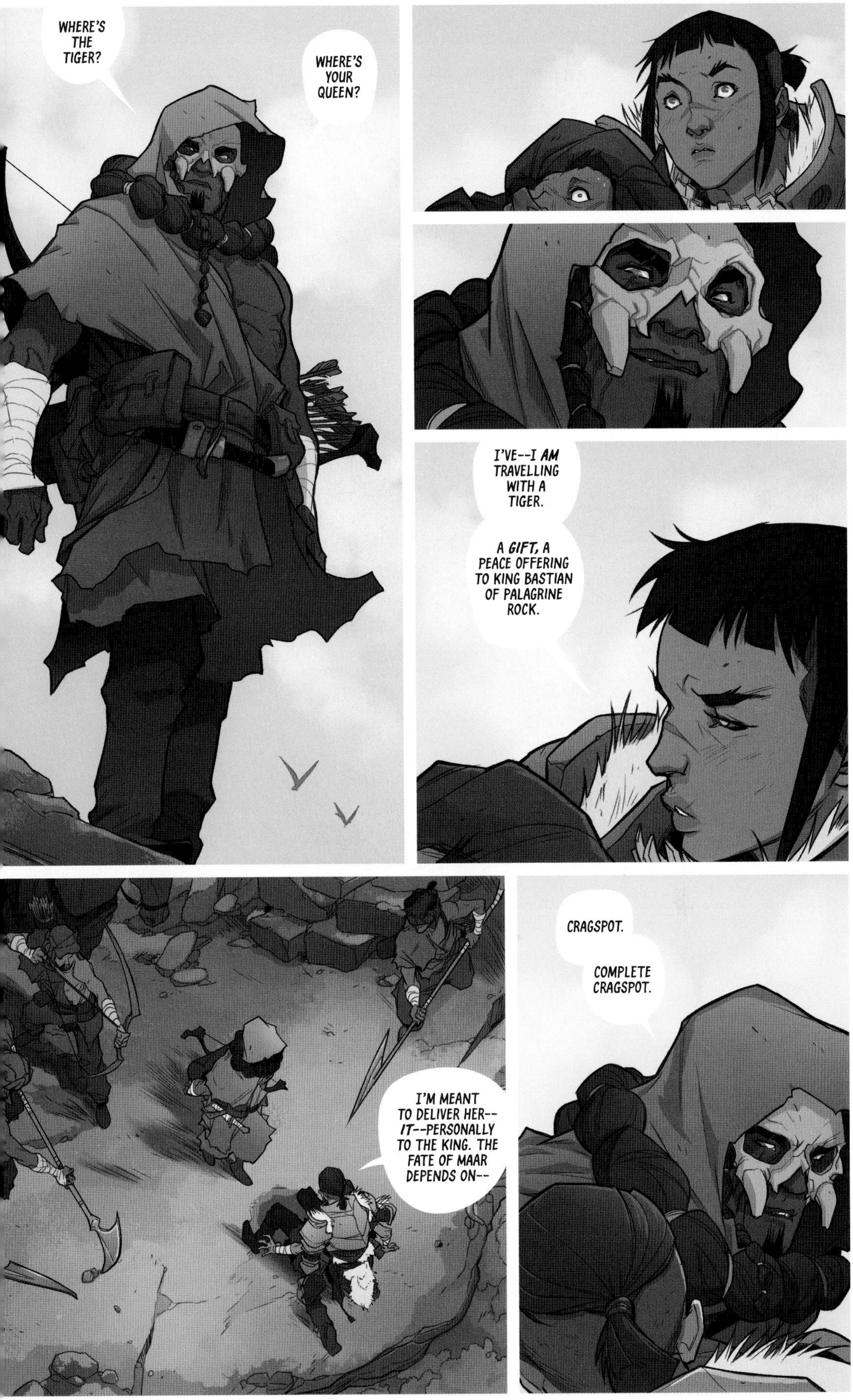
WHERE'S THE TIGER?
WHERE'S YOUR QUEEN?
I'VE--I *AM* TRAVELLING WITH A TIGER.
A *GIFT,* A PEACE OFFERING TO KING BASTIAN OF PALAGRINE ROCK.
I'M MEANT TO DELIVER HER-- *IT*--PERSONALLY TO THE KING. THE FATE OF MAAR DEPENDS ON--
CRAGSPOT.
COMPLETE CRAGSPOT.

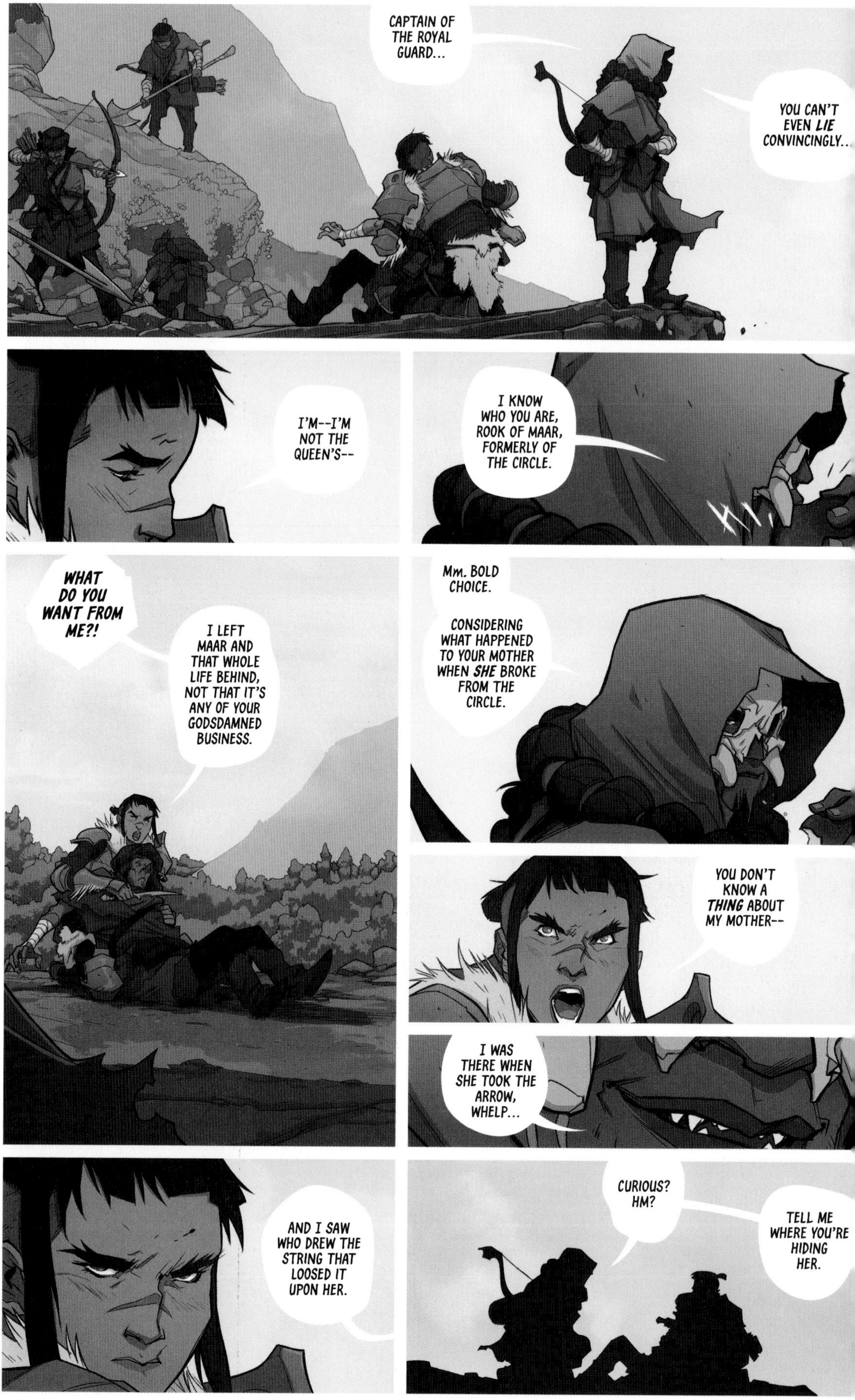

CAPTAIN OF THE ROYAL GUARD...
YOU CAN'T EVEN LIE CONVINCINGLY...
I'M--I'M NOT THE QUEEN'S--
I KNOW WHO YOU ARE, ROOK OF MAAR, FORMERLY OF THE CIRCLE.
WHAT DO YOU WANT FROM ME?!
I LEFT MAAR AND THAT WHOLE LIFE BEHIND, NOT THAT IT'S ANY OF YOUR GODSDAMNED BUSINESS.
Mm. BOLD CHOICE.
CONSIDERING WHAT HAPPENED TO YOUR MOTHER WHEN SHE BROKE FROM THE CIRCLE.
YOU DON'T KNOW A THING ABOUT MY MOTHER--
I WAS THERE WHEN SHE TOOK THE ARROW, WHELP...
AND I SAW WHO DREW THE STRING THAT LOOSED IT UPON HER.
CURIOUS? HM?
TELL ME WHERE YOU'RE HIDING HER.

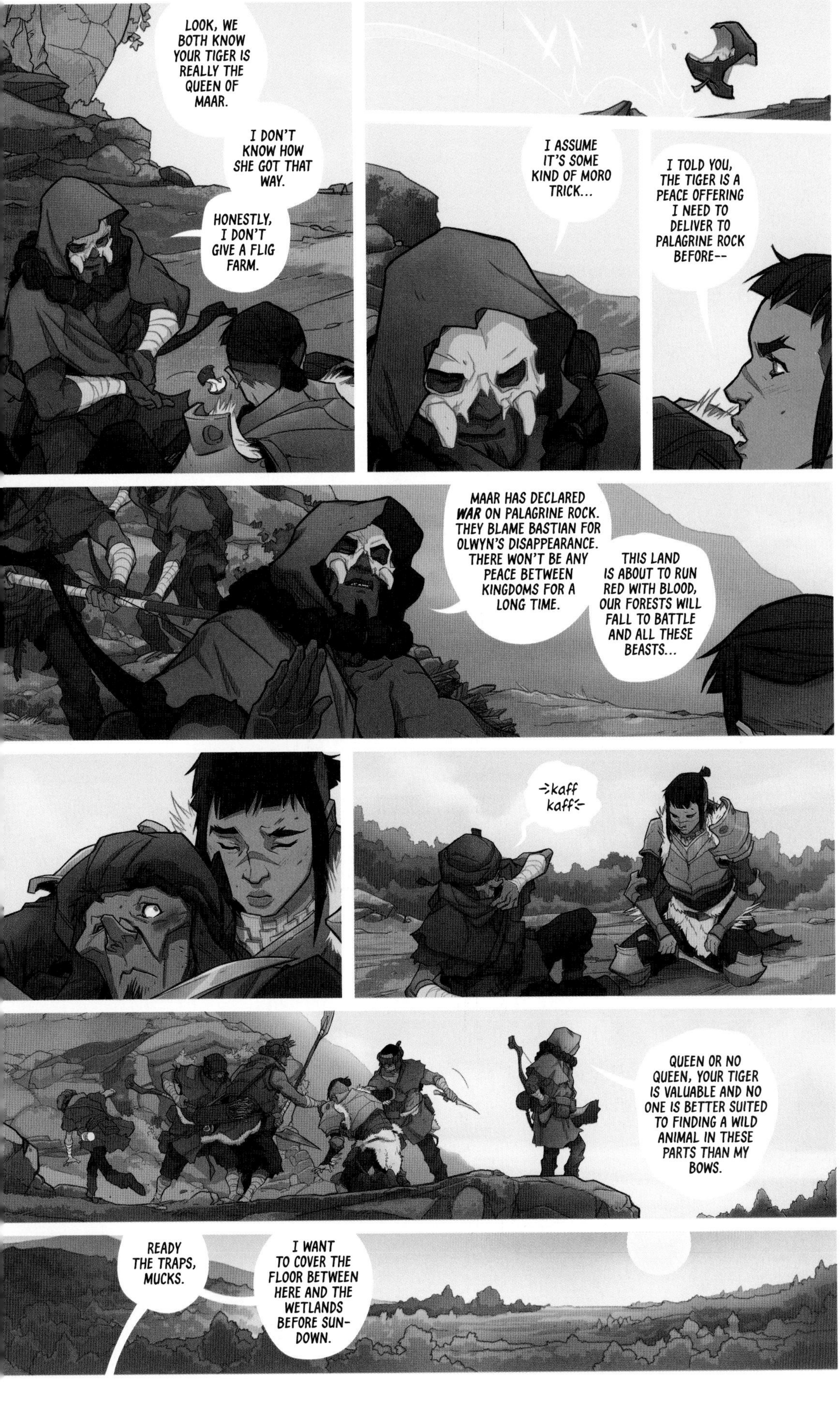
LOOK, WE BOTH KNOW YOUR TIGER IS REALLY THE QUEEN OF MAAR.
I DON'T KNOW HOW SHE GOT THAT WAY.
HONESTLY, I DON'T GIVE A FLIG FARM.
I ASSUME IT'S SOME KIND OF MORO TRICK...
I TOLD YOU, THE TIGER IS A PEACE OFFERING I NEED TO DELIVER TO PALAGRINE ROCK BEFORE--
MAAR HAS DECLARED WAR ON PALAGRINE ROCK. THEY BLAME BASTIAN FOR OLWYN'S DISAPPEARANCE. THERE WON'T BE ANY PEACE BETWEEN KINGDOMS FOR A LONG TIME.
THIS LAND IS ABOUT TO RUN RED WITH BLOOD, OUR FORESTS WILL FALL TO BATTLE AND ALL THESE BEASTS...
kaff kaff
QUEEN OR NO QUEEN, YOUR TIGER IS VALUABLE AND NO ONE IS BETTER SUITED TO FINDING A WILD ANIMAL IN THESE PARTS THAN MY BOWS.
READY THE TRAPS, MUCKS.
I WANT TO COVER THE FLOOR BETWEEN HERE AND THE WETLANDS BEFORE SUN-DOWN.

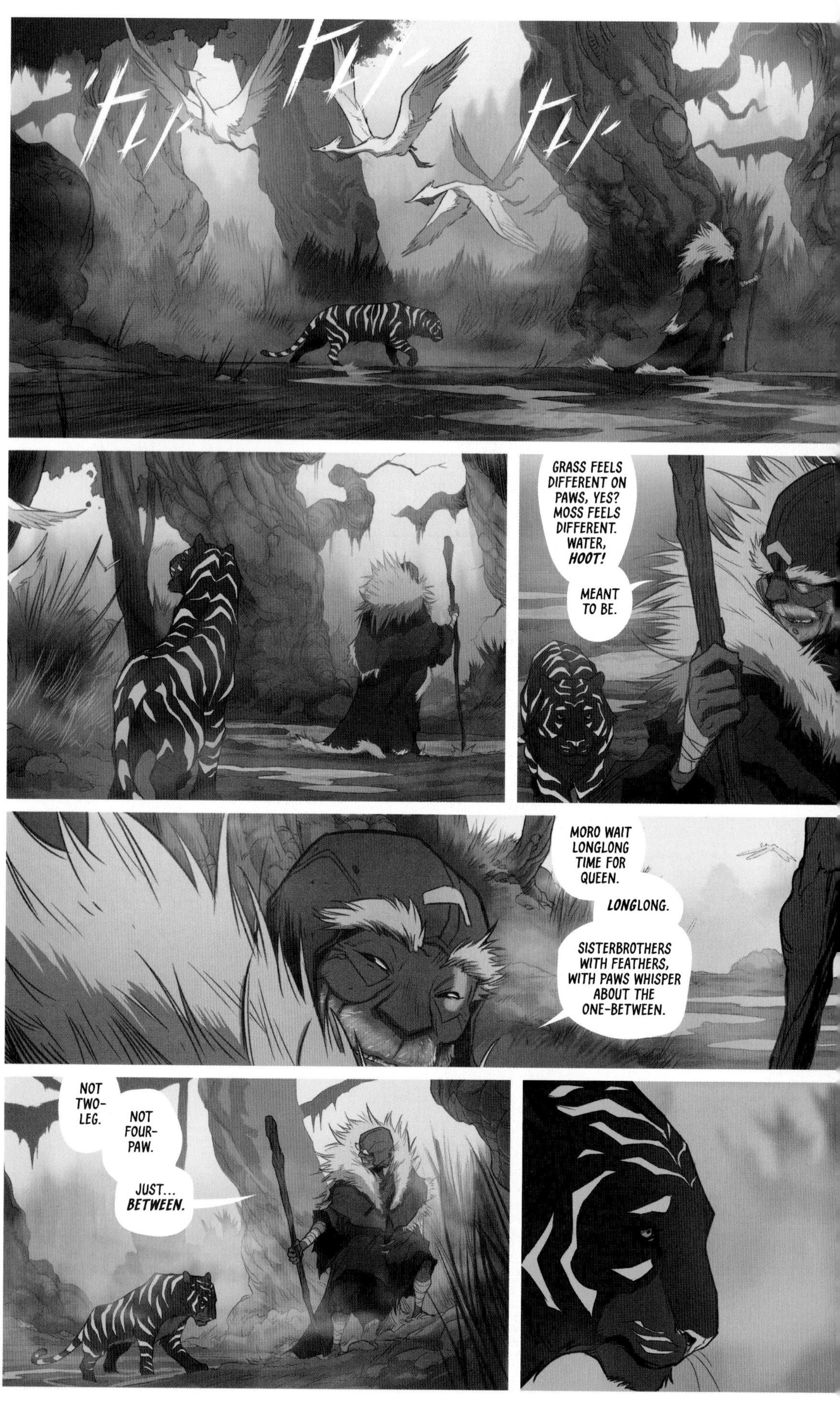
TKTK
TKTK
TKTK
GRASS FEELS DIFFERENT ON PAWS, YES? MOSS FEELS DIFFERENT. WATER, HOOT!
MEANT TO BE.
MORO WAIT LONGLONG TIME FOR QUEEN.
LONGLONG.
SISTERBROTHERS WITH FEATHERS, WITH PAWS WHISPER ABOUT THE ONE-BETWEEN.
NOT TWO-LEG.
NOT FOUR-PAW.
JUST... BETWEEN.

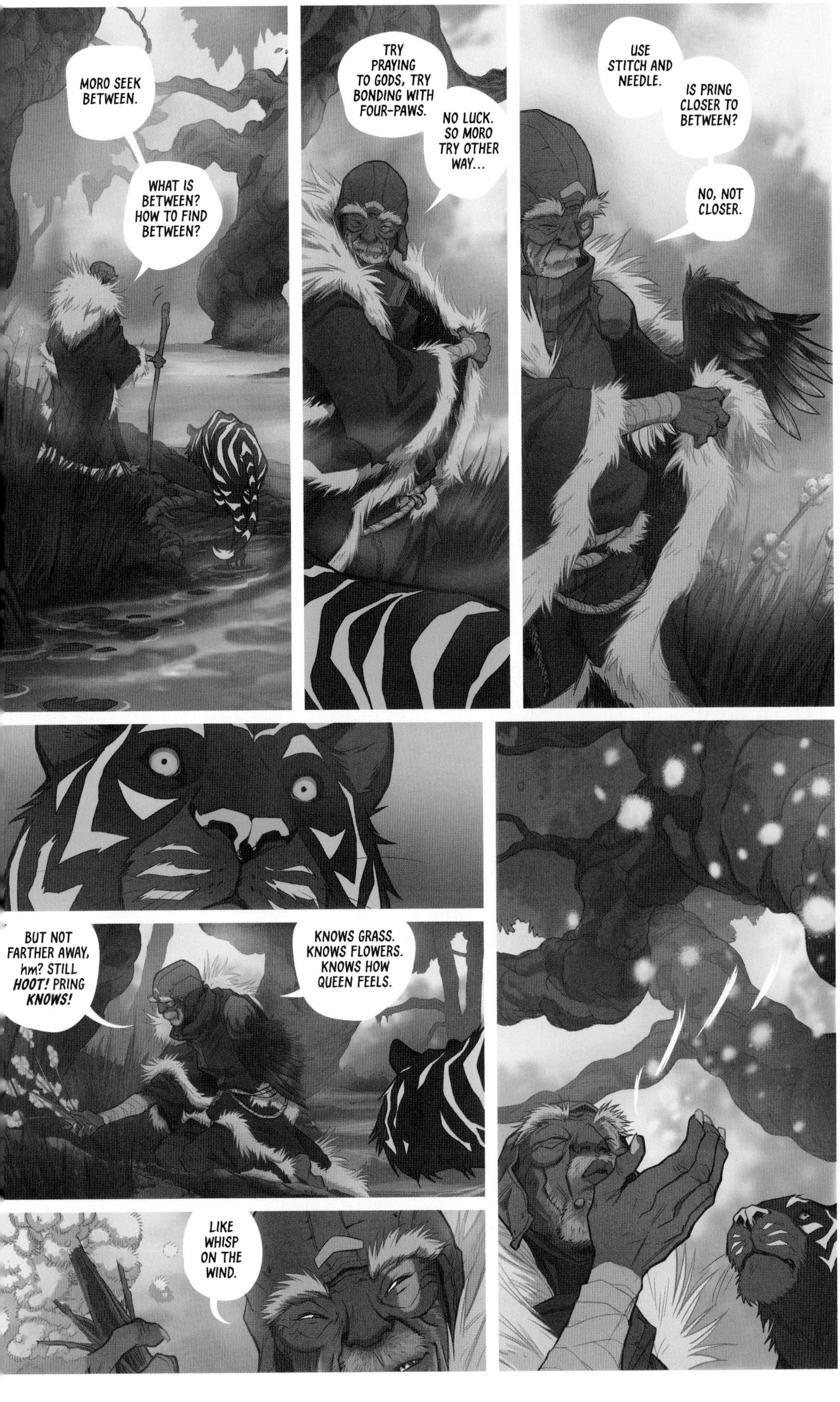
MORO SEEK BETWEEN.
WHAT IS BETWEEN? HOW TO FIND BETWEEN?
TRY PRAYING TO GODS, TRY BONDING WITH FOUR-PAWS.
NO LUCK. SO MORO TRY OTHER WAY...
USE STITCH AND NEEDLE.
IS PRING CLOSER TO BETWEEN?
NO, NOT CLOSER.
BUT NOT FARTHER AWAY, hm? STILL HOOT! PRING KNOWS!
KNOWS GRASS. KNOWS FLOWERS. KNOWS HOW QUEEN FEELS.
LIKE WHISP ON THE WIND.

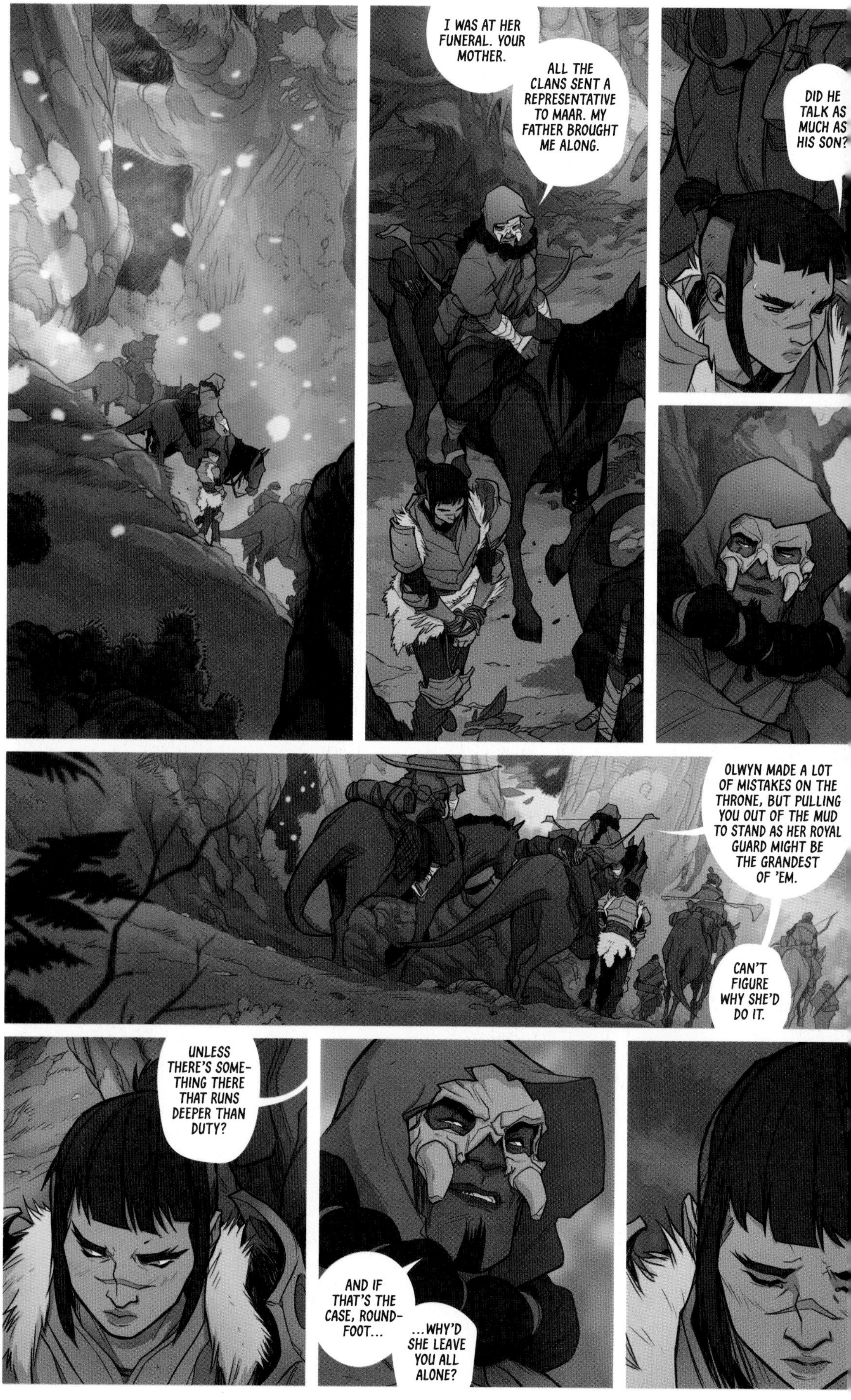
I WAS AT HER FUNERAL. YOUR MOTHER.
ALL THE CLANS SENT A REPRESENTATIVE TO MAAR. MY FATHER BROUGHT ME ALONG.
DID HE TALK AS MUCH AS HIS SON?
OLWYN MADE A LOT OF MISTAKES ON THE THRONE, BUT PULLING YOU OUT OF THE MUD TO STAND AS HER ROYAL GUARD MIGHT BE THE GRANDEST OF 'EM.
CAN'T FIGURE WHY SHE'D DO IT.
UNLESS THERE'S SOMETHING THERE THAT RUNS DEEPER THAN DUTY?
AND IF THAT'S THE CASE, ROUNDFOOT...
...WHY'D SHE LEAVE YOU ALL ALONE?

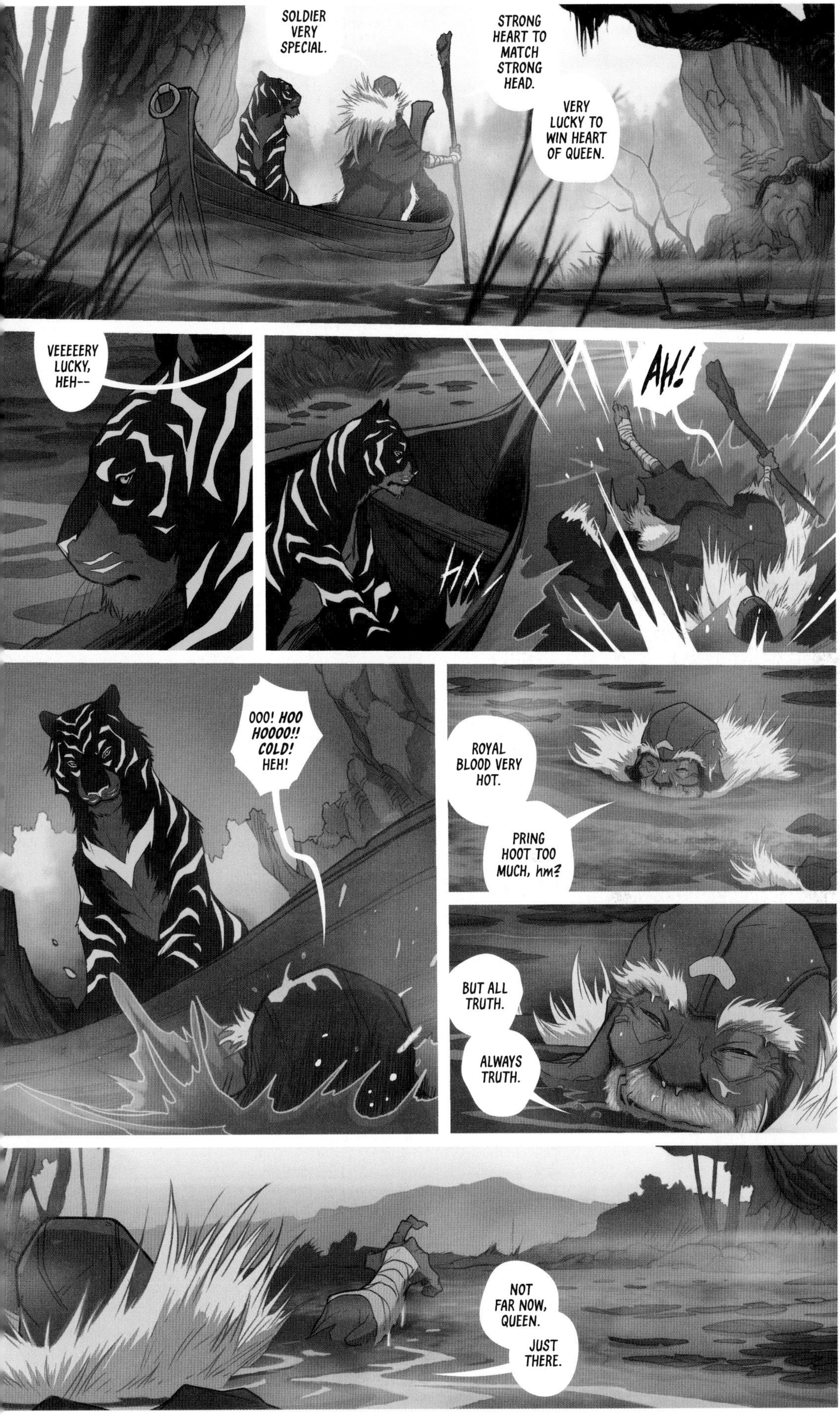
SOLDIER VERY SPECIAL.
STRONG HEART TO MATCH STRONG HEAD.
VERY LUCKY TO WIN HEART OF QUEEN.
VEEEEERY LUCKY, HEH--
AH!
OOO! HOO HOOOO!! COLD! HEH!
ROYAL BLOOD VERY HOT.
PRING HOOT TOO MUCH, hm?
BUT ALL TRUTH.
ALWAYS TRUTH.
NOT FAR NOW, QUEEN.
JUST THERE.

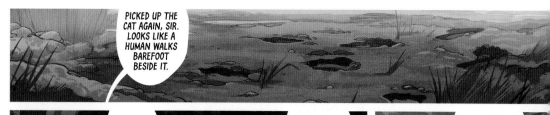

PICKED UP THE CAT AGAIN, SIR. LOOKS LIKE A HUMAN WALKS BAREFOOT BESIDE IT.

THE MORO HAVE GOT HER.

MOVE ON THE TRAIL NOW. IF WE LOSE THEM, IT'S ALL OVER.

AYE, BOSS.

ONCE THE MORO GET HER INTO THE WETLANDS THEY'LL BE INVISIBLE TO US.

WAIT!

I CAN FIND THEM. I KNOW WHERE THEY'RE GOING.

JUST--I'M THE ONLY ONE WHO KNOWS.

IF YOU CAN GET THESE ROPES OFF...

NOT A CHANCE.

THERE'S A BOOK IN MY PACK! IT'S FILLED WITH DIRECTIONS AND NOTES AND...

IT SHOWS THE WAY TO THE MORO.

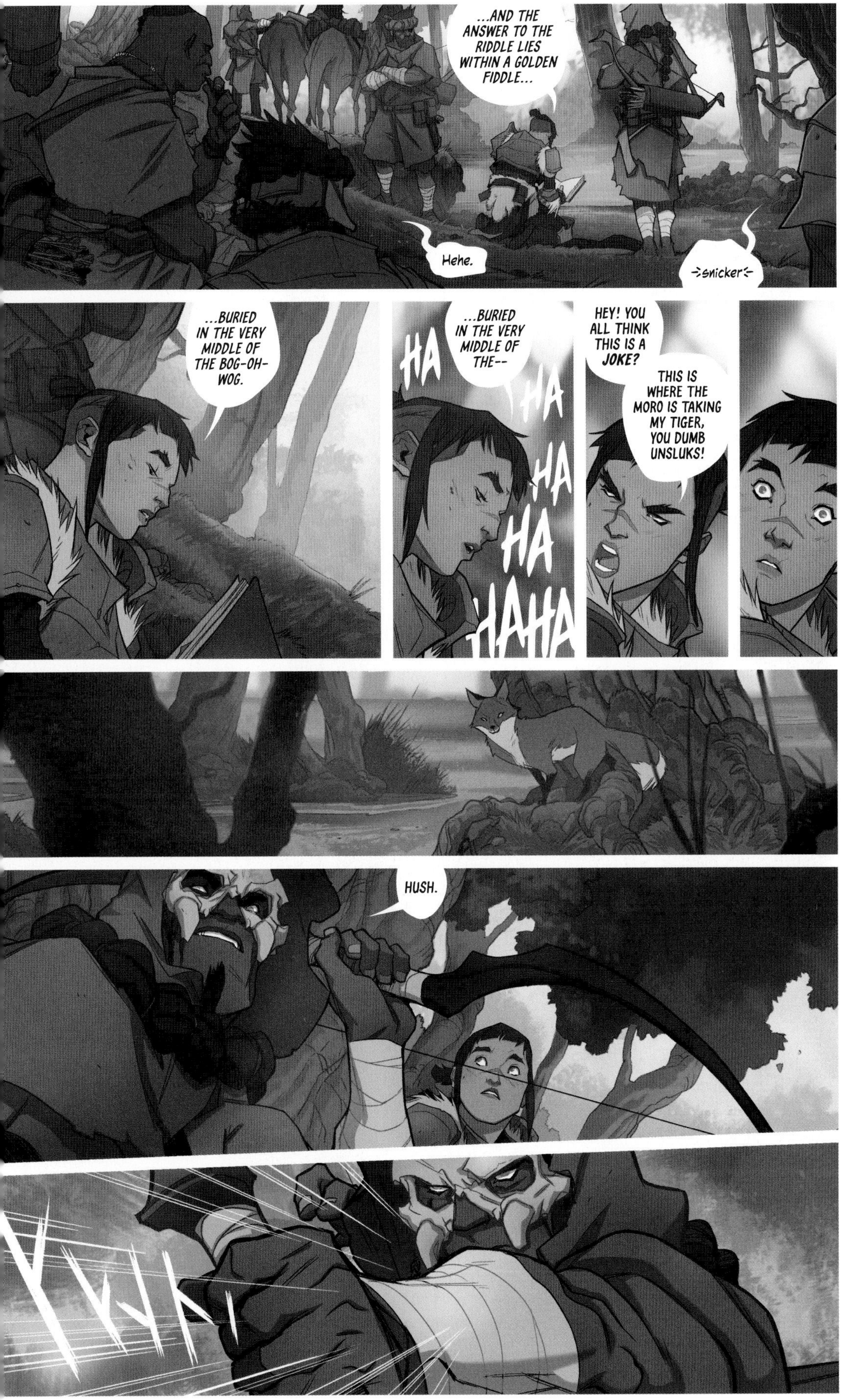

...AND THE ANSWER TO THE RIDDLE LIES WITHIN A GOLDEN FIDDLE...
Hehe.
snicker
...BURIED IN THE VERY MIDDLE OF THE BOG-OH-WOG.
...BURIED IN THE VERY MIDDLE OF THE--
HA HA HA HA HA HAHA
HEY! YOU ALL THINK THIS IS A JOKE?
THIS IS WHERE THE MORO IS TAKING MY TIGER, YOU DUMB UNSLUKS!
HUSH.

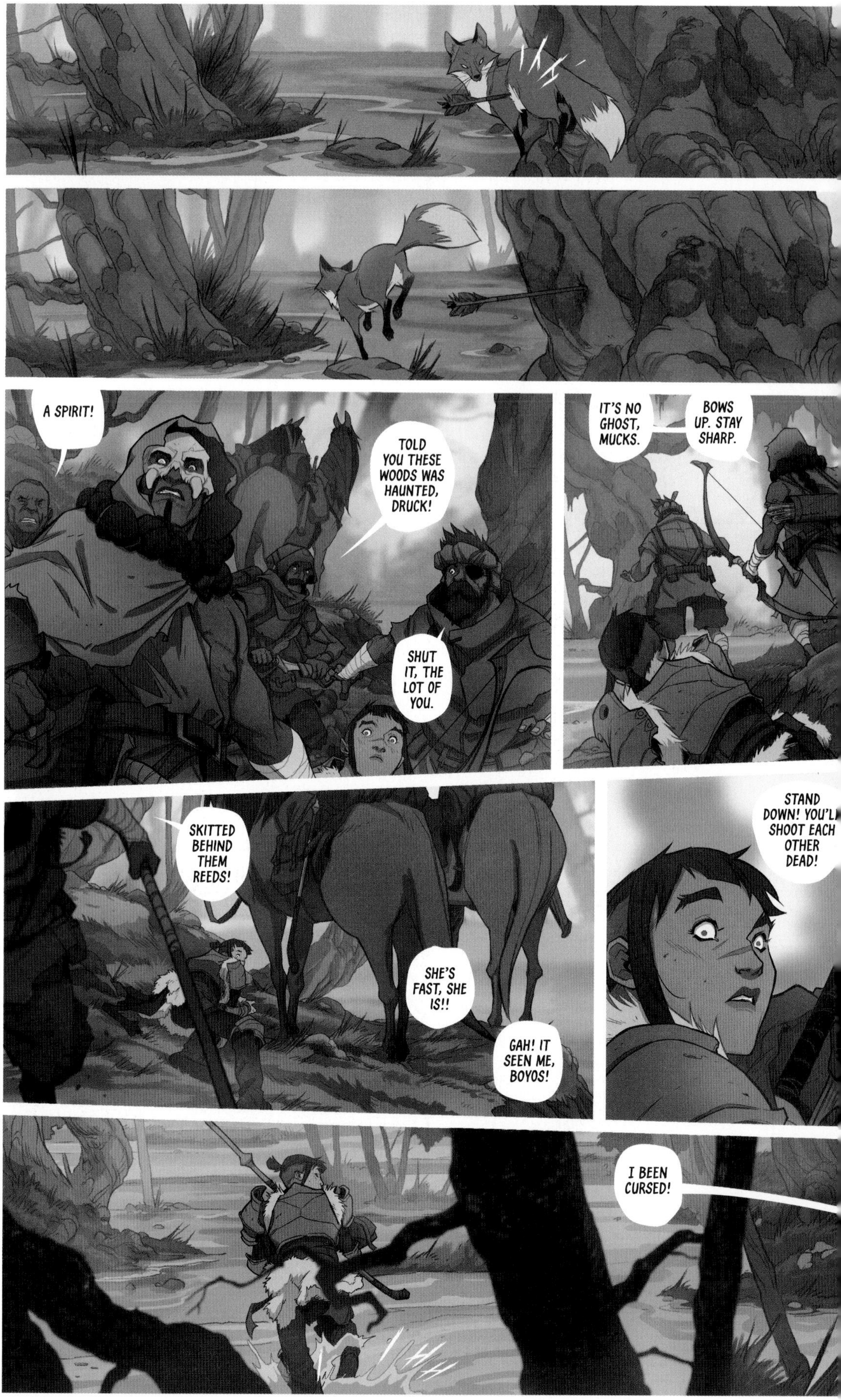
A SPIRIT!
TOLD YOU THESE WOODS WAS HAUNTED, DRUCK!
SHUT IT, THE LOT OF YOU.
IT'S NO GHOST, MUCKS.
BOWS UP. STAY SHARP.
SKITTED BEHIND THEM REEDS!
SHE'S FAST, SHE IS!!
GAH! IT SEEN ME, BOYOS!
STAND DOWN! YOU'LL SHOOT EACH OTHER DEAD!
I BEEN CURSED!

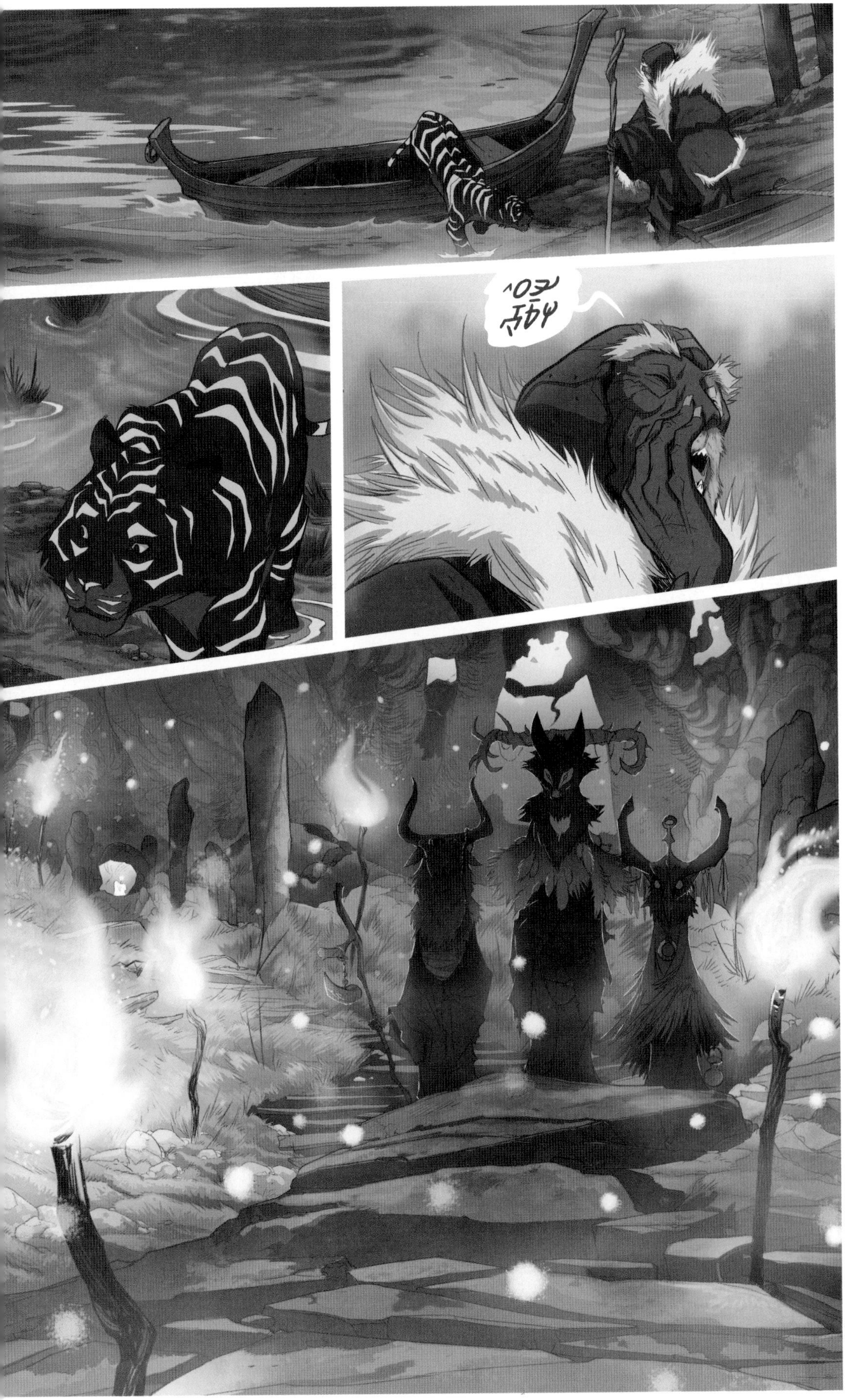

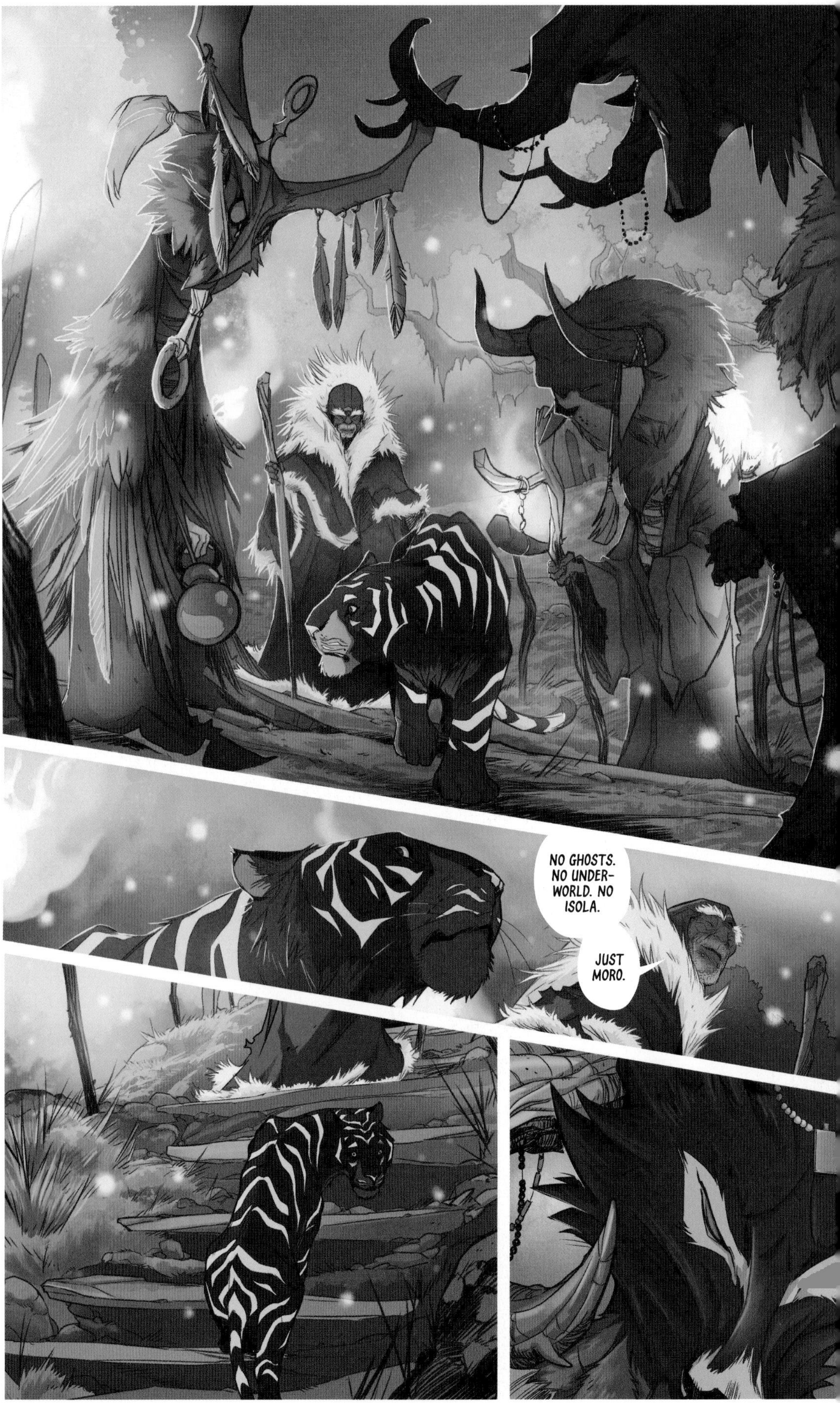
NO GHOSTS. NO UNDER-WORLD. NO ISOLA.
JUST MORO.

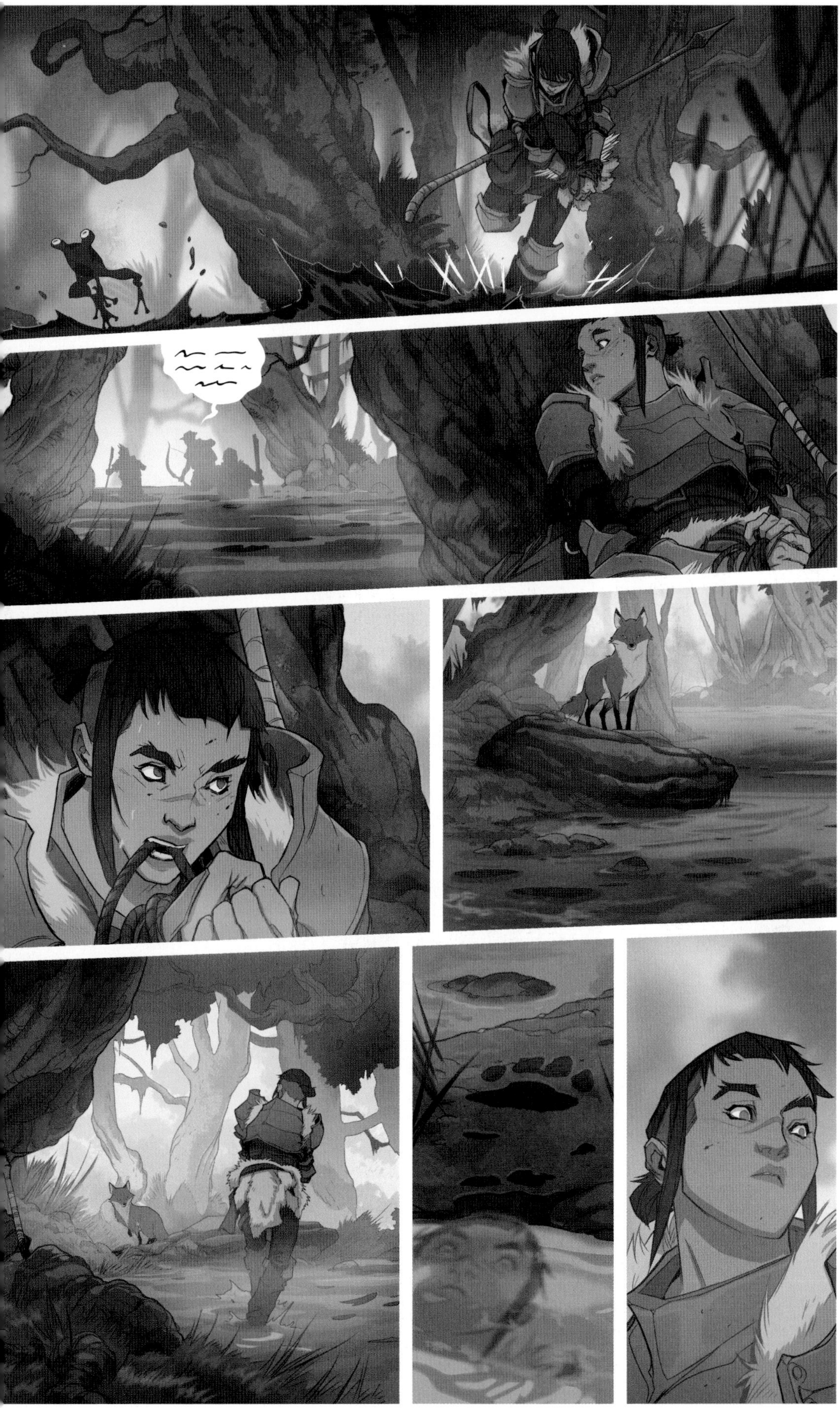

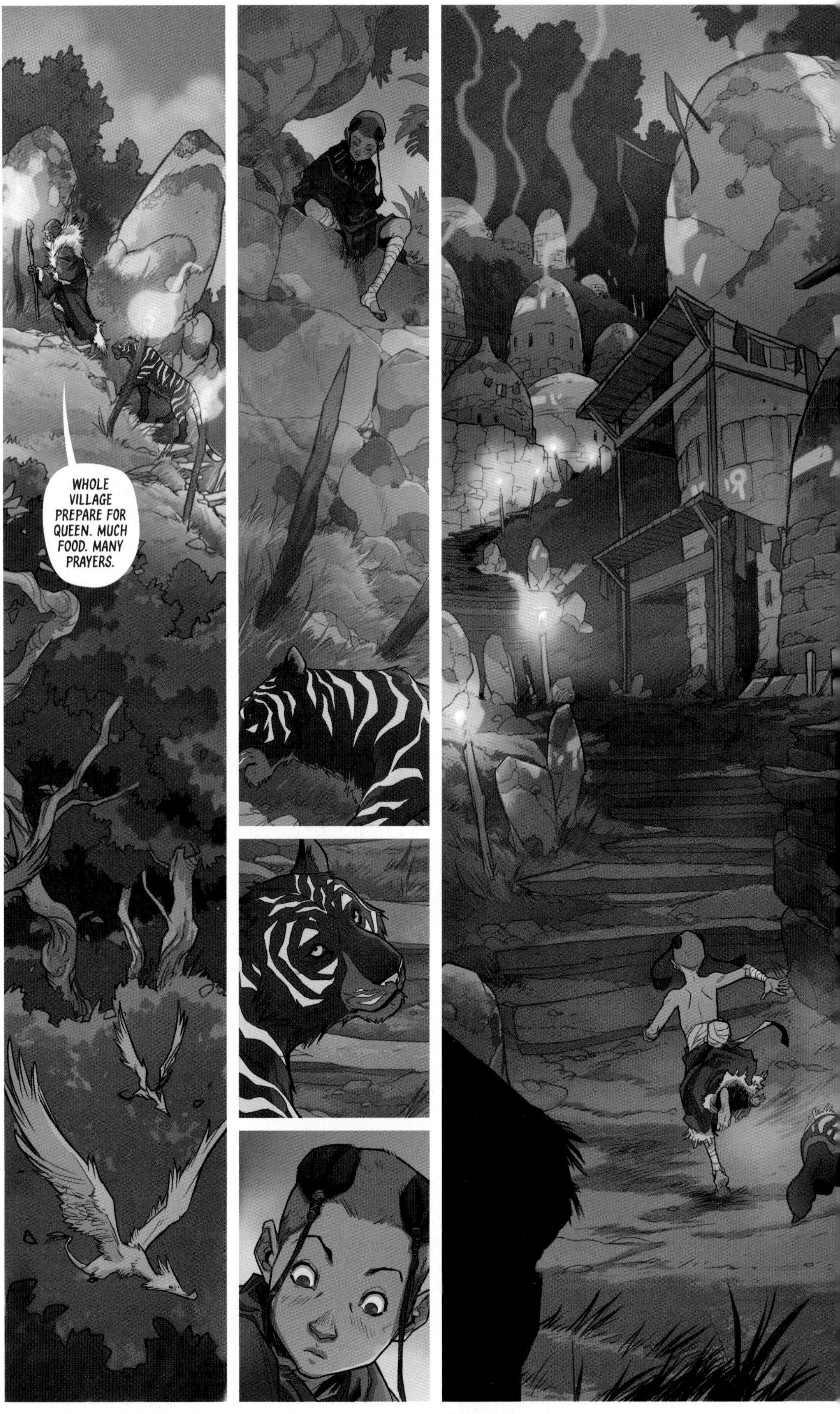
WHOLE VILLAGE PREPARE FOR QUEEN. MUCH FOOD. MANY PRAYERS.

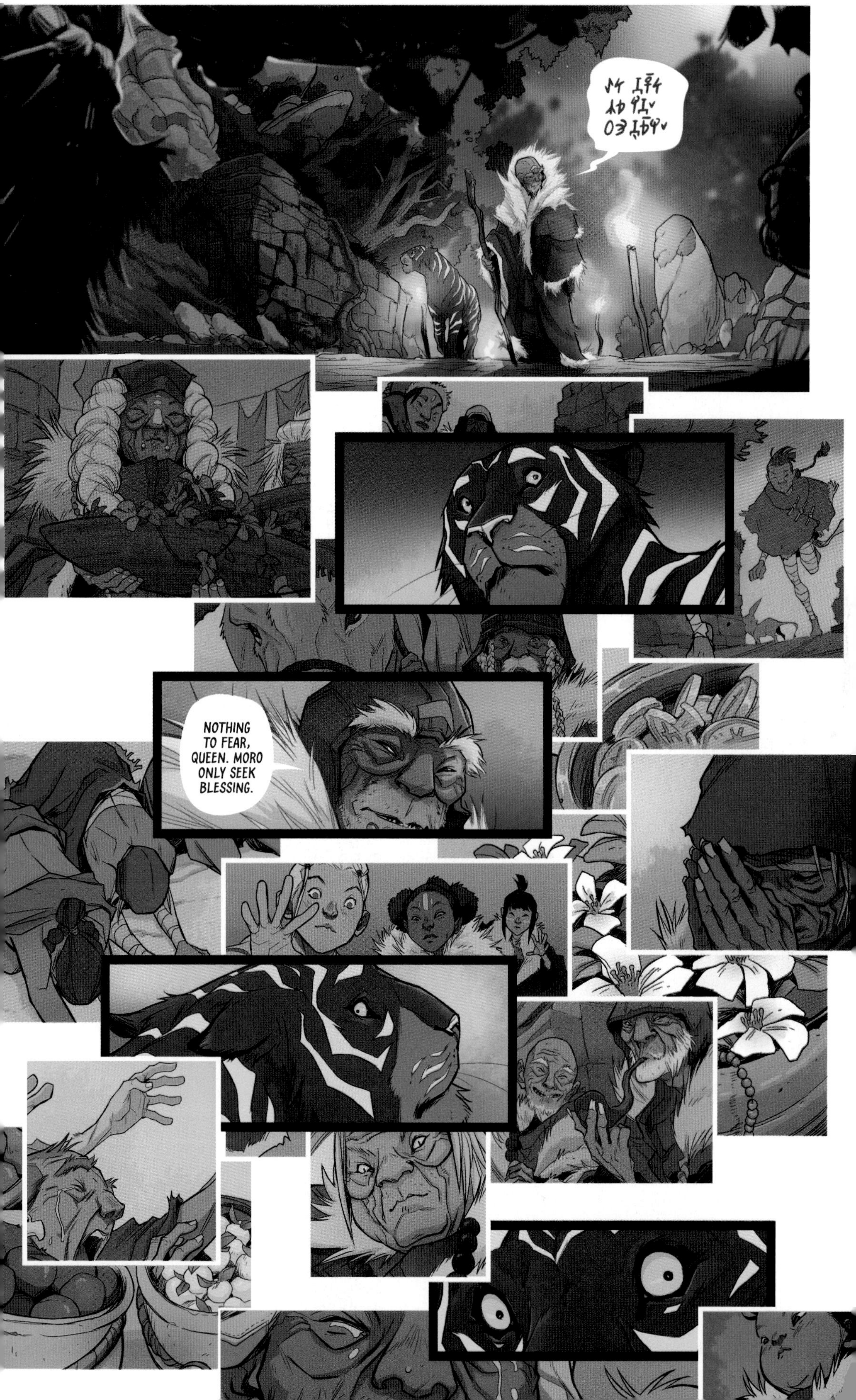
NOTHING TO FEAR, QUEEN. MORO ONLY SEEK BLESSING.

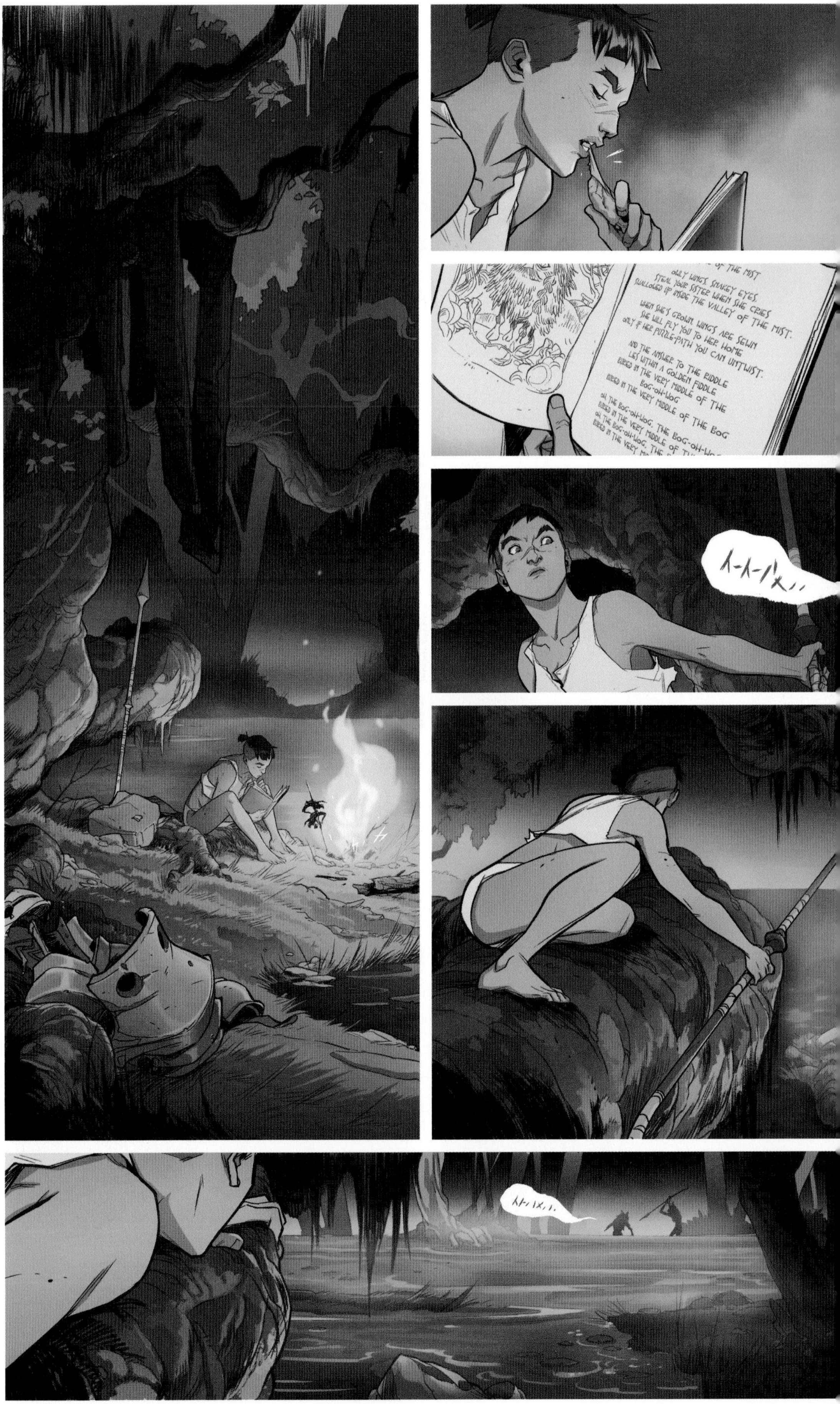
OF THE MIST
ONLY WINGS, SMOKEY EYES,
STEAL YOUR SISTER WHEN SHE CRIES
SWALLOWED UP INSIDE THE VALLEY OF THE MIST.
WHEN SHE'S GROWN, WINGS ARE SEWN
SHE WILL FLY YOU TO HER HOME
ONLY IF HER PUZZLE-PATH YOU CAN UNTWIST.
AND THE ANSWER TO THE RIDDLE
LIES WITHIN A GOLDEN FIDDLE
BURIED IN THE VERY MIDDLE OF THE
BOG-OH-WOG
BURIED IN THE VERY MIDDLE OF THE BOG

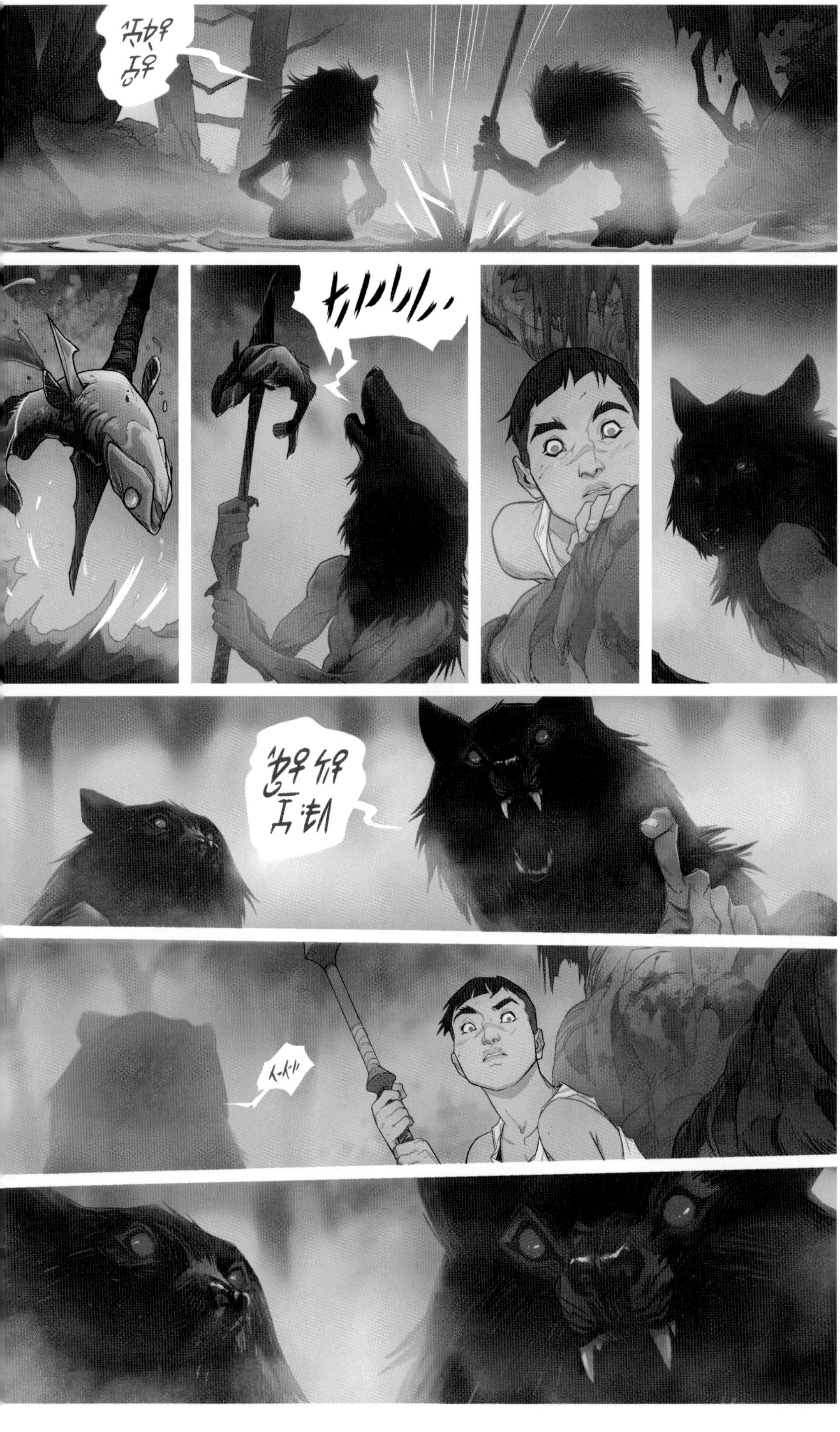

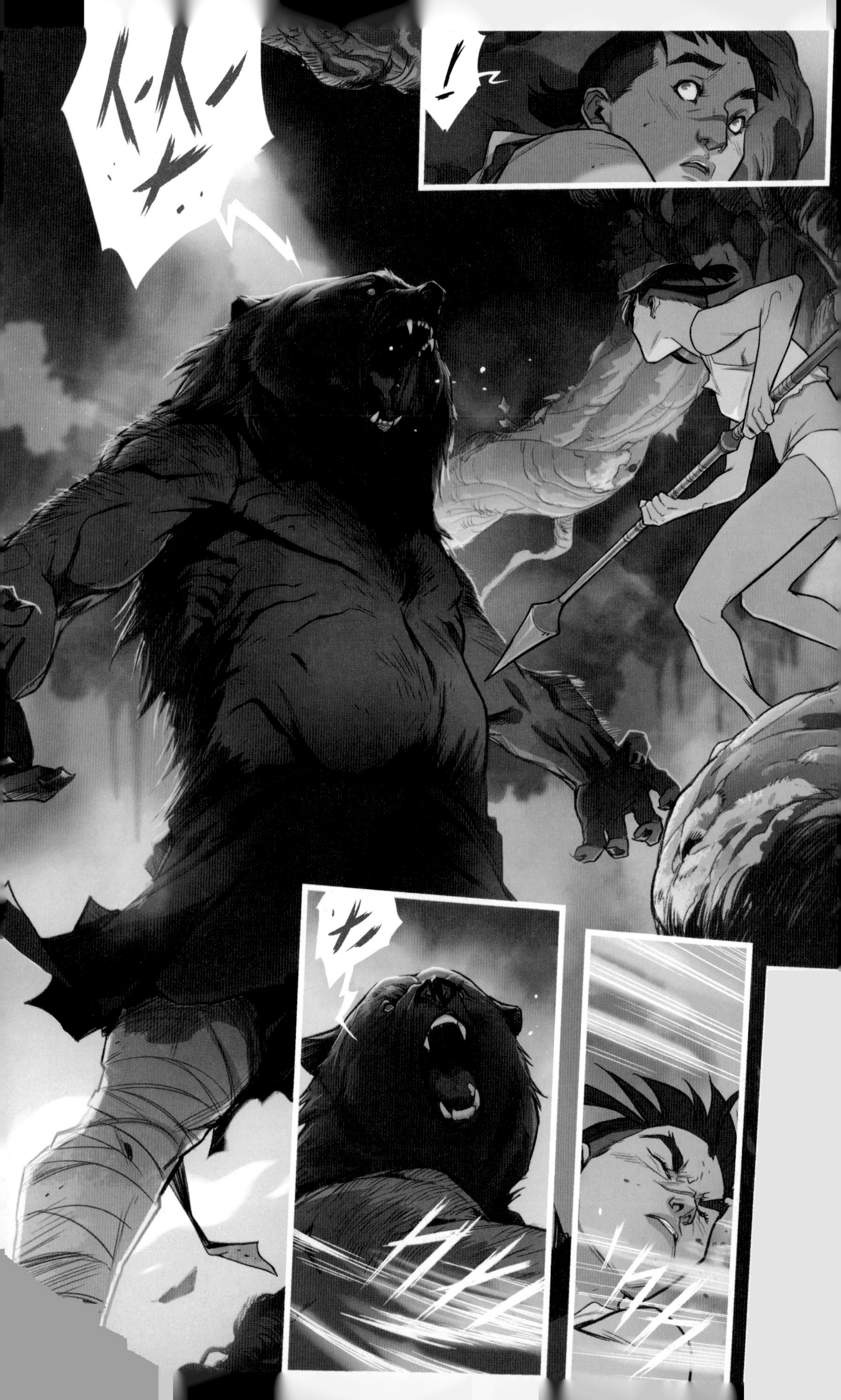
!

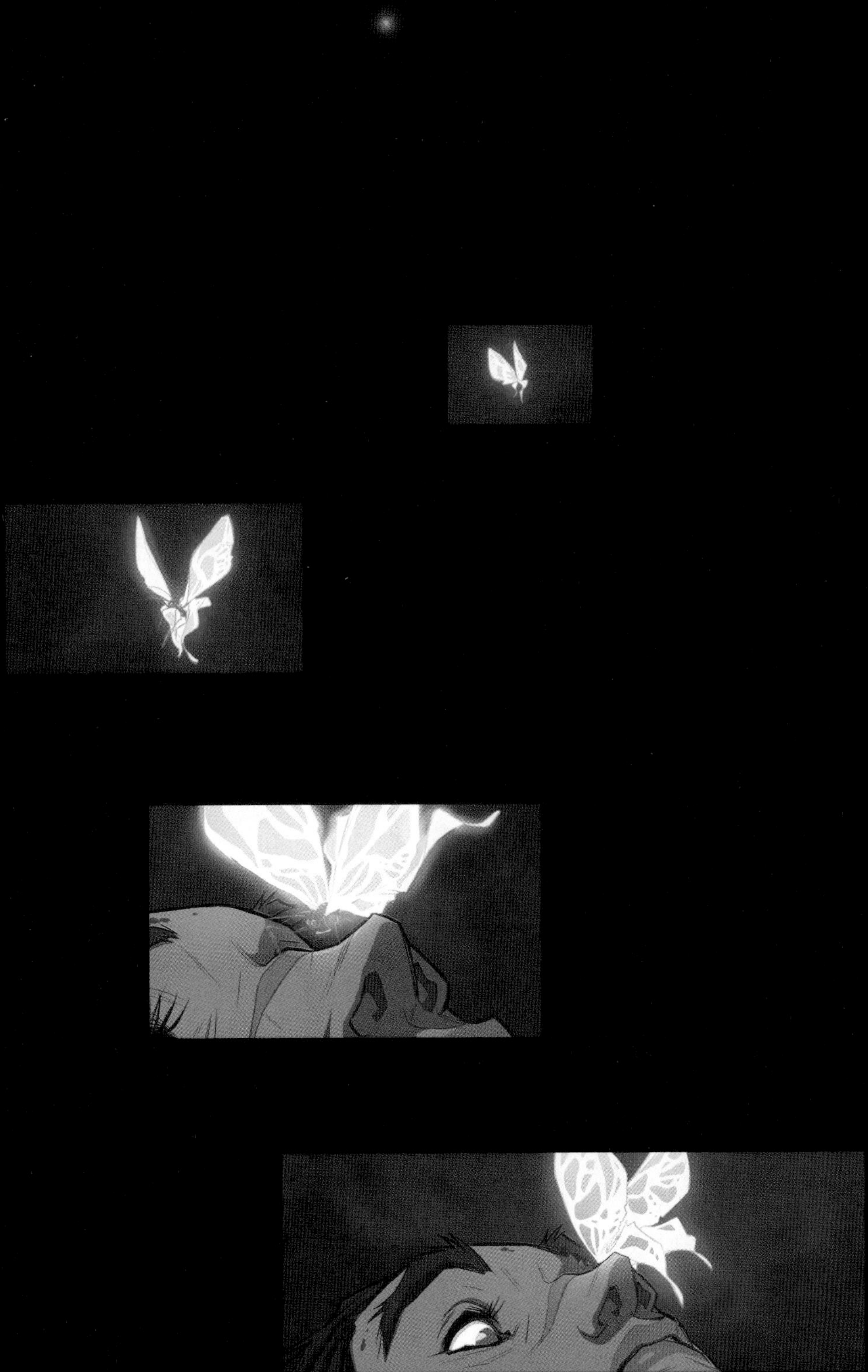

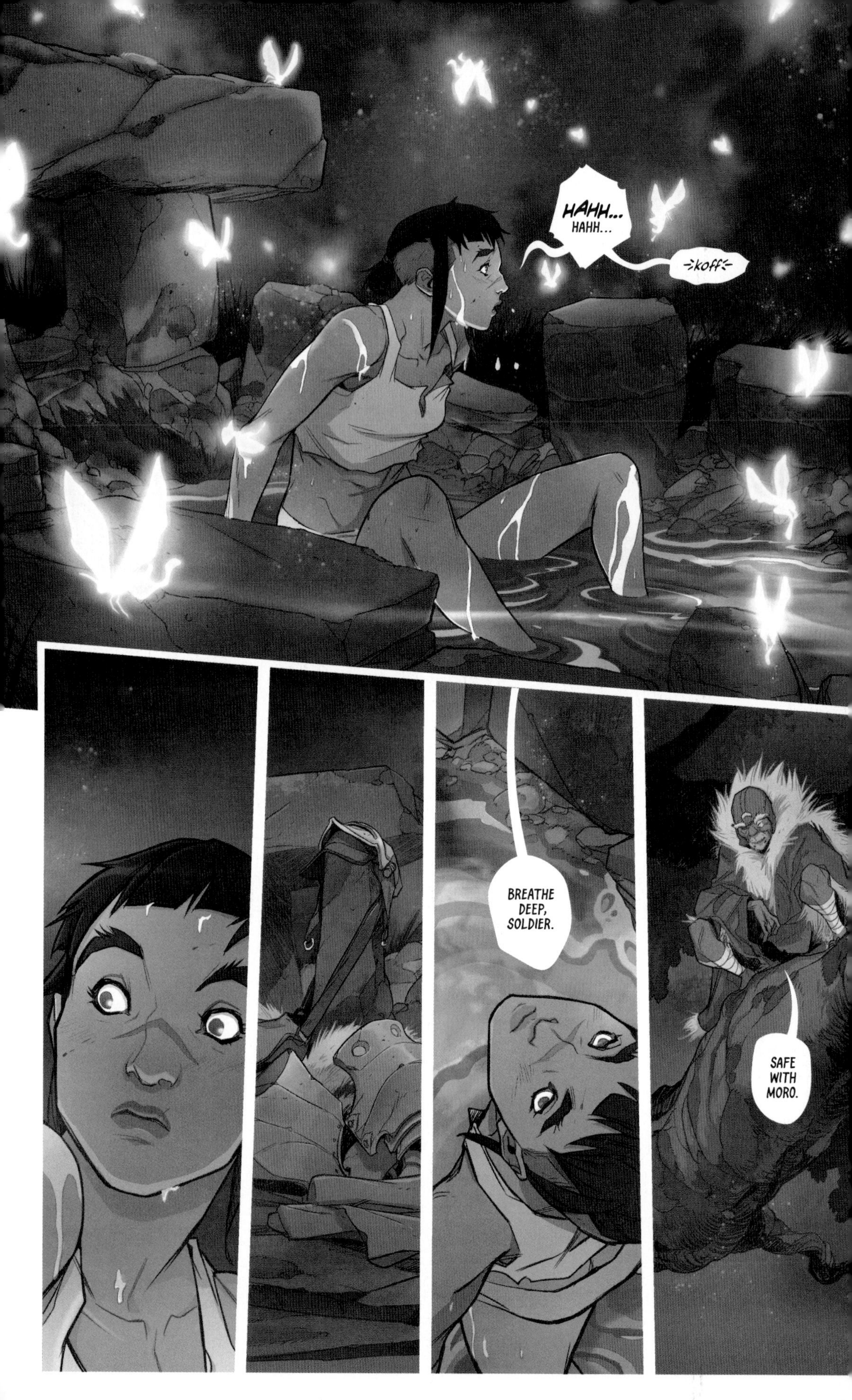
HAHH... HAHH...
koff
BREATHE DEEP, SOLDIER.
SAFE WITH MORO.

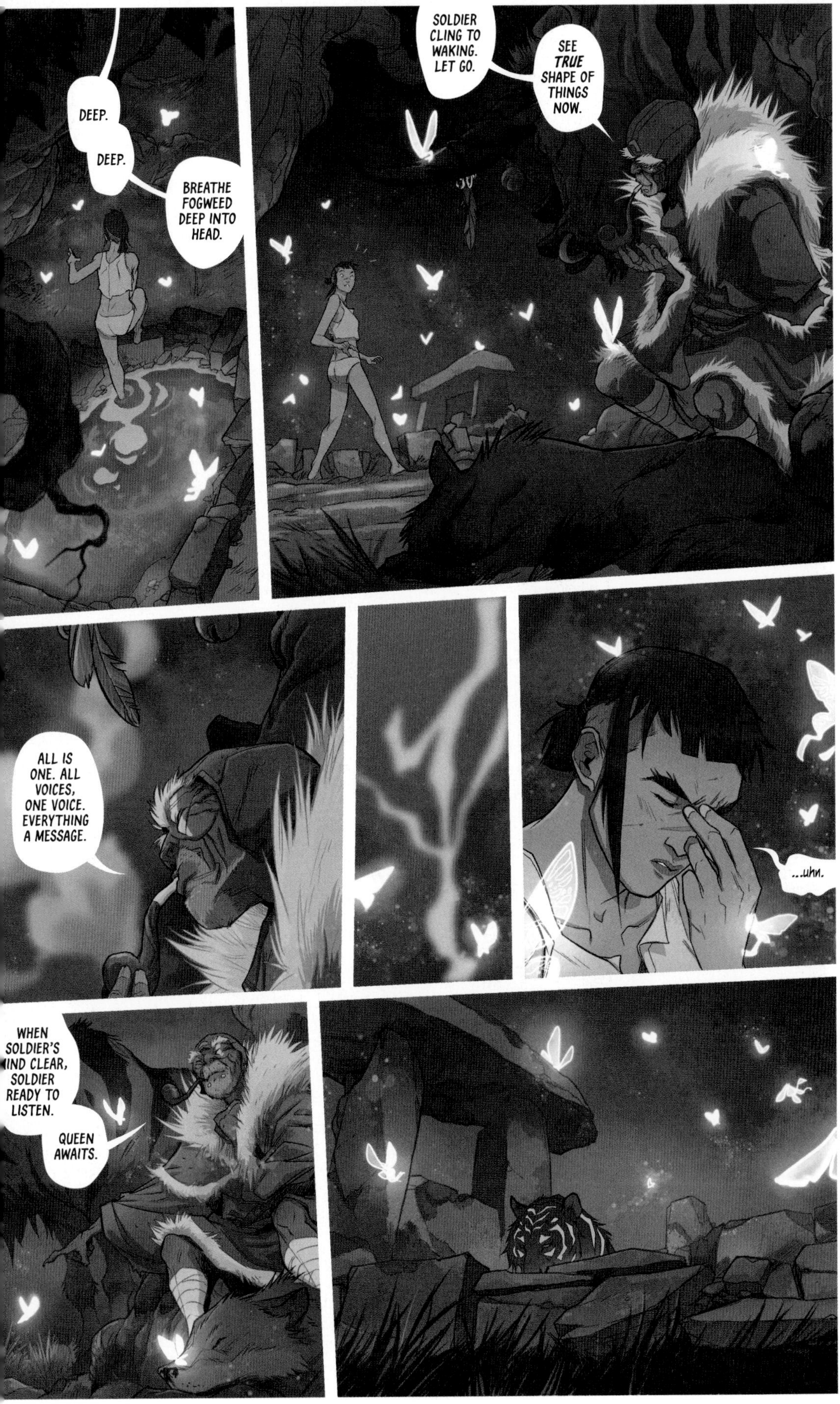
DEEP.
DEEP.
BREATHE FOGWEED DEEP INTO HEAD.
SOLDIER CLING TO WAKING. LET GO.
SEE TRUE SHAPE OF THINGS NOW.
ALL IS ONE. ALL VOICES, ONE VOICE. EVERYTHING A MESSAGE.
...uhn.
WHEN SOLDIER'S IND CLEAR, SOLDIER READY TO LISTEN.
QUEEN AWAITS.

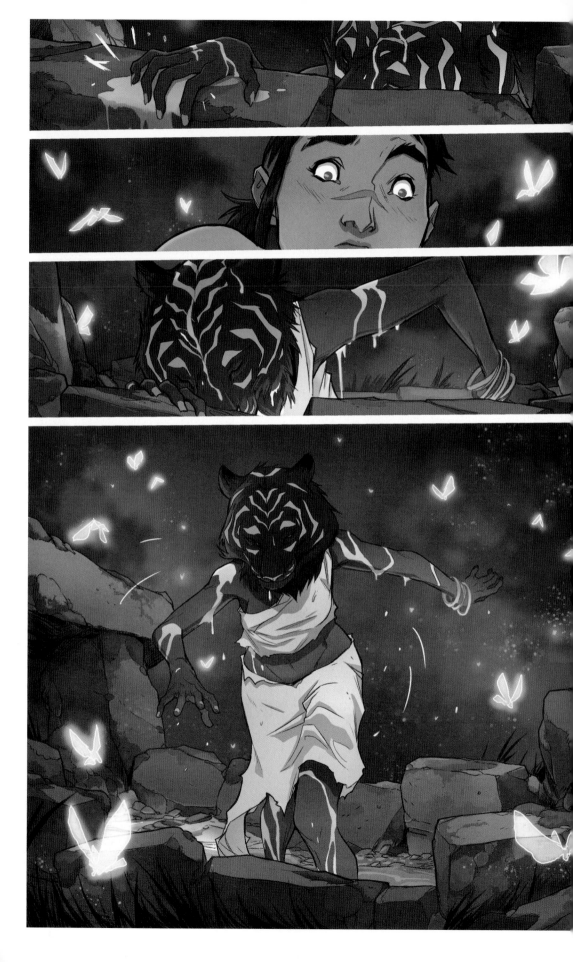

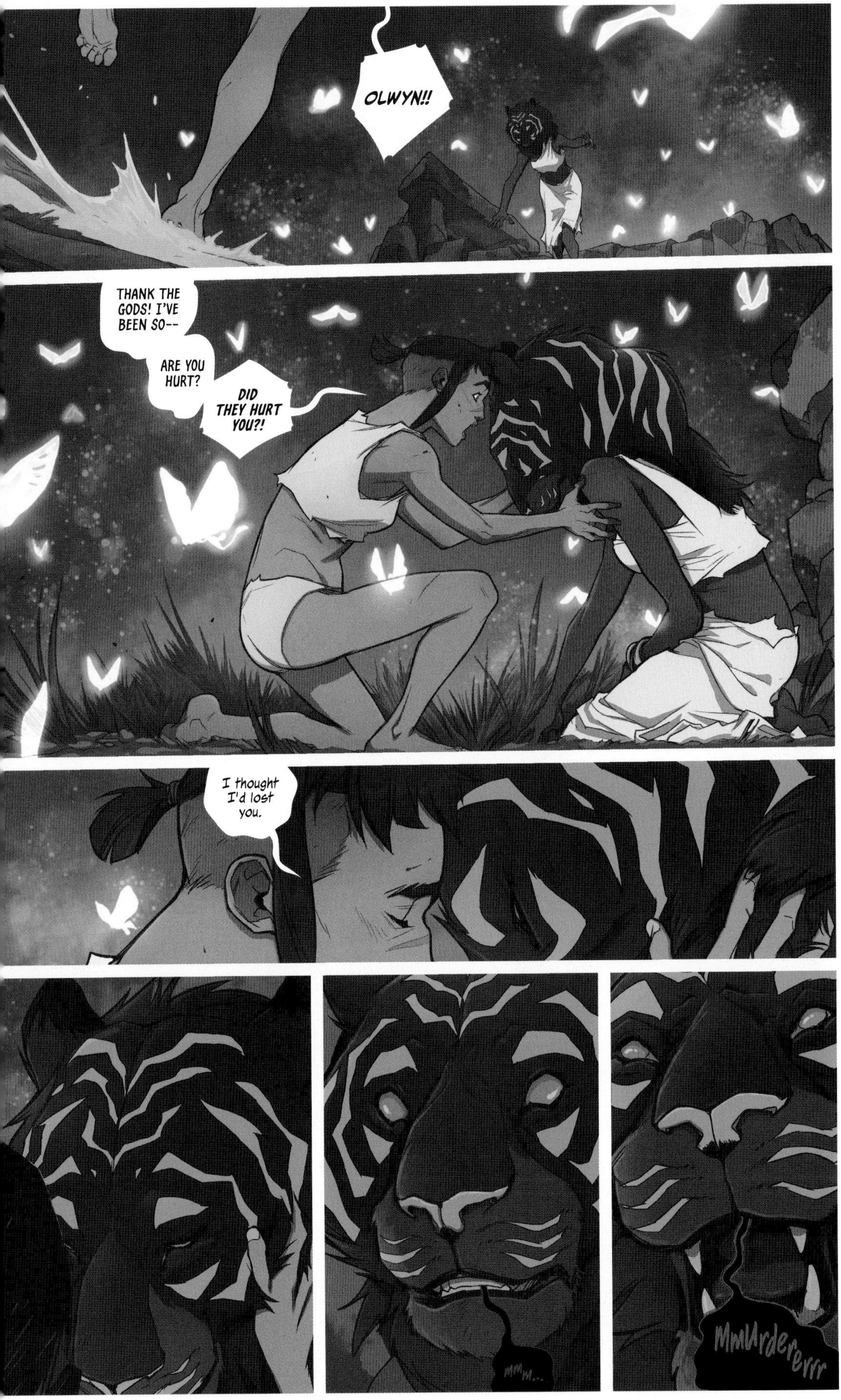
OLWYN!!
THANK THE GODS! I'VE BEEN SO--
ARE YOU HURT?
DID THEY HURT YOU?!
I thought I'd lost you.
MMW...
MmUrdererrr

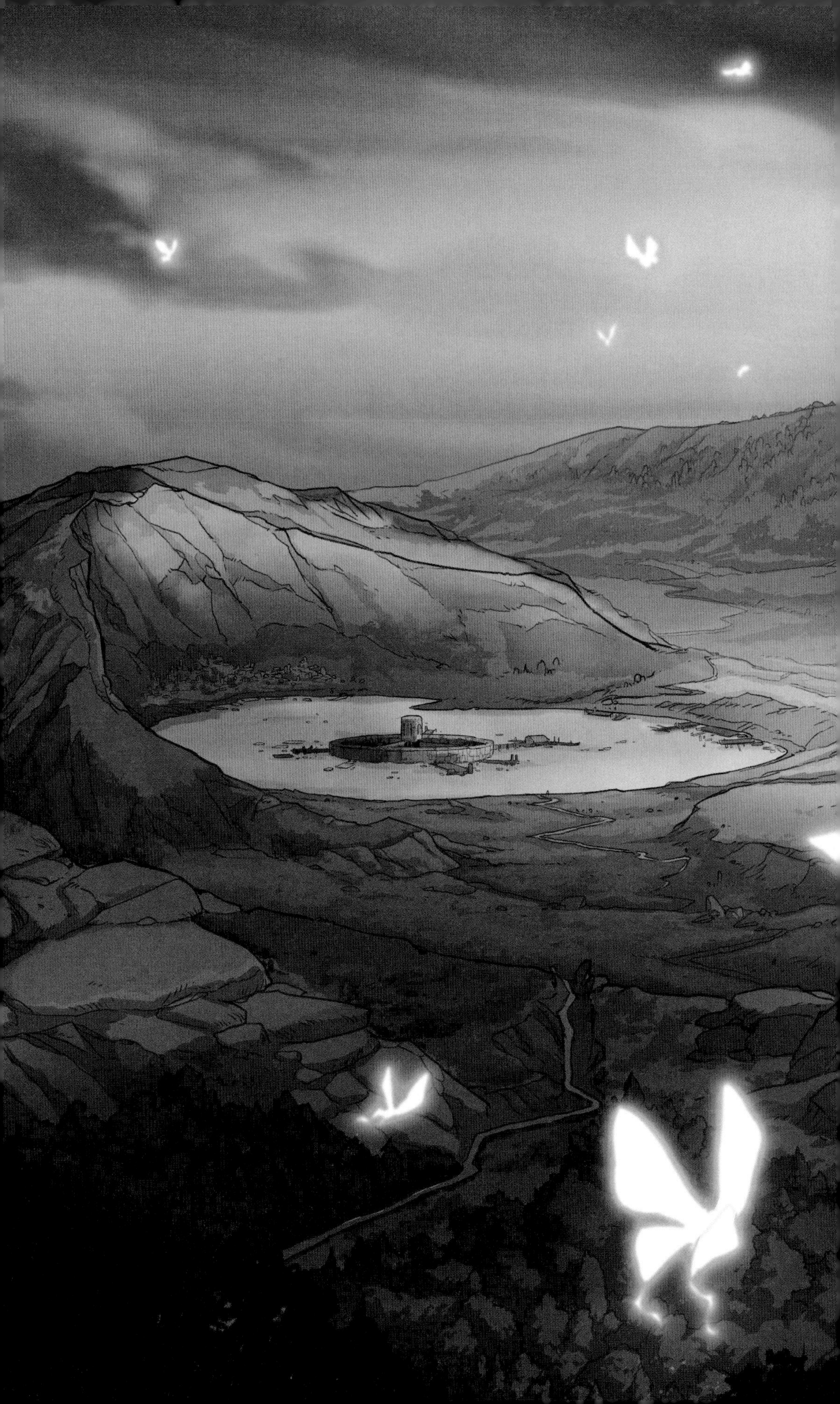

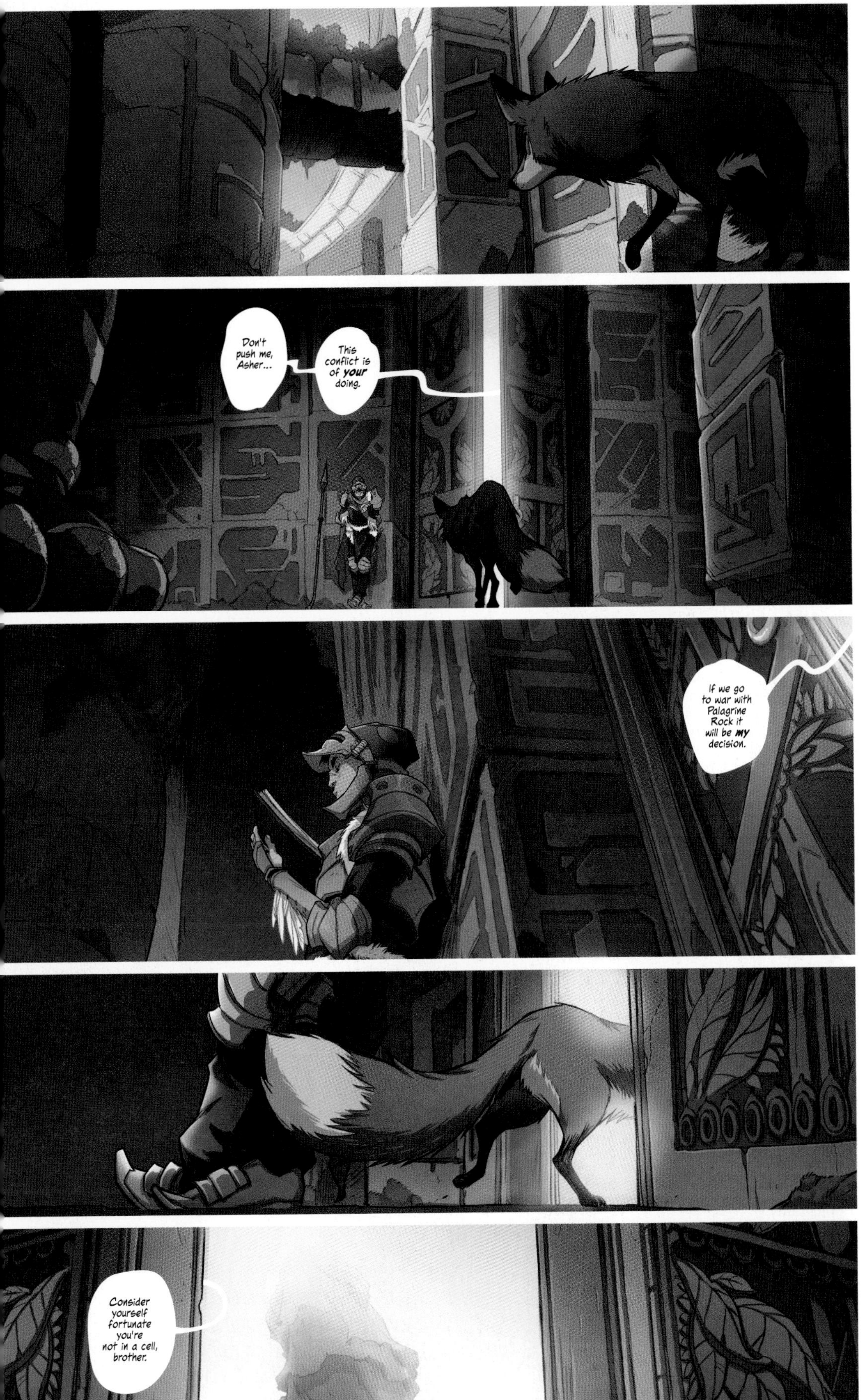
Don't push me, Asher...
This conflict is of *your* doing.
If we go to war with Palagrine Rock it will be *my* decision.
Consider yourself fortunate you're not in a cell, brother.

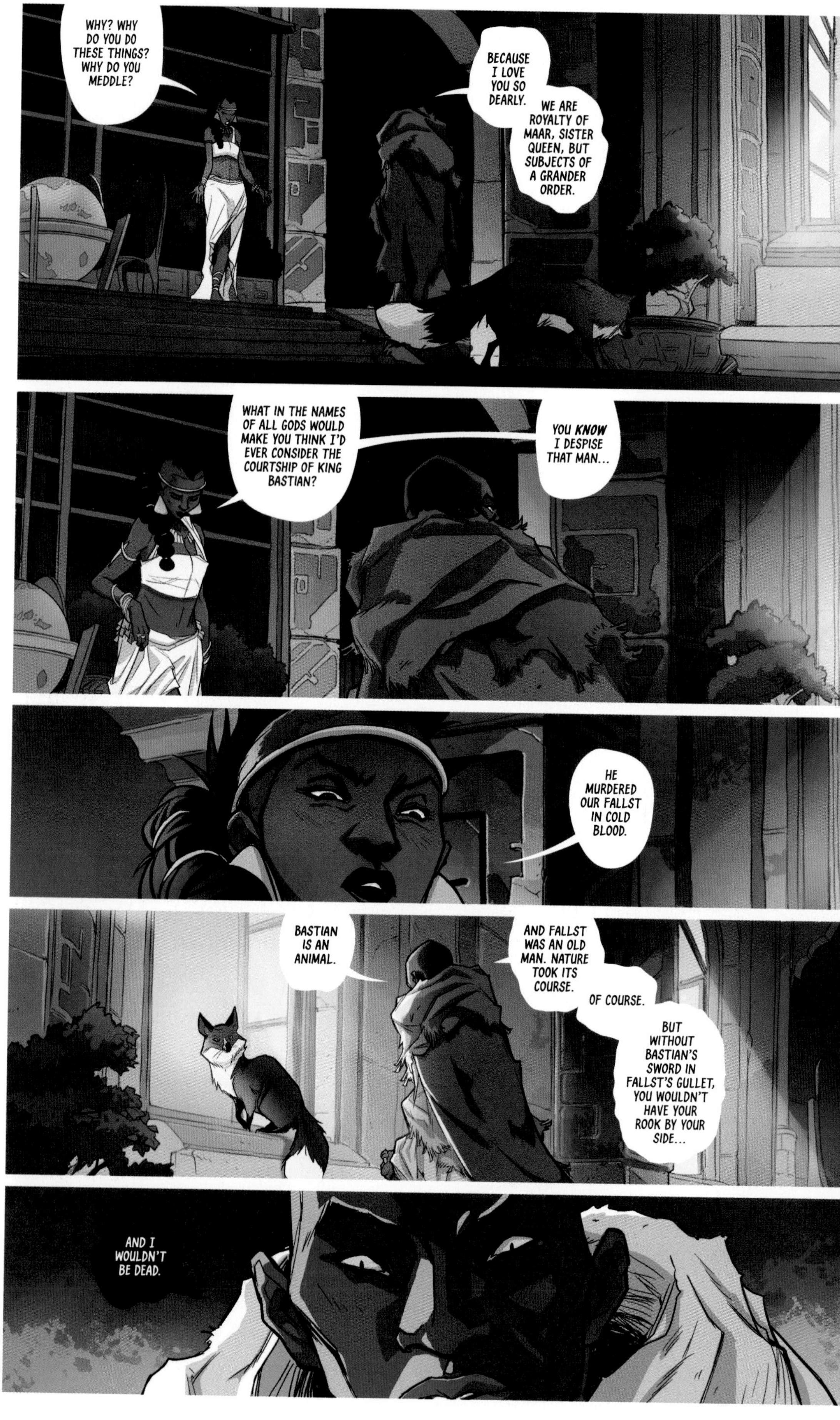
WHY? WHY DO YOU DO THESE THINGS? WHY DO YOU MEDDLE?
BECAUSE I LOVE YOU SO DEARLY.
WE ARE ROYALTY OF MAAR, SISTER QUEEN, BUT SUBJECTS OF A GRANDER ORDER.
WHAT IN THE NAMES OF ALL GODS WOULD MAKE YOU THINK I'D EVER CONSIDER THE COURTSHIP OF KING BASTIAN?
YOU *KNOW* I DESPISE THAT MAN...
HE MURDERED OUR FALLST IN COLD BLOOD.
BASTIAN IS AN ANIMAL.
AND FALLST WAS AN OLD MAN. NATURE TOOK ITS COURSE.
OF COURSE.
BUT WITHOUT BASTIAN'S SWORD IN FALLST'S GULLET, YOU WOULDN'T HAVE YOUR ROOK BY YOUR SIDE...
AND I WOULDN'T BE DEAD.

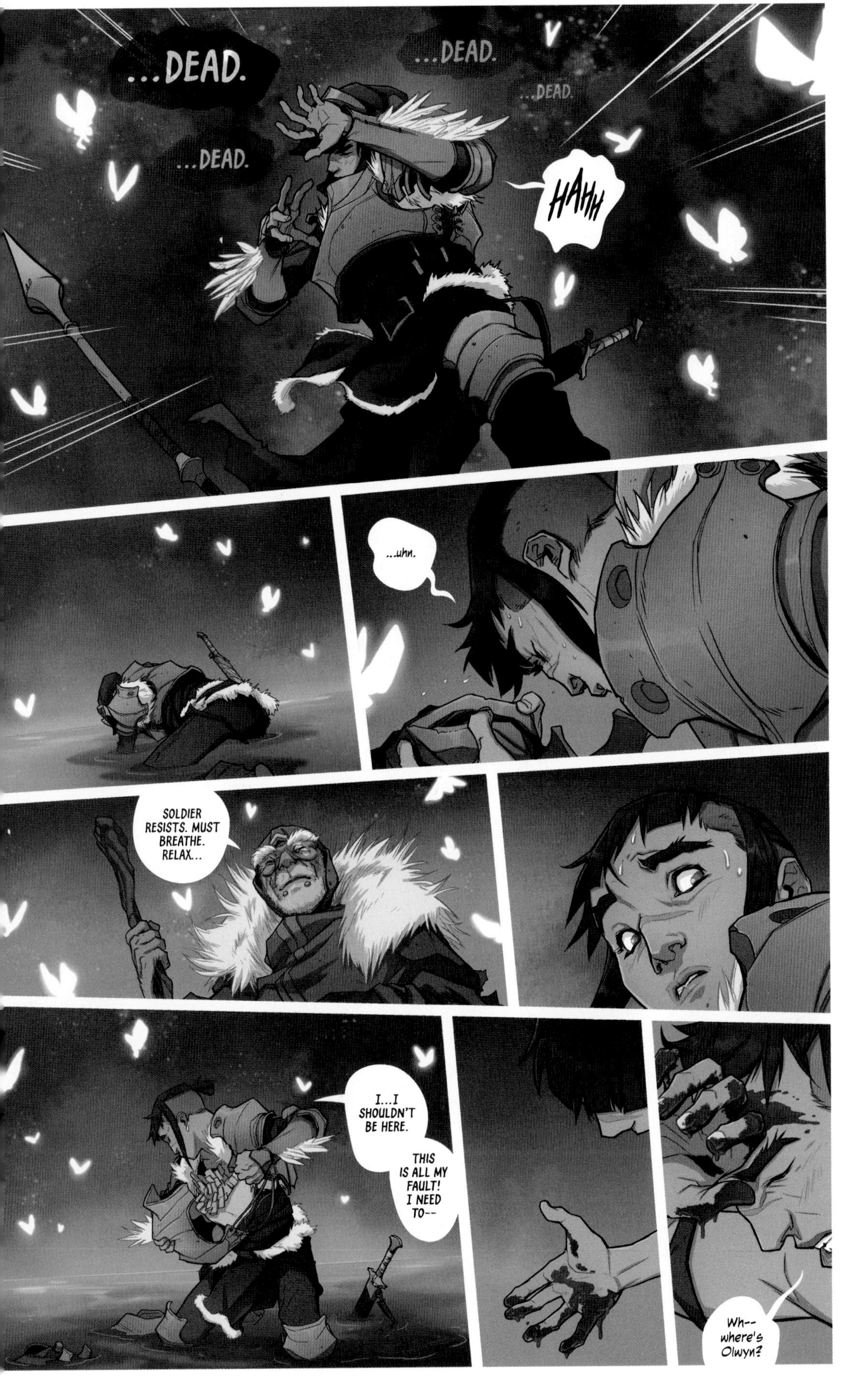
...DEAD.
...DEAD.
...DEAD.
...DEAD.
HAHH
...uhn.
SOLDIER RESISTS. MUST BREATHE. RELAX...
I...I SHOULDN'T BE HERE.
THIS IS ALL MY FAULT! I NEED TO--
Wh-- where's Olwyn?

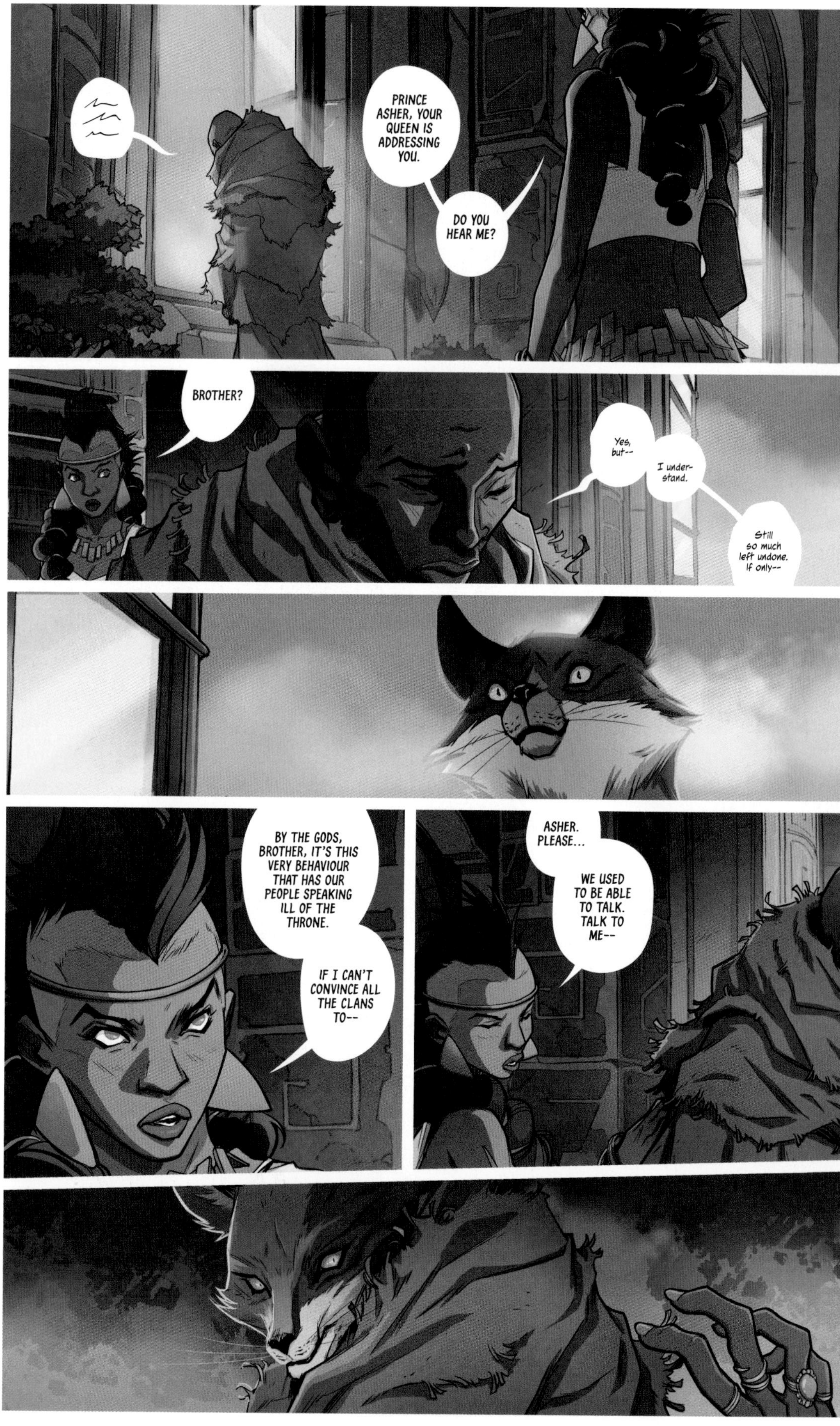
PRINCE ASHER, YOUR QUEEN IS ADDRESSING YOU.
DO YOU HEAR ME?
BROTHER?
Yes, but--
I understand.
Still so much left undone. If only--
BY THE GODS, BROTHER, IT'S THIS VERY BEHAVIOUR THAT HAS OUR PEOPLE SPEAKING ILL OF THE THRONE.
IF I CAN'T CONVINCE ALL THE CLANS TO--
ASHER. PLEASE...
WE USED TO BE ABLE TO TALK. TALK TO ME--

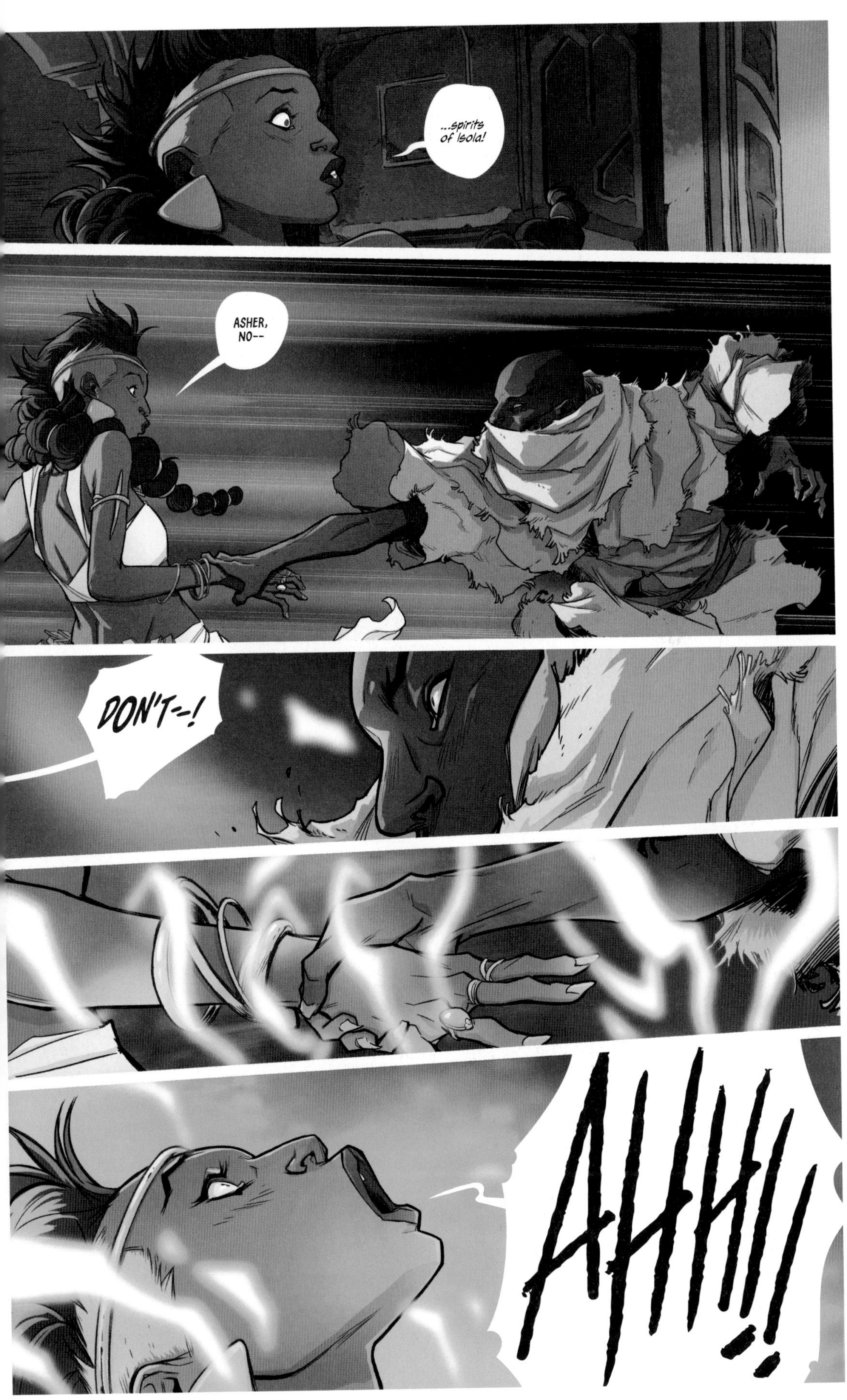

...spirits of Isola!
ASHER, NO--
DON'T--!
AHH!!

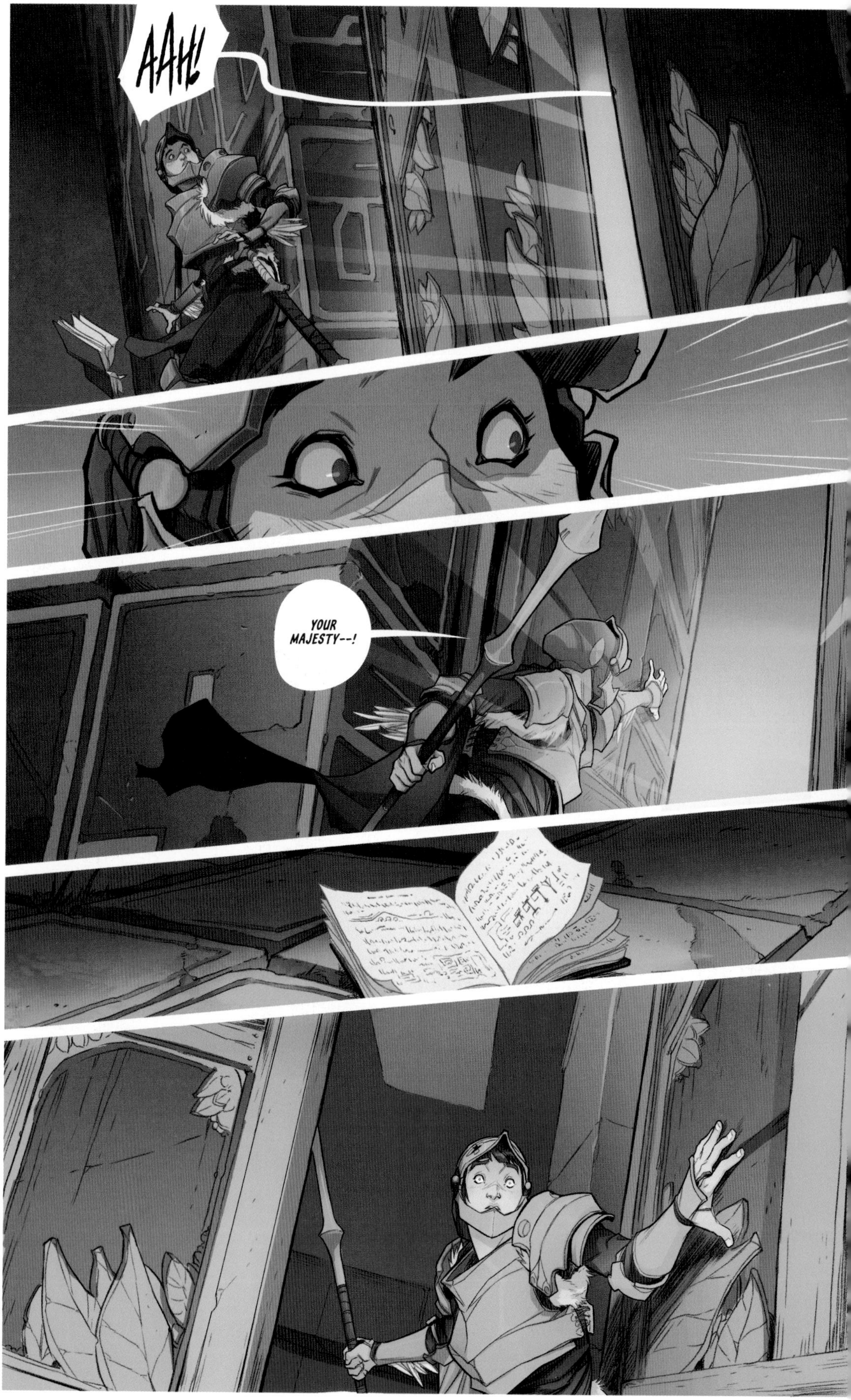
AAH!
YOUR MAJESTY--!

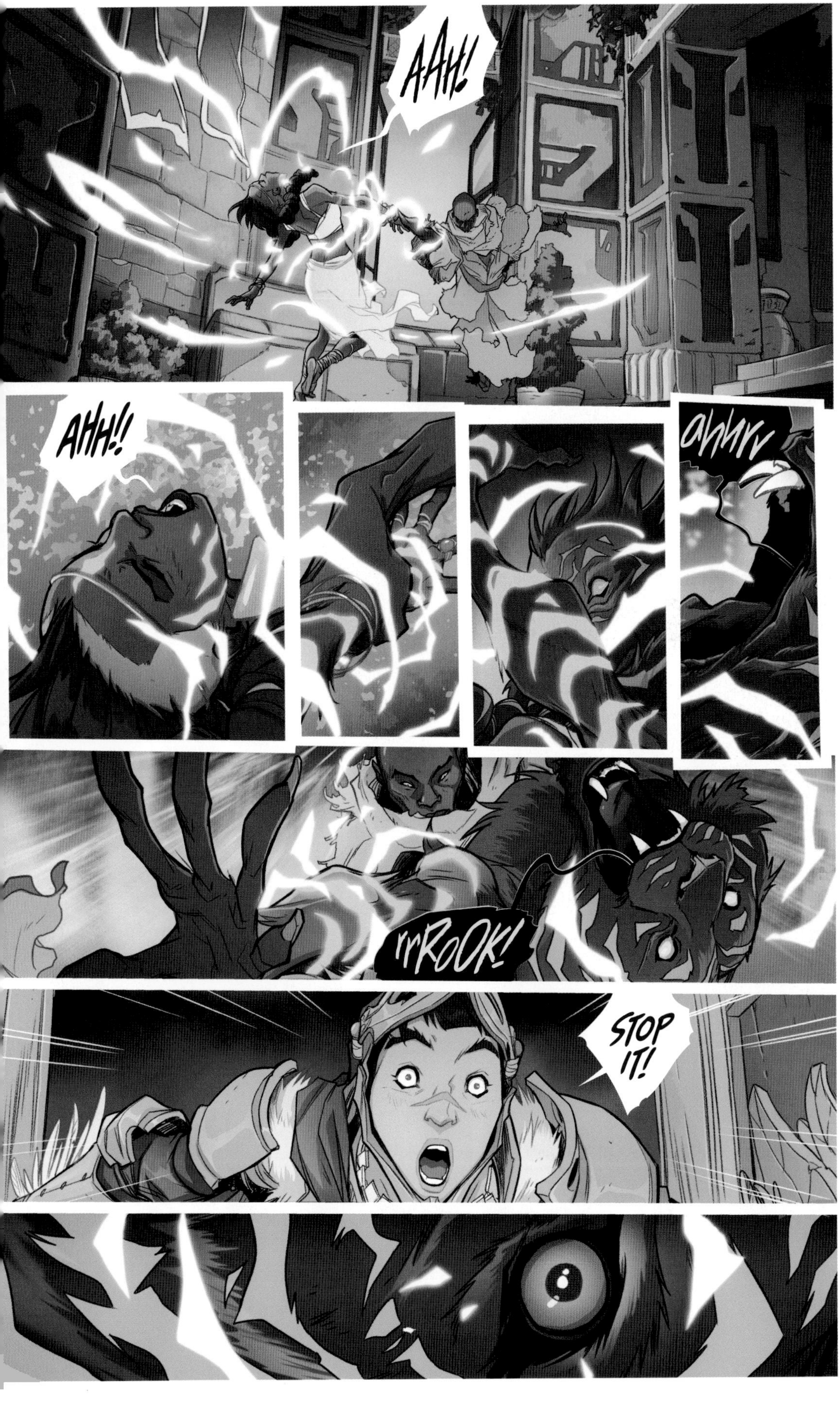
AAH!
AHH!!
ahhrr
rrROOK!
STOP IT!

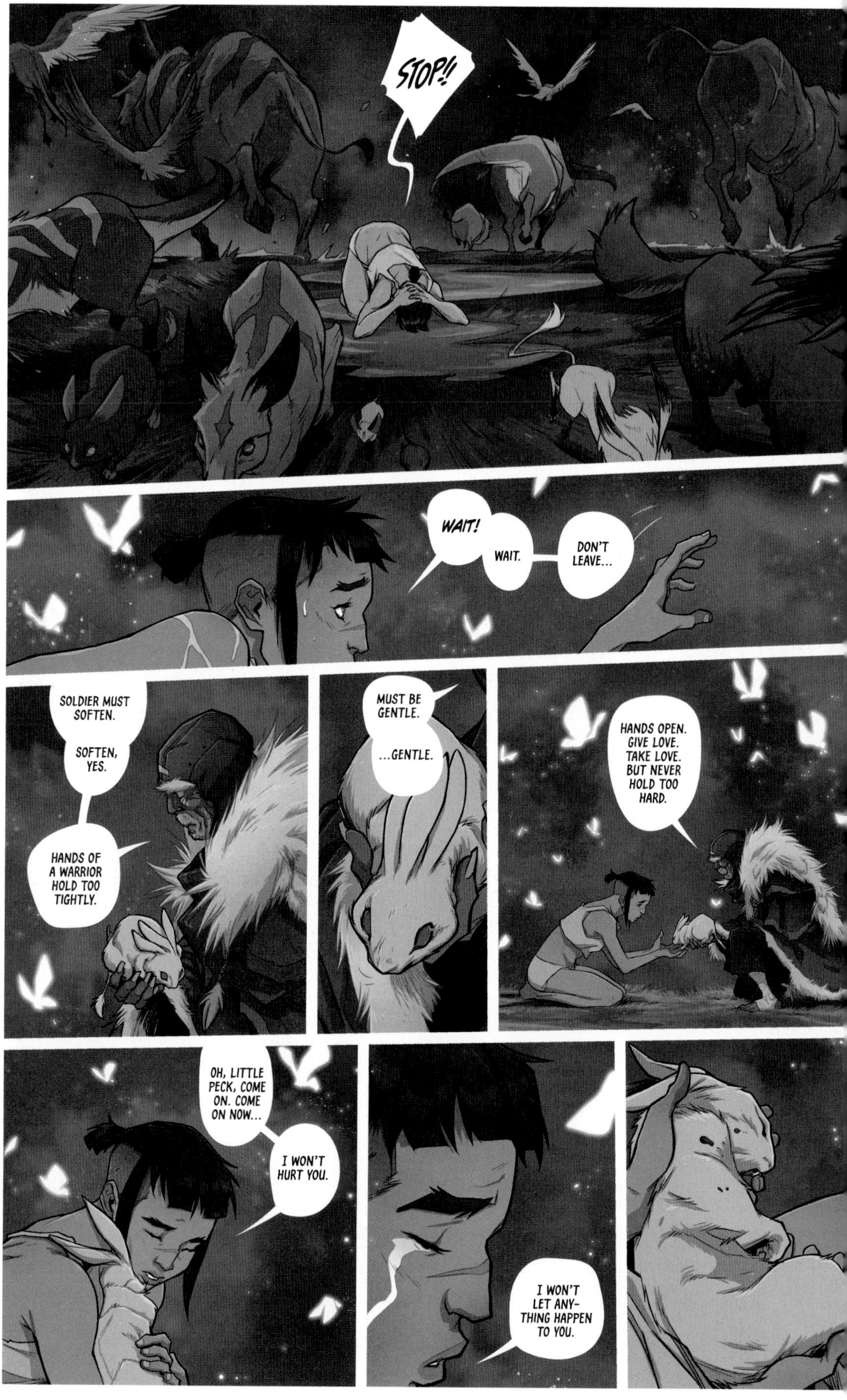
STOP!!
WAIT!
WAIT.
DON'T LEAVE...
SOLDIER MUST SOFTEN.
SOFTEN, YES.
HANDS OF A WARRIOR HOLD TOO TIGHTLY.
MUST BE GENTLE.
...GENTLE.
HANDS OPEN. GIVE LOVE. TAKE LOVE. BUT NEVER HOLD TOO HARD.
OH, LITTLE PECK, COME ON. COME ON NOW...
I WON'T HURT YOU.
I WON'T LET ANY-THING HAPPEN TO YOU.

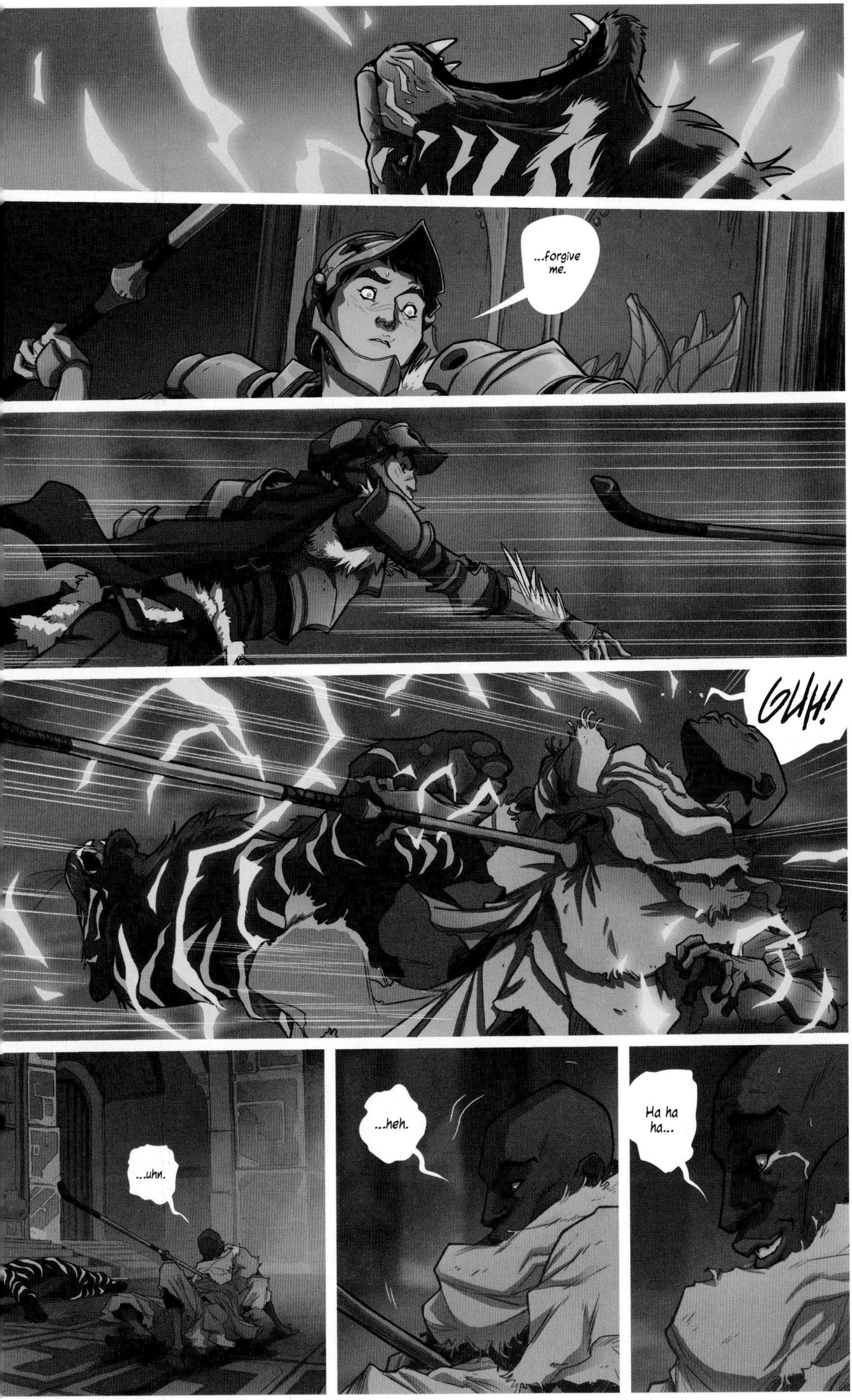
...forgive me.
GUH!
...uhn.
...heh.
Ha ha ha...

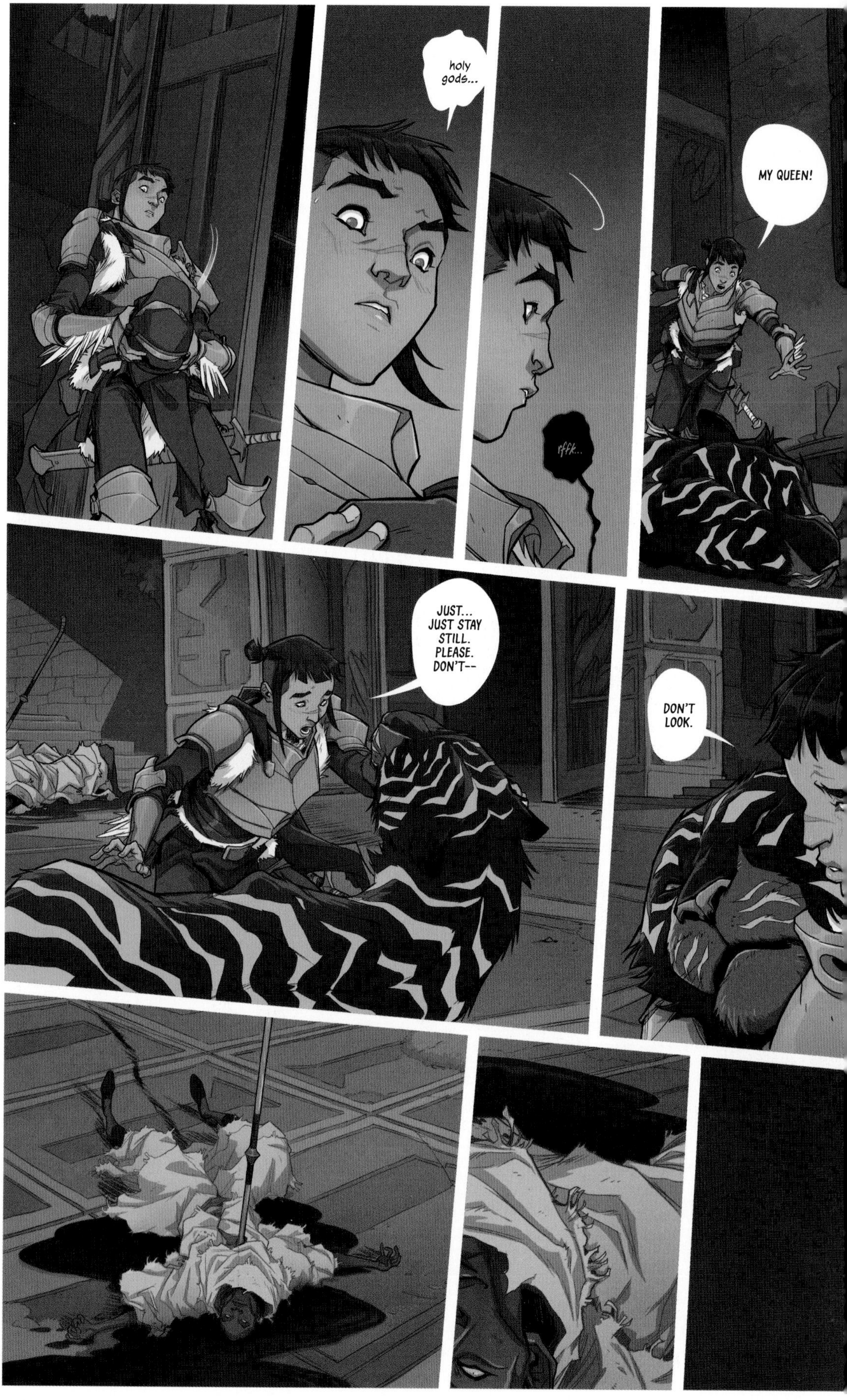
holy gods...
rffk...
MY QUEEN!
JUST... JUST STAY STILL. PLEASE. DON'T--
DON'T LOOK.

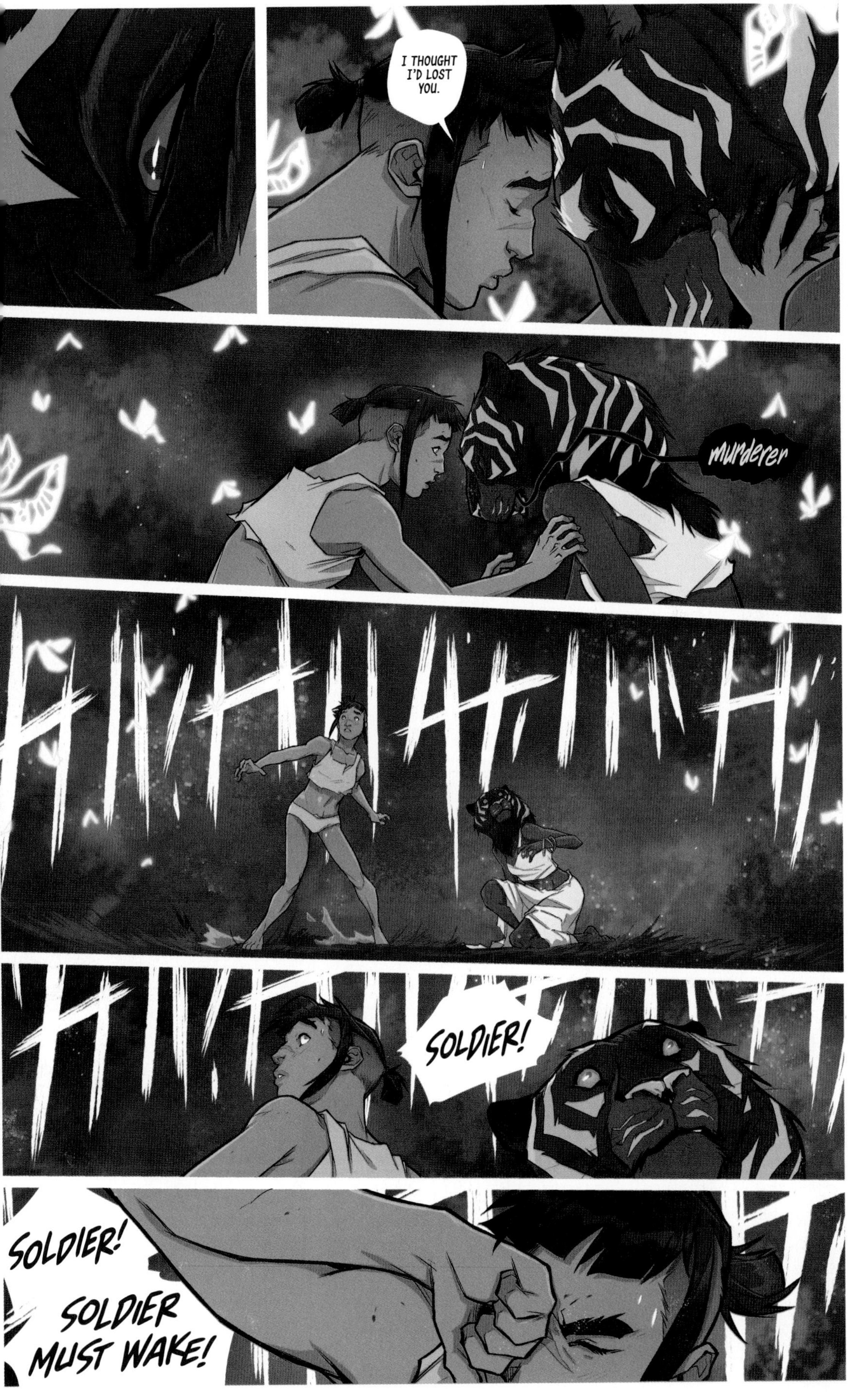
I THOUGHT I'D LOST YOU.
murderer
SOLDIER!
SOLDIER!
SOLDIER MUST WAKE!

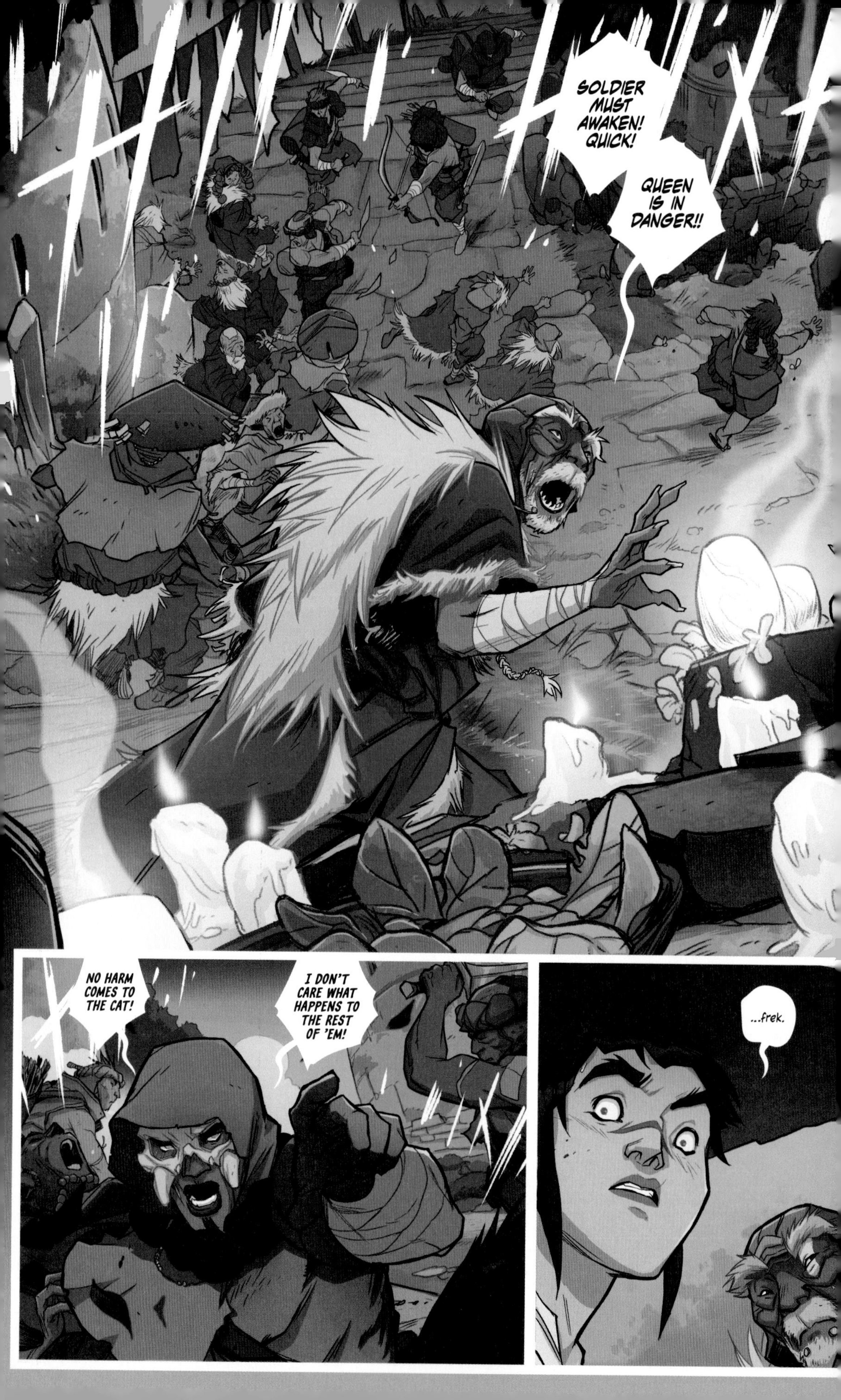

SOLDIER MUST AWAKEN! QUICK!
QUEEN IS IN DANGER!!
NO HARM COMES TO THE CAT!
I DON'T CARE WHAT HAPPENS TO THE REST OF 'EM!
...frek.

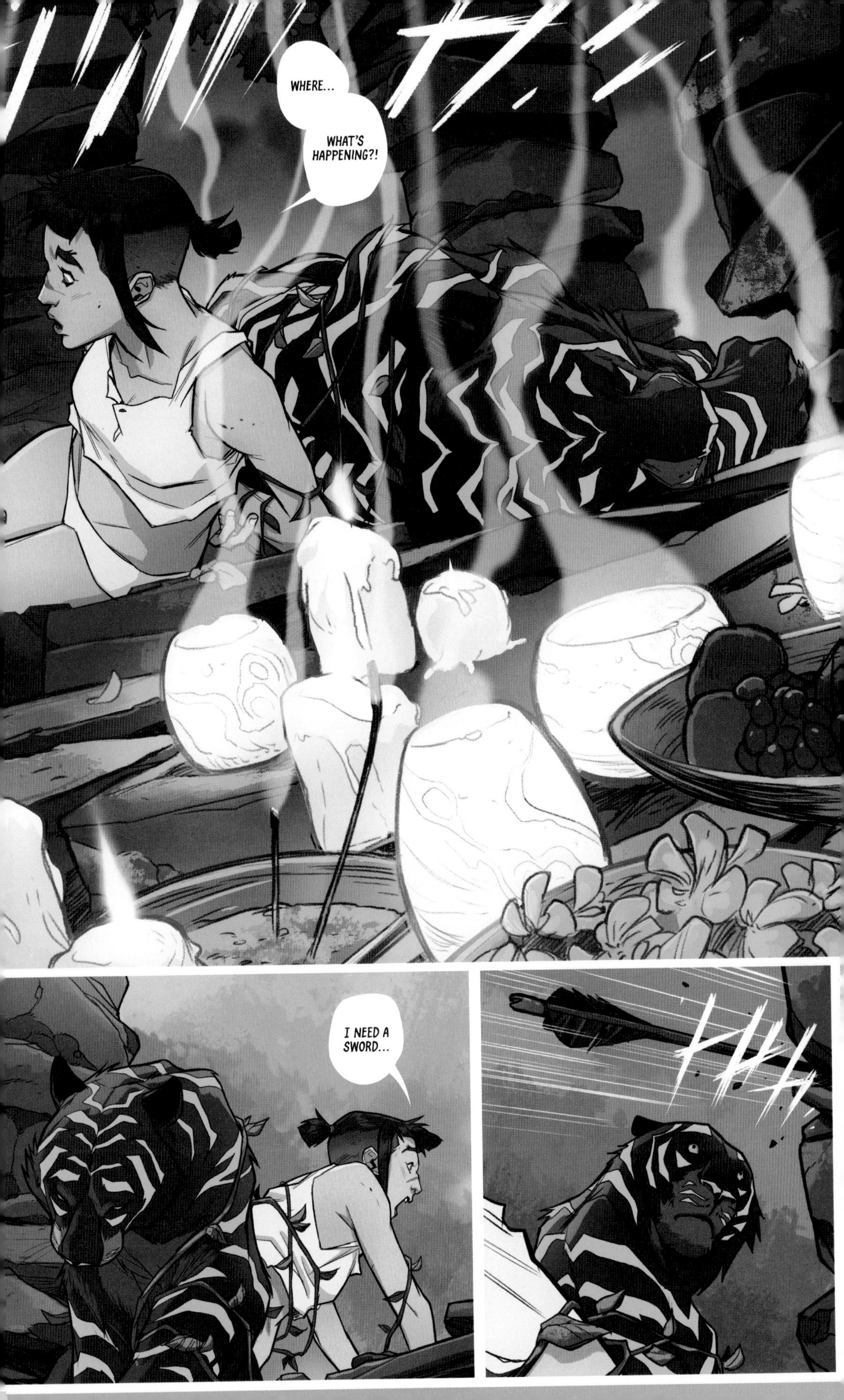
WHERE...
WHAT'S HAPPENING?!
I NEED A SWORD...

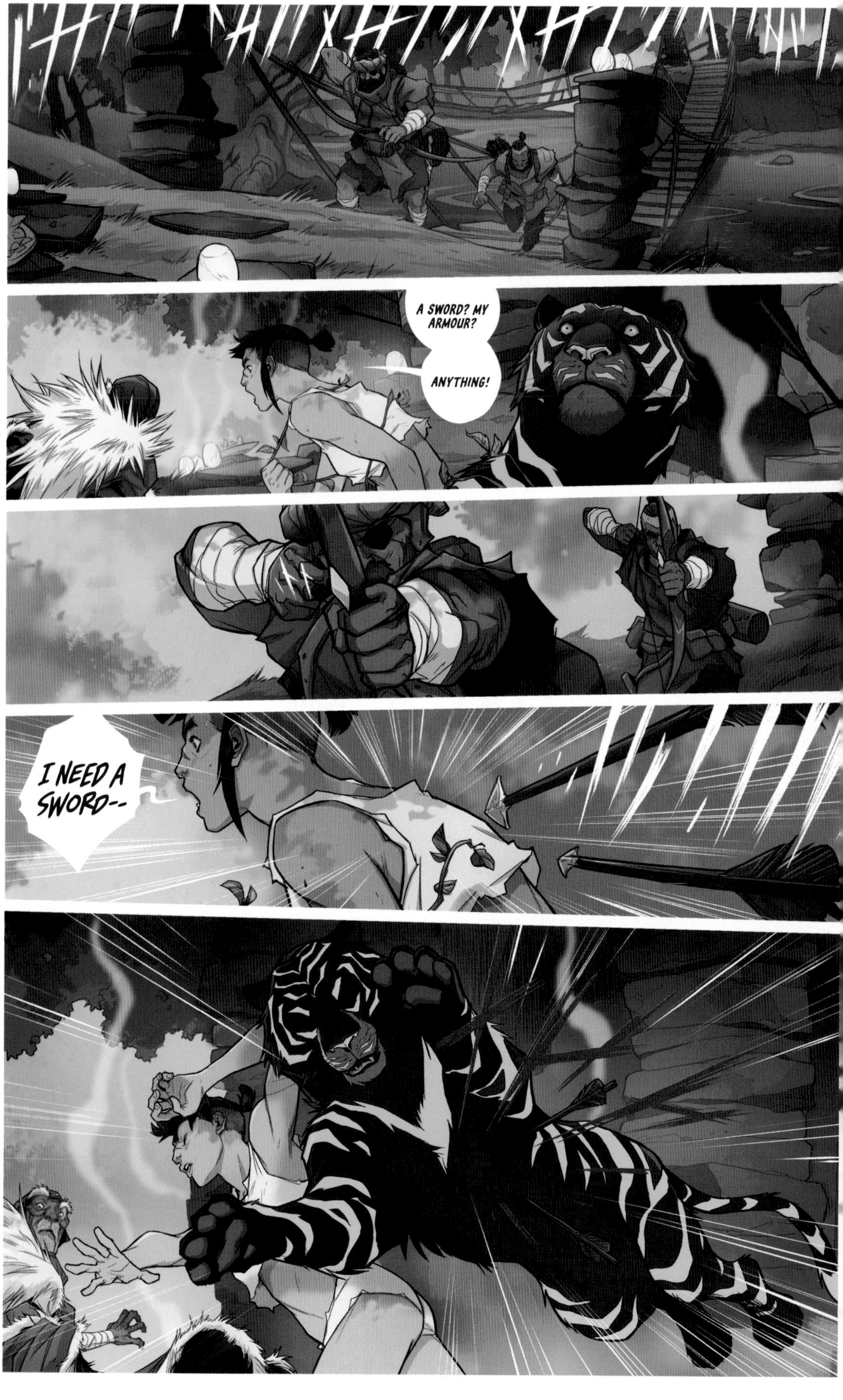

A SWORD? MY ARMOUR?
ANYTHING!
I NEED A SWORD--

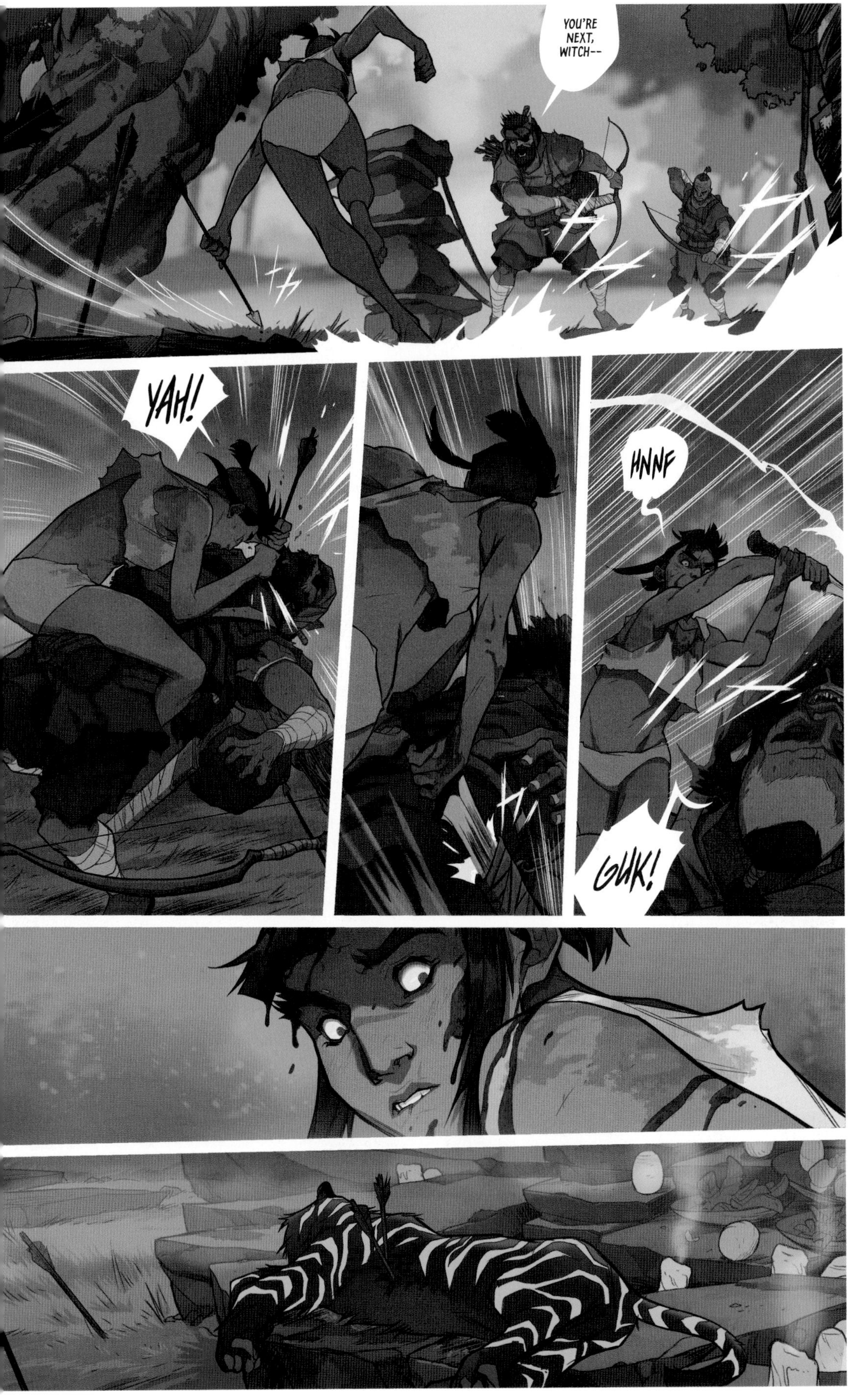
YOU'RE NEXT, WITCH--
YAH!
HNNF
GUK!

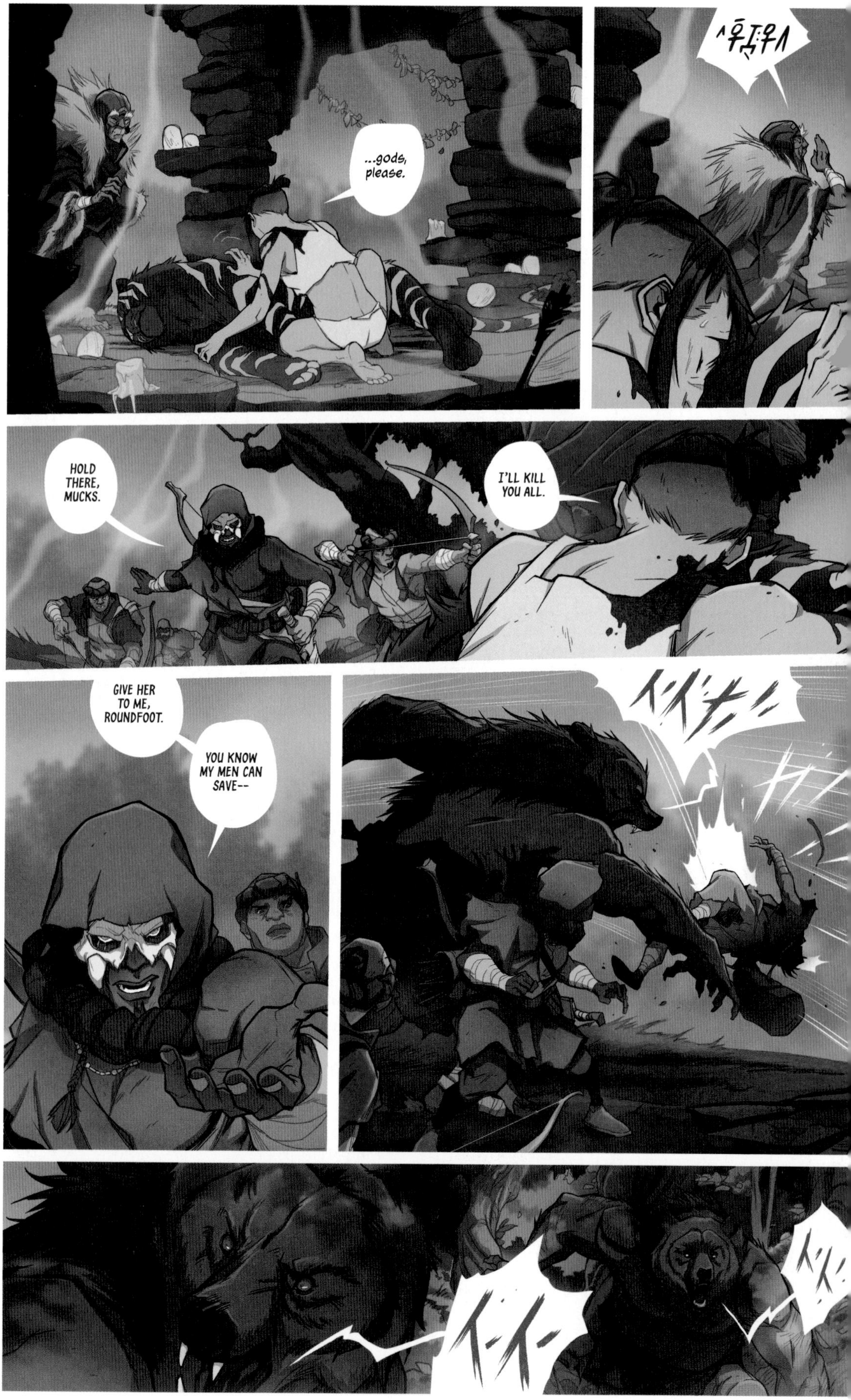

...gods, please.
HOLD THERE, MUCKS.
I'LL KILL YOU ALL.
GIVE HER TO ME, ROUNDFOOT.
YOU KNOW MY MEN CAN SAVE--

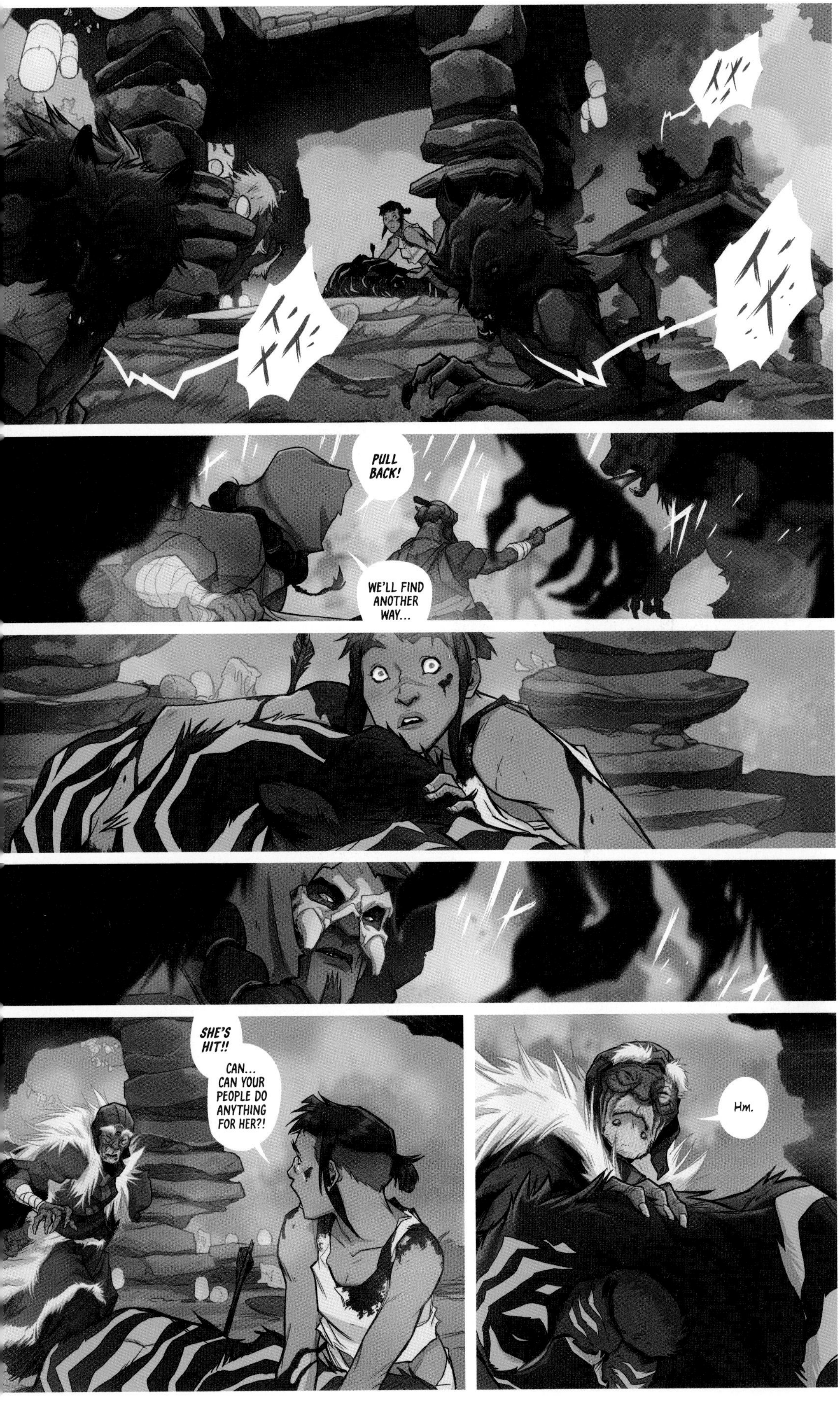
PULL BACK!
WE'LL FIND ANOTHER WAY...
SHE'S HIT!!
CAN... CAN YOUR PEOPLE DO ANYTHING FOR HER?!
Hm.

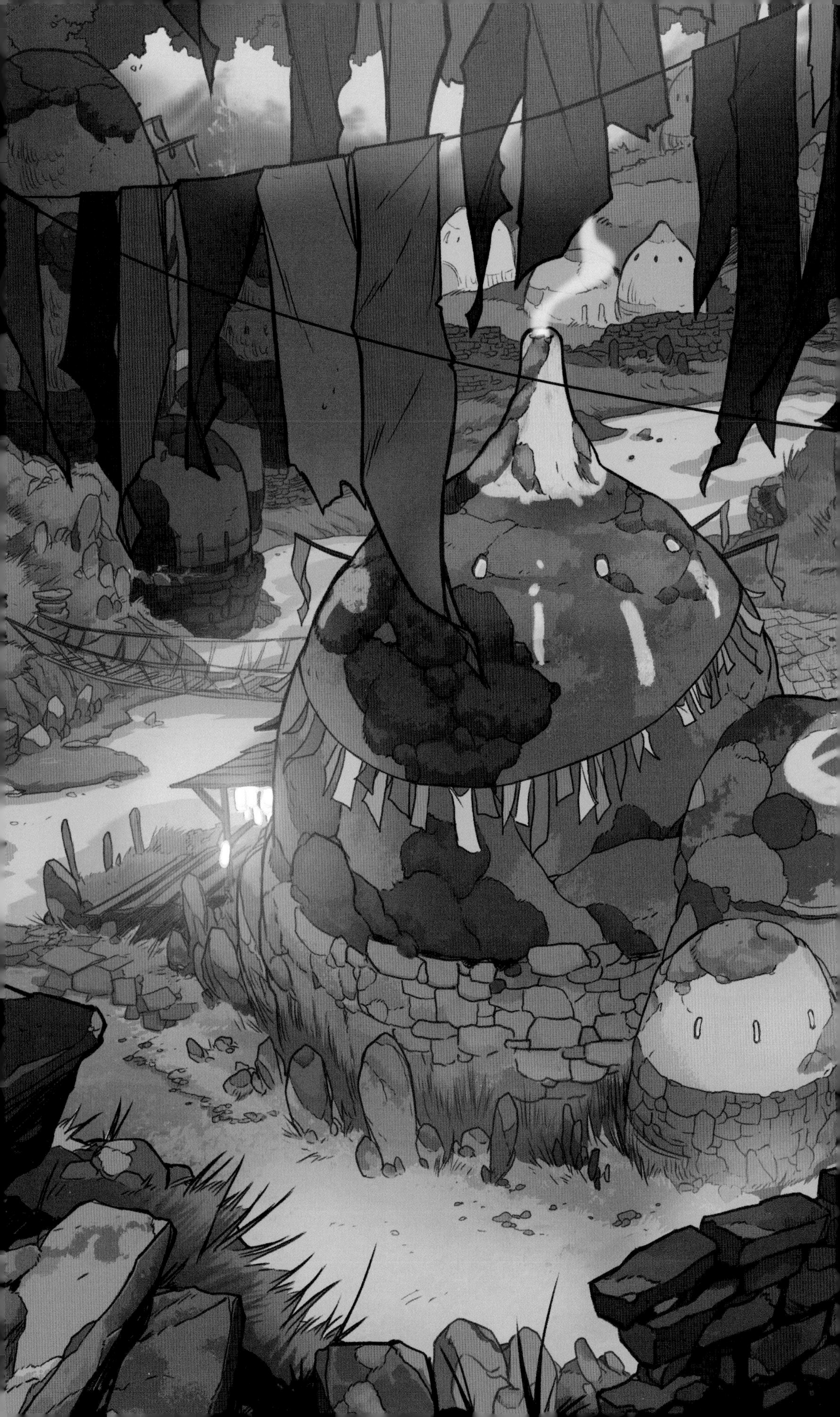

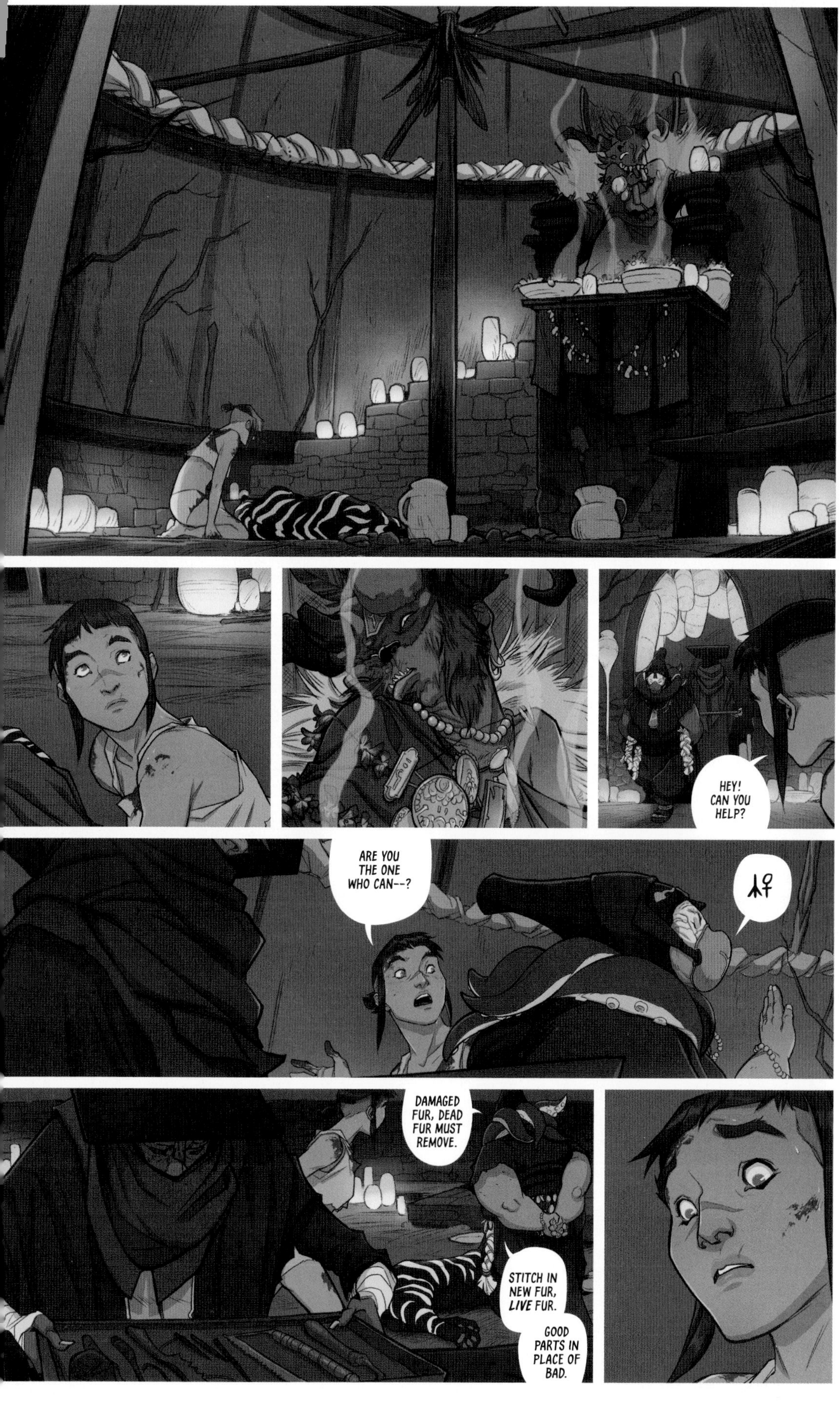
HEY! CAN YOU HELP?
ARE YOU THE ONE WHO CAN--?
DAMAGED FUR, DEAD FUR MUST REMOVE.
STITCH IN NEW FUR, *LIVE* FUR.
GOOD PARTS IN PLACE OF BAD.

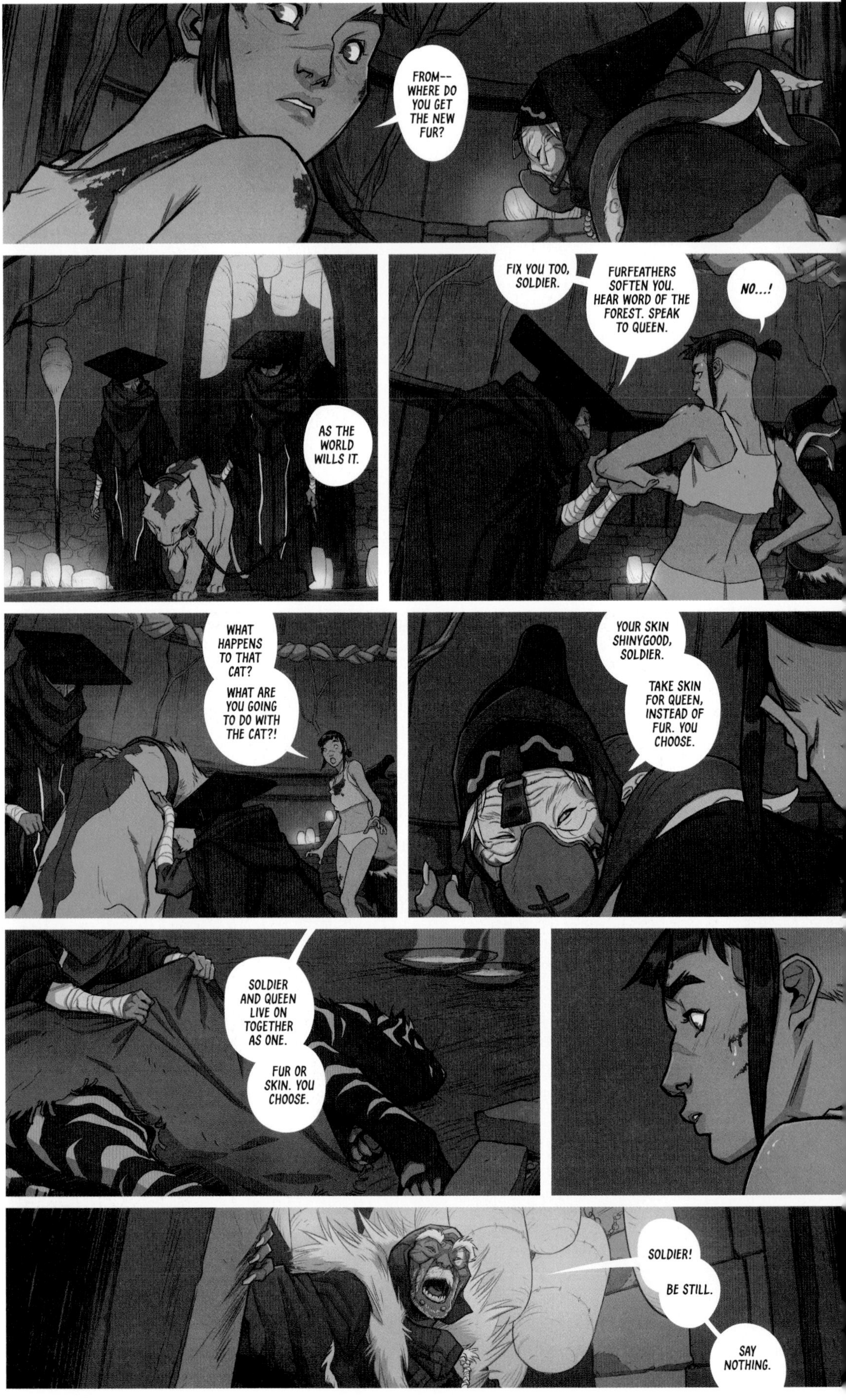
FROM--
WHERE DO YOU GET THE NEW FUR?
AS THE WORLD WILLS IT.
FIX YOU TOO, SOLDIER.
FURFEATHERS SOFTEN YOU. HEAR WORD OF THE FOREST. SPEAK TO QUEEN.
NO...!
WHAT HAPPENS TO THAT CAT?
WHAT ARE YOU GOING TO DO WITH THE CAT?!
YOUR SKIN SHINYGOOD, SOLDIER.
TAKE SKIN FOR QUEEN, INSTEAD OF FUR. YOU CHOOSE.
SOLDIER AND QUEEN LIVE ON TOGETHER AS ONE.
FUR OR SKIN. YOU CHOOSE.
SOLDIER!
BE STILL.
SAY NOTHING.

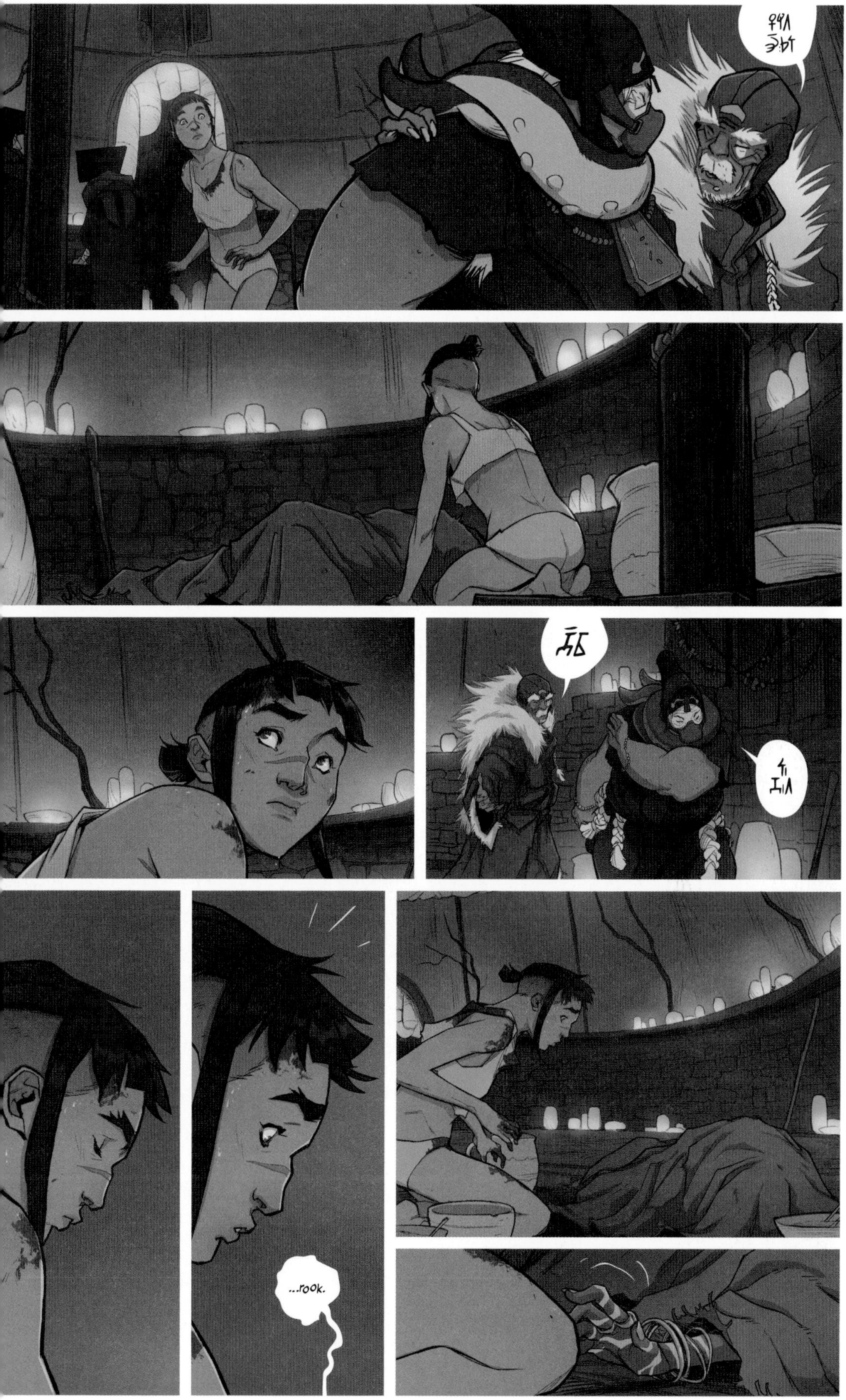
...rook.

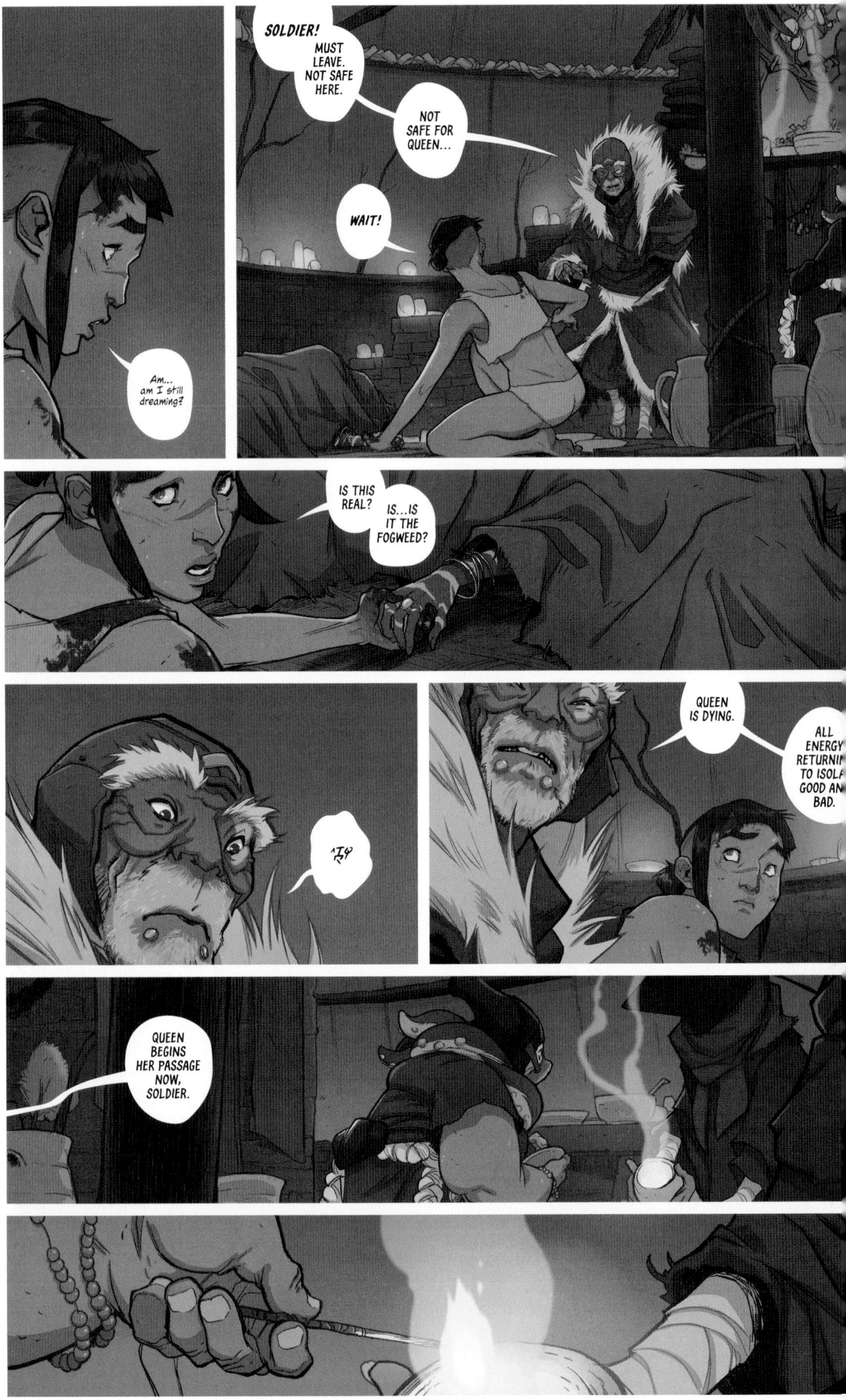

Am... am I still dreaming?
SOLDIER! MUST LEAVE. NOT SAFE HERE.
NOT SAFE FOR QUEEN...
WAIT!
IS THIS REAL?
IS...IS IT THE FOGWEED?
QUEEN IS DYING.
ALL ENERGY RETURNI TO ISOL GOOD AN BAD.
QUEEN BEGINS HER PASSAGE NOW, SOLDIER.

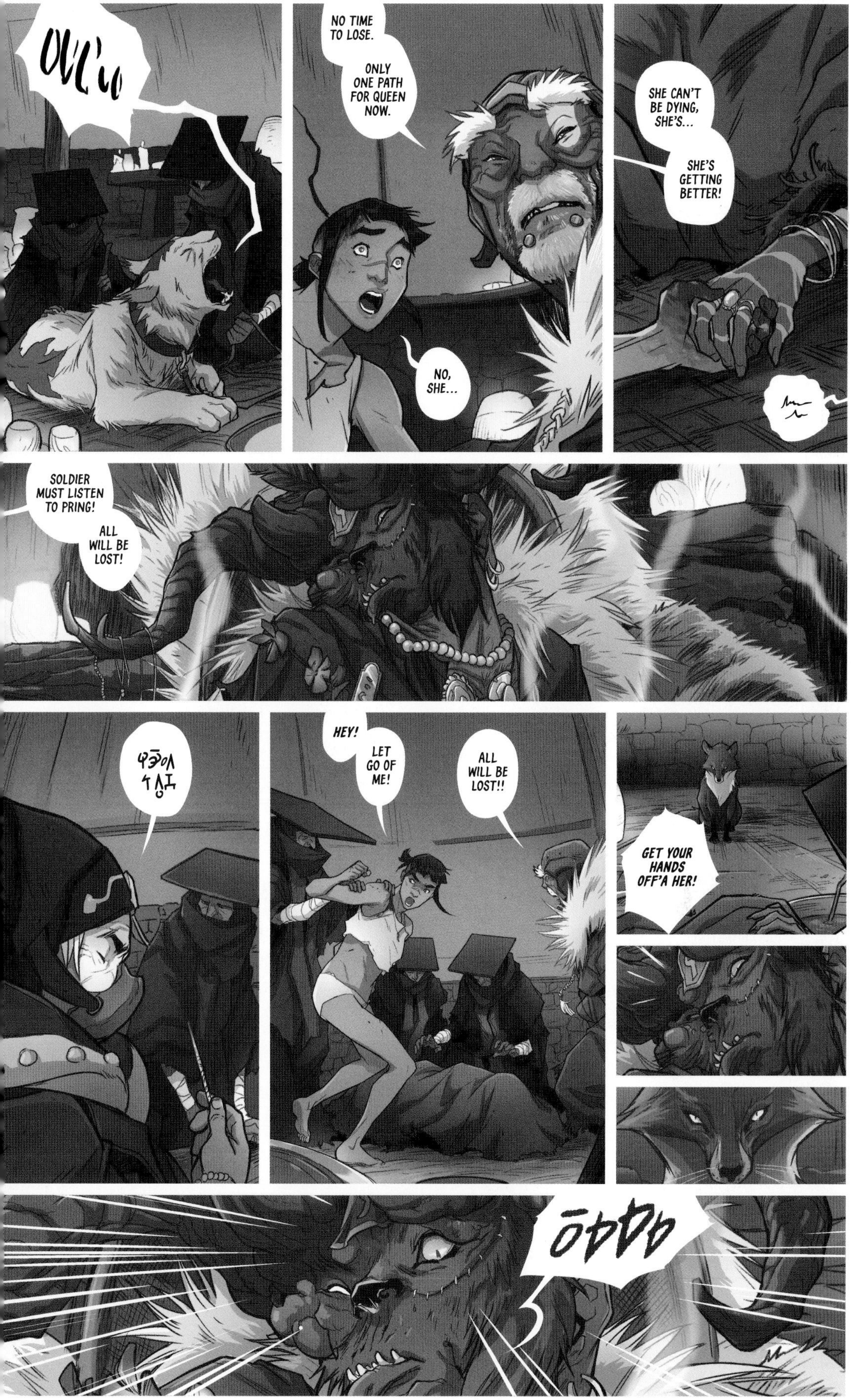
NO TIME TO LOSE.
ONLY ONE PATH FOR QUEEN NOW.
NO, SHE...
SHE CAN'T BE DYING, SHE'S...
SHE'S GETTING BETTER!
SOLDIER MUST LISTEN TO PRING!
ALL WILL BE LOST!
HEY!
LET GO OF ME!
ALL WILL BE LOST!!
GET YOUR HANDS OFF'A HER!

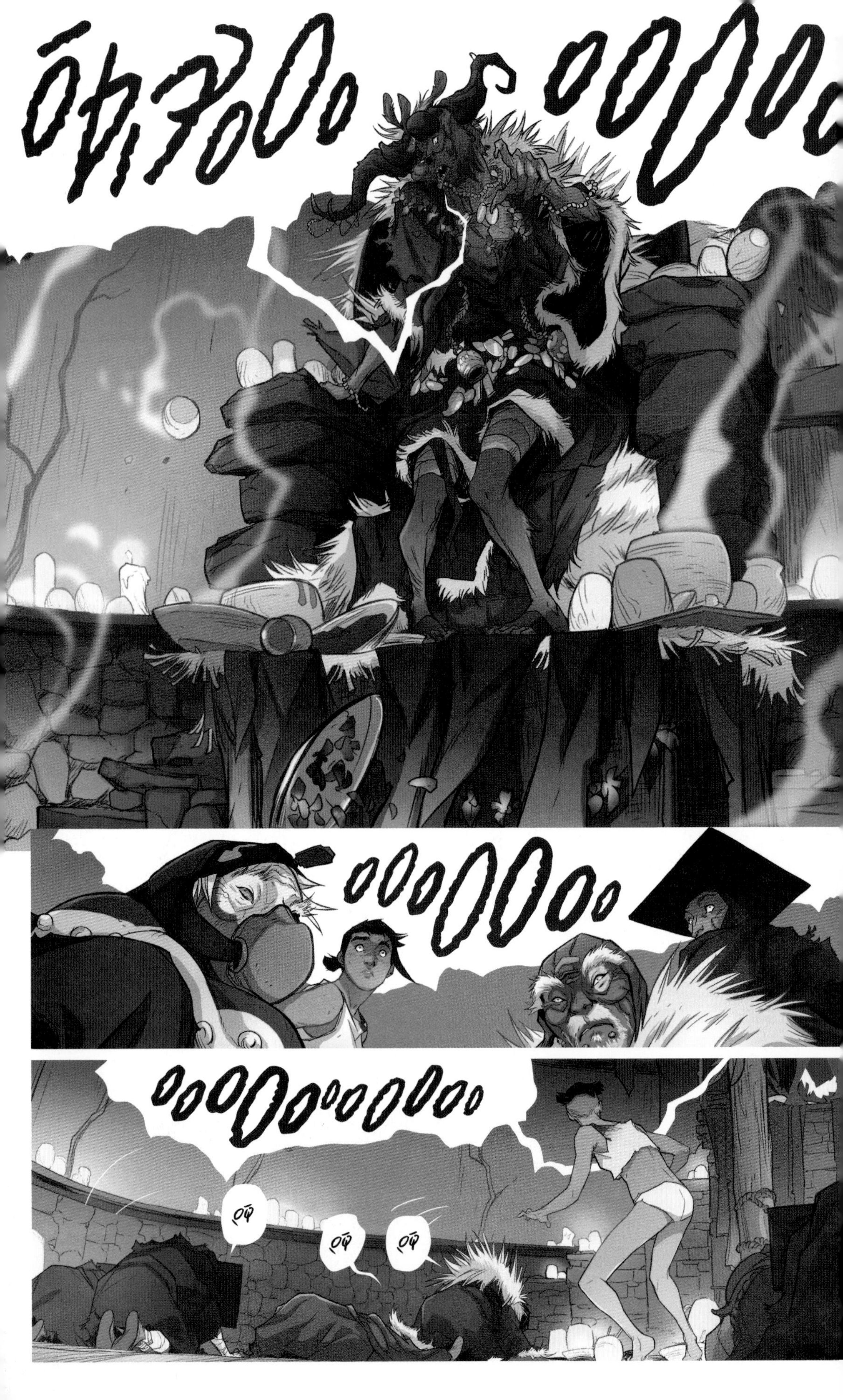
OOOOoo
oooOOOoo
oooOOOooooooo

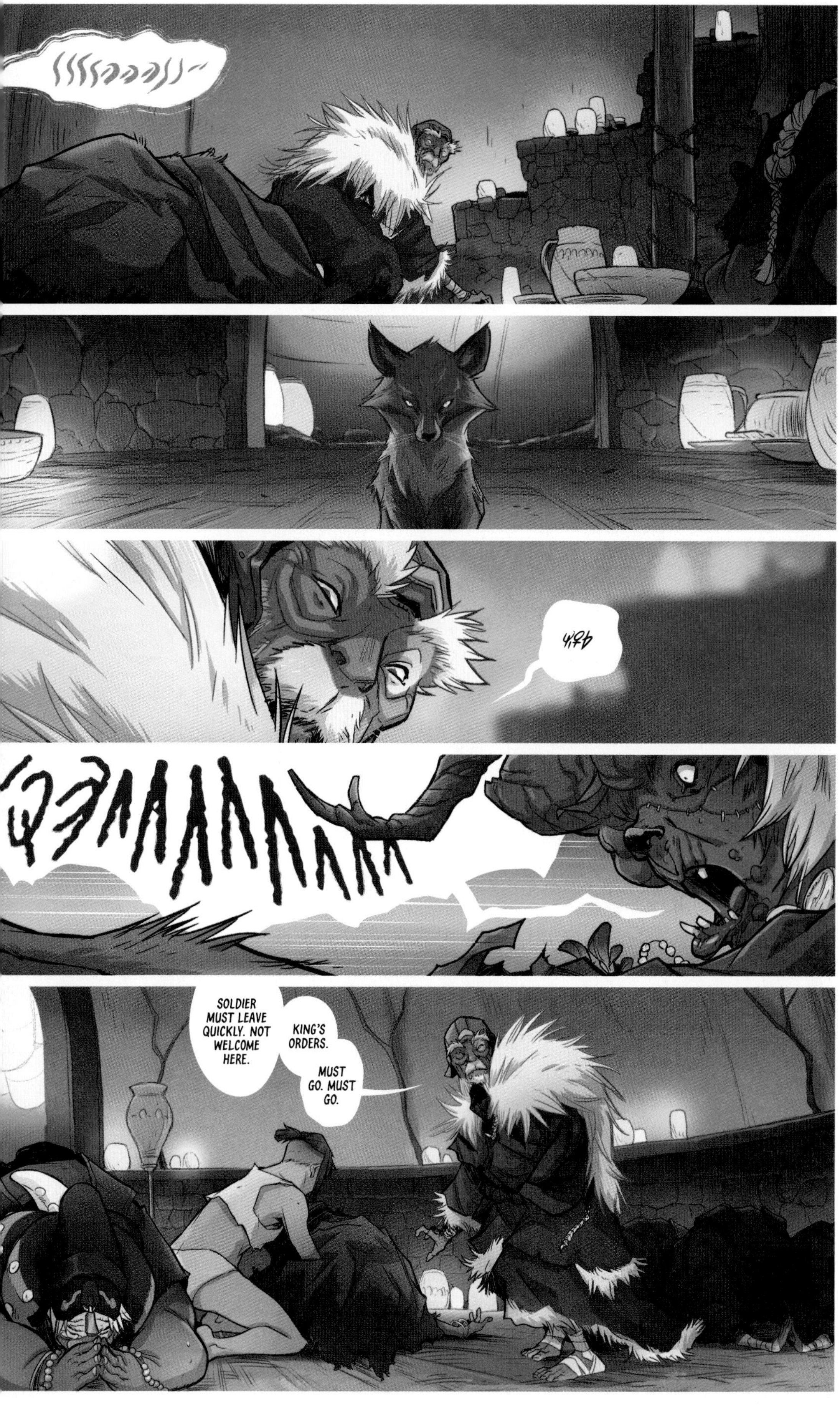
SOLDIER MUST LEAVE QUICKLY. NOT WELCOME HERE.
KING'S ORDERS.
MUST GO. MUST GO.

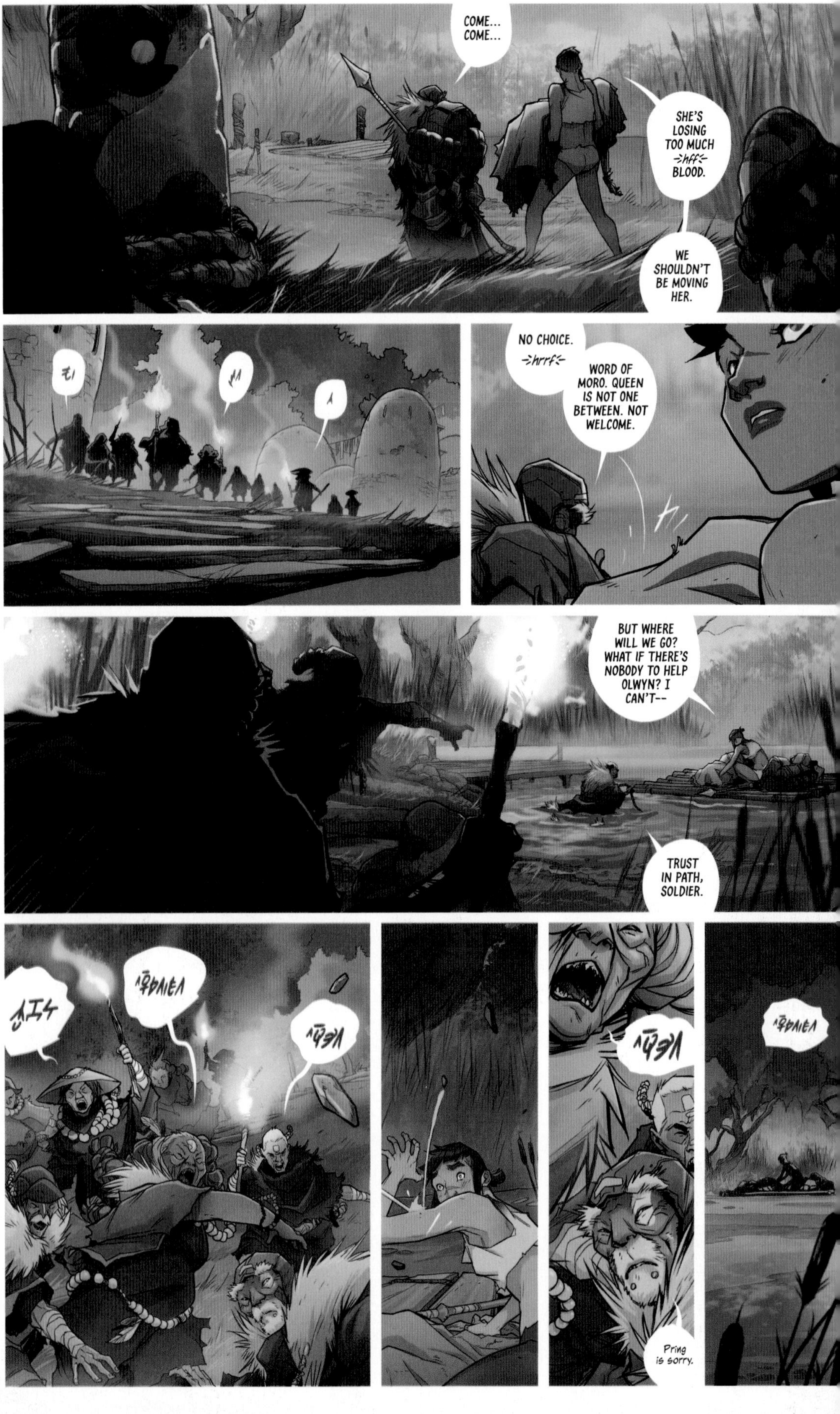
COME... COME...
SHE'S LOSING TOO MUCH
-hff-
BLOOD.
WE SHOULDN'T BE MOVING HER.
NO CHOICE.
-hrrf-
WORD OF MORO. QUEEN IS NOT ONE BETWEEN. NOT WELCOME.
BUT WHERE WILL WE GO? WHAT IF THERE'S NOBODY TO HELP OLWYN? I CAN'T--
TRUST IN PATH, SOLDIER.
Pring is sorry.

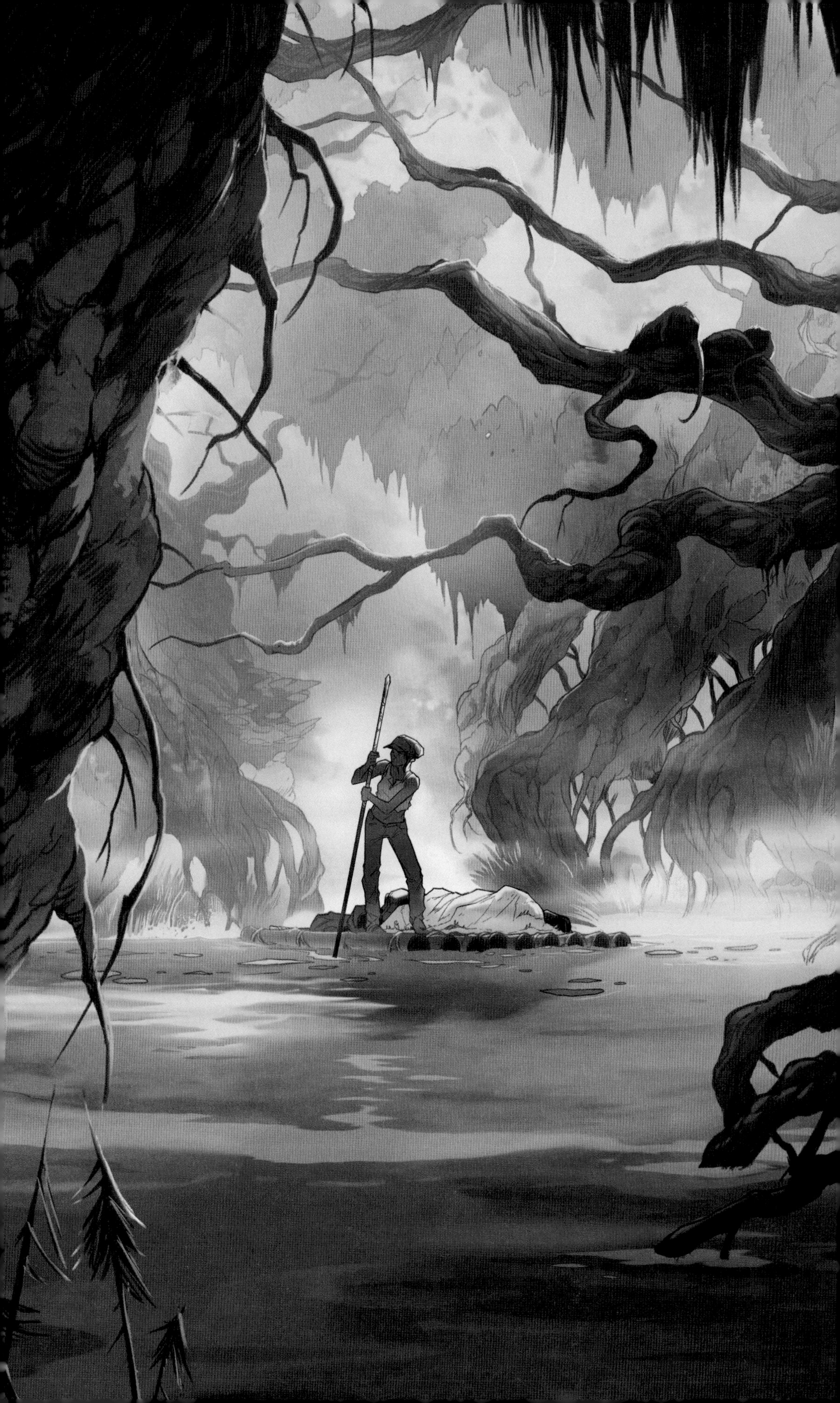

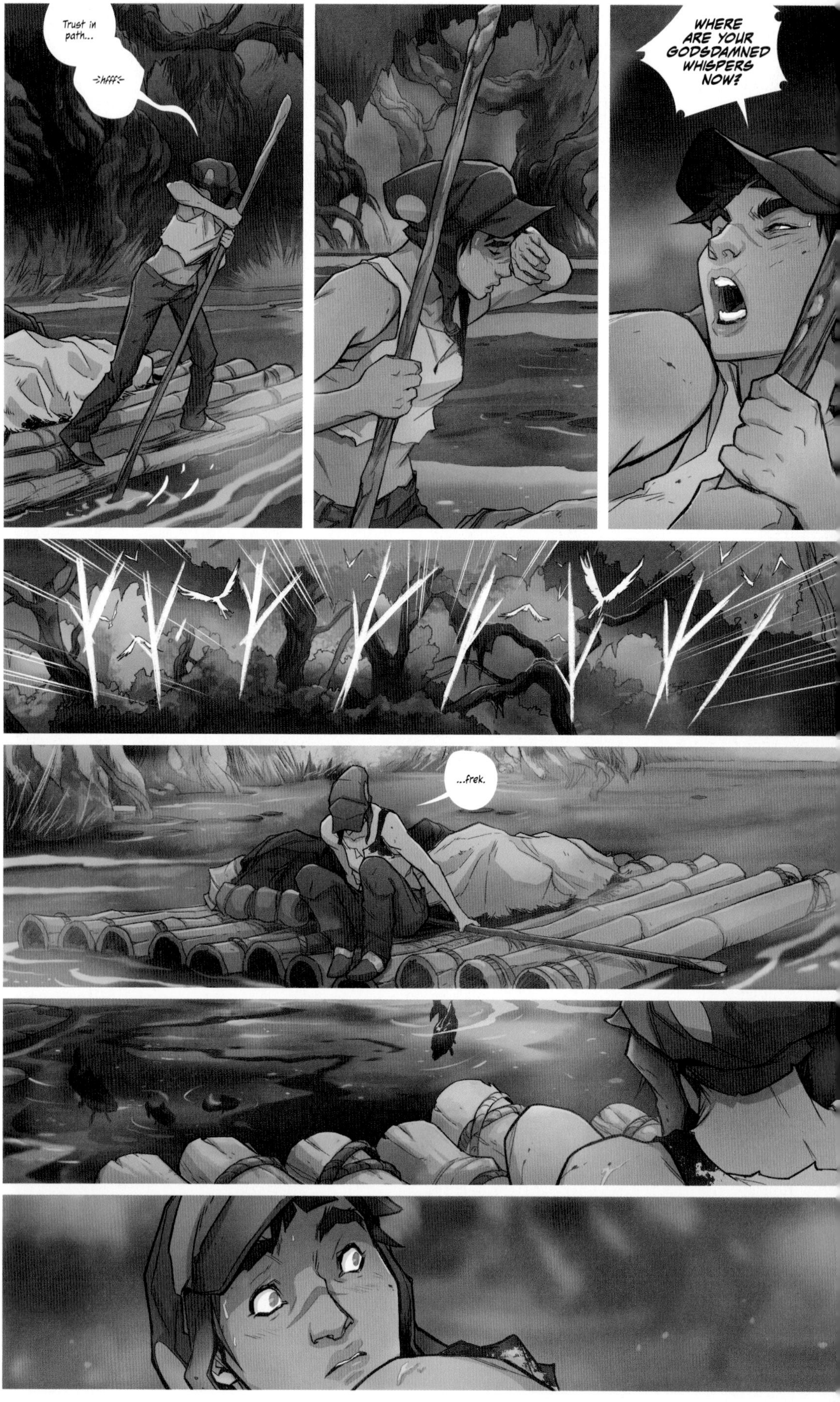
Trust in path...
-hfff-
WHERE ARE YOUR GODSDAMNED WHISPERS NOW?
...frek.

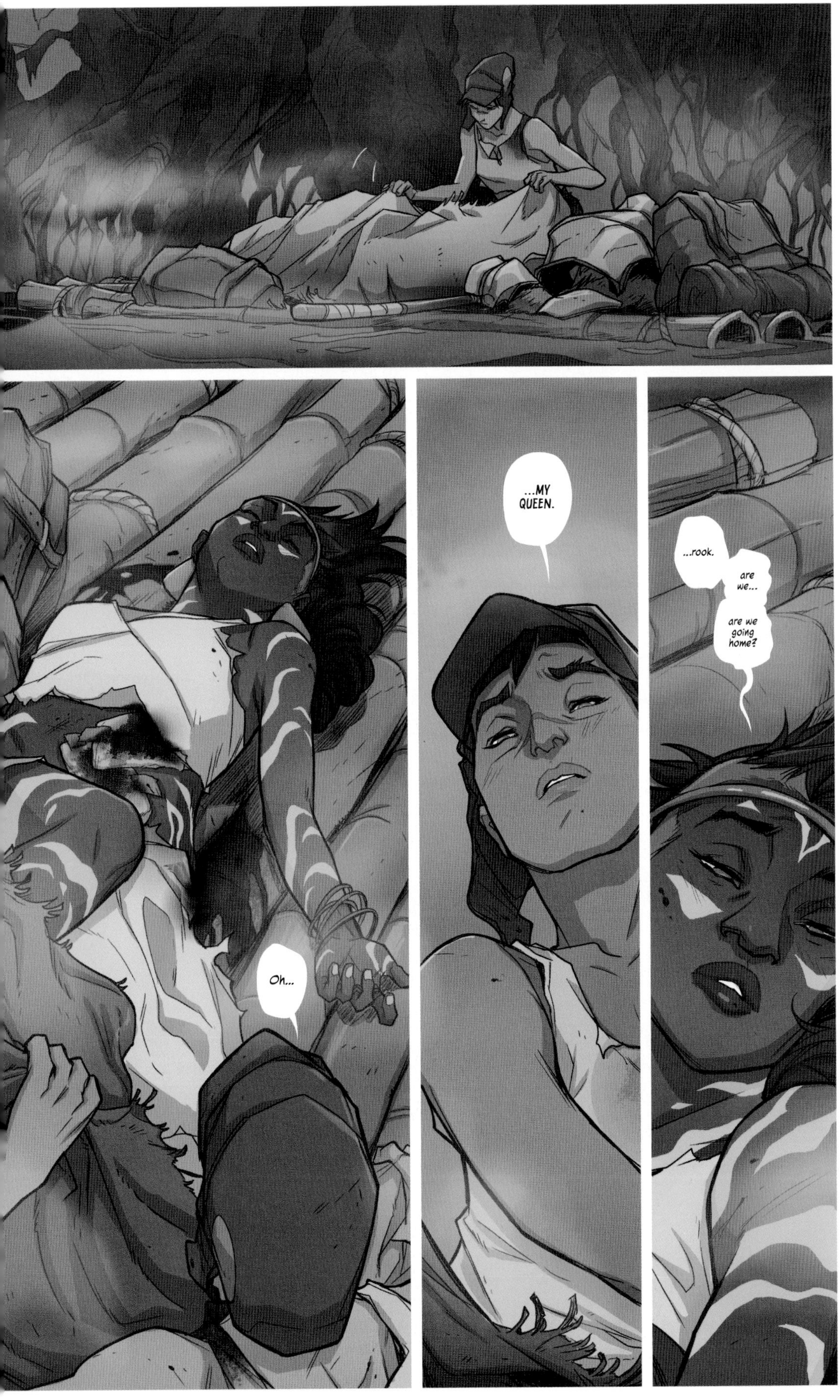
Oh...
...MY QUEEN.
...rook.
are we...
are we going home?

OH GODS! I SENT HIM THERE. I KILLED HIM.

THIS IS ALL MY FAULT.

...no. no, captain.

rook...

YOUR MAJESTY, I--

WE WERE TRAVELLING TO ISOLA, REMEMBER? TO FIND THE PRINCE AND--

you did... nothing wrong.

you were protecting your queen, as was your sworn--

->hnnf<-

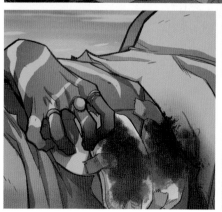

WHAT CAN I DO?

...just-- ->hnnf<- just stay with me...

...beside me.

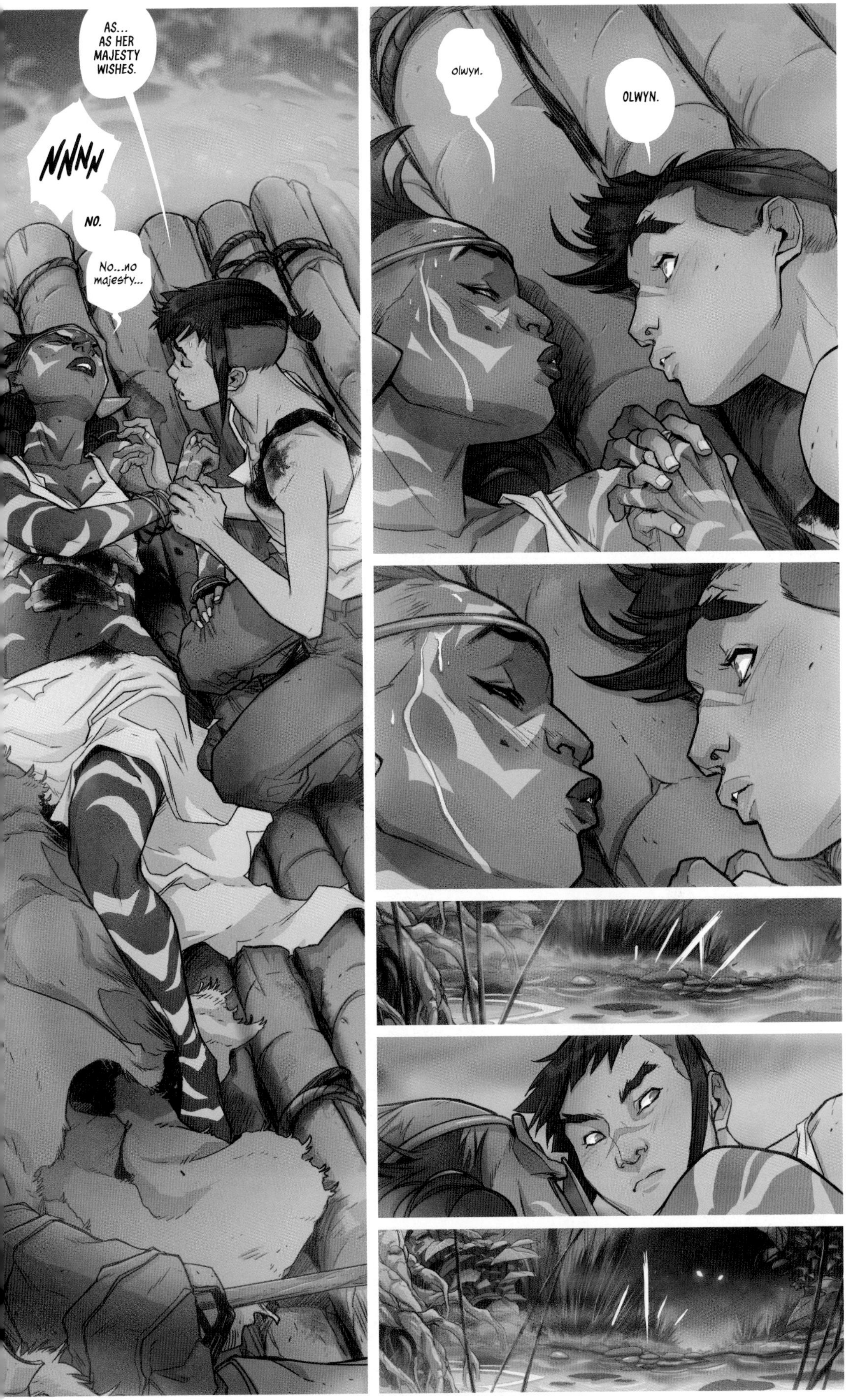
AS... AS HER MAJESTY WISHES.
NNNN
NO.
No...no majesty...
olwyn.
OLWYN.

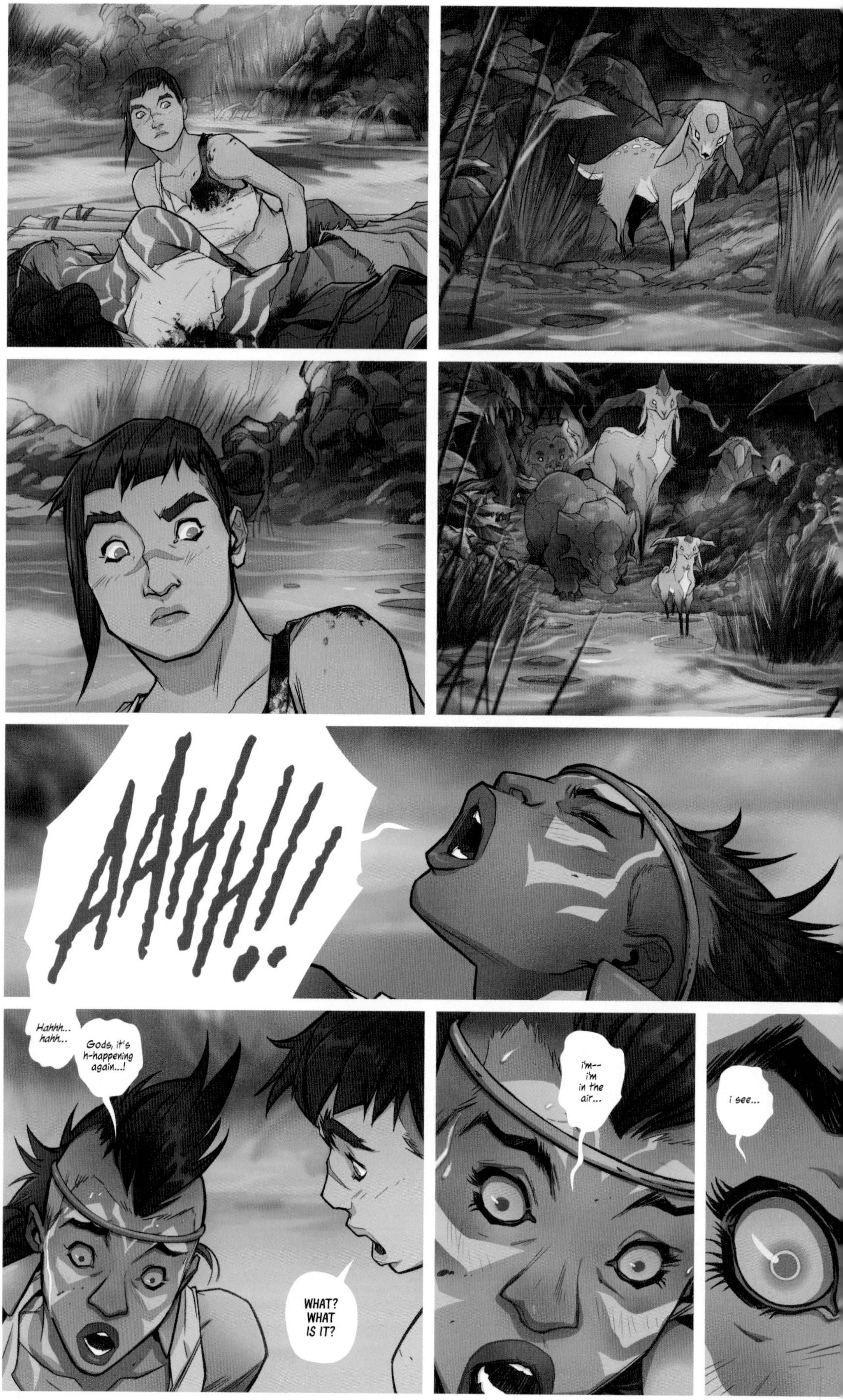
AAHH!!
Hahhh... hahh...
Gods, it's h-happening again...!
WHAT? WHAT IS IT?
i'm-- i'm in the air...
i see...

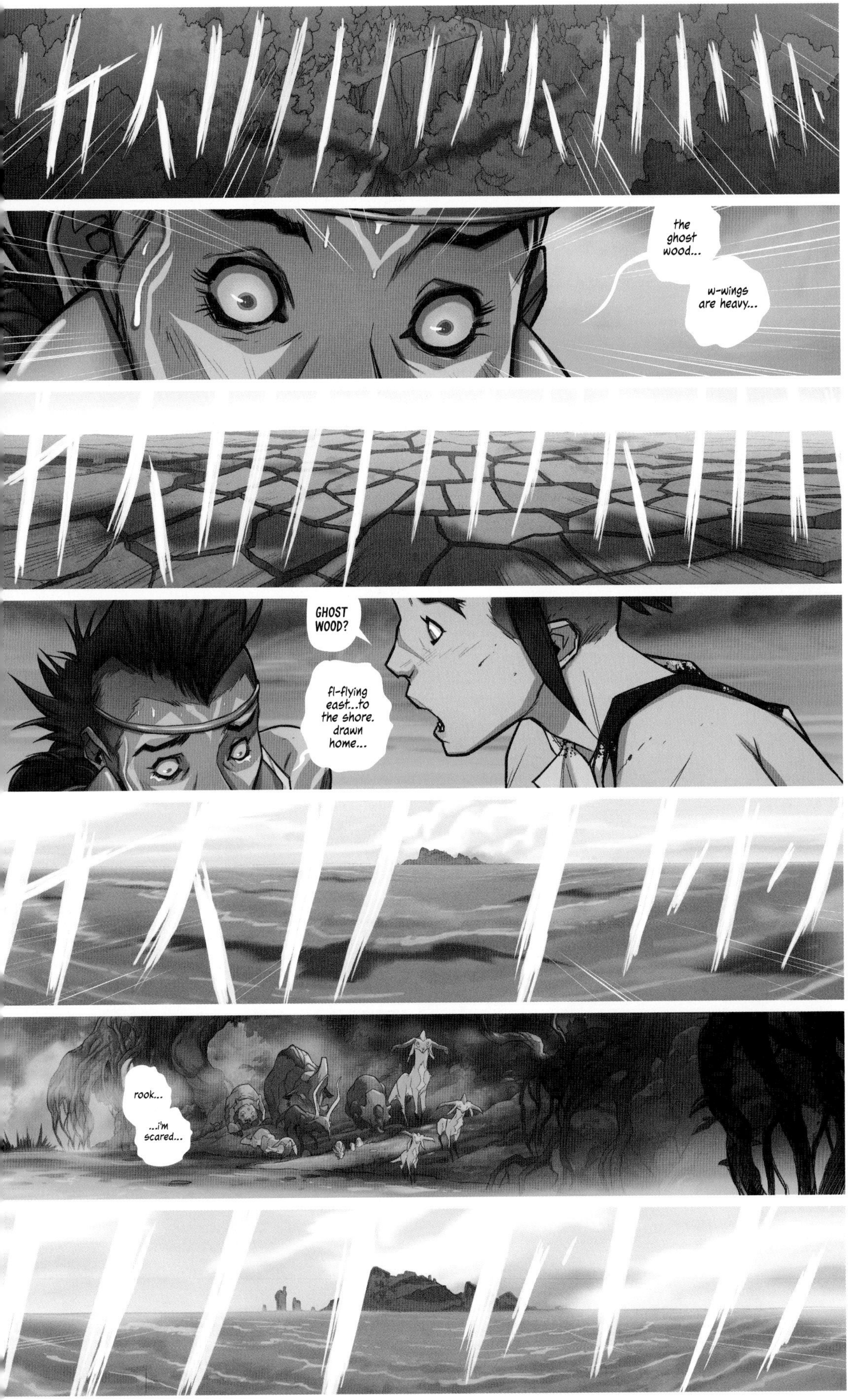
the ghost wood...
w-wings are heavy...
GHOST WOOD?
fl-flying east...to the shore. drawn home...
rook...
...i'm scared...

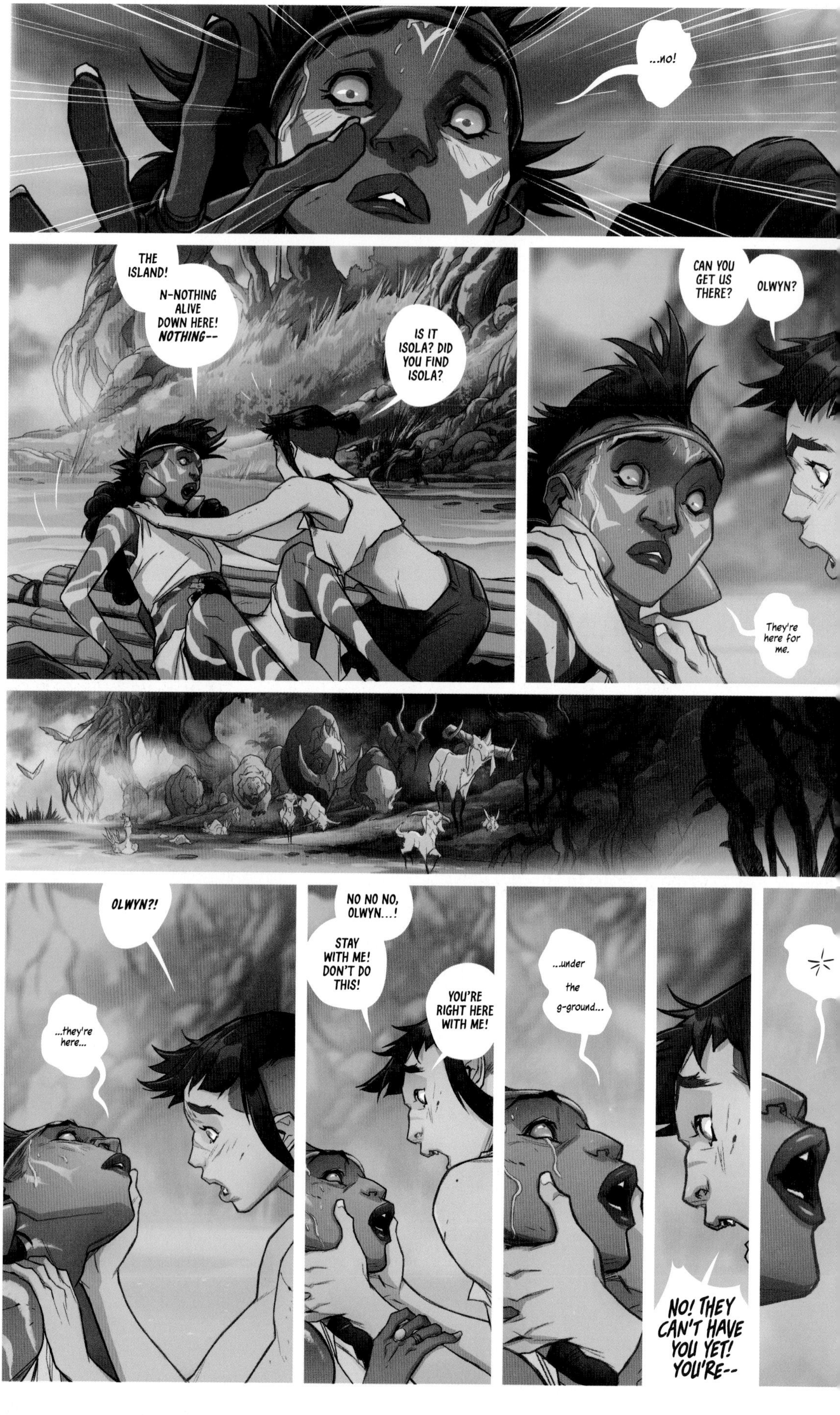
...no!
THE ISLAND!
N-NOTHING ALIVE DOWN HERE! NOTHING--
IS IT ISOLA? DID YOU FIND ISOLA?
CAN YOU GET US THERE?
OLWYN?
They're here for me.
OLWYN?!
...they're here...
NO NO NO, OLWYN...!
STAY WITH ME! DON'T DO THIS!
YOU'RE RIGHT HERE WITH ME!
...under the g-ground...
NO! THEY CAN'T HAVE YOU YET! YOU'RE--

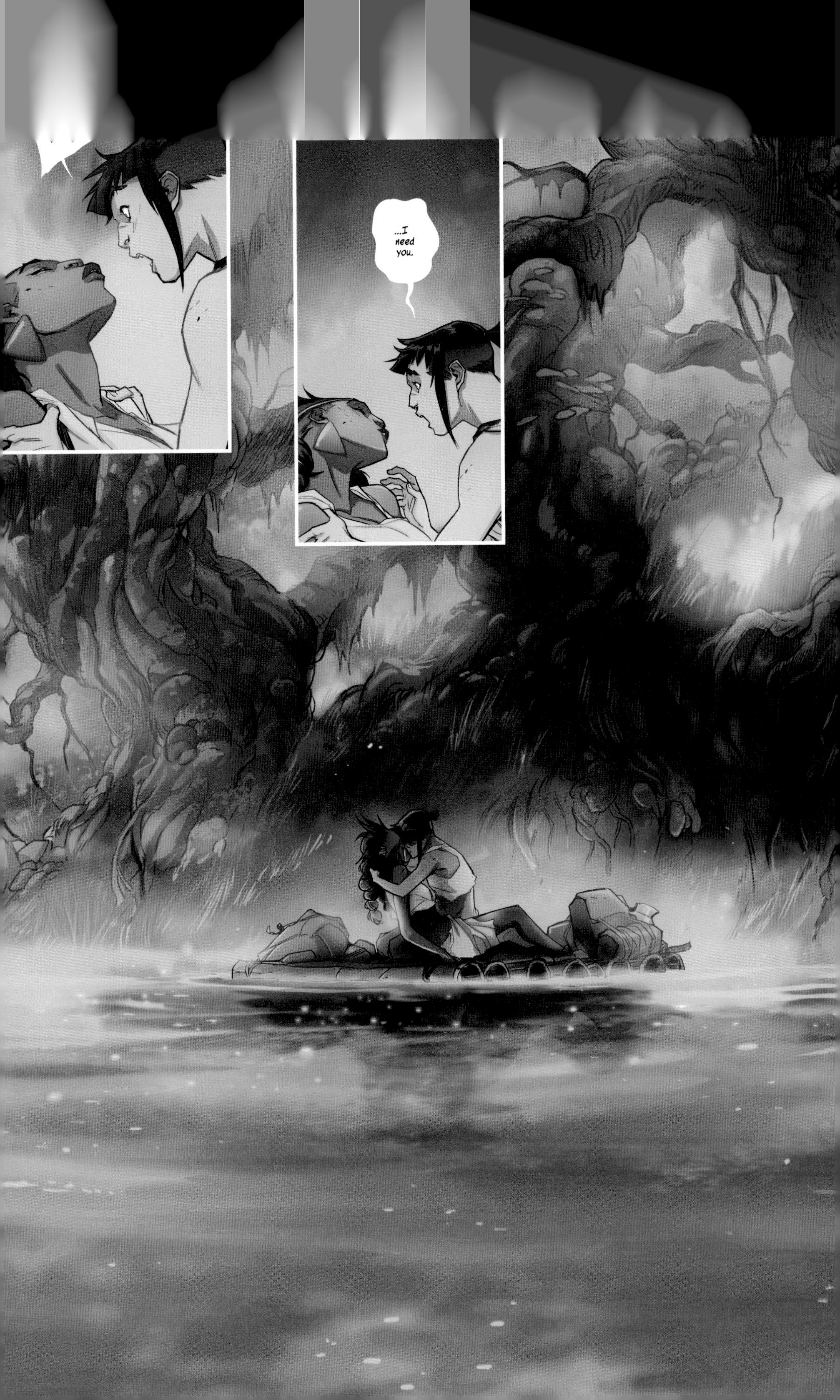
...I need you.

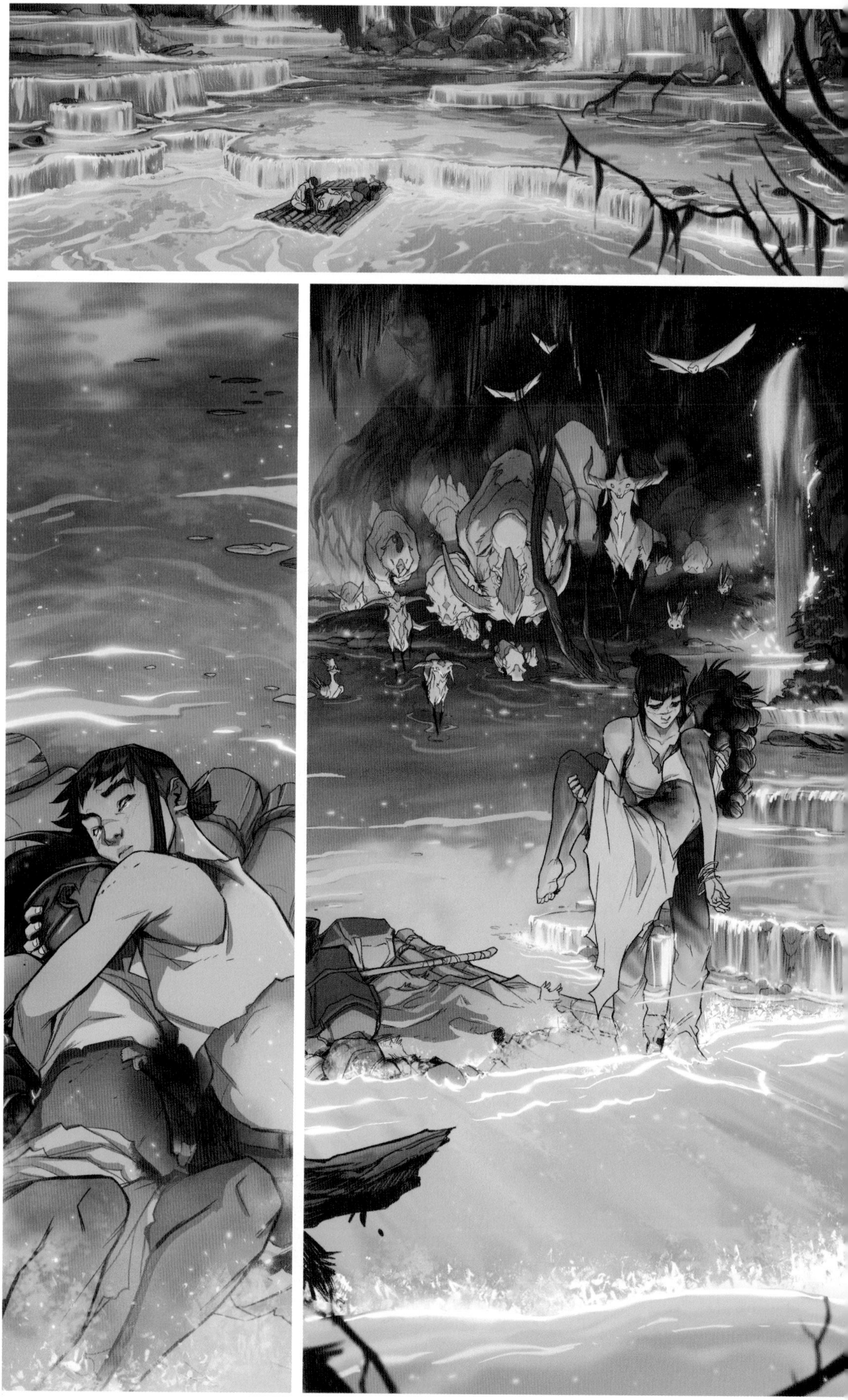

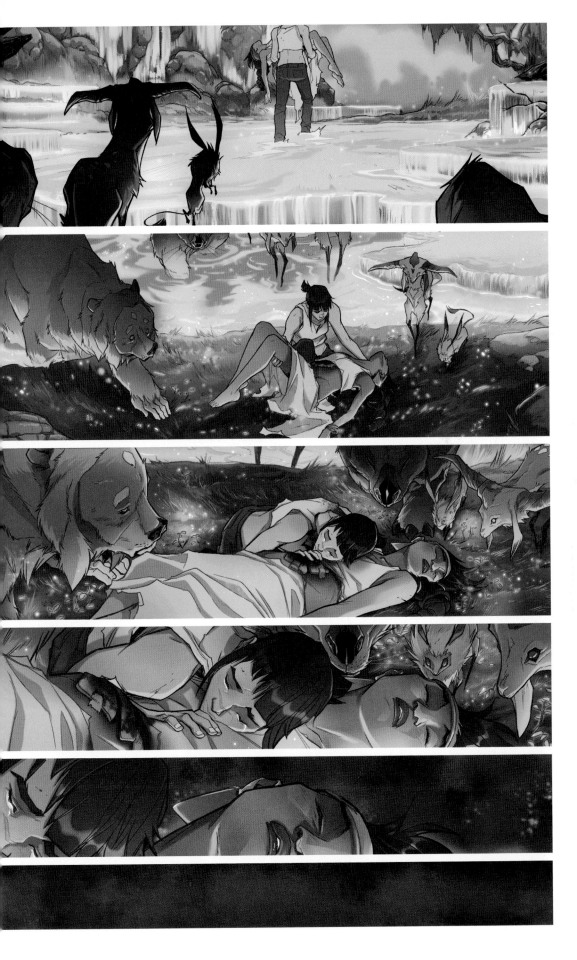

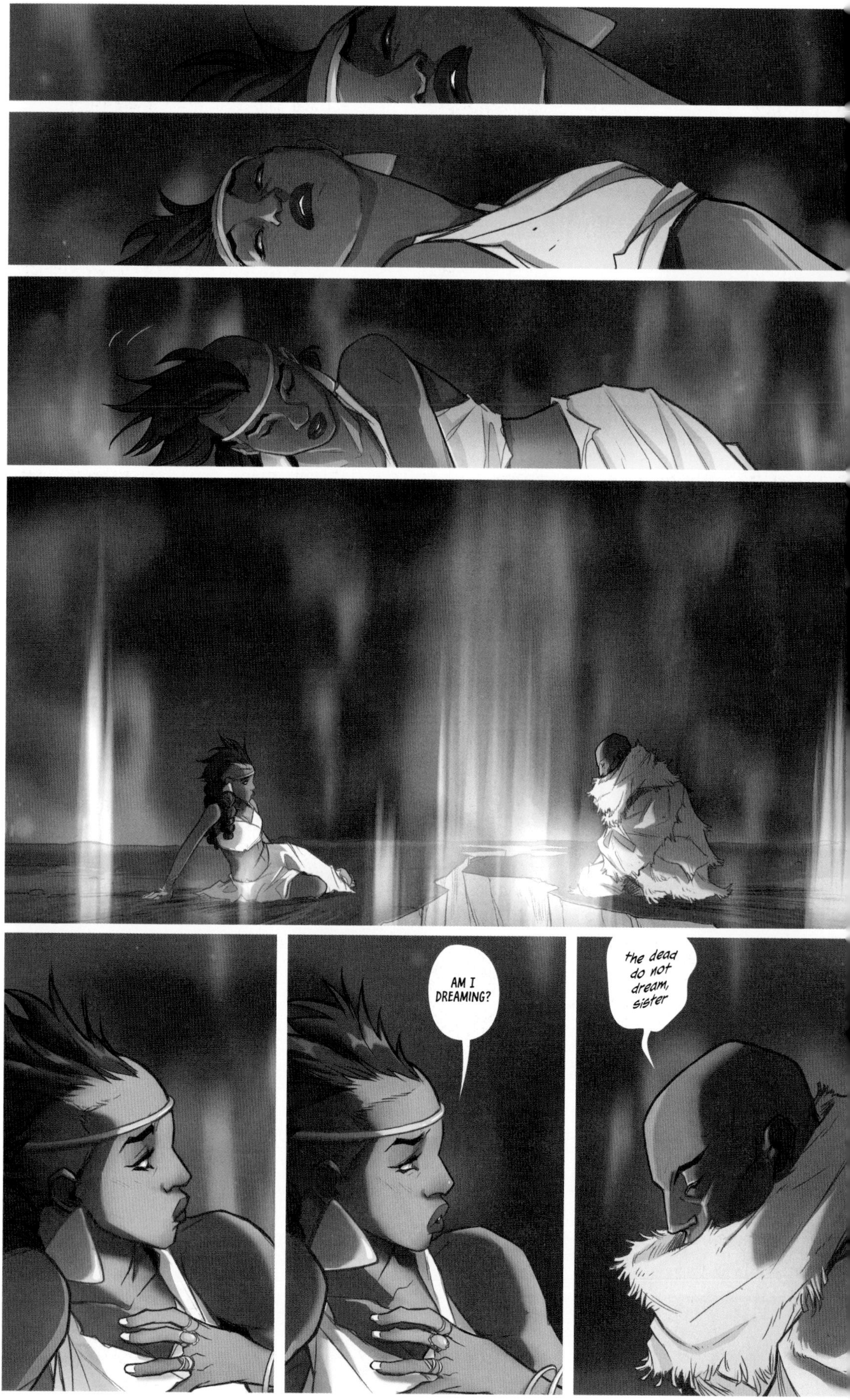
AM I DREAMING?
the dead do not dream, sister

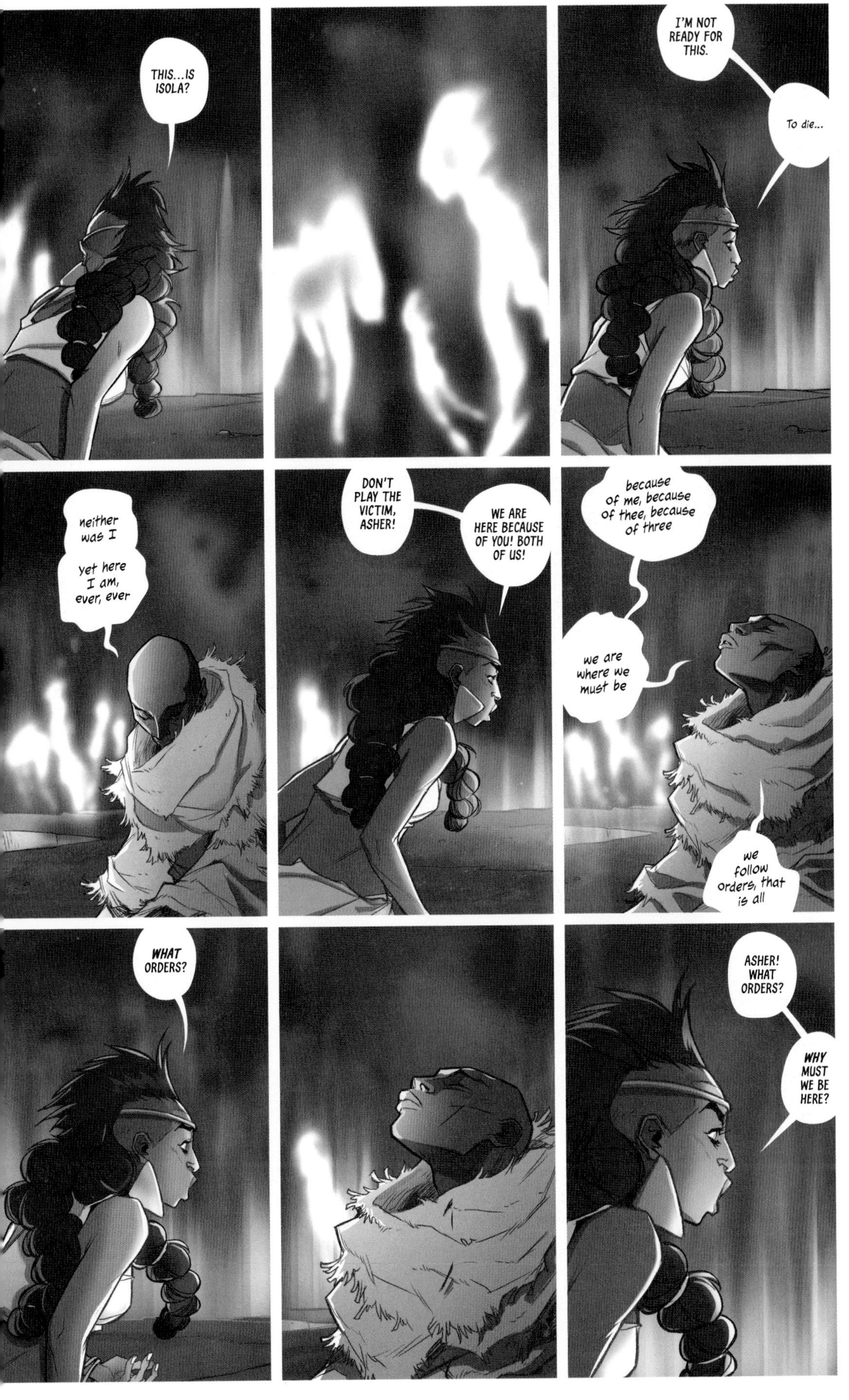
THIS...IS ISOLA?
I'M NOT READY FOR THIS.
To die...
neither was I
yet here I am, ever, ever
DON'T PLAY THE VICTIM, ASHER!
WE ARE HERE BECAUSE OF YOU! BOTH OF US!
because of me, because of thee, because of three
we are where we must be
we follow orders, that is all
WHAT ORDERS?
ASHER! WHAT ORDERS?
WHY MUST WE BE HERE?

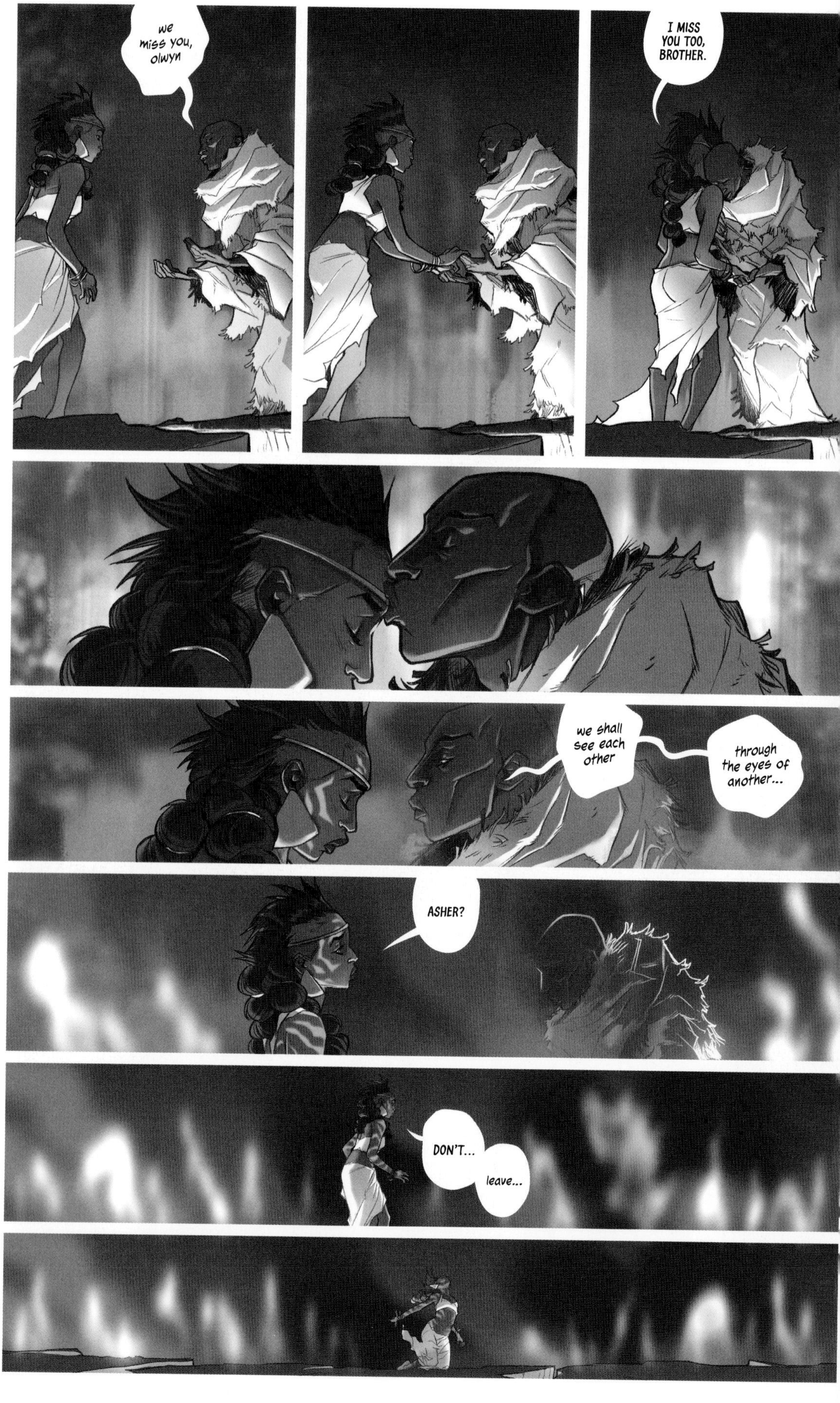
we miss you, olwyn
I MISS YOU TOO, BROTHER.
we shall see each other
through the eyes of another...
ASHER?
DON'T...
leave...

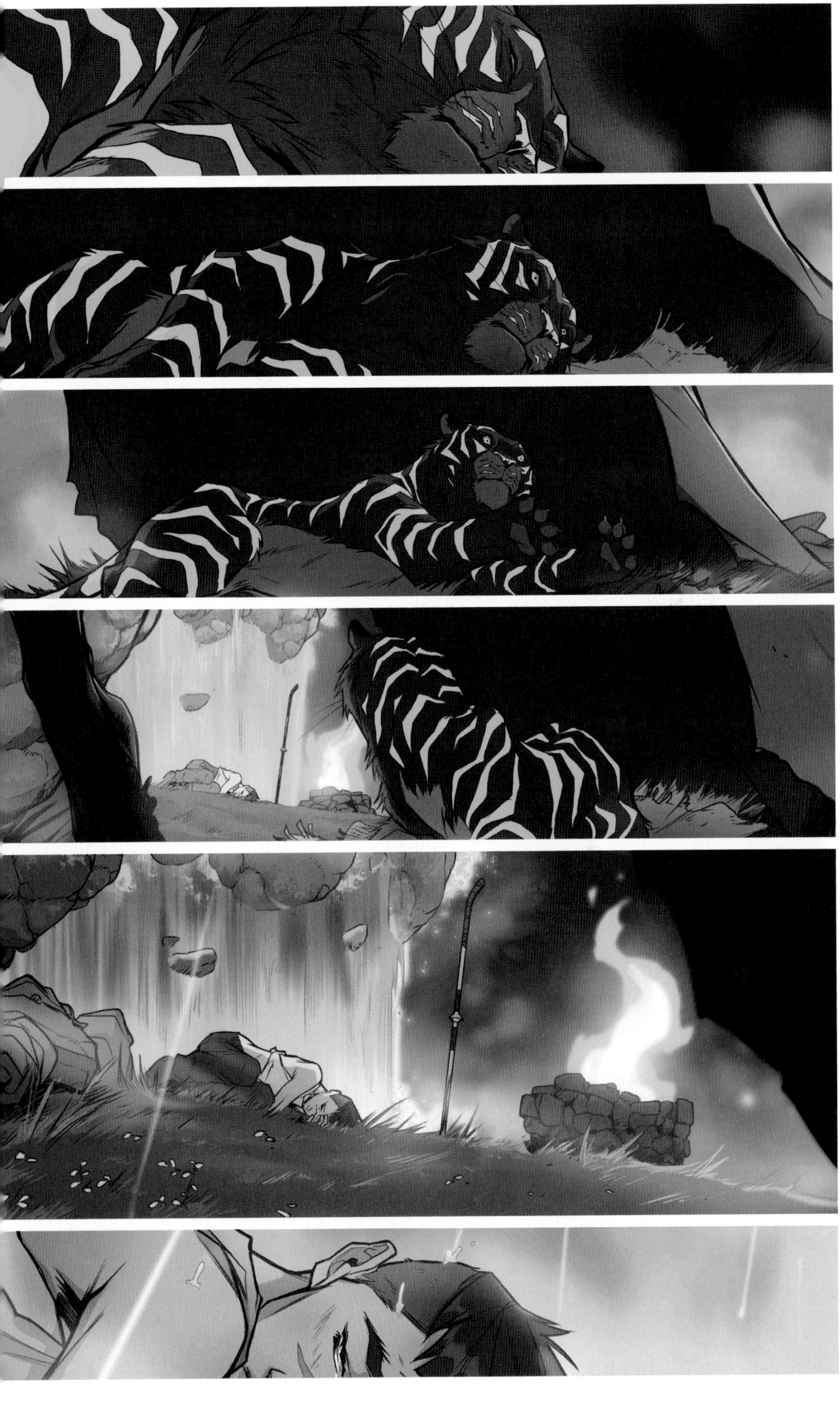

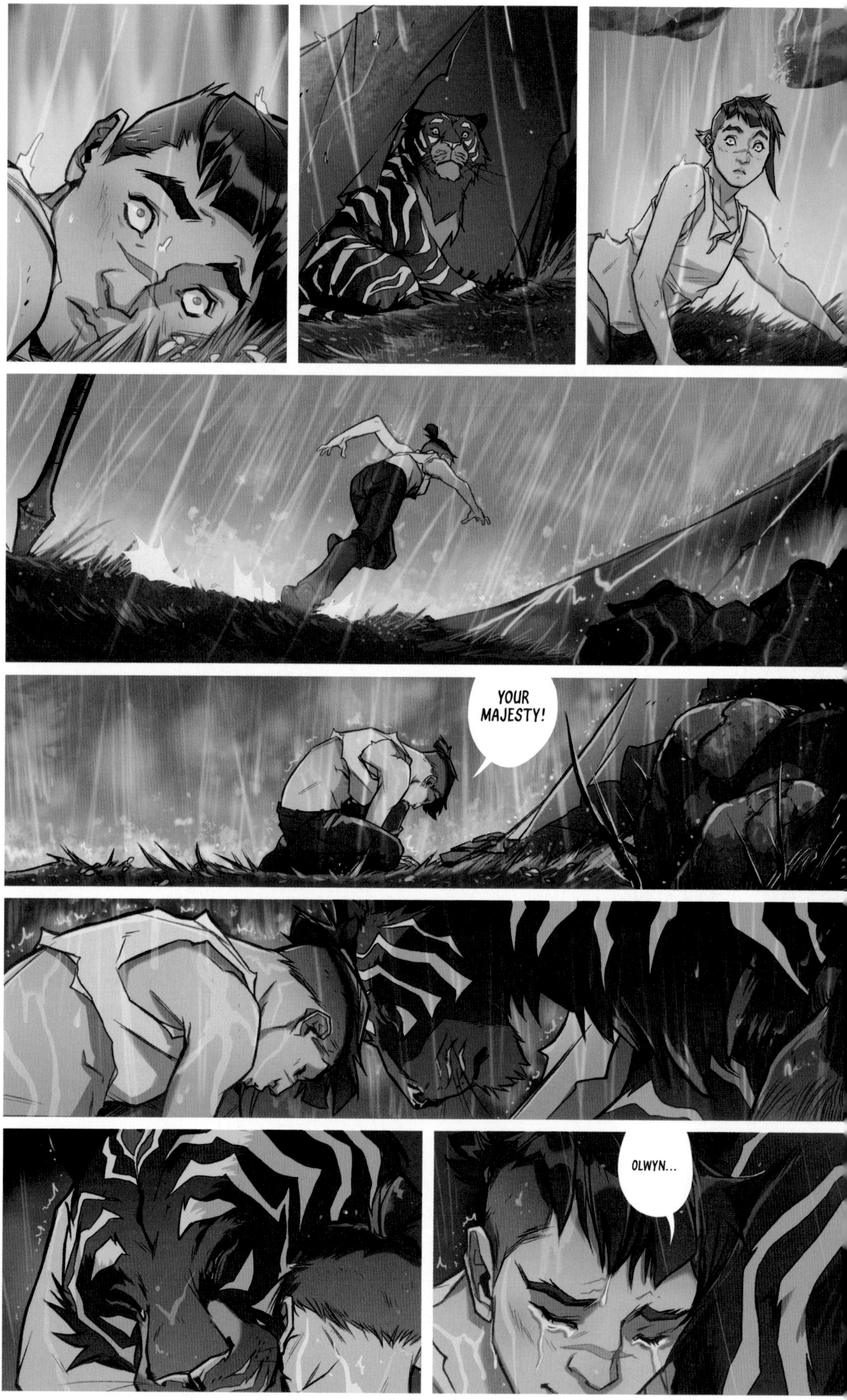
YOUR MAJESTY!
OLWYN...

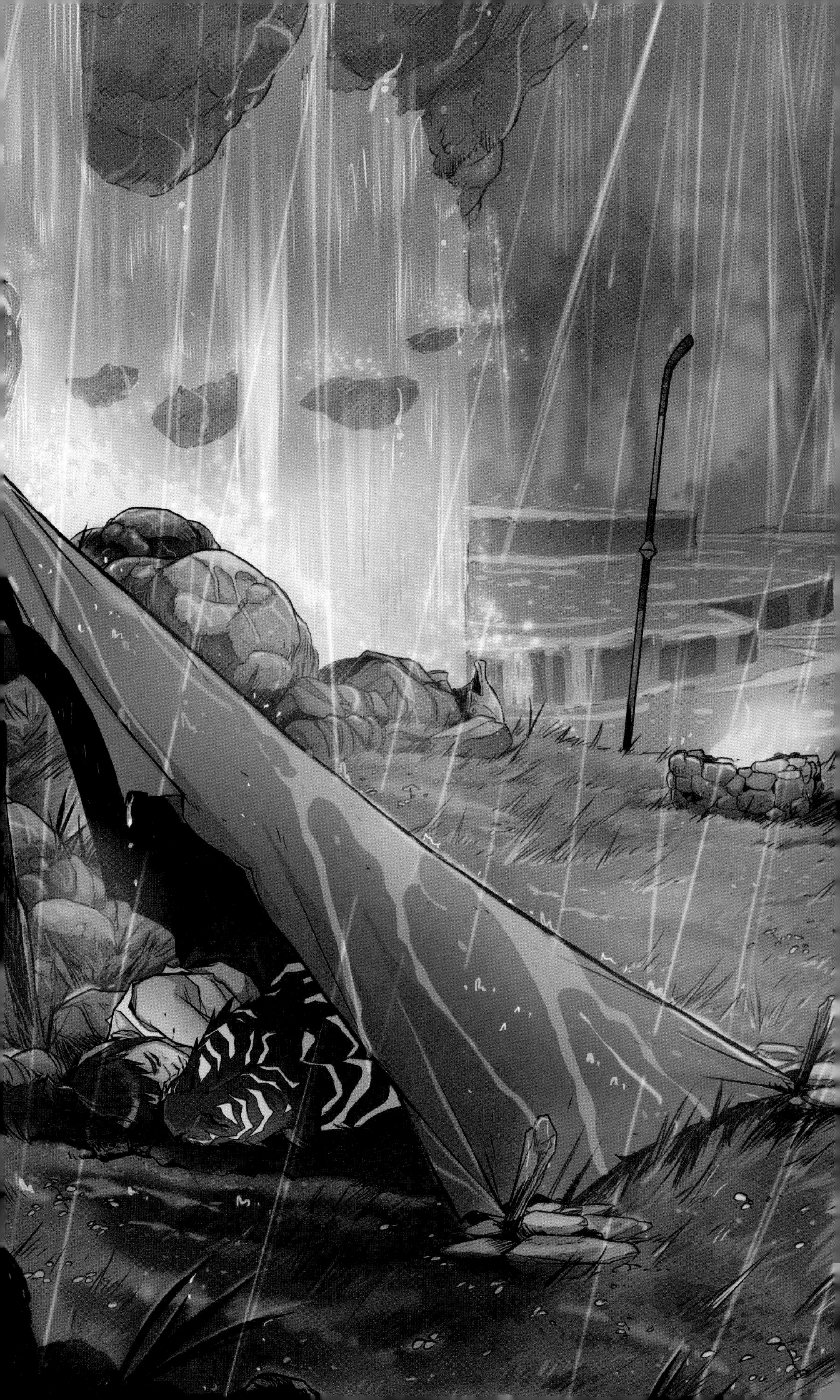

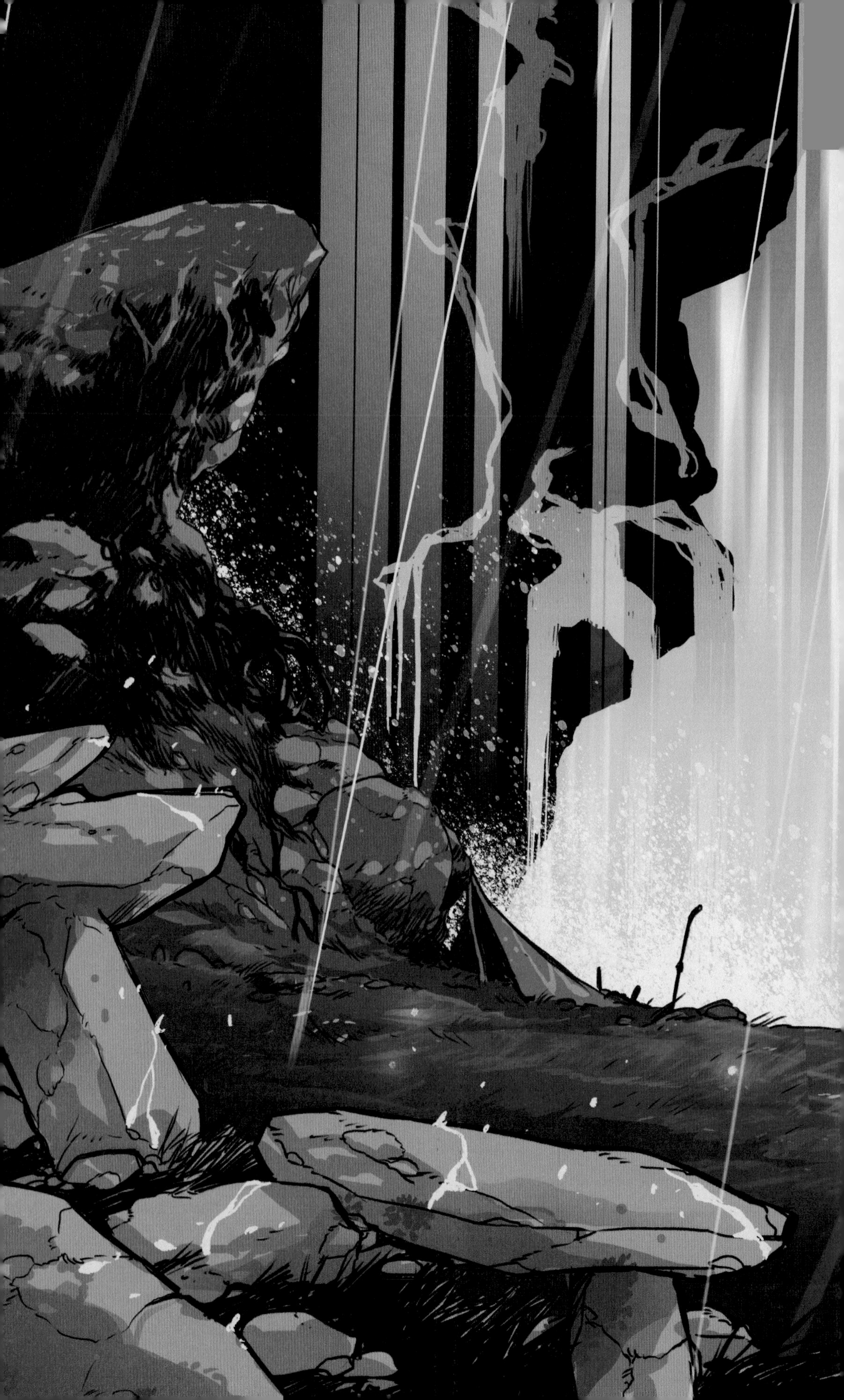

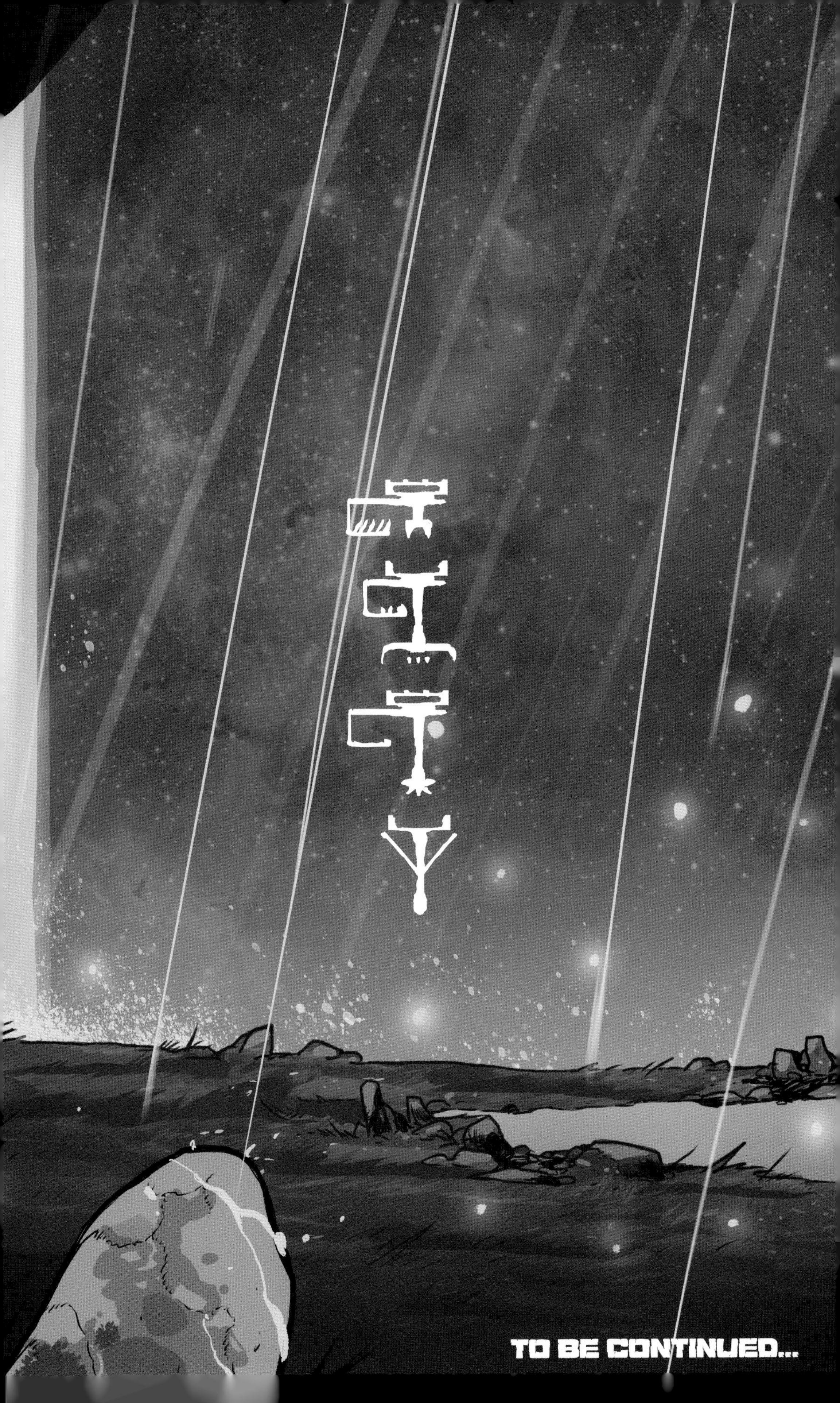
TO BE CONTINUED...

ISOLA

COVER GALLERY

Each monthly issue of ISOLA shipped with two different cover options — the 'A' covers offered a unified, graphic presentation of the series' characters and the variant 'B' covers depicted lush scenery indicative of the art and world inside.

'A' COVERS - Art by Karl Kerschl

'B' COVERS - Art by Karl Kerschl & MSassyK

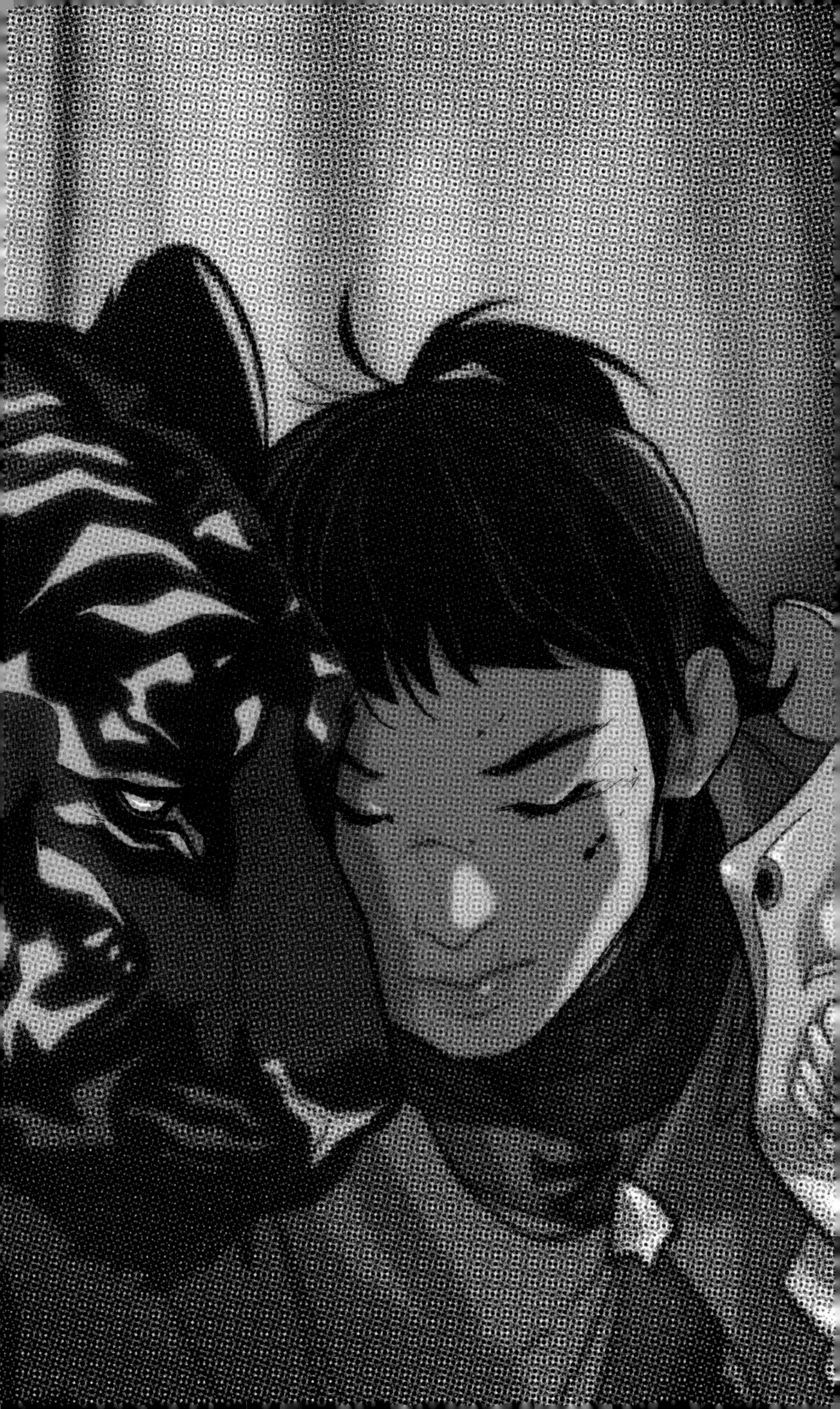

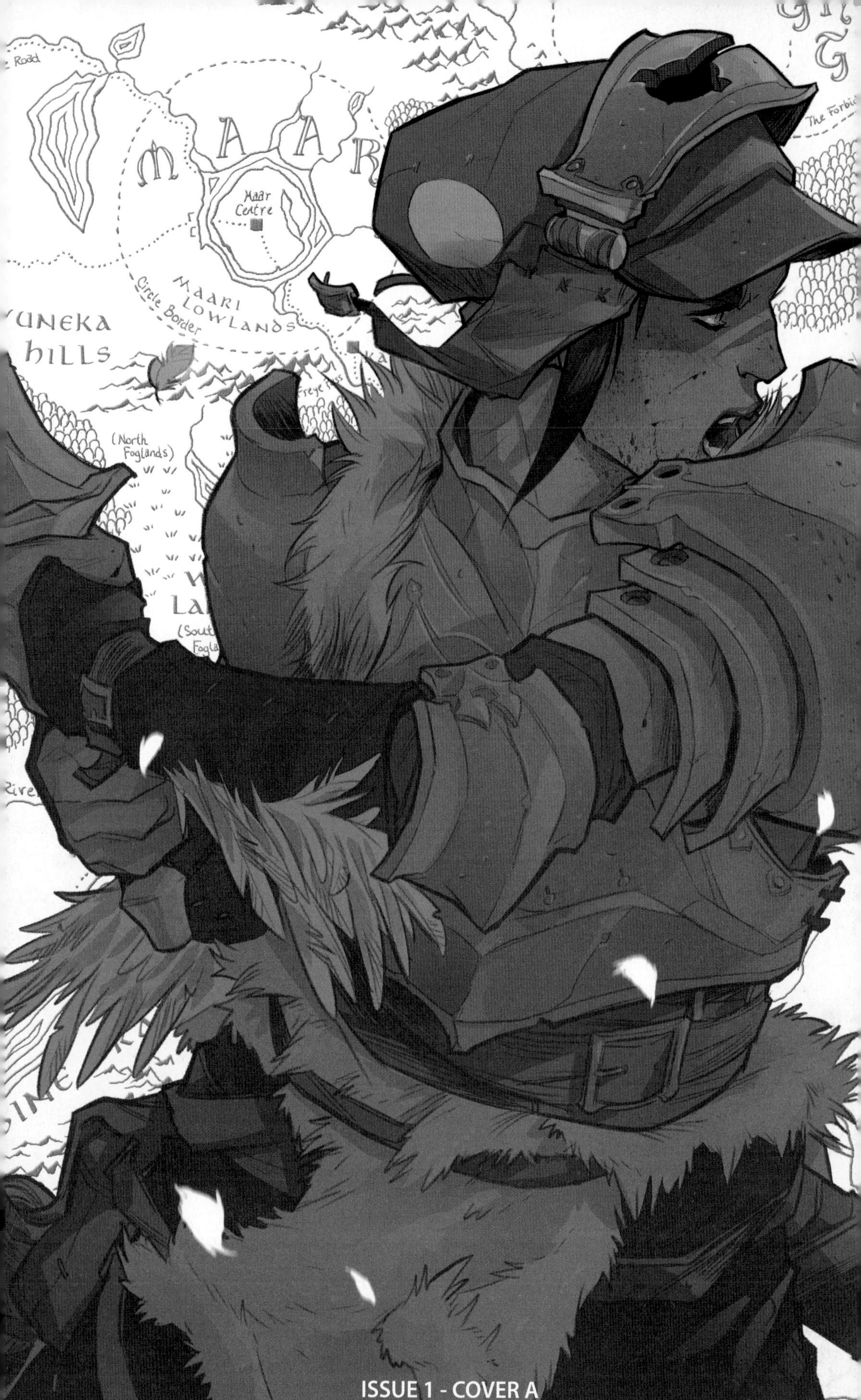
Road
Maar Centre
MAARI LOWLANDS
Circle Border
hILLS
(North Foglands)
Freye Pass

ISSUE 1 - COVER A

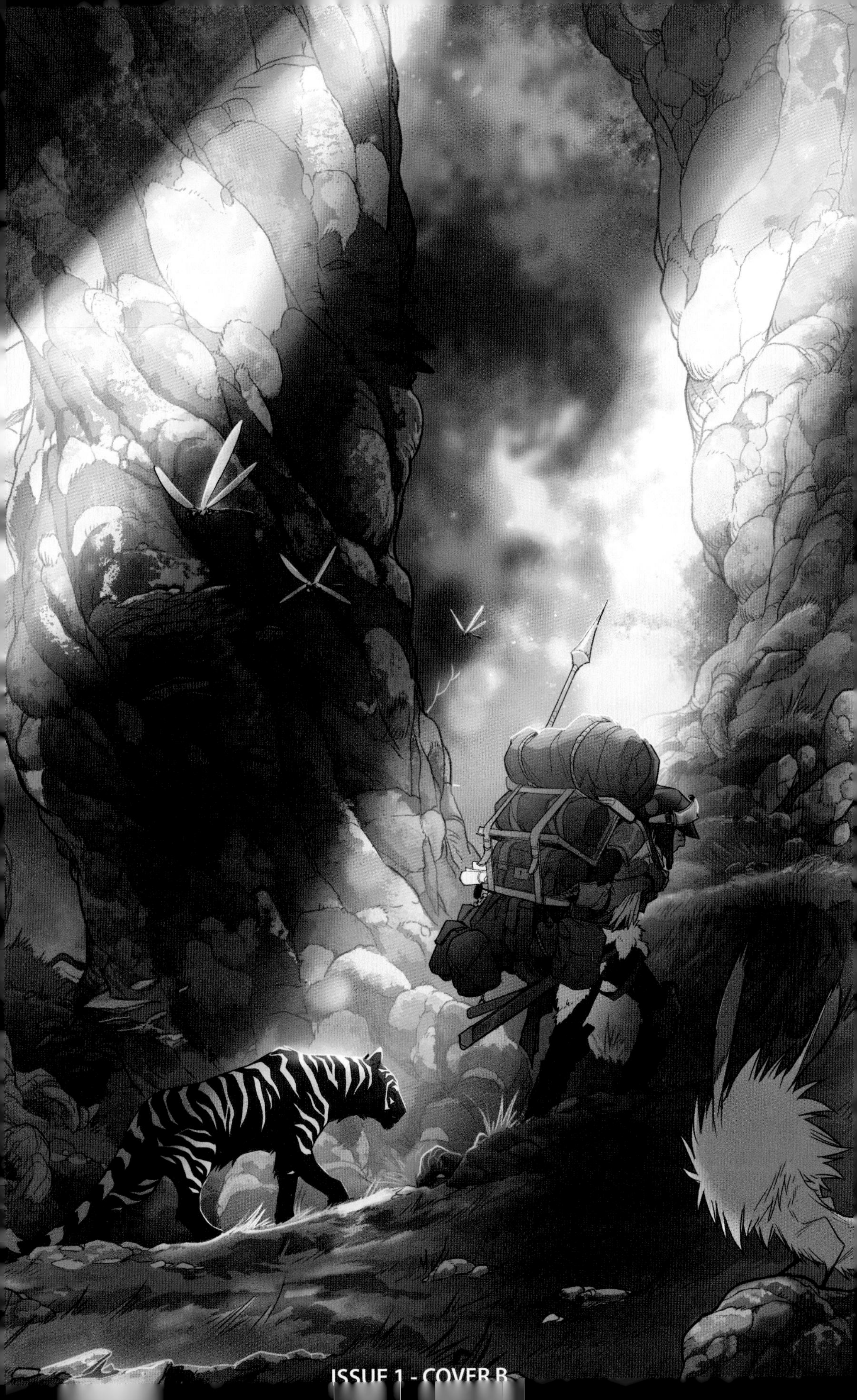

ISSUE 1 - COVER B

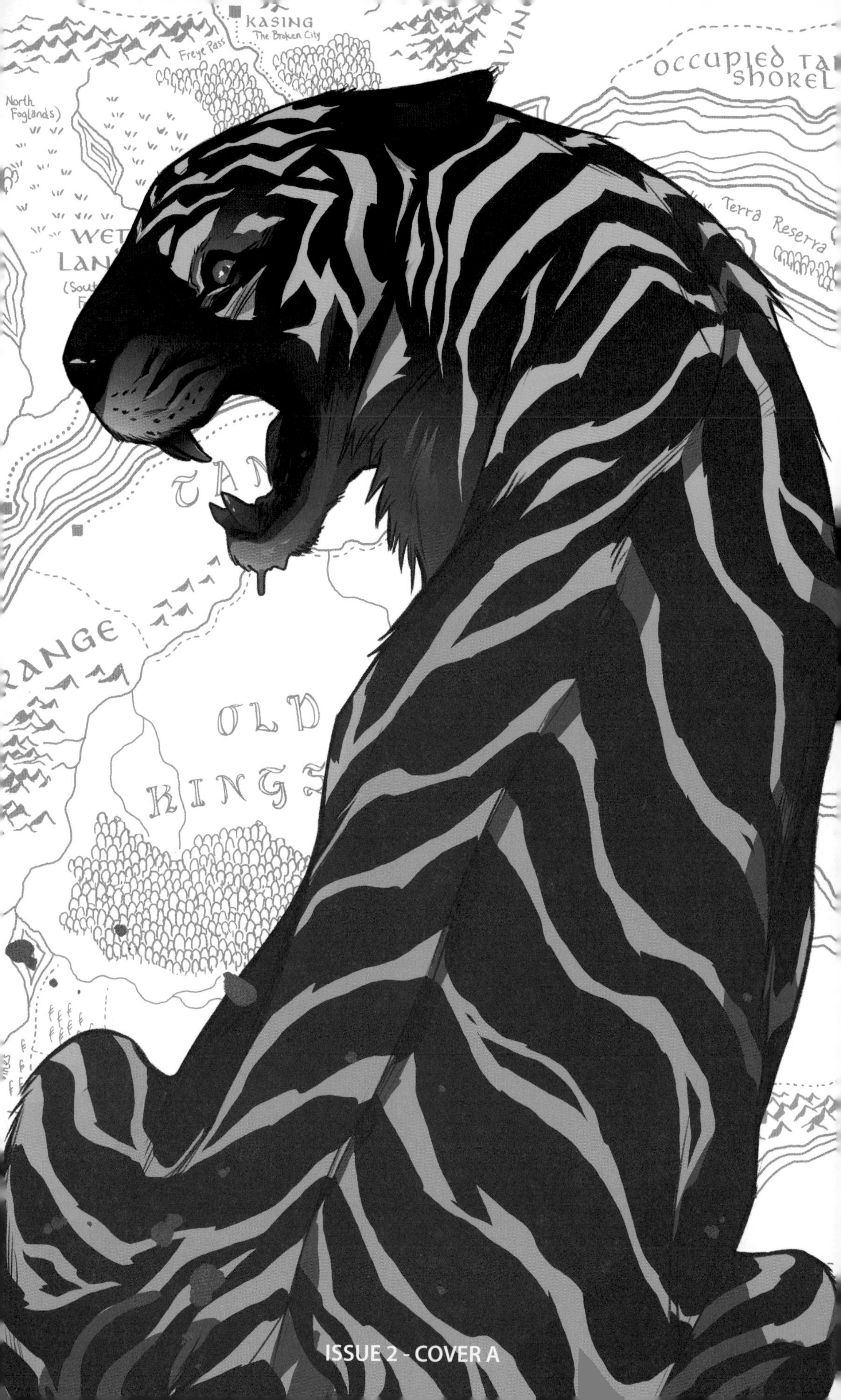
KASING
The Broken City
Freye Pass
North
Foglands)
OCCUPIED TA
SHOREL
Terra Reserra
RANGE
OLD
KINGS

ISSUE 2 - COVER A

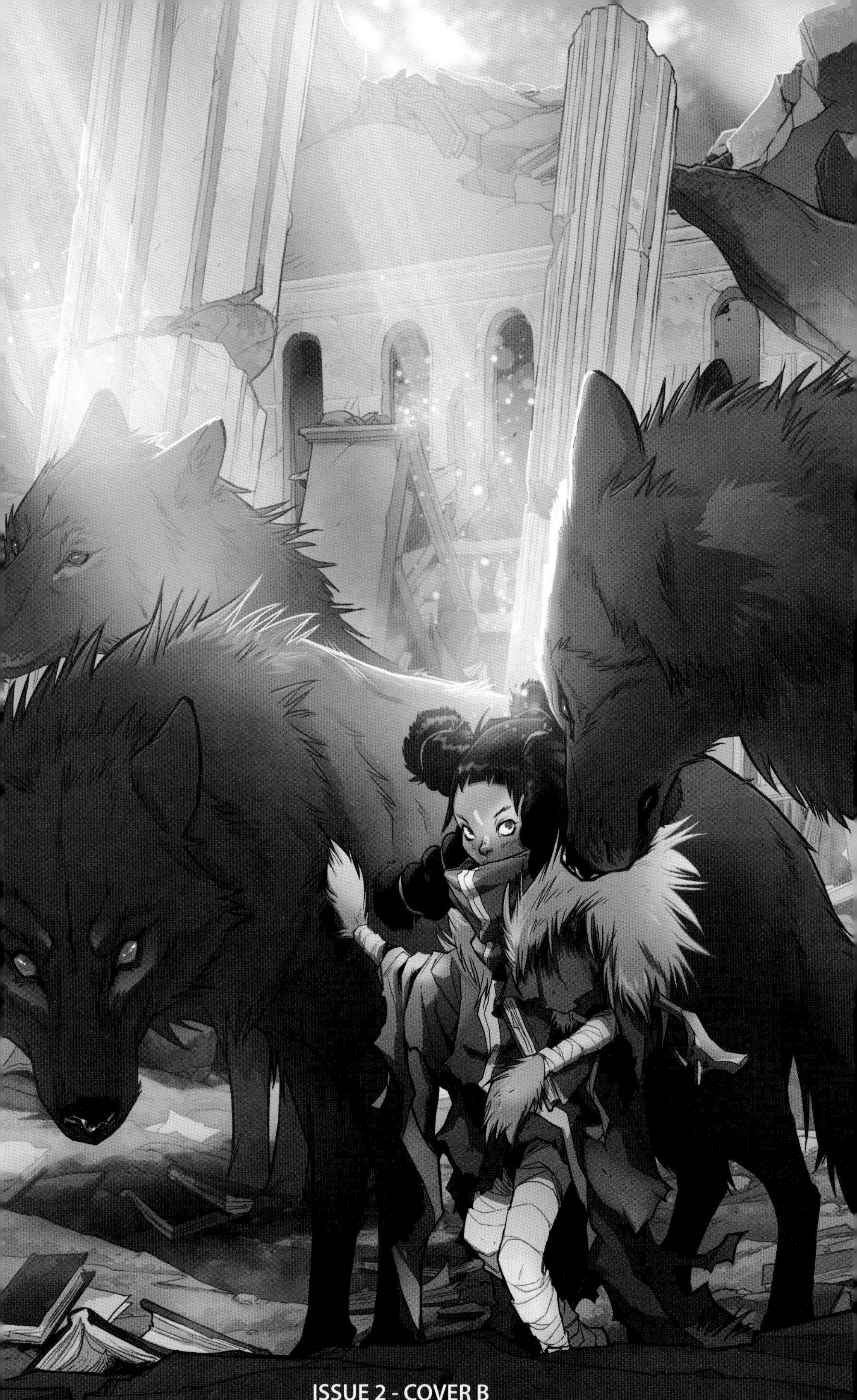

ISSUE 2 - COVER B

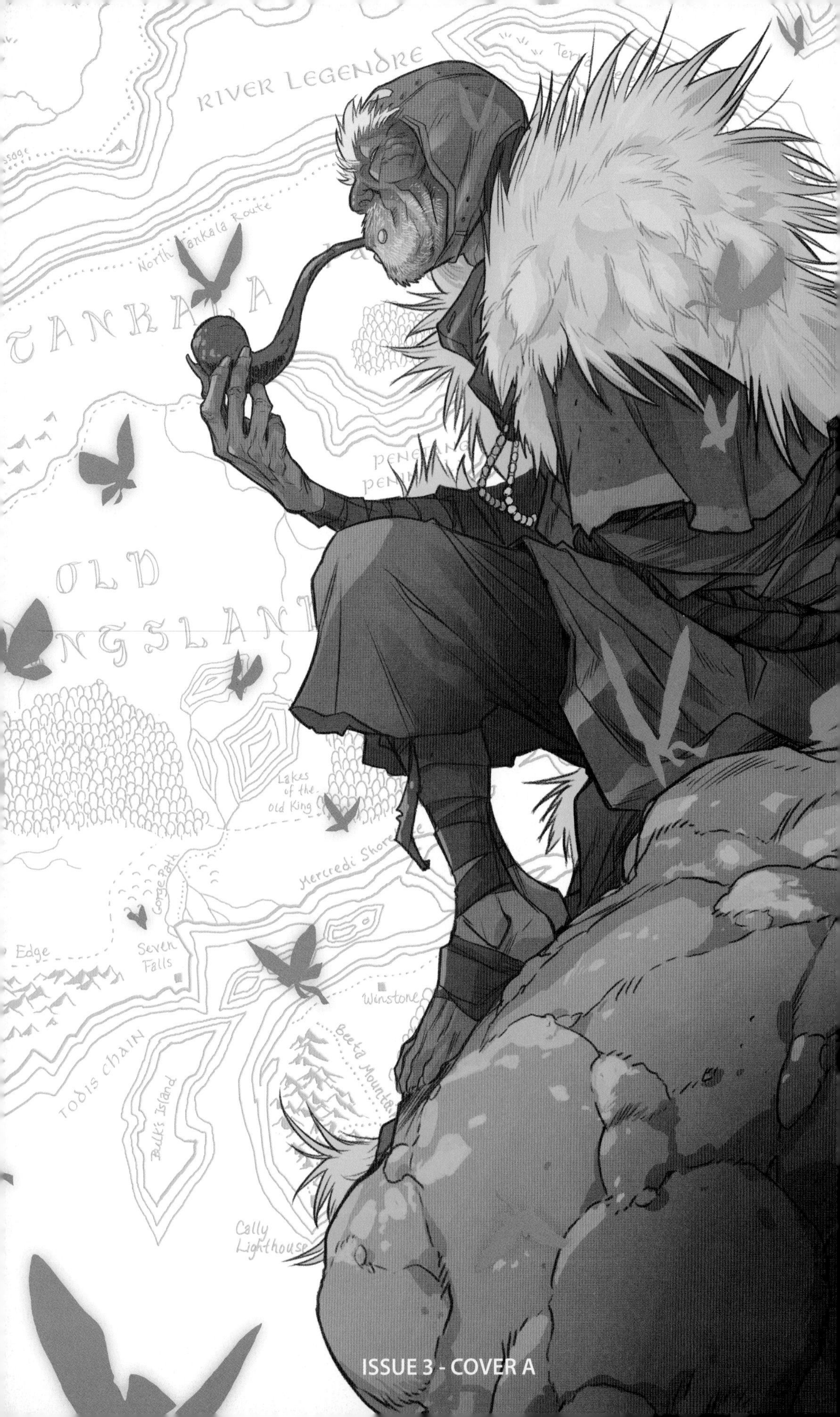
RIVER LEGENDRE
Lakes of the Old King
Gorge Path
Edge
Seven Falls
Winstone
TODIS CHAIN
Bulk's Island
Cally Lighthouse

ISSUE 3 - COVER A

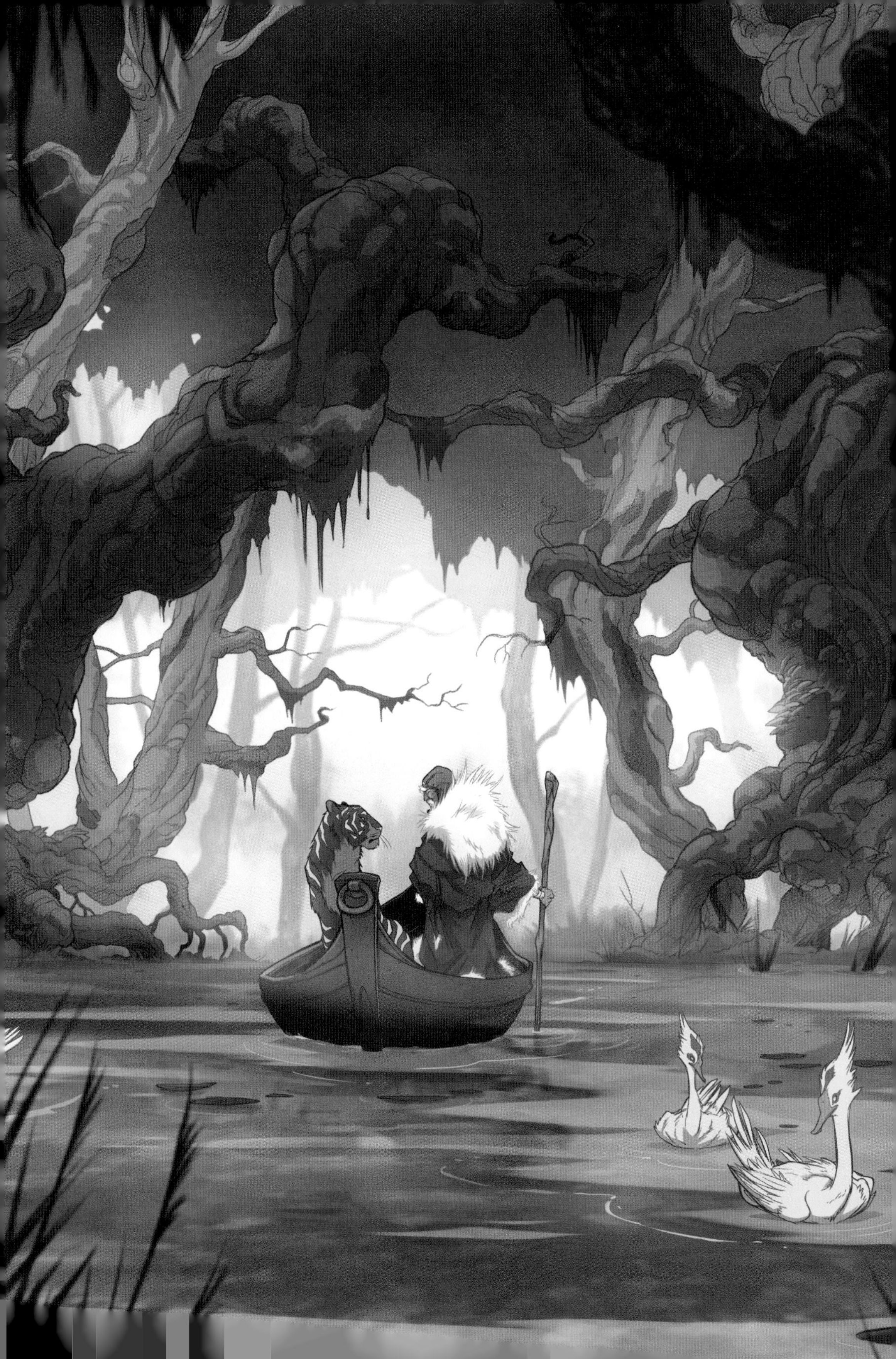

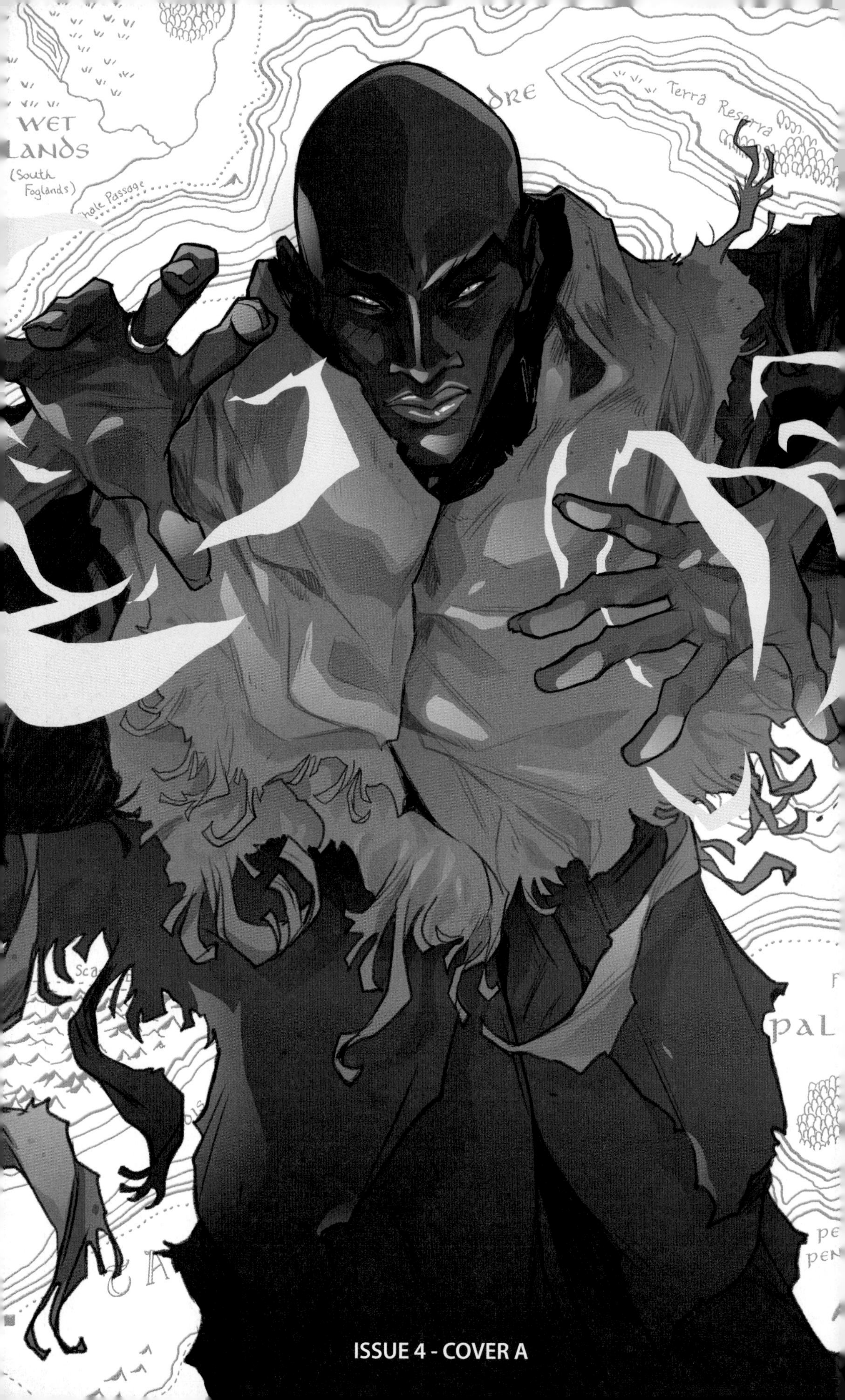
WET LANDS
(South Foglands)
ISSUE 4 - COVER A

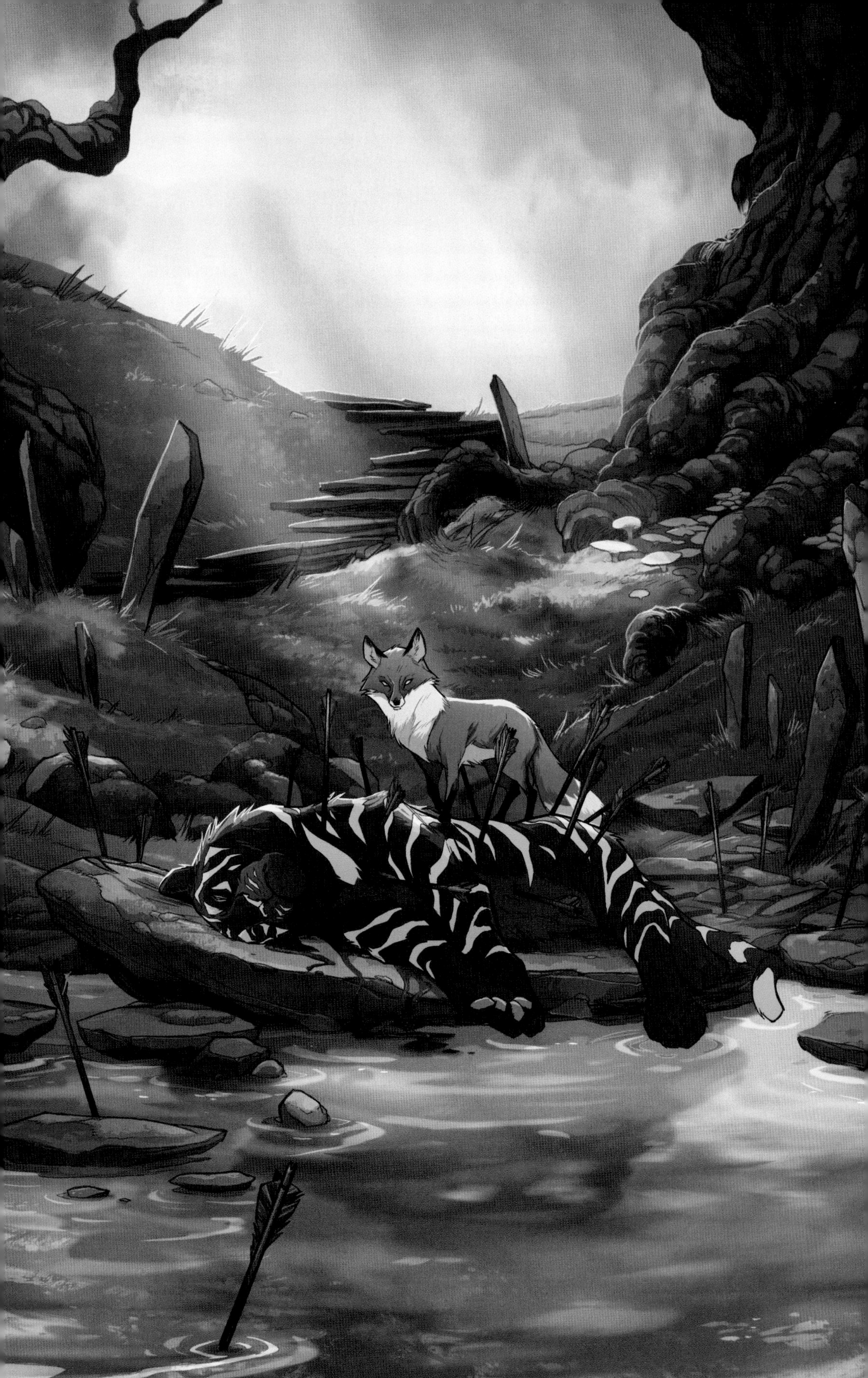

ISSUE 4 - COVER B

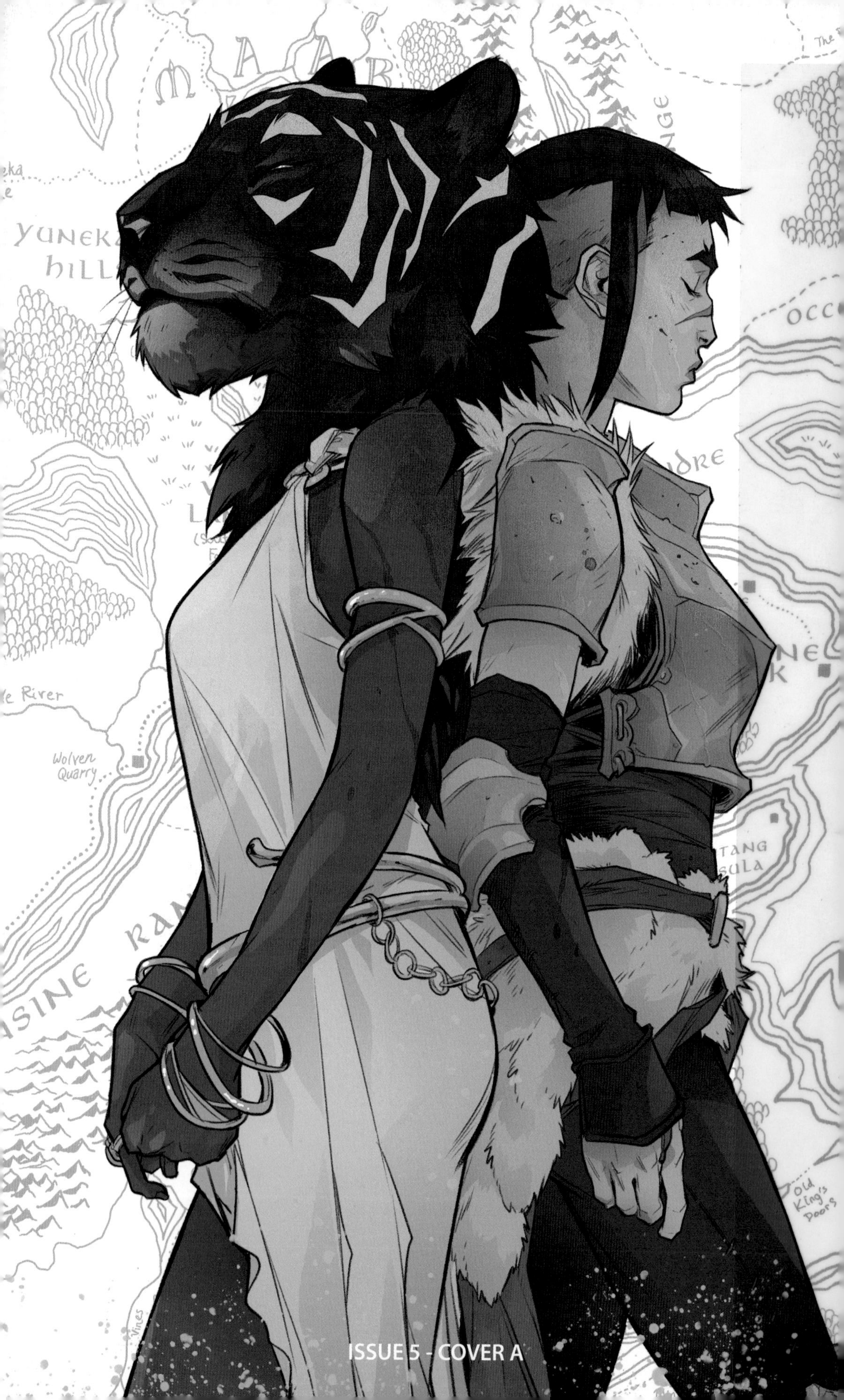
Wolven
Quarry
River
Old
King's
Doors

ISSUE 5 - COVER A

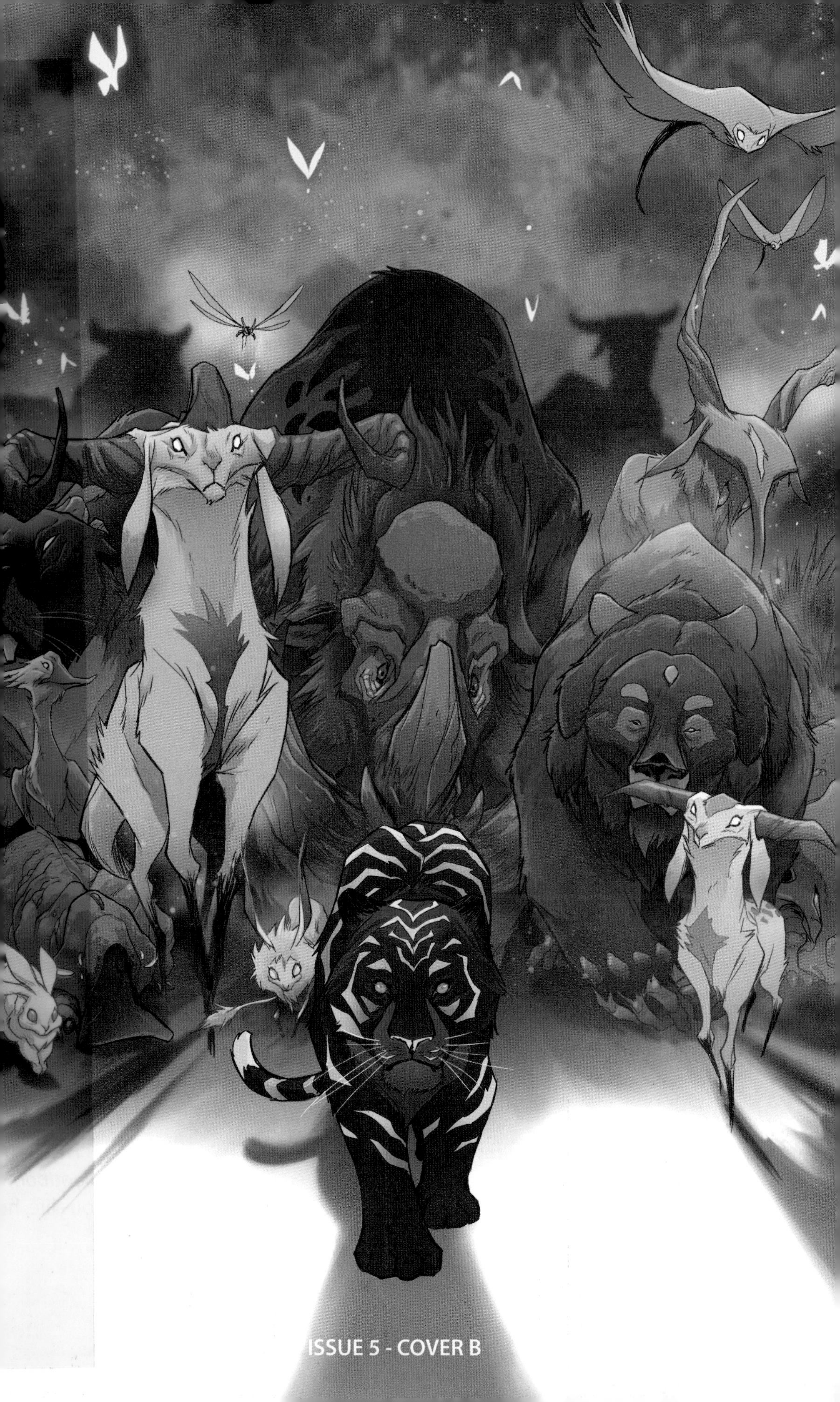

ISSUE 5 - COVER B

BRENDEN FLETCHER is a *New York Times* bestselling writer of comics and cartoons many of which he's been lucky enough to create with childhood friend, Karl Kerschl. He's known for his work on DC Comics' titles *Batgirl, Black Canary* and *Gotham Academy* (with Karl and MSassyK,) his acclaimed Image Comics series, MOTOR CRUSH (with Aditya Bidikar) and various other illustrated/animated bits and bobs in books and TV. He lives in Brooklyn, NY with his wife and two cats.

KARL KERSCHL has been drawing comics professionally since the age of eighteen. He has worked on a number of titles for Marvel and DC Comics, including *Superman, The Flash, Deadpool, Spider-Man, Teen Titans* and *Wonder Woman* and co-created the YA series *Gotham Academy*.
His ongoing webcomic, *The Abominable Charles Christopher*, won the Eisner Award for best webcomic in 2011.
He lives in Montréal with his family but is proud to have grown up in Welland, Ontario.

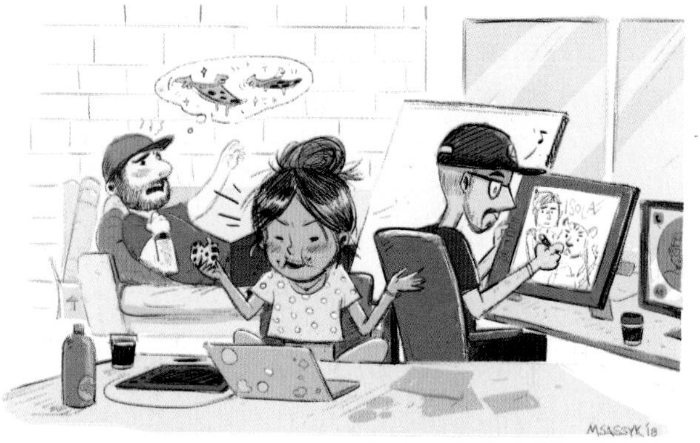

TEAM ISOLA. (HARD AT WORK)

MSASSYK (MICHELE ASSARASAKORN) worked in the animation, film and game industry before debuting as a colourist on DC Comics' *Gotham Academy*. She later joined the same creative team (Karl Kerschl & Brenden Fletcher) on the *Wonder Woman* anniversary anthology before beginning her role as colourist on ISOLA.
She spends half her time playing outside and the other half working from her current home in Vancouver.

ADITYA BIDIKAR is currently lettering MOTOR CRUSH, VS, and DAYS OF HATE for Image Comics, *Deep Roots* and *These Savage Shores* for Vault Comics, and *Bloodborne* and *The Beatles: Yellow Submarine* for Titan Comics, among others. In a previous life, he has been a comics editor, and sometimes dabbles in prose short stories.

He lives and works out of Pune, India, with a cat called Loki for company.

www.isola.ca